burning deck translations

Xue Di, *Heart Into*
Crook, Janet Tan, Hil

Dichten=

Friederike Mayröcker, *Heiligenanstalt*
[tr. Rosmarie Waldrop] Prose, 96 pp., ISBN 0-930901-95-9, original pbk., $8

Elke Erb, *Mountains in Berlin*
[tr. Rosmarie Waldrop] Poems, 96 pp., ISBN 1-886224-06-4, original pbk., $8

Ilma Rakusa, *Steppe*
[tr. Solveig Emerson-Möring] Stories, 80 pp., ISBN 1-886224-27-7, orig. pbk., $10

Ernst Jandl, reft and light [multiple versions by American poets] Poems, 112 pp., ISBN 1-886224-34-x, original pbk., $10

Oskar Pastior, *Many Glove Compartments* [tr. Harry Mathews, Christopher Middleton, Rosmarie Waldrop, with a guest appearance by John Yau] Poems, 120 pp., ISBN 1-886224-44-7, original pbk., $10

Série d'Ecriture

Jean Daive, *A Lesson in Music*
[tr. Julie Kalendek] Poem, 64 pp., ISBN 0-930901-80-0, original pbk. $6

Paol Keineg, *Boudica*
[tr. Keith Waldrop] Poem, 64 pp., ISBN 0-930901-94-0, original pbk. $6

Marcel Cohen, *The Peacock Emperor Moth*
[tr. Cid Corman] Stories, 112 pp., ISBN 1-886224-07-2, original pbk. $8

Jacqueline Risset, *The Translation Begins*
[tr. Jennifer Moxley] Poem, 96 pp., ISBN 1-886 224-09-9, original pbk. $10

Alain Veinstein, *Even a Child* [tr. Robert Kocik, Rosmarie Waldrop] Poems, 64 pp., ISBN 1-886224-28-5, original pbk. $10

Emmanuel Hocquard, *A Test of Solitude: Sonnets*
[tr. Rosmarie Waldrop] Poems, 72 pp., ISBN 1-886224-33-1 original pbk. $10

Crosscut Universe: Writing on Writing from France
[ed./tr. Norma Cole, Pieces by Albiach, Collobert, Daive, Fourcade, Guglielmi, Hocquard, Roubaud, Royet-Journoud et al.]
Prose, 160 pp., offset, smyth-sewn, ISBN 1-886224-39-0, original pbk. $15

Pascal Quignard, *On Wooden Tablets: Apronenia Avitia*
[tr. Bruce X] Novel, 112 pages, ISBN 1-886224-45-5, original pbk. $10
—, *Sarx* [tr. Keith Waldrop] Poem, 40 pp., ISBN 1-886224-20-x, $5

Claude Royet-Journoud, *i. e.*
[tr. Keith Waldrop] Poem, 20 pp., ISBN 1-886224-08-0, saddlestitched, $5

Anne-Marie Albiach, *A Geometry* [tr. Keith & Rosmarie Waldrop] Poems, 28 pp., ISBN 1-886224-31-5, saddlestitched, $5

www.burningdeck.com
Distributed by Small Press Distribution, 1341 Seventh St., Berkeley, CA 94710 1-800/869-7553 orders@spdbooks.org

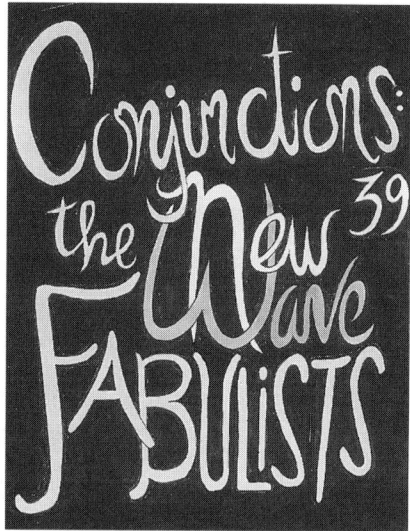

CONJUNCTIONS

Bi-Annual Volumes of New Writing

Edited by
Bradford Morrow

published by Bard College

CONJUNCTIONS is published in the Spring and Fall of each year by Bard College, Annandale-on-Hudson, NY 12504. This issue is made possible in part with the generous funding of the National Endowment for the Arts, and with public funds from the New York State Council on the Arts, a State Agency.

SUBSCRIPTIONS: Send subscription orders to CONJUNCTIONS, Bard College, Annandale-on-Hudson, NY 12504. Single year (two volumes): $18.00 for individuals; $25.00 for institutions and overseas. Two years (four volumes): $32.00 for individuals; $45.00 for institutions and overseas. Patron subscription (lifetime): $500.00. Overseas subscribers please make payment by International Money Order. For information about subscriptions, back issues, and advertising, call Michael Bergstein at (845) 758-1539 or fax (845) 758-2660.

All editorial communications should be sent to Bradford Morrow, *Conjunctions,* 21 East 10th Street, New York, NY 10003. Unsolicited manuscripts cannot be returned unless accompanied by a stamped, self-addressed envelope.

Conjunctions is listed and indexed in the American Humanities Index.

Visit the *Conjunctions* Web site at www.conjunctions.com.

Cover design by Jerry Kelly, New York. Cover art by Ilya Kabakov, "Agonizing Surikov," colored pencil and ink on paper, 51.5 by 35 centimeters, 1972, courtesy of the artist.

Available through D.A.P./Distributed Art Publishers, Inc., 155 Sixth Avenue, New York, NY 10013. Telephone: (212) 627-1999. Fax: (212) 627-9484.

Printers: Edwards Brothers

Typesetter: Bill White, Typeworks

ISSN 0278-2324
ISBN 0-941964-54-X

Manufactured in the United States of America.

TABLE OF CONTENTS

REJOICING REVOICING

Easter Rain

Vladimir Nabokov

Translated from Russian by Dmitri Nabokov and Peter Constantine

THAT DAY A LONELY OLD SWISS woman named Joséphine, or Josefina Lvovna, as the Russian family she had once lived with for twelve years had dubbed her, bought half a dozen eggs, a black brush, and two buttons of carmine watercolor. That day the apple trees were in bloom. A cinema poster on the corner was reflected upside down on the smooth surface of a puddle, and, in the morning, the mountains on the far side of Lake Léman were all veiled in silky mist, like the opaque sheets of rice paper that cover etchings in expensive books. The mist promised a fair day, but the sun barely skimmed over the roofs of the skewed little stone houses, over the wet wires of a toy tram, and then dissolved once again into the haze. The day turned out to be calm, with springtime clouds, but, toward evening, a weighty, icy wind wafted down from the mountains, and Joséphine, on her way home, broke into such a fit of coughing that she lost her balance for a moment by the door, flushed crimson, and leaned on her tightly furled umbrella, thin as a black walking stick.

It was already dark in her room. When she turned on the lamp, it illuminated her hands—thin hands with tight, glossy skin, ecchymotic freckles, and white blotches on the fingernails.

Joséphine laid out her purchases on the table and dropped her coat and hat on the bed. She poured some water into a glass and, putting on a black-rimmed pince-nez that made her dark gray eyes look stern beneath the thick funereal brows that grew together over the bridge of her nose, began painting the eggs. For some reason the carmine watercolor would not stick. Perhaps she should have bought some kind of chemical paint, but she did not know how to ask for it, and was too embarrassed to explain. She thought about going to see a pharmacist she knew—while she was at it, she could get some aspirin. She felt so sluggish, and her eyeballs ached with fever. She wanted to sit quietly, think quietly. Today was the Russian Holy Saturday.

At one time, the peddlers on the Nevsky Prospect had sold a special kind of tongs. These tongs were very practical for fishing out the eggs from the hot, dark blue or orange liquid. But there were also the wooden spoons: They would bump lightly and compactly against the thick glass of the jars from which rose the heady steam of the dye. The eggs were then dried in piles, the red with the red, the green with the green. And they used to color them another way too, by wrapping them tightly in strips of cloth with decalcomanias tucked inside that looked like samples of wallpaper. After the boiling, when the manservant brought the huge pot back from the kitchen, what fun it was to unravel the cloth and take the speckled, marbled eggs out of the warm, damp fabric, from which rose gentle steam, a whiff of one's childhood.

The old Swiss woman felt strange remembering that, when she lived in Russia, she had been homesick, and sent long, melancholy, beautifully written letters to her friends back home about how she always felt unwanted, misunderstood. Every morning after breakfast she would go for a ride in the large open landau with her charge, Hélène. And next to the coachman's fat bottom, reminiscent of a gigantic blue pumpkin, was the hunched-over back of the old footman, all gold buttons and cockade. The only Russian words she knew were: "Coachman," "good," "fine." [*kutcher, tish-tish, nichevo (coachman, hush-hush, so-so,* all mispronounced*).*]

She had left Petersburg with a dim sense of relief, just as the war was beginning. She thought that now she would delight endlessly in chatty evenings with her friends and in the coziness of her native town. But the reality turned out to be quite the opposite. Her real life—in other words, the part of life when one most keenly and deeply gets used to people and things—had passed by there, in Russia, which she had unconsciously grown to love and understand, and where God only knew what was going on now. . . . And tomorrow was Orthodox Easter.

Joséphine sighed loudly, got up, and closed the window more firmly. She looked at her watch, black on its nickel chain. She would have to do something about those eggs. They were to be a gift for the Platonovs, an elderly Russian couple recently settled in Lausanne, a town both native and foreign to her, where it was hard to breathe, where the houses were stacked at random, in disorder, helter-skelter, along the steep, angular streets.

She grew pensive, listening to the drone in her ears. Then she shook herself out of her torpor, poured a vial of purple ink into a tin can, and carefully lowered an egg into it.

The door opened softly. Her neighbor Mademoiselle Finard entered, quiet as a mouse. She was a thin little woman, a former governess herself. Her short-cropped hair was all silver. She was draped in a black shawl, iridescent with glass beads.

Joséphine, hearing her mouselike steps, awkwardly, with a newspaper, covered the can and the eggs that were drying on some blotting paper.

"What do you want? I don't like people simply coming in like that."

Mademoiselle Finard looked askance at Joséphine's anxious face and said nothing, but was deeply offended, and, without a word, left the room with the same mincing steps.

By now the eggs had turned a venomous violet. On an unpainted egg, she decided to draw the two Easter initials[1], as had always been customary in Russia. The first letter, "X," she drew well, but the second she could not quite remember, and finally, instead of a "B," she drew an absurd, crooked "Я." When the ink had dried completely she wrapped the eggs in soft toilet paper and put them in her leather handbag.

But what tormenting sluggishness. . . . She wanted to lie down in bed, drink some hot coffee, and stretch out her legs. . . . She was feverish and her eyelids prickled. . . . When she went outside, the dry crackle of her cough began rising in her throat again. The streets were dark, damp, and deserted. The Platonovs lived nearby. They were seated having tea, and Platonov, bald-pated, with a scanty beard, in a Russian serge shirt with buttons on the side, was stuffing yellow tobacco into cigarette papers when Joséphine knocked with the knob of her umbrella and entered.

"Ah, good evening, Mademoiselle."

She sat down next to them, and tactlessly, verbosely started discussing the imminent Russian Easter. She took the violet eggs out of her bag one by one. Platonov noticed the egg with the lilac letters "X Я" and burst out laughing.

"Whatever made her stick on those Jewish initials?"

His wife, a plump woman with a yellow wig and sorrowful eyes, smiled fleetingly. She started thanking Joséphine with indifference, drawing out her French vowels. Joséphine did not understand why they were laughing. She felt hot and sad. She began talking again, but

---

[1]The Cyrillic letters X (Kh) and B (V) stand for *Khristos vorkresye,* "Christ has risen."

she had the feeling that what she was saying was out of place, yet she could not restrain herself.

"Yes, at this moment there is no Easter in Russia. . . . Poor Russia! Oh, I remember how people used to kiss each other in the streets. And my little Hélène looked like an angel that day. . . . Oh, I often cry all night thinking of your wonderful country!"

The Platonovs always found these conversations unpleasant. They never discussed their lost homeland with outsiders, just as ruined rich men hide their poverty and become even haughtier and less approachable than before. Therefore, deep down, Joséphine felt that they had no love at all for Russia. Usually when she visited the Platonovs she thought that, if she only began talking of beautiful Russia with tears in her eyes, the Platonovs would suddenly burst into sobs and begin reminiscing and recounting, and that the three of them would sit like that all night reminiscing, crying, and squeezing each other's hands.

But in reality this never happened. Platonov would nod politely and indifferently with his beard, while his wife kept trying to find out where one could get some tea or soap as cheaply as possible.

Platonov began rolling his cigarettes again. His wife placed them evenly in a cardboard box. They had both intended to take a nap until it was time to leave for the Easter Vigils at the Greek church around the corner. They wanted to sit silently, to think their own thoughts, to speak only with glances and special, seemingly absent-minded smiles about their son, who had been killed in the Crimea, about Easter odds and ends, about their neighborhood church on Pochtamskaya Street. Now this chattering, sentimental old woman with her anxious dark gray eyes had come, full of sighs, and might well stay until they left the house themselves.

Joséphine fell silent, hoping avidly that she too might be asked to accompany them to church, and, afterward, to break fast with them. She knew they had baked Russian Easter cakes the day before, and although she obviously could not eat any because she felt so feverish, still it would have been so pleasant, so warm, and so festive.

Platonov ground his teeth and, stifling a yawn, looked furtively at his wrist, at the dial under its little screen. Joséphine saw they were not going to invite her. She rose.

"You need a small rest, my dear friends, but there is something I want to say to you before I leave." And, moving close to Platonov, who also got up, she exclaimed in sonorous, fractured Russian, "Hath Christs rised!"

This was her last hope of eliciting a burst of hot, sweet tears, Easter kisses, an invitation to break fast together. . . . But Platonov only squared his shoulders and said with a subdued laugh, "See, Mademoiselle, you pronounce Russian beautifully."

Once outside, she broke into sobs, and walked pressing her handkerchief to her eyes, swaying slightly, tapping her silken, canelike umbrella on the sidewalk. The sky was cavernous and troubled—the moon vague, the clouds like ruins. The angled feet of a curly-headed Chaplin were reflected in a puddle near a brightly lit cinema. And when Joséphine walked beneath the noisy, weeping trees beside the lake, which seemed like a wall of mist, she saw an emerald lantern glowing faintly at the edge of a small pier and something large and white clambering onto a black boat that bobbed below. She focused through her tears. An enormous old swan puffed itself up, flapped its wings, and suddenly, clumsy as a goose, waddled heavily onto the deck. The boat rocked; green circles welled over the black, oily water that merged into fog.

Joséphine pondered whether she should perhaps go to church anyway. But in Petersburg the only church she had ever gone to was the red Catholic one at the end of Morskaya Street, and she felt ashamed now to go into an Orthodox church, where she did not know when to cross herself or how one held one's fingers, and where somebody might make a comment. She felt intermittent chills. Her head filled with a confusion of rustling, of smacking trees, of black clouds, and Easter recollections: mountains of multicolored eggs, the dusky sheen of St. Isaac's. Deafened and woozy, she somehow managed to make it home and climb the stairs, banging her shoulder against the wall, and then, unsteadily, her teeth chattering, she began undressing. She felt weaker, and tumbled onto her bed with a blissful, incredulous smile.

A delirium, stormy and powerful as the surge of bells, took hold of her. Mountains of multicolored eggs scattered with rotund tapping sounds. The sun—or was it a golden-horned sheep made of creamery butter?—came tumbling through the window and began to grow, filling the room with torrid yellow. Meanwhile, the eggs scurried up and rolled down glossy little strips of wood, knocking against each other, their shells cracking, their whites streaked with crimson.

All night she lay delirious like that, and it was only the following morning that a still-offended Mademoiselle Finard came in, gasped, and ran off in panic to call a doctor.

"Lobar pneumonia, Mademoiselle."

Through the waves of delirium twinkled wallpaper flowers, the old woman's silver hair, the doctor's placid eyes—it all twinkled and dissolved. And again an agitated drone of joy engulfed her soul. The fable-blue sky was like a gigantic painted egg, bells thundered, and someone came into the room who looked like Platonov, or maybe like Hélène's father—and on entering he unfolded a newspaper, placed it on the table, and sat down nearby, glancing now at Joséphine, now at the white pages with a significant, modest, slightly cunning smile. Joséphine knew that in this paper there was some kind of wondrous news, but, try as she might, she could not decipher the Russian letters of the black headline. Her guest kept smiling and casting significant glances at her, and seemed on the very point of revealing the secret, to confirm the happiness that she foretasted—but the man slowly dissolved. Unconsciousness swept over her like a black cloud.

Then came another motley of delirious dreams: The landau rolled along the quay, Hélène lapped the hot bright color from a wooden spoon, the broad Neva sparkled expansively, and Czar Peter suddenly leapt off his bronze steed, the hooves of both its forelegs having simultaneously alighted. He approached Joséphine, and, with a smile on his green-tinted, stormy face, embraced her, kissed her on one cheek, then on the other. His lips were soft and warm, and when he brushed her cheek for the third time, she palpitated, moaning with bliss, spread out her arms, and suddenly fell silent.

Early in the morning, on the sixth day of her illness, after a final crisis, Joséphine came to her senses. A white sky shimmered brightly through the window and perpendicular rain was rustling and rippling in the gutters.

A wet branch stretched across the windowpane, and at its very end a leaf kept shuddering beneath the patter of the rain. The leaf leaned forward and let a large drop fall from the tip of its green blade. The leaf shuddered again, and again a moist ray rolled downward, then a long, bright earring dangled and dropped.

And it seemed to Joséphine as if the rainy coolness were flowing through her veins. She could not take her eyes off the streaming sky, and the pulsating, enraptured rain was so pleasant, the leaf shuddered so touchingly, that she wanted to laugh; the laughter filled her, though it was still soundless, coursing through her body, tickling her palate, and was on the very point of erupting.

To her left, in the corner, something scrabbled and sighed. Aquiver with the laughter that was mounting in her, she took her eyes off the window and turned her head. The little old woman lay facedown on the floor in her black kerchief. Her short-cropped silver hair shook angrily as she fidgeted, thrusting her hand under the chest of drawers, where her ball of wool had rolled. Black yarn stretched from the chest to the chair, where her knitting needles and a half-knitted stocking still lay.

Seeing Mademoiselle Finard's black back, her squirming legs, her button boots, Joséphine broke out in peals of laughter, shaking as she gasped and cooed beneath her down comforter, feeling that she was resurrected, that she had returned from faraway mists of happiness, wonder, and Easter splendor.

Editor's Note

Vladimir Nabokov wrote "Easter Rain" in 1925, and the story was originally published in the Russian émigré weekly *Russkoye Ekho* on April 12, that same year, under the author's pen name, Sirin. This is its first appearance in print in English. "Easter Rain" is not yet included in *The Stories of Vladimir Nabokov* (Knopf 1995; Vintage 1996) because the only known extant copy of *Russkoye Ekho* (Berlin) was discovered in the late 1990s by Dieter Zimmer—the German Nabokov scholar and editor for Rowohlt Verlag of the Nabokov *Gesammelte Werke*—in the Deutsche Bucherei, Leipzig. There have been, to date, two other translations of this important early story, one into German by Zimmer (for Rowohlt, *Literaturmagazin,* September 1997), the other into French (for Gallimard, *La nouvelle revue Française,* September 1999).

The Deep Zoo

Rikki Ducornet

Writing is the uncovering of that which was unrevealed.

—Ghani Alani, *Dreaming Paradise*

◆ IN THE TRADITION OF Islam, the first word that was revealed to Mohammed was *Igrá* (Read!). The world is a translation of the divine, and its manifestation. To write a text is to propose a reading of the world and to reveal its potencies. Writing *is* reading and reading a way back to the initial impulse. Both are acts of revelation.

◆ The Ottoman calligraphers delighted in creating mazes of embellishments in which the text was secreted like a treasure. The text needed to be deciphered and the task proved the worthiness of the reader. These calligrapher's mazes remind us that if the text is the mirror of an exorbitant, mutable universe, it is playful, too. The maze places the text within an intimate space, very like a garden, where the text hides, then reveals itself; perhaps it could be said such a text is *irresistible.* Writes Gaston Bachelard: *All the spaces of intimacy are designated by an attraction (Poetics of Space).*

◆ The texts we write are not visible until they are written. Like a creature coaxed from out a deep wood, the text reveals itself little by little. The maze evokes a multiplicity of approaches, the many tricks we employ to tempt the text hither. The maze is both closed and open; it demands to be approached with a *thoughtful lightness* (Calvino). The powers lurking within it are like stars. Despite their age and inaccessibility, their light continues to reach us and to reveal us to ourselves.

◆ A playful mind is deeply responsive to the world and informed by powers instilled during infancy and childhood, powers that animate the imagination with primal energies. A playful mind is guided as much by attraction as consistency and coherence—and I am thinking here of Lewis Carroll's Looking Glass world—its consistent tyrants, the coherence of its nonsense, and the energy of Alice's fearless lucidity. The Looking Glass reminds us that the world's maze is attractive to eager thinkers. After all, playfulness describes as much the mind of the scientist as the artist (and Lewis Carroll was both).

◆

The idea that the world was engendered by the spoken word comes to us from Egypt. Here language flourished, mirroring and delighting in the phenomenal world. Here Paradise persisted; the gods and their creatures dwelling together in good understanding or, phrased differently, in *knowledge* of one another. And if the world of nature and its book indicated the divine, it also provided a place of unlimited encounters. To name a thing was to acknowledge and evoke its primary potencies—religious, medical, and magical. Plants, minerals, and animals were not only animated by the divine breath (*nous*), they were its vessels. Each tree, bird, river, and star was an altar, the dwelling place of a god. To gaze upon the world's image reflected in the waters of the Nile was to gaze into and reflect upon a sacred face or body: Hathor, the cow-faced goddess, embodied by the moon; Horus, the falcon, perched among the reeds.

Deep in the desert, each fossil shell was seen as Hathor's gift, tossed to earth from the sky; the fossil sea urchin's five-pointed star needled to its back indicated its stellar origins and explains why such things are found placed near the dead in ancient tombs. To use a lovely term of Gaston Bachelard's, such a reverie—and to leap from stone to star can only be called a reverie—*digs life deeper, enlarge(s) the depth of life.* Bachelard offers these lines from the poet Vincent Huidobro:

> *In my childhood is born a childhood burning like alcohol.*
> *I would sit down in the paths of night*
> *I would listen to the discourse of the stars*
> *And that of the tree.*
>
> —*The Poetics of Reverie*

Such *sympathies*—the stone, the moon caught in the branches of the willow, the gods, the stars—are born of a deep looking at the world and a deep dreaming. The ancient world of sympathies, rooted in inquisitiveness and informed by imaginative seeing, gave us marvelous aesthetic and scientific achievements; alchemy, for example—that exemplary amalgam of science and poetry, that "immense word reverie," says Bachelard. It would be a mistake to dismiss such *sympathies* as mere foolishness, for they were born of qualities of mind that illustrate what Italo Calvino calls *the lightness of thoughtfulness (Six Memos for the Next Millennium)* and illumine his phrase *Poetry is the enemy of chance.* The moment one reaches for the starstruck stone, the reverie begins; the moment its star is recognized as a piece of the night sky fallen to earth, the poem begins. Chance gives way to a deep seeing and the recognition of a pattern that informs the mind with light, a pattern that incandesces and *burns like alcohol.* If poetry is the enemy of chance, it is also *the daughter of chance* (Calvino).

If I have chosen to open this essay with an evocation of an ancient world and its *sympathies,* it is because the urgencies concealed within the maze of the mind that animate our imaginations provoke incandescence on the page. I am not calling for magical thinking, obscurity, or preciousness, but for an eager access to memory, reverie, and the unconscious—its powers, beauties, terrors, and, perhaps above all, its rule-breaking intuitions, and to celebrate with you the mind's longing to become lighter, free of the weight of received ideas and gravity-bound redundancies. If we were scientists and not writers, we would not waste our time reinventing gravity. Speaking of a poet he especially admires, Calvino says:

> *The miraculous thing about his poetry is that he simply takes the weight out of language to the point that it resembles moonlight.*
>
> —*Six Memos for the Next Millennium*

And Bachelard:

> *For things as for souls, the mystery is inside. A reverie of intimacy—of an intimacy which is always human—opens up for the (one) who enters into the mysteries of matter.*
>
> —*The Poetics of Reverie*

The mysteries of matter are the potencies that in the shapes of dreams, landscapes, exemplary instants, and so on inform our imagining minds; they are potencies; they are powers. For Bachelard, they take the form of shells, a bird's nest, an attic; for Borges, a maze, mirrors, the tiger; for Calvino, moonlight, the flame, and the crystal; for Cortázar, ants on the march and the cry of the rooster.

Potencies are never static but in constant flux within our minds and what's more, they *fall in sympathy* with one another. For example, for Borges there is an evident sympathy between the tiger's stripes, the world's maze, language, and the maze of the mind; for Calvino, between moonlight and the lucent transparency of clear thinking; for Bachelard, between attics and a love of solitude; for Cortázar, between the cock's cry and the knowledge of mortality, of finitude.

◆

> *The world of animals is an ocean of sympathies from which we drink only drops whereas we could drain torrents from it.*
>
> —Lamartine (as quoted by Giovanni Mariotti in his essay on Aloys Zötl, *F.M.R.* #1)

◆

One evening years ago, a family circus set up its shabby tent in the park of a French village—Le Puy Notre Dame in the Val de Loire—I called home. As I approached the park I heard the sound of a powerful motor and searched the sky for an airplane—a rarity at that time in that place. The sky was empty of everything, even clouds, and the thrumming I heard was the purring of tigers. An instant later I saw the cage and two exquisite tigers, surely drugged; their contentment in such small quarters was uncanny. If I recall this distant evening, its circus, and its tigers for you now, it is in the guise of an introduction to *potencies in the shape of beasts.*

For the first issue of Franco Maria Ricci's magazine *F.M.R.,* Julio Cortázar was asked to write an essay on the bestiary of a little-known and eccentric nineteenth-century painter from the foothills of the Bohemian mountains whose name is Aloys Zötl. From 1832 to 1887—the year of his death—Zötl painted 170 achingly beautiful watercolors of animals inhabiting the ideal landscapes of his imagination. Years were kingdoms: 1832 ruled by fish, 1835 by reptiles, 1837 by the gentle tyranny of birds. André Breton called his bestiary "the most sumptuous ever seen."

Instead of describing Zötl's bestiary, Cortázar chooses to walk us through his own Deep Zoo. His essay is titled "A Stroll among the Cages" and it is a parallel journey on a path *burning like alcohol* that generously leads straight to Cortázar's own holding ground of totems, just as it prepares our eyes for the sight to come: Zötl's lucent tigeries and tigered lucencies:

In the beginning it was a cock, Cortázar tells us; *before that there was no memory.* Our journey with Cortázar is announced by the crowing of the cock.

> *And then a cock crowed, if there is a memory it is because of that, but there was no notion of what a cock was, no tranquilizing name, how was I to know that was a cock, that horrible rending of the silence into a thousand pieces, that shattering of space throwing its tinkling glass down on me, a first and frightful Roc.*

This shattering of silence precipitates the infant Cortázar into a waking nightmare that would never abandon him entirely. It informs the beasts that follow—in both Cortázar's essay and Zötl's painted bestiary—with a vaguely menacing shimmer.

What comes next, writes Cortázar, *has a Guarani Indian name: mamboretá, a name that's long and beautiful just like its green and prickly body, a dagger that suddenly plunges into the middle of your soup or drops onto your cheek when the summer table is set . . .* and there is always an aunt who flees in terror, and a father who authoritatively proclaims the inoffensive nature of the *mamboretá* while thinking, perhaps, but not mentioning the fact that the female devours the male in the midst of copulation. And Cortázar recalls the terrible moment when the *mamboretá would become enraged* with him for past torments and look at him from its branch, accusingly. Barking frogs come next (Zötl, by the way, was especially partial to frogs and the lion's part of his bestiary belongs to them), and swarming ants that *pass through a house like a detergent, like the fearsome machine of fascism,* locusts whose devastation brings Attila to mind, and a couple of amorous lions, their bodies trembling *slightly with the orgasm.* Cortázar fulfills his promise to us and admirably; we have strolled among the animals, although, to tell the truth, there were no cages anywhere. The vision is clear, unobstructed, and hot. Cortázar has given us totemic potencies; he has given us Aloys Zötl.

Now, because I cannot offer you Zötl's paintings and because Cortázar chose not to describe them, the task falls to me.

> *The imagining consciousness holds its object (such images as it imagines) in an absolute immediacy.*
>
> —Gaston Bachelard, *The Poetics of Reverie*

Immediacy is precisely the word that characterizes Aloys Zötl's bestiary. With few exceptions, he had seen his subjects in books only, yet painted them with feverish deliberation. I imagine it was chronic and unrequited longing that drove him on, for his bestiary surges with all the kaleidoscopic opulence of a mushroom-enhanced daydream. Spangled and lucent, Zötl's beasts have been conjured hair by hair; one can count their whiskers, their feathers, and their teeth. (One thinks of Borges's magician dreaming hour after hour and one by one the infinite elements that make for a living man.) Zötl's creatures take their ease in gardens as lavish as wonder-rooms; he has packed his pictures with rarities so that the overall effect recalls the haunting superabundance of Max Ernst's experiments with rough surfaces and sopping rags, those hieroglyphic landscapes haunted by hierophantic lop lops. Or Borgesian dream gardens that are the amalgam of all the gardens one has ever loved. Zötl's pictures provide a glimpse of paradise: It is a first glimpse, prodigal and unfettered. In other words, Zötl has painted the potencies of Old Time, when to name a thing was to bring it surging into the real. Even his scattered stones are poised for speech.

But—what about tigers? It seems there are none. However, there is a leopard, completed in April 1837. He is the same leopard that haunts the fables of the Maya and, as all the rest, he is meticulously painted *and he is very still.* Clearly he has heard a sound that has frightened him. Perhaps he has heard, and for the first time, the crowing of a cock. And perhaps this is the writer's task: to make audible a sound of warning—which is also the sound of awakening?

◆

> *The subconscious is ceaselessly murmuring, and it is by listening to these murmurs that one hears the truth.*
>
> —Gaston Bachelard, *The Poetics of Reverie*

Back to Egypt where things and their names were not seen as separate entities, but were instead in profound sympathy with one another. These perceived sympathies are often very playful, as in this story of Isis and Seth:

Seth, in the form of a bull, attempts to overcome Isis. Fleeing, she takes the form of a little dog holding a knife in its tail and evades him. In his thwarted excitement, Seth ejaculates and his seed spills to the ground. When Isis sees this she cries: *What an abomination!*

To have thus scattered your seed!

Where Seth's seed has fallen, a plant grows called the coloquint (or bitter apple). In ancient Egypt the word for *coloquint* and *your seed* is one and the same.

Within a writer's life, words, just as things, acquire powers. For Borges, *Red* is such a word, as are *Labyrinth* and *Tiger.* And if Beauty in the form of a yellow tiger or a red rose *waits in ambush for us (Seven Nights),* beautiful words are the mind's animating flame.

In his essay on his blindness, Borges recalls a cage he saw as a child holding leopards and tigers; he recalls that he *lingered before the tiger's gold and black.* Nearly blind, he is no longer able to see red, *that great color, that color which shines in poetry, and which has so many beautiful names,* but it is the yellow of the tiger that persists, as does its beauty and the power of its beautiful name. In his story "The Zahir," the Tiger *is* the Zahir; it is the face of God, God's name, the sound he uttered when he created the world, the *Shadow of the Rose* and the *Rending of the Veil (Labyrinths).* Tiger is the power that brings the unborn universe surging into the real and, what's more, it is the name of the infinite book you and I are writing; it is the letters of each word of this book; Tiger is the calligrapher's maze and also the text hidden within that maze.

It is the *shell* that tigers Bachelard—that lover of intimacy and solitude. A creature with a shell is a *mixed creature;* it reveals and conceals itself simultaneously. You will recall that in ancient times a fossil shell acquired the potencies of the moon. Stones of unusual shapes were empowered by Osiris also; they evoked the myth of his dismemberment and his own scattered limbs. In the myth, Isis gathers the pieces of her husband's broken body and makes him whole; she revives him. For Bachelard, *the fossil is not merely a being that once lived but one that is still asleep in its form.* He is speaking of the *spaces of our intimacy, the centers of (our) fate;* he is speaking of our memories, those powers that, *securely fixed in space,* remain coiled within us ready to spring and inform our lives with immediacy and our thoughts with urgency.

In his *Poetics of Space,* Bachelard writes:

> *We have the impression that by staying in the motionlessness of its shell, the creature is preparing temporal explosions, not to say whirlwinds of being.*

And in *The Poetics of Reverie:*

> *The passionate being prepares his explosions and his exploits in . . . solitude.*

The shell, the yellow tiger, the crowing cock, the moon—these are among the potencies in which time is compressed in the form of memories. To write is to engage a waking dream, to, in solitude, prepare a whirlwind. Says Bachelard:

> *. . . daydreams illuminate the synthesis of immemorial and recollected. In this remote region, memory and imagination remain associated, each one working for their mutual deepening.*

For Bachelard, Time has but one reality—that of the instant. The instant is our solitude stripped bare, stripped down to its essential potencies—its Deep Zoo.

◆

> *The shapes of time are the prey we want to capture.*
> —George Kubler, *The Shape of Time*

When I was a child, I came upon the dead body of a red fox in the woods; it was early summer and the fox's belly was burning brightly with yellow bees. A species of animate calligraphy, the bees rose and fell in a swarm that revealed, then concealed, the corpse. Yellow and black they tigered it and they glamorized it, too—transforming what otherwise might have seemed horrible into a thing of rare beauty. It is no accident that my first novel opens with the death of a creature in a wood.

If I have, throughout this essay, dwelled on the potencies of what I've been calling the Deep Zoo, it is because it is the work of the writer to move beyond the simple definitions or descriptions of things—which is of limited interest, after all—and to bring a dream to life through the alchemy of language; to move from the street—the place of received ideas—into the forest—the place of the unknown.

But the Deep Zoo's attraction is not sufficient. We must take care that our books do not resemble those seventeenth-century wonder-rooms or nineteenth-century parlors with their meaningless jumbles of stuffed bears, kayaks, giant lobsters, and exotic stools. In other words, just as the Museum of Natural History has contributed to, perhaps *enabled* our practical knowledge of the phenomenal world—and do not forget that the development of the museum coincides with the exclusion of Christian orthodoxy from the process of scientific inquiry—so must the books we write be free of those restraints that impede aesthetic invention; so must they be *enabled* by the rigors of intellectual coherence. Again, if we are to be quickened by the prime qualities of the Deep Zoo, we cannot, nevertheless, allow our books to be determined by excess or arbitrariness. Ideas and language deserve our chronic, our acute attention. After all, a book is above all a place to think, and the lightness of thoughtfulness our way of approaching the truth.

It is our capacity for moral understanding that enables us to interpret the world and to act thoughtfully and with autonomy. As psychoanalysis demonstrates, knowledge of ourselves and the world allows us to heal, to transcend the moral darkness that suffocates and blinds us. The process of writing a book is similar as it reveals to the writer what is hidden within her: Writing is a reading of the self and of the world. *It is a process of knowledge.* This is why the lost roads and uncharted territories of the world's maze deserve our interest. If a book is a place to think, it is a pragmatic place, a place of experiment and discovery, a *battleground* (Calvino's word) where the orthodoxies—religious, political, neurotic—that interfere with clairvoyance, are dismantled and replaced by a new order. In other words, to write in the light of childhood's burning alcohol, with the irresistible ink of tigers and the cautious uncaging of our own Deep Zoo, we need to be attentive and fearless—above all, very curious—and all at the same time.

In Maria Dermout's *The Ten Thousand Things,* a living sea snail in a box guards memories in the shapes of small, disparate objects. When the snail dies it is replaced—a spiritual manipulation that is also an act of magic. Resurgent, the memories continue to inform the world with a playful, essential, and erotic mystery. Writes Borges:

> *In my soul the afternoon grows wider and I reflect.*
>
> *—Dream Tigers*

Anita's Diary
Julia Alvarez

June 3, 1961, Saturday, time of day, hard to say

WE ARE FINALLY settled in and Mami says, go ahead, write in your diary as much as you want, we're in trouble already, maybe you can leave a record that will help others who are in hiding, too.

Mami now speaks in spurts of panic instead of sentences. I tell her that all I want to do is keep a diary, not save the world.

I don't want any freshness here, Anita, I've just about had it, I'm up to four Equanil a day, that's sixteen hundred milligrams, I can't take it.

You see why I need this diary.

June 5, 1961, Monday morning, while Mami showers in the bathroom next door

I can only write a little bit at a time, as I don't get much privacy around here even though it's just me and Mami in the walk-in closet in the Mancinis' bedroom. When the Mancinis lock their bedroom door, we can visit with them in their room and do things like take a shower. Otherwise, we have to stay in the closet.

Last night in the middle of the night, Mrs. Mancini shook us awake and whispered, I don't know which one of you is doing it, but I'm afraid you don't have the luxury of snoring in this house.

Our sounds have to sound like their sounds.

June 6, 1961, Tuesday, early—or so it seems from the light streaming in the bathroom window

Mrs. Mancini says it's a good thing she has always been in the habit of locking their bedroom door in order to get some privacy. Also, she has always cleaned the master bedroom herself, as the help have enough to do what with five kids. Besides, she doesn't trust anyone since she learned of the undercover training at the Domestic Academy. So the Mancinis' habits make their bedroom as safe a hiding place as any private residence can be right now.

The Mancinis have this kind of strange house like an apartment. The first floor is basically a large garage and laundry room and kitchen. They live on the second floor since it's cooler up here with a gallery running all along the back and stairs going down to the garden.

From their bathroom window, I have a bird's-eye view of the grounds of the embassy. But unlike a bird, I can't fly free . . . except in my imagination.

Later, evening

According to Mr. Mancini, loads of people are being arrested. The whole town of Moca was imprisoned because one of the conspirators comes from there! El Jefe's son, Trujillo Junior, says he will not rest until he has punished every man, woman, and child associated with the assassination of his father. Actually, Mr. Mancini says that people are secretly calling it an *ajusticiamiento,* which means *bringing to justice,* the way criminals have to face the consequences of their evil deeds.

I feel so much better thinking that Papi and Tío Toni were doing justice, not really ~~murdering~~ ~~killing~~ hurting someone. But still . . . just the thought of my own father—

Have to go. One of the little Marías is calling at the bedroom door.

June 7, 1961, Wednesday afternoon, a cloudy day, I can tell rain is coming

Once the Mancinis go out, we have to stay quietly in the closet and can't move around or use the bathroom. (We have a chamber pot but you'd be surprised how noisy peeing is, and how messy in the dark.)

Only two human beings in the house know we are here, Tío Pepe and Tía Mari (they insist I call them that now), and their two teensy Yorkshire terriers. Thank goodness Mojo and Maja remember me from school and Mami from the times the canasta group met here, so they don't bark at us. No one else knows. Tía Mari says it's going to be a job keeping a secret in this curious family. But it's just too dangerous right now to tell anyone where we are.

It is so strange to be in the very same house as Oscar, and he doesn't even know! Every time Tía Mari or Tío Pepe mentions his name, I can feel my face burn. I wonder if they notice my special interest.

The emergency procedure is, if the SIM start a search or anyone comes into the bedroom (besides the Mancinis), we slip into the bathroom, where there are two narrow closets; Mami goes in one and I go in the other, all the way to a crawl space in back, and we stay there and pray we are not discovered.

June 8, 1961, Thursday, right after supper, in bathroom

During supper tonight, Tía Mari turned on Radio CARIBE kind of loud. It's the government station, so it's fine if we listen to it. Meanwhile, Tío Pepe tuned his shortwave radio to Radio SWAN real low since that station is still illegal, and he and Mami and Tía Mari leaned forward listening closely to the "real" news. It was like night and day, what each station was reporting.

CARIBE: *The OAS is here to help the SIM maintain stability.*

SWAN: *The OAS is here investigating human rights abuses.*

CARIBE: *Prisoners praise treatment to OAS investigation committee.*

SWAN: *Prisoners complain of atrocities to OAS investigation committee.*

CARIBE: *Consul Washburn has been recalled.*

SWAN: *Consul Washburn has been airlifted by helicopter to protect his life.*

Both stations agreed on one thing: The plot did not work. Pupo, the head of the army, just wasn't there to announce the liberation over the radio, and instead, Trujillo Junior has taken over, and it's a bloodbath out there. The SIM are doing house-to-house searches. Over 5,000 people have been arrested, including family members of the conspirators.

I wanted to block my ears and not listen to this stuff!

Whenever I feel this way, I start writing in my diary so there's another voice that I can listen to. A third radio, tuned to my own heart.

So I snuck off to the bathroom with my diary, and soon enough, Mami was calling me, saying it was rude for me to be off by myself, come join them and be sociable, but then Tía Mari told her to let me be, that it's a good thing that I'm writing, that ever since I started keeping this diary, I'm talking a lot more.

It took her saying so for me to realize it's true.

The words are coming back, as if by writing them down, I'm fishing them out of forgetfulness, one by one.

June 9, 1961, Friday—evening

Mami has heard from Tío Pepe that Mr. Washburn is back in Washington and pushing to get Papi and Tío Toni on the OAS list of prisoners interviewed, as their lives are then much safer. Once the OAS has a name on record, it's harder for the SIM to get rid of that individual.

Mami and Tía Mari have begun praying a rosary to the Virgin Mary every night to take care of all the prisoners, but most especially to take care of Papi and Tío Toni.

I always kneel with them. But even though I'm talking again, I can't seem to fish the words for an Our Father or Hail Mary out of my brain.

June 10, 1961, Saturday, late night

The electricity goes on and off all the time. Tía Mari bought Mami and me little flashlights. Tonight, a total blackout again. So I'm writing by the light of this tiny beam.

I never know exactly what time it is anymore—except when the siren sounds at noon and then again at six for curfew. The Mancinis don't have a clock in their bedroom because it would never tell the right time anyhow. The kind you wind drives Tía Mari crazy because it tick-tocks too loud. She says she feels like someone is timing her life.

The truth is, when you live in such close quarters, you find out the most private things about people—like Tío Pepe always having to wear white socks to bed or Tía Mari tweezing little hairs from her upper lip.

I wonder what they've noticed about me. How I stroke a spot on my left cheek (where Oscar once kissed me) whenever I'm feeling scared or lonely?

June 11, 1961, after supper, second Sunday in hiding

Sundays are especially hard, as that was always the day of our big family gathering. But we were reduced to just the Garcías and us, then just us, then just us minus Lucinda, and now it's even less than a nuclear family, just Mami and me, like survivors after a bomb drops, a fallout family.

Every day, I ask Mami about Papi and Tío Toni. But on Sundays, I probably ask her more than once. (No, not "countless times," like she accuses me of!)

Today, I promised myself I wouldn't ask her even once. But by evening, I couldn't stand it anymore. Mami, I said, just tell me if they're okay.

She hesitated. They're alive, she said, and started crying.

Tía Mari pulled her into the bathroom, and meanwhile I was left alone in the bedroom with Tío Pepe. We were quiet for a while and then he said, Anita, one must think positively. That is how the greatest minds in history have survived tragedy.

I felt like reminding him I'm not one of the greatest minds, but Tío Pepe is so smart, maybe his advice is worth a try.

I close my eyes and think positively. . . . After a while, a picture pops into my head of Papi and Tío Toni and me walking on the beach. I'm real little, and they're holding me between them and swinging me out over the waves like they're going to throw me into the sea, and I'm giggling and they're laughing, and Papi is saying, fly, *mi hijita,* fly, like I am a little kite that is catching the wind!

Then, like on a birthday, I make a wish: that Papi and Tío Toni will soon be free and that we will all be together again as a family.

June 12, 1961, Monday night, bathroom, about ten o'clock

Sometimes, I try to think of my life in hiding like a movie that will be over in three hours. It makes it a lot easier to put up with Mami's nerves!

So here's the scene every night when I want to write after lights-out:

SETTING: Dark inside of closet. Mother on her mat, not the most comfortable of beds, but a lot better than sleeping in prison or in a coffin!

ACTION: Girl feels for diary and flashlight under her pillow. Absolutely silently, she begins to slip out of the closet.

MOTHER (whispering, loud enough to wake up sleeping couple in bedroom beyond closet): *Remember, the Mancinis are asleep!*

GIRL: *I know.* (Rolls her eyes in the dark, makes disgusted face, which, of course, mother can't see. Girl goes into bathroom, props flashlight on back of the toilet, and begins writing. Screen goes blurry and scene of what she's writing unfolds before our very eyes!)

Back to my diary—

I want to write down everything that happened the night that Tío Pepe rescued us from the compound—not that I'm likely to forget. I don't think I've ever been so scared!

Mami and I crouched down in the back of Tío Pepe's Pontiac with some sacks over us. Good thing, too, since the streets were crawling with tanks. When we got to the Italian embassy, Mundín was already there, and though Mami had sworn that she was going to kill him, she was so pleased to see him alive and well and biting his nails that she just hugged him and kept touching his face and hair. Poor Mundín looked like he had suddenly turned from fifteen to fifty, his eyes glazed over with the horrible news of Papi and Tío Toni being taken away.

Meanwhile, Tío Pepe and the Italian ambassador came up with a plan.

Since Mundín was most at risk, being a guy, he'd stay at the embassy, since it's off-limits to the SIM if they're obeying rules anymore. But the place was so packed with refugees seeking protection, we couldn't all stay there. So Mami and I were moved next door to the Mancinis', which is not as safe. (Private residences do not have amnesty privileges.) The plan is to get us all out of the country as soon as a way can be found. Meanwhile, we have to lay low, not a peep from us, as the SIM close in with their house-to-house searches.

When we got to the Mancinis' bedroom that first night, Tía Mari showed us "the accommodations." Here is the dining room, she said, pointing to her little bedside table with magazines, and here is your bedroom, she added, showing us the walk-in closet, then crossing the narrow hallway, here is your bathroom-living-room-patio. She was trying to make us smile.

I started unpacking, and what a surprise to find my diary among my things! Then, I remembered Chucha scooping it up and stuffing it in my laundry bag.

Ay, how I miss Chucha!

June 13, 1961, Tuesday evening

Tío Pepe says he drove by the compound today and the whole place was crawling with SIM. He heard through Radio BEMBA, which is how people are referring to gossip, Radio BIG MOUTH, that the compound is now a SIM interrogation center. It makes me sick just to think what might be happening in my old bedroom.

What about Chucha? I asked. The thought of anything happening to Chucha . . .

Chucha is fine! Tío Pepe assured me. It seems that the day after he evacuated us, Chucha also left the compound. She wandered into town on foot, to Wimpy's, and has gotten a job there sweeping out the aisles, which is near impossible to believe. But Wimpy is one of Tío Pepe's contacts, so maybe Chucha feels that by being there, she is close to us. Who can tell.

Just the thought of Chucha at Wimpy's makes me smile.

June 14, 1961, Wednesday morning, after breakfast

Poor Tía Mari has to think of meals on top of everything else!

For breakfast, she always fixes Tío Pepe's tray first thing, before the cook is up, and carries it to their bedroom. So that meal is never a problem. Tía Mari just brings some extra waterbreads and marmalade and cheese and a pot of coffee and one of milk, and fresh fruits. She locks the door, and Mami and I slip out of the closet and eat breakfast, taking turns drinking out of one cup while Tía Mari and Tío Pepe share the other one.

As for supper, Tía Mari and Tío Pepe used to eat out in the dining room, but now, with the excuse that they want to listen to the news quietly in their bedroom, they bring their trays in here and we all eat off the two plates.

The big midday meal is the difficulty as the family always eats together in the formal dining room. So what Tía Mari does is hide a plastic bag under her napkin on her lap, and she serves herself lots of food and eats slowly so that the little girls and María de los Santos and Oscar are excused long before she is done, and then quick, she scrapes her plate into the bag for us. It's not the most appetizing meal, a bag of mixed-up food, but when I think—which I don't want to—of what Papi and Tío Toni and the other prisoners are eating, I feel grateful and make myself eat so Tía Mari doesn't have to worry about getting rid of leftovers. (Mojo and Maja can only eat so much.)

Tío Pepe likes to tease Tía Mari that she has gotten so good with that plastic bag, if she ever needs a job, the SIM would surely hire her!

June 15, 1961, Thursday evening, already two weeks in hiding!!!

Earlier this afternoon, I was in the bathroom writing and I heard the three little Marías playing out in the yard. I felt such envy for them, enjoying the warm sun on their skin and the blue sky above.

Then, I started thinking how Papi and Tío Toni might not even have a glimpse of sky and fresh air or a bite of food and all my positive thinking went out the window. I stroked my cheek, but that didn't help either. I burst into tears. So much for the girl who never cried.

Mami caught me crying and began scolding, what is the matter with you, Anita, you're going to have to make an effort, please, you're too old for this.

Which made me cry even more.

Tía Mari pulled me into the bathroom and shut the door and whispered, Anita, you have to understand that your mother is under tremendous pressure, tremendous pressure, and so take that into account, and just keep writing, don't stop. Stay calm. Pray to la Virgencita.

My brave and beautiful niece, she added, hugging me.

June 16, 1961, Friday, after supper

Believe it or not, we get mail here!

Mundín writes out notes that he gives to the ambassador, who gives them to Tío Pepe, then we answer back by reverse method. It seems so strange that we should be writing back and forth when we're only a house away! Mundín won't say where exactly he is hidden in case the note should fall into the wrong hands, but he tells us he is fine, though very worried about Papi and Tío Toni. Today's note was just to me. I guess from his hiding place, Mundín caught a glimpse of María de los Santos sitting on the gallery with some young fellow, and he wants to know what I know.

I couldn't believe that Mundín was thinking about a girlfriend at a time like this!

But then . . . I'm thinking a lot about Oscar! As Chucha would say, the hunchback laughing at the camel's hump!

Tonight at supper, I'll drop a question about María de los Santos and see if the Mancinis volunteer any news of a boyfriend.

Mojo and Maja are making it hard for me to write—they climb up on my lap and chew at my pen. They look like two little waterfalls of hair, with a pink and a blue ribbon tied in a teensy pigtail on top of their heads.

Stay calm, I say to them. Keep writing, I say to myself.

June 17, 1961, Saturday night

Another scene from the movie of my life in hiding:

SETTING: Girl and mother sitting in bedroom with husband and wife who are hiding them. Radio they have been listening to is turned off.

GIRL (very innocently): *How is María de los Santos?*

WIFE: Muy bien, *she is fine,* gracias *to la Virgencita María.*

GIRL: *Does she have a boyfriend?*

WIFE (shaking her head): *When hasn't that girl had a boyfriend?*

HUSBAND (looking up from shortwave radio, alarmed): *What's this? I didn't know you were allowing María de los Santos to have gentlemen callers.*

WIFE (hand on her hip): *Allowing her? Who can tell that girl what to do? And where have you been that you didn't notice? Even the Chinese in Bonao know this.*

(Soon, a full-blown disagreement is in progress. Mother and girl slip back into closet, and mother turns on girl.)

MOTHER: *Look at what you started, Anita, I hope you're satisfied, such nice people, after all they have done for us.*

(Girl keeps her mouth shut—someone has to keep the peace around here!)

June 18, 1961, Sunday, late afternoon, sunny and bright

My least favorite day . . . but today has been tolerable because Tía Mari invited Mami's old canasta friends for a Sunday barbecue. Of course, none of them know we are hiding here. But Mami has been so depressed that Tía Mari thought that just seeing her old friends secretly from the window would lift Mami's spirits. It turns out that the whole canasta group are wives of supporters of the plot.

So why aren't they in hiding, too? I asked Mami.

Their husbands weren't directly involved, Mami explained. And we're in the most trouble because El Jefe was found in the trunk of Papi's Chevy.

Suddenly, it struck me that for a day or so, we were living with a dead body in our garage! It seemed so spooky as well as dumb. Why would Papi and Tío Toni leave El Jefe's body lying around where the SIM could find it if they searched us?

The plan was to bring Pupo over to the house, Mami explained some more. Pupo had said he wouldn't start the revolution until he saw the dead body.

Usually, Mami starts to cry or gets upset with me when I ask her about all this stuff, but today she was the calmest I've seen her since we came into hiding. We took turns peeking out the high window in the bathroom, standing on the toilet. Mami reported on everyone she saw, *Ay, pero* Isa has gotten so thin, and look at Maricusa, she's cut her hair, *y esa* Anny is going to have twins.

When it was my turn, my eye was caught by a young man, off by himself, reading. Suddenly, I realized, it was Oscar! Maybe it was from not seeing him for several weeks, but he seemed a lot older and very handsome. I kept watching him, every time I had a turn.

I've decided that I want to read more myself. I've been here almost three weeks now and all I've done is page through Tía Mari's magazines, play cards with Mami, listen to the radio, and write in my diary. Reading would make the time pass and take my mind off gloomy thoughts about what is happening to Papi or Tío Toni or us.

So I asked Tía Mari if she'd get me a book out of our old classroom.

Which book? she wanted to know.

I shrugged and told her to get me anything she thought I'd like.

June 19, 1961, Monday night

Tonight, Tía Mari said, oh dear, I keep forgetting to get a book for you from the children's library. Here's one to start. And she gave me this book about the life of the Virgin Mary.

I tried to read some of it, but it was not very interesting.

Instead, I experimented with some new hairdos in the mirror, wondering what Oscar would think of a young lady with her hair pulled back in a pony tail.

June 20, 1961, Tuesday, late night

I talked to Tío Pepe about how I want to read more, and he said it was an excellent idea. He told me all about famous people in prisons and dungeons who did incredible stuff, like this nun way back in colonial times, who I guess wrote tons of poetry in her head, and the Marquis de Sade, who wrote whole novels, and someone else who worked on a dictionary, and another person who came up with some new kind of printing press. It was real inspiring, but not for me. I think I'll just stick to reading some books and writing in my diary.

Tío Pepe said that one thing all these famous prisoners found while they were locked up was that it was important to keep a schedule so as not to go crazy. Right then, remembering how Charlie Price called me crazy, I decided to draw one up and try to follow it every day.

ANITA DE LA TORRE'S SCHEDULE IN HIDING:

MORNING:

WAKE UP—Slip out so as not to wake Mami and touch my toes (20 times) and do waist exercises (25), plus the ones that Lucinda taught me so my breasts will grow (do 50 of those).

SHOWER AND DRESS—Brush my teeth for at least a minute so as not to end up toothless like Chucha, shampoo hair twice a week, and definitely do not spend the whole day in my pajamas or muumuu! Tío Pepe said the Marquis de Sade put on his powdered wig and morning jacket while he was locked up. Also, British lords used to dress in their white linens in the jungle and look at how long they ruled the world. I was going to remind Tío Pepe how El Jefe was real finicky about what he wore, too, and look at what a monster he was . . . but I decided I better keep my mouth shut.

DURING BREAKFAST—Try to learn one new thing from Tío Pepe, who must be a genius, as he knows about everything and speaks five languages perfectly.

AFTER BREAKFAST—Read good book (once Tía Mari remembers to bring me one), write in diary, try not to be bored, as Tío Pepe says boredom is a sign of the poverty of the mind—definitely do not want that!!!

NOON:

LUNCH TIME—Try to keep my stomach from growling before Tía Mari comes back with her hidden lunch bag, try to be nice about the eggplant squashed up with the rice and beans and leftover chicken (always dark meat, my least favorite) because, as Mami says, beggars cannot ask for cebollitas with their *mangú*. (But I don't like onions with my mashed plantains!) Most of all, try to be nice to Mami.

AFTERNOON:

FREE TIME—Write in diary, talk with Mami about happy times in past. Tía Mari says this will really help improve her spirits. Try not to think about the tanks we keep hearing rolling down the street or the gunshots from the direction of the national palace, the dead quiet once curfew sounds at six.

NIGHT:

EAT DINNER—Usually the best meal, as Tío Pepe has to have his pasta once a day, which is my favorite food, too. Tío Pepe says I must have Italian blood in me. And, of course, that gets Mami and Tía Mari started on the Family Tree.

AFTER DINNER—Listen to Radio SWAN, try not to think of the sad news, of the 7,000 arrests, of the bodies thrown off cliffs to the sharks, of the army generals in their tanks shooting at neighborhoods where they think people are hiding, and instead . . . think positively! Join in discussions, think positively! Write in diary, look through Tía Mari's magazines, anything to avoid bad thoughts that might drive me crazy.

SLEEP—Lights out around 10 P.M., but I can stay up in the bathroom reading or writing, provided—Mami does love a lecture—that I am very quiet, so as not to bother the Mancinis. Listen politely, try not to roll eyes and make disgusted face at Mami when she gives this lecture every night.

BEFORE GOING TO SLEEP—Think about Tío Toni and Papi on the beach, try not to think of bodies thrown into the sea, think positively, think of the sand and wind in my hair, and Papi saying, Fly, and Tío Toni laughing as they swing me up in the air.

X X X X X
X X X X

(One mark for each day I missed writing in my diary!!!)

June 30, 1961, Friday, bathroom, very hot night

I know, I know, it's been ten days and I haven't written a word.

I just couldn't after the fright we had the night I wrote up my schedule.

What happened was just awful!!! I was getting ready to cross back from the bathroom to the closet to bed when I heard someone moving around in the yard. The night watchman had already made his rounds at 10 P.M. or so, and this was after 11 P.M.

So I woke up Mami, who "never sleeps a wink," but I always seem to find her fast asleep, and we woke up the Mancinis, who turned Mojo and Maja loose on the gallery, and they scampered off and down the steps into the yard, barking and growling, and then there were gunshots, and Tía Mari was screaming from the gallery, MOJO! MAJA! but no answer, and Tío Pepe was trying to drag her back inside, while also hurrying into his dressing gown as there was now loud knocking downstairs at the front door.

We went into emergency procedure—Mami and I slipped into the bathroom closets and back into the crawl space—one of the boards is loose and it made a terrible WHACK!!! sound—scared us half to death! We waited for what must have been 20 minutes but seemed forever. My heart was pounding so loud, I thought surely it could be heard throughout the house, and then, oh my God, I remembered I had left my diary on the back of the toilet when I rushed to the closet to wake up Mami! I didn't dare sneak out to get it and I didn't dare tell Mami because she would just die of one of her nerve attacks right then and there.

In a little while Tío Pepe was back, and we all sat on the floor of the closet, and Tío Pepe told us the story.

The SIM had come to the door to say they had been called by the embassy (a lie!) and told that there were intruders on the grounds. It turned out the SIM agent in charge recognized Tío Pepe, whose brother-in-law, Dr. Mella, had saved his little daughter's life after a ruptured appendix. Anyhow, when Tío Pepe invited them inside to search the house, this grateful man said that would be unnecessary. Tío Pepe stood talking to them a little longer at the door and then they left.

Tía Mari quieted while Tío Pepe told the story, but then she started to cry again about Mojo and Maja.

The next morning, the night watchmen reported the two dead dogs.

Poor Tía Mari was just crying and crying. Mami and I felt terrible, as it was our fault that this happened. And I felt doubly terrible leaving my diary out in the open! What if the SIM had come in and found it there? I could have cost us our lives on account of my carelessness.

For days, I wasn't able to write a single word. The third radio was turned off. But then, I started thinking, if I stop now, they've really won. They've taken away everything, even the story of what is happening to us.

So, tonight, I picked up my pen and, sure enough, I've been writing my heart out even if my hand is shaking.

July 1, 1961, Saturday morning

Two resolutions for new month:

1—Try to write something every day!

2—Keep diary hidden at all times!!! At night under my mat, and during the day when we roll up the mats, in the pocket of Tía Mari's fur coat she wears when she travels to cold countries. It's become so much me that finding it would be like finding me. So it's got to be a diary in hiding.

When I write in it, I feel as if I've got a set of wings, and I'm flying over my life and looking down, thinking, Anita, it's not as bad as you think.

July 2, 1961, Sunday afternoon

Another dreary Sunday, worrying about Papi. It's been over a month since I saw him. Sometimes I find myself forgetting what he even looks like, and then I feel bad, like my forgetfulness means he is gone forever.

When I get this way, I don't care about following my schdule or writing in my diary or daydreaming about Oscar. All I want to do is lie on my mat in the closet. Mami gets upset with me.

Come on, Anita, she scolds. You can't lie around all day. Who do you think you are, the Queen of Sheba?

Queen of the Walk-in Closet is more like it.

July 3, 1961, Monday night

The little Marías gave us such a scare this afternoon. Tía Mari was out grocery shopping at Wimpy's, and she must have thought she locked up her bedroom door as usual, but she hadn't. Mami and I were in the walk-in closet, with the door open for some ventilation and light, playing concentration, being quiet but not especially careful, when suddenly we heard the little girls coming into the bedroom.

Mami's going to be mad, one of them was saying, I couldn't tell which one.

She is not! said another. She won't even know.

Then there were sounds of opening drawers, and giggles, and one of them saying, you put on too much. They were at the vanity, trying on the lipsticks and perfumes, which I've done in my own mami's bedroom countless times.

Look what you did! You spilled it.

Then, one of them said, Let's go see Mami's bear, which is the way they refer to their mother's fur coat hanging in this closet.

Mami and I froze. Our concentration game was spread out on the floor. We had no time to pick it up or cross over to the bathroom closets, so we just backed in among the clothes.

Suddenly, we heard someone else coming in the room. What are you girls doing? You know you're not supposed to be in here. It was Oscar! I hadn't heard his voice in so long. It sounded deeper, more like a man's voice than a boy's.

The little girls scrambled off, but curious Oscar stayed on, looking around. Soon, the steps came around the corner and into the narrow hall, and then Oscar stepped inside the closet and ran his hand over the hanging suits and dresses, then stopped cold. Something had caught his eye. Very quietly, he backed out of the closet and shut the door.

Mami and I stayed hidden until we heard Tía Mari coming back. Virgen María! she cried. I believe I left the door unlocked.

On the floor of the closet, our concentration game was undisturbed—all the center cards facedown. But one card had been turned over: the queen of hearts!

July 4, 1961, Tuesday morning

Before breakfast, I heard a little pebble strike the window of the bathroom. Then another. I didn't dare look out just in case. But when a third went *ping!*, curiosity got the better of me, and I peeked out the high window—

Oscar was standing in the yard, looking up. I ducked down before he saw me.

Later

I've been wondering if Oscar did see me?

So just now, I took the queen of hearts, slipped it out the window, and watched it sailing down to the yard below.

July 5, 1961, Wednesday, after siesta

Yesterday being the day of independence for the United States, Wimpy had a barbecue behind his store. The Mancinis were invited. Tío Pepe says that Wimpy knows where we are and is doing all he can to ensure our safety, whatever that means.

Was Chucha there? I asked Tía Mari.

Was she there! She and Oscar would not stop talking.

I touched the spot on my cheek, trying to calm myself down. But my imagination has been going wild. Could they have been talking about . . . me?

Oscar was again outside early this morning, looking up!

July 6, 1961, Thursday evening news

This evening, a surprise: Tía Mari brought me *The Arabian Nights*, which has to be one of my all-time favorite storybooks. When she saw the smile on my face, she said, so he was right.

It turns out Tía Mari asked Oscar this morning what book he might recommend for someone about his age, and he pulled this one out.

I opened the book, and there it was as a bookmark—the queen of hearts!

July 7, 1961, Friday night

Just knowing that I might have a secret communication going with Oscar makes every day brighter. I'm spending a lot more time in the bathroom, trying out hairstyles.

This afternoon, Mami saw me fussing and said, Who's going to see you here, for heaven's sake, Anita?

My face burned. Of course, she's right. But still, I told her what Tío Pepe had said about the Marquis de Sade. Mami just answered with one of Chucha's sayings: Dress the monkey in silk, he's still a monkey!

During supper tonight, Tío Pepe got into a long explanation about how human beings aren't using their full potential. If the brain were this plate, he said, we're using this grain of rice. Einstein maybe used this wedge of avocado. Galileo, this yucca patty.

(To think how much potential I'm wasting combing my hair and wondering if I'm pretty enough!)

How do you know when you're using your full potential? I asked Tío Pepe. But before he could get a word out, Tía Mari said, I'll tell you when you're using your full brain power—when you're smart enough to eat your supper before it gets cold. That made even Tío Pepe smile and dig in.

July 8, 1961, Saturday evening

Reading *The Arabian Nights* again has started me thinking . . . can stuff like this really happen? A girl who saves her life by telling a cruel sultan a bunch of stories? Let's say El Jefe had taken me away to his big bedroom, like he wanted to do with Lucinda. Could I have told him some stories that would have changed his evil heart? Or are some people so awful nothing can really get inside them and make a difference?

I asked Tío Pepe, and he said that is the million-dollar question. He said many great thinkers like Knee-chi (sp??) and Hide-digger (sp???) tried but never came up with a satisfactory answer (and they were working with a lot bigger plate of brains than I am).

Tía Mari has promised to ask Oscar for another book recommendation.

July 9, 1961, Sunday, late afternoon

Mami and I have been alone all day, as the Mancinis went to the beach to visit friends. They shut up the house and sent all the servants away. The place is so creepy and quiet. And of course, every little noise scares us.

Mami and I played cards for a while, and then we went into the bathroom, and Mami herself put my hair up in a bun like a ballerina and made me up with a little lipstick and rouge.

Mami, I asked as we studied the results in the mirror, do you think I look just the tiniest bit like Audrey Hepburn?

Much prettier, Mami said.

She couldn't have said anything nicer! I forgave her all her nerve attacks and how she hasn't said one nice thing to me in ages. I turned around and gave her a bone-crunching hug.

Watch you don't break something, Mami said, laughing, I can't exactly go to the doctor's right now.

Later, Sunday night

Tía Mari came back from the beach with some seashells Oscar and the little girls collected.

I picked one to take with me to the closet, a shiny spiral with brown freckles. But then I remembered how Chucha used to say girls who keep seashells die old maids, and I took it back to Tía Mari and said, keep this for me until I'm married.

She looked a little surprised.

Tío Pepe just returned from the embassy next door with some exciting news—Mundín is going to be evacuated soon! It seems there is an Italian cruise ship in the harbor headed for Miami. The ambassador was hoping to get us all on board, but the captain said he could only take one mysterious passenger, as more would be too high a risk in view of how the SIM are carefully monitoring all ports of exit.

Mami is worried about Mundín and whether the transfer will go okay, and that starts her worrying about Papi and Tío Toni. She isn't sleeping as well anymore, as she doesn't have any Equanil left. Tía Mari says that the drugstores are all out. It seems the whole country is taking tranquilizers.

July 11, 1961, Tuesday night

Last night, as we lay on our mats in the closet, Mami started telling me stories about growing up on a sugar estate where her father was the resident doctor. It was like old times again, when we used to get along so well.

The best story was about when she turned fifteen, and her parents threw her a big *quinceñera* party. She wore a long white dress like a bride's and a tiara of sugar flowers made especially for her by the plantation pastry cook.

When the party was over, Mami really wanted to save that crown, but her little brother Edilberto found that sweet crown and sucked off the sugar rosettes. All that was left was the wire frame!

You laugh now, Mami laughed, but I cried as if he'd eaten up my heart.

Speaking of queens, Mami said, I don't know if you remember how six years ago, El Jefe's daughter was crowned Queen Angelita the First? You were just a little girl, but when you saw her in the papers wearing that ridiculous silk gown that cost 80,000 dollars, you said, Mami, is that our queen? And I didn't know what to say because the help was all around, and so I said, we don't actually have a royal family here, but Angelita was made into a queen by her father, and for a while afterward when we asked you what you wanted for your birthday or for Christmas or Vieja Belén or Los Tres Reyes Magos, you'd say you wanted your father to make you a queen.

And so for your next birthday, you remember? Your father made you a marshmallow crown. You wore that thing all day long in the sun, you wouldn't take it off, and those soft marshmallows began to melt on your hair. We had a time washing them out.

The thought of Papi made us both fall silent. I lay in the dark, remembering Papi and Tío Toni, walking on the beach with me, and the sand and the wind, and Tío Toni joking, let's throw her in, and Papi holding on tight and laughing—

I reached out for Mami's hand just as she was reaching out for mine.

July 12, 1961, Wednesday night

Wimpy and Mr. Washburn have been trying to do all they can. But Papi's name and Tío Toni's were not listed among those of the prisoners the OAS interviewed when they came. I don't need Mami to tell me that's not a good sign.

I heard some of the stories the prisoners told during those interviews. Mami and the Mancinis were listening to the OAS report on Radio SWAN tonight. They thought I was writing in my diary in the bathroom, but I was still in the hallway. The announcer read out passages, his voice matter-of-fact, but the facts themselves were horrible.

Prisoners complained about how their fingernails were pulled out, their eyes sewn open. About being put on an electric chair called the Throne and given shocks so they would tell who else was involved. About how one of them was fed a steak only to find out it was the flesh of his own son.

For the first time in a long time, I slipped my little crucifix in my mouth and said an Our Father. Then I went in the bathroom and threw up my supper.

July 13, 1961, Thursday night

What a surprise!

We were out in the bedroom with the Mancinis, listening to the news, when there was a knock: the maid announcing that the Mancinis had visitors.

Who is it? Tía Mari asked through the locked door.

El embajador with a lady, the maid replied.

Tía Mari and Tío Pepe were not expecting the ambassador, and so of course they suspected a SIM trick. We instantly went into emergency procedure.

A little later, we heard Tía Mari coming back into the bedroom with someone else. We heard her locking the bedroom door. Then she came into the bathroom and said, it's okay. You can come out now.

So we crept out of the crawl-space closets, thinking the other person was Tío Pepe or the ambassador himself, but as Mami and I headed out, there was a blonde girl sitting on Tía Mari's bed with her back to us.

We hurried back to the bathroom.

But Tía Mari called, come on out here, somebody wants to see you.

Mami and I were shocked. We all know that we are not to show our faces to anyone, except our two hosts.

Tía Mari appeared at the door of the bathroom with this blonde girl wearing sunglasses and a dress that you could tell she didn't much like by the way she was looking down, disgusted at herself. Then she glanced up with the most familiar eyes in the world.

Mundín! Mami cried out.

Hush! Tía Mari said, laughing. So it works, she said. I told *el embajador* that the best test would be if his own mother and sister didn't recognize him!

Mundín was on his way to the boat. He hugged us goodbye. I'm not all that happy about this, he said, and I don't mean the disguise. I mean leaving you. Papi always said if anything should happen—

He stopped when Mami started to cry.

Tía Mari let me walk with Mundín to the door of the bedroom. With every step, I felt my heart falling apart like that torture I heard about on the radio where a man was slowly cut up alive.

Mundín turned to me, and they say boys don't cry, so maybe it was because he was dressed as a girl, but there were tears in my big brother's eyes.

As for me, I was sobbing so hard, I could barely breathe.

July 15, 1961, Saturday morning

Mami and I stayed up late last night talking. Earlier, we had been listening to Radio SWAN, and the announcer closed the program by saying, *¡Que Vivan Las Mariposas!* Long Live the Butterflies!

That must have got Mami thinking about Papi because she started talking about the old days and how Papi and my uncles became involved in the underground movement against the dictator.

After your father came back from college in the States, Mami explained, he got so busy working and raising his own family that he didn't pay much attention to politics. Mami was whispering real low, so as not to disturb the Mancinis. I had to roll to the very edge of my mat to hear her.

But things began to go from bad to worse. Our friends were disappearing. One of your uncles was arrested. But we didn't know what to do.

Then we heard about these sisters who were organizing a movement to bring freedom to the country. Everyone called them las Mariposas, the Butterflies, because they had put wings on all our hearts.

Some of your uncles, like Tío Carlos and Tío Toni, joined right away, Mami went on. But Papi held back, afraid to risk all our lives.

Somehow, the SIM found out about the movement. They started arresting people, and their families, torturing them, and getting more and more names. Mamita and Papito and your uncles got out while they could. Tío Carlos made it just in time.

As for the Butterflies, they were ambushed and murdered on a lonely mountain road. Their car was thrown over a cliff to make it all look like an accident.

And it was then that your father and I took up the torch of the Butterflies and began the struggle again.

I couldn't believe my own mother with her bad nerves was part of a secret plot! But suddenly, like one of those lamps you click one more turn, and it throws an even brighter light, I saw her at Papi's old Remington, typing up declarations, or out in the yard, burning incriminating stuff, or in the garden shed, covering a sack of guns with an old tarp. My Joan-of-Arc mother, my Butterfly Mami! I felt so proud of her!

Mami went on telling about how the movement spread all over the country. Everyone was joining up. Papi contacted Wimpy and Mr. Farland, whom he knew from his college days, and the Americans agreed to help them. Some other men even persuaded General Pupo to join the plot. The General said that once he had proof that El Jefe was out of the way, he, Pupo, would take control of the government and hold free elections.

But then, things started to fall apart, Mami said. She sounded like one of those wind-up toys winding down. Washington got cold feet. The night of the *ajusticiamiento,* no one could find Pupo. The SIM moved in fast.

The end, Mami finished. Her voice was barely a whisper.

I closed my eyes, remembering the promise Papi wanted me to make, and I thought, no Mami, not the end. Long live the Butterflies!

July 17, 1961, Monday, late night

As we were getting ready for bed tonight, Tía Mari said, oh yes, I almost forgot. Chucha came up to me at Wimpy's today and said something I didn't quite understand. All three of us were in the bathroom, brushing our teeth. We have to do all our noise simultaneously.

She said to tell you to get ready to use your wings again.

Mami looked surprised. I thought no one but you and Wimpy knew we were here.

Believe me, Tía Mari said, I didn't let on. But she followed me all through the store and then out to the car. And again, she said the same thing. I said, Chucha, I don't know what you're talking about. And she just gave me that look of hers and then she took this out of her pocket.

It was a holy card of San Miguel lifting his huge wings above the slain dragon.

My heart has a pair of wings, too—one wing fluttering with excitement because maybe we'll soon be free! The other shaking with fear because I don't really want to be free without Papi and Tío Toni.

July 18, 1961, Tuesday night

I'm using my little flashlight Tía Mari gave me, as the electricity is out again all over the capital today. Tío Pepe's theory is that it's a SIM sabotage, one more reason to roll out the army tanks.

We are all feeling very hopeful, as there is a big rally planned for tomorrow. There was also a letter that took up a whole page in the paper, stating the rights of man, and signed with a lot of important people's names.

Tío Pepe says this is our Magna Carta, and I'm so glad I was paying attention that day in history class so I don't have to ask what that is.

July 19, 1961, Wednesday—we can hear the rally going on, shouts of LIBERTAD!

There is a very small chance, very small, Tío Pepe says, holding his thumb and forefinger so close they almost seem to be touching, that we might be able to get on a private flight that will be taking a bunch of Americans to Florida. Wimpy has been trying to work it so that Mami and I can board that plane at the last minute.

Suddenly, the thought of leaving our hideaway is scary.

Tío Pepe once told me about this experiment with monkeys who were caged for so long that when the doors were left opened, they wouldn't come out.

I wonder what it will be like to be free. Not to need wings because you don't have to fly away from your country.

July 20, 1961, Thursday

Oscar and I have a secret language of books going. So far, he has picked out *El Pequeño Príncipe, Poesías de José Martí, Cuentos de Shakespeare para Niños, The Swiss Family Robinson.* When I'm done with each book, I give it back to Tía Mari with the queen of hearts card back in it.

Then, when the next book arrives, sure enough, there's the queen of hearts bookmark!

What will become of Oscar and me? I wonder if there'll be a movie about us, like *Romeo and Juliet?* I just hope and pray our story has a happier ending!

July 28, 1961, Friday, another rally on the street

Because of all these rallies, the SIM have started arresting people again and conducting their house-to-house searches.

We are on the alert from Wimpy that our evacuation might be sooner rather than later. The problem is how to move us to an undisclosed location where we can take a flight to freedom.

The Mancinis are trying to figure something out.

There have been no more book deliveries. On Monday, Tía Mari sent the girls and Oscar and Doña Margot away to their friends with the beach house. Because of the rallies, there's lots of gunfire and massive arrests. Several bullets came through our old classroom window that faces the street. Thank goodness the children were already out of the house. Tía Mari refuses to go in there.

Mami and I are getting on each other's nerves again with all the tension. I try to do my pacing where she isn't doing hers, but there's not much room inside a closet.

It's hard to concentrate on anything, even writing in my diary. I haven't had the energy to keep to my schedule.

Tía Mari suggests we entertain ourselves playing cards, but when Mami sorts through the deck, she says, what on earth happened to the queen of hearts?

July 30, 1961, Sunday—most BORING day so far!

This morning the Mancinis drove out to the beach for the day to see the kids, so it has been like a tomb around here. All I've done is read and nap and look at magazines and eat the leftover waterbreads from breakfast, and now I'm going to try to write—

We're in the crawl space right now—and I'm scribbling down this note by flashlight just in case anyone finds this diary

—There was a huge roar in the backyard like a plane landing—now, a crashing sound at the downstairs door—

Oh my God—they're coming through the house!!!!

My hand is shaking so hard—but I want to leave this record just so the world knows—

Nychthemeron[1]
Rick Moody

I. Thus he lived and sojourned among us, and as he lived so he died

A hot, sultry Washington morning

She loosened my tie, but I opened my suit jacket myself—
Those sons of bitches are killing me

Shoots from the hip, misses the target

They beat me exceedingly, threw me down,
and turned me over a hedge,
afterward dragged me through a house into the street,
stoning and beating me,
so that I was all over besmeared with blood and dirt

It repels him to do these horrible things, but they've got to be done.

*

Never in history a more sensational investigation
started by a less impressive witness;
his main stock-in-trade is he's a master of disguise.[2]

Over the dark Atlantic, stewards and stewardesses plied him with
fine viands

[1]Sources: *Abuse of Power,* edited by Kutler; *The Coven* and *Return to Vorkuta,* by "David St. John"; *Six Crises of Richard M. Nixon; The Journal of George Fox;* miscellaneous pamphlets on Quakerism.
[2]I am also fond of birds.

I had a strange dream last night:
I saw things which cannot be uttered

He pressed a concealed button and the cartridge began to turn—

I could visualize my naked, beaten body collapse and sink into a mire of bottomless ooze;
then I spoke to the people from the graveyard.

Among his followers were those whose sole function was to maintain his peace of mind.

*

Therefore what the man does God does

Standing there in their expensive, well-made business suits,
wearing rubber gloves,
shouting "Don't shoot." The police came in.

The infinite can be reached by wiping out all marks of the finite[3]

As I age, I find my life increasingly disordered;
the constables gave me some blows over my back with their willow rods.

He talked about the whimpering, simpering weaklings at the university:

Oh the blows, punchings, beatings that we underwent!

Survivors all, unreasoning

*

They should not have bugged the candidate's plane. The beer was a false friend.

[3]It is as lawful to baptize a cat, a dog, or a chicken as to baptize an infant.

Because I would not drink with them, they struck me with their clubs—
I was moved to cry against all sorts of music

History shows that Truth has generally appeared first among a small minority.
Goddamn people around here won't read anything.

The sound of my door closing on the day's last client
was louder than a detonating grenade.
The back of my neck began to feel cold.

There are two things and each is bad. One is to lie and the other is to cover up.

II. After the narrative of an attempt to push him over the cliffs the account continues

Here is what happened:

The singer sang. It seemed as though her ode was to Darkness, telling of time before man[4]

Stop. My liberal friends don't love me anymore. Stop.

Crisis, by its nature, is usually personal—
Just, whatever it is, slice it off

I lost interest in eating and skipped meals without even being aware of it.
Jolly well bullshit and all that sort of thing.

She freed one arm and unhooked the back of her scarlet dress
At the sight of the woman eating he began to salivate unwittingly

[4]Again, the story was almost too fantastic to believe.

The ability to be cool, confident, and decisive is not inherited.

*

Dangers surrounded a lone agent operating in a foreign milieu:
kidnapping, providing prostitutes, uh, to weaken the opposition

We sat on some dilapidated rocking chairs on his front porch
overlooking the rolling countryside.

He replaced the pumpkin in its original place in the patch.

They brought dog whips and horse whips,
threatening to whip me.
They put me in a nasty, stinking prison.

As he took most delight in sheep, so he was very skillful in them;
he pressed the pocket of his coat and felt the crackle of
documents.

Well, I didn't, but he did,
and so on and so on and so on;
We are caught in a tragedy of history.

An unsuccessful attempt at suicide that same night.

*

The danger of throwing any baby to the wolves is you always just make
the wolves more hungry

Looking back, I can understand how he must have felt.
His career was gone.
His reputation was ruined. His wife and
children had been humiliated.

The cushion hurtled into the pistol, deflecting it, then into the man's
face.[5]

[5] I asked if he had had any work done on his teeth.

Fangs of flame shot from under the bed and an ear-splitting detonation hurled him against the wall.

Mind the light. God is not far off. He needs no vicar.

I saw something—an awareness of light rather than light itself.

Unfortunate that there were so few television sets.

*

Death reigned from Adam to Moses

See these are very moral men. They don't drink,
they don't smoke,
they don't screw around, they love their families

They haled me out, and stoned me.

He answered in a voice full of despair and resignation,
like Lady Macbeth, saying, in effect, "Out, damned spot!"

Those who fail are those who are overcome. Keep to yea and nay in all things.

I was struck even blind, that I could not see.[6]

Oh, the incredible treachery of that son of a bitch. This damn thing is a chicken shit thing.

All his poise gone now. The burden of the presidency,
the, the awful loneliness.

Hope you liked "God Bless America" at the end.

[6] I should have been elated. The case was broken.

Three Poems

James Tate

A SUNDAY DRIVE

We were out in the middle of nowhere when
Margot said, "Stop the car. I've got to pee."
"Jesus," I said, "where are you going to pee?"
"Behind a tree or something. It doesn't matter.
I just have to pee," she said. "Okay, but I just
hope that nobody sees you," I said, and pulled over.
I watched her walk into the woods. She was gone a
long time. I was beginning to worry, but, then, I
caught a glimpse of her, flying. The woods were
thick, and she seemed to be gliding between the
trees with the greatest of ease. I got out of
the car and walked in there for a better look.
"Margot, come down," I cried. "I can't," she yelled.
"Something bit me on the butt, and now I've got
the flying disease." I was speechless, and in awe
of her grace. It appeared so effortless and natural.
"What am I supposed to do?" I said. "I think you'd
have to put an arrow through me," she replied.
"I don't have an arrow," I said, "and besides I
could never do that. I love you!" "I think the
flying disease is for life," she said, gliding
over me. Then she was gone in a blur of light.
I walked around in circles and kicked an innocent
tree. She was being called. By who, I don't know.
But I could feel it, and it was very strong. A
Sunday drive, a pee in the woods, and now this.

James Tate

ELYSIUM

I had been sitting under an apple tree
in a meadow not far from town, when I spotted
a bluebird. They're quite rare these days, at
least around here, so I was excited. It flew
around my head, and then landed on a branch above
me. I was musing on my good fortune when I noticed
another nearby, and that made me smile even more.
The midday sun lulled me into an unexpected nap.
I'm not sure how long I dozed, but when I awoke
there were dozens of bluebirds darting and alighting
all about me. I was giddy with delight and almost
disbelief. Never in my dreams had I seen such a
congregation of delicately hued creatures. They
seemed to be flirting with me, swarming about my
head and shoulders, grazing my cheeks with the tips
of their wings. They were so playful and friendly,
I was not surprised when several of them landed
on the top of my head. I sat there, mesmerized.
But through the haze of blue in front of me, something
else was going on, something even stranger. Two
men in silver jumpsuits with gas masks were climbing
the hill toward me. They had power packs on their
backs, and were carrying long hoses or flamethrowers,
I couldn't tell which. The bluebirds continued to
flutter before my eyes, and I was suddenly consumed
by an hallucinatory fear. The men kept trudging
toward me with all their bulky equipment. My heart
was pounding. Then suddenly, there was this horrible
sucking sound, almost deafening. It lasted about
fifteen seconds, but felt much longer. The men
took off their masks and all was quiet. "Soul-suckers,"
one of them said. "What?" I said. "They look like
bluebirds, but they're really Soul-suckers. The ones
on your head were sucking your soul. We may have
gotten them just in time. Or they may have succeeded
in getting just part of your soul," he said. "There's
a device down at headquarters that can assess the loss
if you'd like to know," the other one said. I was
still feeling disoriented. I stood up, but my legs

shook. I started to ask them how they knew I was there, but didn't. "I'll be all right," I said. "And thanks for the good work." I started walking. Even a part of my so-called soul inhabiting those bluebirds for just a few moments before their untimely end thrilled me beyond words. I felt like a wild balloon in the wind filled with secrets.

WHAT IS TAUGHT IN SCHOOLS

I had been lost for over an hour when I saw Vicky sitting on a fallen log. I was so happy I ran up to her and gave her a hug. "Vicky," I said, "I can't tell you how great it is to find you here. What in the world are you doing way out here in the middle of nowhere?" "I'm lost," she said. "I was taking a walk, and the next thing I knew I was completely lost." "Well, together we'll find our way out of here," I said. "Two minds are better than one in this kind of situation. Come on, you'll see." We followed a stream for a while, but that just seemed to get us deeper into the thicket. We ate some red berries from a bush. We both felt dizzy after that. When a deer leapt right in front of us, we took it for an omen of good luck. So when we found Marty sleeping under a maple tree, we figured the omen had come true. "Marty, wake up," I said. He rubbed his eyes and opened them with a start. "Gosh, what are you guys doing here?" he asked. "We're lost, Marty. Can you help us out of here?" Vicky said. "I'm lost, too," he said. "I've been lost so long I decided to take a little nap to give me strength." "Well, if we put our heads together, surely we can figure this thing out. Too bad it's so cloudy. I can't even tell where the sun is in the sky," I said. "When I was sleeping, I thought I heard a train, but that may have been in my dreams," Marty said. "We'll get out of here," Vicky said, "I just know we will." "Let's just be sure not to walk in circles," I said. We hiked on, picking up

bits of trails here and there. We tried to be cheerful,
but that was a struggle. After crawling up one
particularly steep bank, we were shocked to find Justine
standing there looking down on us. "Can you guys help
me out of here?" she said. "It sure is good to see you."
"We're lost," Marty said, "but I think the four of us
together are sure to find our way." "Oh, I believe you,
Marty, it's just that my feet hurt and I'm hungry,"
she said. We drew lines in the dirt with a stick,
which made us all feel better. Then we followed the one
we all felt best about. Marty started to whistle, but
we all gave him looks and he stopped. After an hour of
walking in what we hoped was a straight line, we bumped
into Earl and Dolly. They weren't lost, they were just
out for a stroll. I told Earl that we were lost, and
he said, "You're not lost, you're standing right here
talking to us." I said, "Well, perhaps our stray wanderings
have tapered off a bit, but, technically, we're still lost.
When our lostness has found its end, I think we'll know it."

Sleep, Sleepwalker

Eleni Sikelianos

—For Barbara Guest

Sleep, sleepwalker

on a small half-earth found in a world
  of floating
      fluid gold

I think it strange
          to fly over the sea—
& see there the little whirlpools of thought
          streaking across the water—

          the imaginative imagines it made
          the rivers & beasts & sea

& all the Animal forms of wisdom
(mathematics, instinct)

The female, pale, dark & dense

depicts the hardened crust
that protects the material universe
& all its fallen dimensions

our state in soft mention
clothed in penultimate night

when the lineaments of the human form
are revised   in sleep

Everywhere we go the earth keeps
        tight trees, loose
    houses, blue
lights flickering on the Washington Bridge

& little bones housed in the seahorse's skull

Vulgar fish
        in a father's pouch
    the embryo has no mouth

with which to say
of tiny ghost horses floating transparent, hippocampic

By artificially slowing the heart
we can see
the stoned cherry at its wobbled pitch, independent
    sun rays of a
seahorse's fin, go to seahorse
heaven, a sea house to which
        we spin 3 x 3

When the Cuyahoga River burst
into flames, our
ancestors never dreamed
the face of the Earth
blanketed brown over the broken
shore choked with us

The same smile
as the world's smile?
The cracked face
of the Earth?

& so our animals weave
a small success at the edges
red fox, horned beetle

Razor wire around the garden
of Eden, I'm seeing all the seeded lakes
from the air, seeking

air-borne hairs, a soul's detritus

This is a snake-free environment,
sneak-free, but poison blazing is our secret

The Falls curve around
the collarbone of Niagara

the sun withdraws its hand
to caress a lazy smile riding
weathered lips up
toward a stunned star

What have I chosen for the shape
of my epiphany?—
Was it this

river, this

republican,
this,
the white soft gift
of the sheep?

This eidolon of my wild
career as a ghost's ghost, one shade
down there around Hercules' knees, one up here striding

under clicking leaves

Of all the let-go secrets
of all the wild beasts-world below

birds first
in my horizontal gesture

of sound to regesticulate the world once-prisoner-
to-world-view back to pure sound   Let's
make a vertical noise
above the lakes, attach it
to an (unknown) unowned
object—Is there still one
left in the world?

Planes like black
& silver gnats
slide down
the sky—oh
that so sucks

when the shining cars like ducks are slicking up & getting snared
in trees

The river is out there sliding
to our right in the darkened
even—we don't have to see it this
Friday night to feel its
sweaty cogitation like
a caterpillar slinking along on its
watery arms & legs

We are stuck at a spot along the tracks waiting
for another train trucking
the opposite
way from us to pass—Here, there are only
single-tracks so can I seem

to slip my mind
from its lazy path or back
to descriptions of delicate
blue the mind might have
received?

          What is your river thinking?

          Silent thoughts of cars
creeping across bridges,
a dark pressure on the tired café-colored
creatures fiddling in mud-bed muck

All our fingers work in this world,
which is good for getting
our hair tied back into rubber bands, & helping us reach
the Bronx, if that's
where you want to go.

Shake the world's dust from your
   feet, William
Blake

feel the furnace
of a genuine quince-shaped storm,
dark & scratchy like the one
on the dream horizon

          I want to go to the elevator
& ascend in the cool
wind that lifts us
in our just-awake traits
into the dusk, & our skirts asking questions

of cringing atoms singing like brass bands in the closet

I will make the music for you, a view
with no pictorial illusion of volumetric space

Eleni Sikelianos

Because how many Saturdays have you wasted
smashing up the mall, tangling
on the briny edge of corpus bones?

Let the west wind
asleep on the lake
leap on the lake

Little drawers of night
demons laugh, the unpredictability of
a negligee
roughed up
by time

Keeper of Bells
Maxine Chernoff

LIFE, THE MUSICAL

WHEN TINA ENTERS THE RECESSION-ERA front room, drab linoleum, blonde plastic end tables, dark, swirly couches covered in nicotine plastic, her grandmother is watching *Ted Mack's Original Amateur Hour.* "A happy show," she says in Yiddish. Tina, sitting across from her, hears a portly, mustached man sing opera. He makes the applause-o-meter go berserk. Tina listens as a teenaged girl in a dirndl skirt sings a medley from *The Sound of Music.* "A *shanie madele,*" or pretty girl, her grandmother says to her. Tina's deaf grandmother loves music.

The television is her grandmother's bright side. Her dark side is located in the unfinished concrete basement, where she goes to moan and howl like a wounded animal. The entire family tries to ignore her with silence or activity. Her father is out of the house, always at work. Tina takes her bicycle and endlessly circles the block singing songs from *South Pacific. Some enchanted evening . . .* she howls at the blazing sun. Her sister, older and freer, flees with her friends. Only her mother has no place to go.

In its aftermath, no one speaks of her grandmother's despair. Foreign and inexplicable, it is some beast that has accompanied her from Russia and lives in a dark corner. If the family pays it any heed, it will mark the entire group with its strange, unmentionable power. Their lives can't hold the explanations that tenderness entails. If they speak of their grandmother's sorrow, they will need to find words for other injuries: for Tina's mother's depression, for her lapses of memory after electroshock therapy, for her occasional disappearances for the rest cures that keep her alive.

Tina isn't to be openly insolent to her grandmother, but showing her favor may incite her parents. They might deny her lemonades and brownies for dessert or refuse to take her to Rainbow Beach. The glittery plastic headband she's been eyeing at Woolworth's or the new box turtle to replace the dead one whose shell has gone soft might go unbought. When Tina's grandmother loves her, which she obviously does, Tina is to ignore it. Too late to comfort her grandmother, Tina shows her incendiary appreciation by loving popular music, by knowing a full century of song lyrics, by singing like a fool as she drives or lies alone in bed.

In the 1970s an anthropologist reported on a tribe that was intentionally cruel to one another. As humor would have it, their name was the Ik. The Ik would laugh when their children got burned or if a stillbirth took place. The Germans have a word for this, *Schadenfreude,* which means lack of empathy. When Tina is in college and learns of the Ik, she wonders if her family might be lost members.

HER MOTHER'S SILENCE

Her mother's silence is an outcome of depression, a persistent one for which there's no explanation. Perhaps, as we now know and correct with a variety of pills, it's all organic. Perhaps her mother's father, the grandfather Tina only knows as a sick elderly man wasting away in a back bedroom, is the cause. Her mother's mother has gone deaf in Russia as a result of spinal meningitis that destroyed the nerve endings in her ears. Upon her arrival in Chicago, she marries a fellow immigrant twice her age and settles down. He has a family he's left behind in Russia, but that is hardly a consideration in his new home.

When Tina's aunt is born, Tina's grandmother takes the child to bed with her so that her husband, a skilled coppersmith by trade, can wake up in time for work without the aggravation of a crying infant. He no longer sleeps with Tina's grandmother. Instead, he sleeps in a different bedroom with his older daughter, Tina's mother. Tina's mother has told her how soft her father's earlobes were and how she'd tickle them before she fell asleep. Maybe he touches her back. Maybe the nights are cold and long, and there is no comfort. The story is closed to Tina, but she can imagine its progress toward some kind of tenderness.

Decades later, Tina and her sister lie naked in bed, bodies close. They hold their heads together and make loud purring sounds that vibrate their skulls, jaws, and throats. The noise is both comforting and shrill. Tina's sister is ten years her senior and already has a mature body when they begin this practice. What Tina remembers is comfort, no harm. Why foist harm upon her mother's report of earlobes?

Did Tina's father tell her to get a bra because her budding figure embarrassed him with its openness, because it caused him to yearn for his own daughter? Or was he concerned that some day without proper care Tina would have sagging breasts and no man to love her? These are the mysteries that stories determine to solve, but in leaving them open, aren't we persuading the story to tell us what it knows, keeping the work open to possibility? Seeking a motive is a vicious game.

EVERYONE GROWS UP DESPITE IT ALL

Tina is twenty-one and working as a waitress at the Drake Hotel. Her friend Michelle is walking away from work every day with parts of the hotel under her coat: glasses and wine openers and wicker baskets and raw steaks. Emboldened by Michelle's example (or perhaps by the Manhattan straight up that she drinks alone at a bar before taking the bus home), Tina enters the local Woolworth's and puts some patchouli oil and watermelon lip gloss into her pocket. When she gets back to her apartment, she throws them away. She doesn't mention the theft to anyone. She never tells anyone about her abortion either.

THERE ARE SO MANY THINGS SHE HAS TO LEARN

There are so many things Tina has to learn, how to leave her mother alone when she comes home from the hospital, how to understand a look of hers that means something special: *I'm trying to die and might succeed if it weren't for my daughters.* Her mother has read about Japan, where women tired of living take their children along. Although, by some logic, it's kinder that way, she won't harm Tina. She won't even tempt herself by taking Tina to the beach that entire summer. She buys her daughter a baby pool and sends her off to day camp. While Tina is at camp, her mother stays in bed. Sometimes it's most humane to almost disappear.

There are so many things she has to learn, how to speak English when she can't hear English spoken. She makes so many mistakes with it, but not even their humor is clear. When she says "Zoop" for 7-UP, thinking the 7 a Z, when she says "Applause" for "applesauce." She is teaching her granddaughters things they can do with their hands: how to play checkers, how to crochet. The little one walks around the house making great crocheted strings long as clotheslines. The grandmother writes poems in Yiddish to these little girls, her only darlings, some of which are published in the *Daily Forward.* Others are lost when the Jewish Home for the Elderly on Chicago's West Side has to be evacuated due to a bomb threat after the killing of Dr. Martin Luther King, Jr. The mottled black-and-white composition book she writes in is never recovered. It is thought by nurse's aides to be a figment of her imagination.

FRANKENSTEIN'S DAUGHTER

It must be Christmastime because it is over a television show Tina associates with that season. It is four P.M. and the house is eerily lit. Outside the sun is setting early, and long shadows are falling on the snow. Her grandmother is in the kitchen starting dinner. Her signature dish, beef stew, filled with huge onions and small cuts of celery, is boiling in a pot. Tina's mother is off with her father getting a shock treatment. Tina is only five and knows nothing of the process, which she has since researched, but knows that her mother comes home changed, her affect zombielike, her speech slower, and her memory and attention affected by lapses. Tina is used to her depression and its signs: the sweater even when the weather is warm, her lack of interest in food and food preparation, her commitment to chair sitting and distance gazing, but the aftermaths of the shock treatments are new.

Tina lets Sherry control the television. After all, Tina has her imagination. She can sit under the dining-room table, where she alternates identities. She is a cowboy shooting an Indian from behind a rock or Flash Gordon's girlfriend, Dale Arden, watching a torture involving bizarre wires and numerous dials. But *The Cinnamon Bear* is compelling viewing. Tina is not willing to switch to Sherry's favorite, *American Bandstand.* Tina guesses that the association of a favorite animal with a comforting taste makes the show worth fighting for. Emulating her mother's eating habits, the only foods Tina allows herself are bacon and pretzels. She would enjoy chewing glass were it available. She is skinny as a rail, and the doctor has asked her mother if she has been feeding Tina, a major insult for a Jewish mother, even a depressed, anorectic one.

Tina, at home with her grandmother, desperately fears being alone with her. If the telephone rings, her grandmother won't hear it, and Tina isn't supposed to answer. If someone comes to their door, Tina is supposed to mediate the situation between the census taker or Fuller Brush man and a wildly gesturing woman. In her mother's absence, Tina is the keeper of bells and the conservator of language in her household. Sherry comes home from the world outside. When her sister throws her furry-collared coat to the floor and enters the front room, Tina feels enormous relief. Without hesitating, as if she were the sole proprietor, Sherry walks over to the television and turns off *The Cinnamon Bear.*

Tina heaves two crashing blows at Sherry's back with her left fist. Sherry turns and pushes Tina to the floor, which vibrates with her weight. The momentum slides Tina toward the wall, where she lands with a thud. The noise causes her grandmother to come into the front room and scream as she rarely has. How can they behave this way at this moment? Their mother will be home soon, and what will she find? Crying, bruised sisters.

The scene goes black here except for the arrival of Tina's mother and the major clue Tina receives when something is seriously amiss: Her mother is wearing no lipstick.

SOUVENIRS

Tina's mother is almost eighty-six, and this is a Sunday outing. She and Sherry have taken her to an American chain restaurant convenient to her retirement home. She's ordered a huge plate of food for herself, French fries, steak well done, and breaded shrimp. Her eating disorders are long in the past. Her husband and mother have been gone for nearly three decades. Although Tina and her sister are grown women with families, their mother makes a remark about a sign reading "KIDS EAT FREE."

"These are my kids," she smiles shrewdly. "So they eat free?"

"Only on Tuesdays," replies the nonplussed waitress.

They begin discussing O.J. Simpson, a topic in the news.

"He's as guilty as hell," Tina's mother says. "I can't believe he got away with it."

"*Proste menschen,*" Sherry adds, meaning *cheap people,* a souvenir of their grandmother's Yiddish.

The talk continues to the news, how in Italy within a year scientists will clone a person.

"Let's clone you," Tina tells her mother, "and then we'll raise you again and see how you turn out."

"I was a cute baby," her mother smiles radiantly.

Aren't we all cute babies, Tina thinks, those we cherish, those we don't, those who raise us, those who are centuries in the ground, all of us starting with so much shape, so much promise.

Clustered

A PLAY

Robert Quillen Camp

SCENE ONE. All is quiet. Suddenly the living room is overcome with the noise of business. Alicia doesn't request anything. A voice comes over the intercom. "Please continue with your noise." Noise and more noise. Bent over like a schoolboy, Alfred is reminded of his own children. Everyone is romantically involved, but these entanglements are red herrings. "Come over here." "No." "Give me your hand." "No." "Let me remember the feeling." "I can't, I'll yell for help." Everyone yells. No one cries. A paperboy decries, "No kissing today." The office is overcome. A piano. Everyone is everywhere at once. Noises of business are slowly replaced by noises of its effects. "Please tell my husband about the disks and drives, the screens and sentences, my monitors and memory." Another noise. Another quiet.

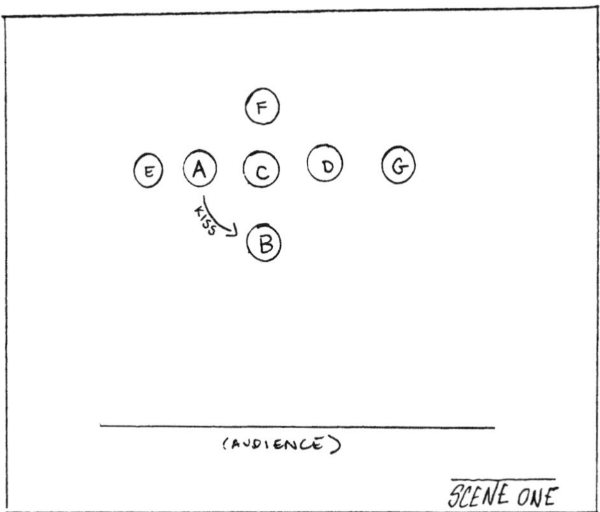

*Note: performers on wheels.

SCENE TWO. A long silence. A ghost town. A freak show. "What's the price of admission?" "Ask the boss." "Where is he?" "In the picnic shed. Having a picnic." "He's busy?" "Not really." "Where's the shed?" "Behind the shooting range. You can't miss it." "I'll be right back." A long silence. 6 ghosts reveal themselves. A freak show. A ghost town. Another ghost enters, in the form of furniture.

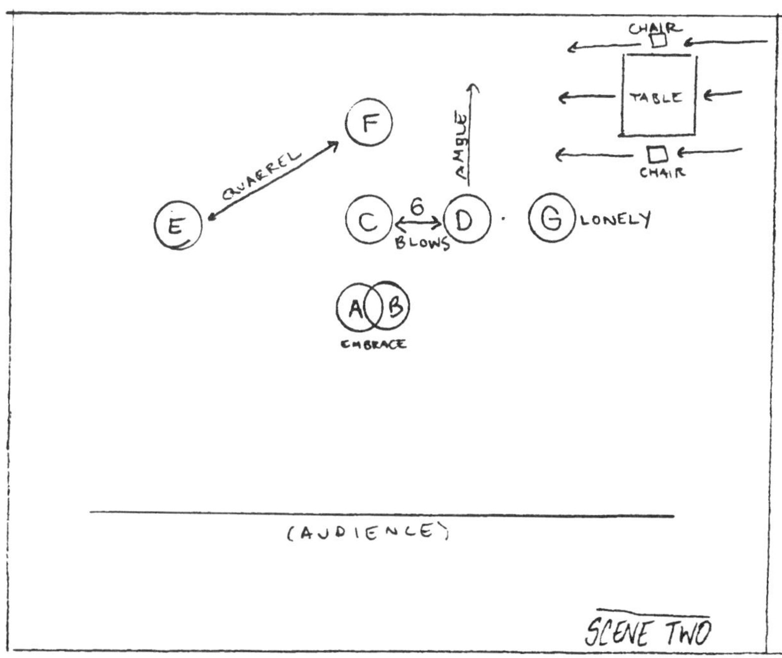

SCENE THREE. Another night at the castle. Bobby falls asleep. Bandits rob the kingdom blind. They escape, naturally. "We would like to ask about your qualifications, we would like to ask about your *quality*." "Naturally." A bell sounds. Everyone starts over again or just goes home. Officials research the official story. They write critical analyses and fax them to one another. They read the papers and are brought to tears.

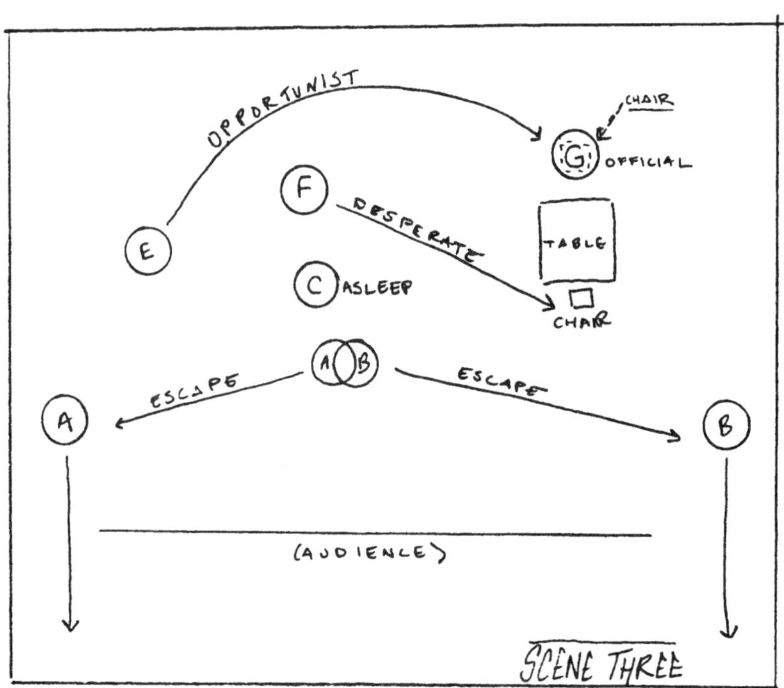

SCENE FOUR. Jimmy stays sleeping. Career ruined, the chair of the commission creeps offstage to do bad things in motel bathrooms. Gary hides in the corner. Gary makes a telephone call. The rooms get comfortable. It's time for a meal, but not one of the usual ones. A Saint Bernard falls asleep on the new rug.

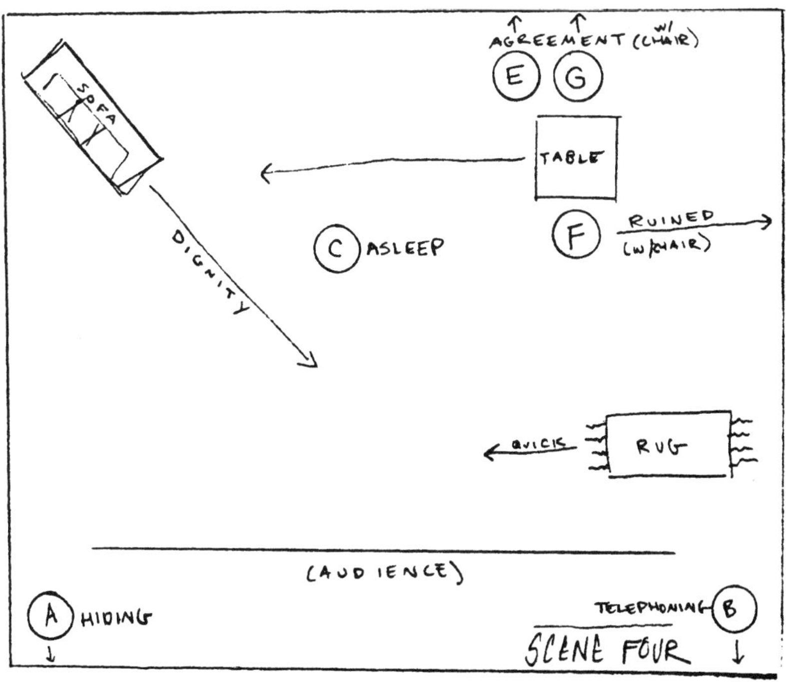

SCENE FIVE. Clustered together, the sailors ready themselves for the big city. "I'm gonna fuck myself blind." "Better yet, find yourself a girl." One of the sailors is sleeping. They take his watch. The moon is out. The sailors look up and it silences them. A paperboy decries, "No kissing today." The sailors think quietly to themselves. Several honeybees find their targets. A cry.

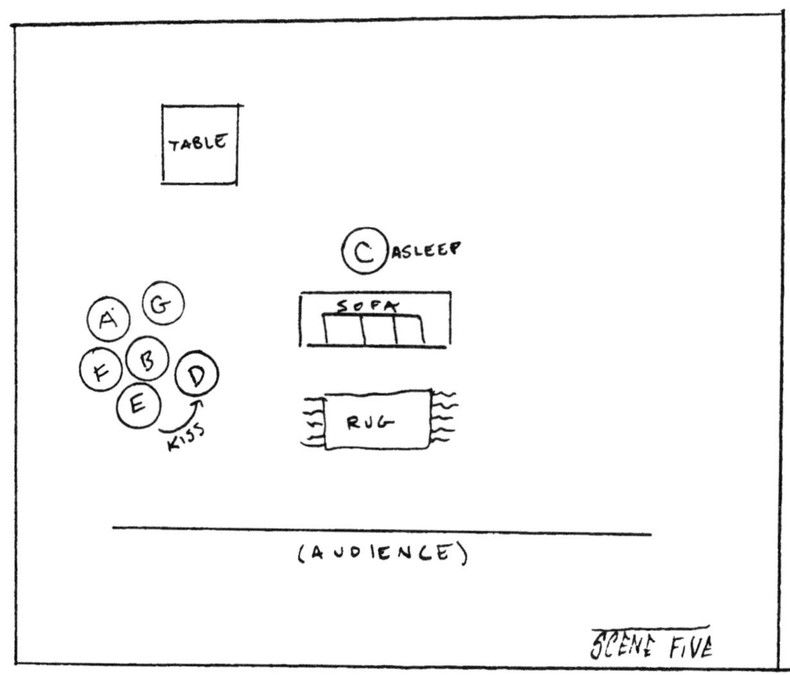

SCENE SIX. Another day on the road. "Rock and roll takes its toll." Mary and Allison arm wrestle. Cara, still asleep, can't stop them this time. "I win. You owe me a dollar, a foot massage, *and* a written apology." The roadies grumble. "St. Louis is for suckers." They get out of town. Mary and Allison repeat themselves. "I win. You owe me a frankfurter, a ticket to the haunted house, *and* a written apology." A breeze blows quick, like Mercury.

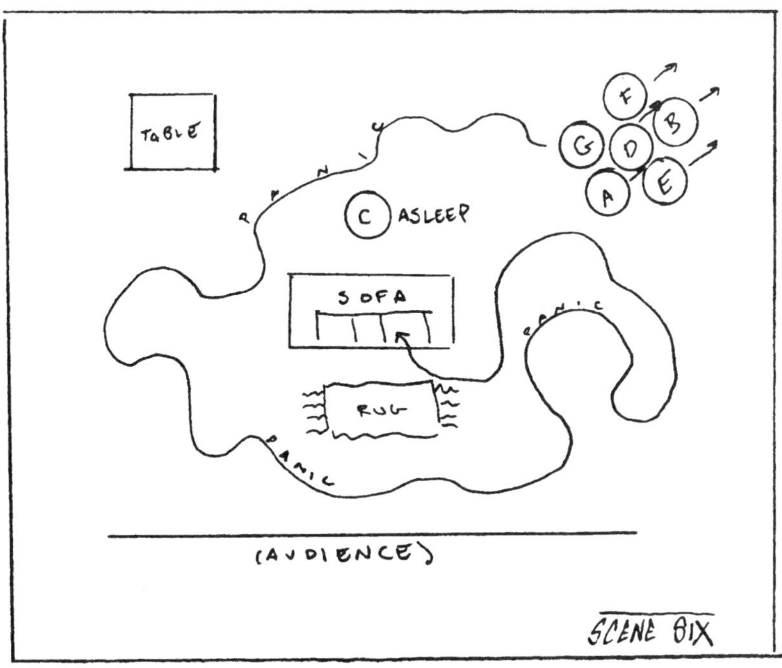

SCENE SEVEN. Gregory espies himself in the shop window. "How now." Store clerks busy themselves over the customer who seems to have fainted. He hasn't. Mary Ann stifles a laugh. Harry stifles a moan. Jonathan stifles a wail. Five lurching drunks make a makeshift parade. Gregory feels around in his pocket for a phone number. He finds it and is reassured. The lights flicker for a moment, but order is restored. Two alley cats run for their lives, one to the east, and one to the west. They are never seen again. "That was a disaster."

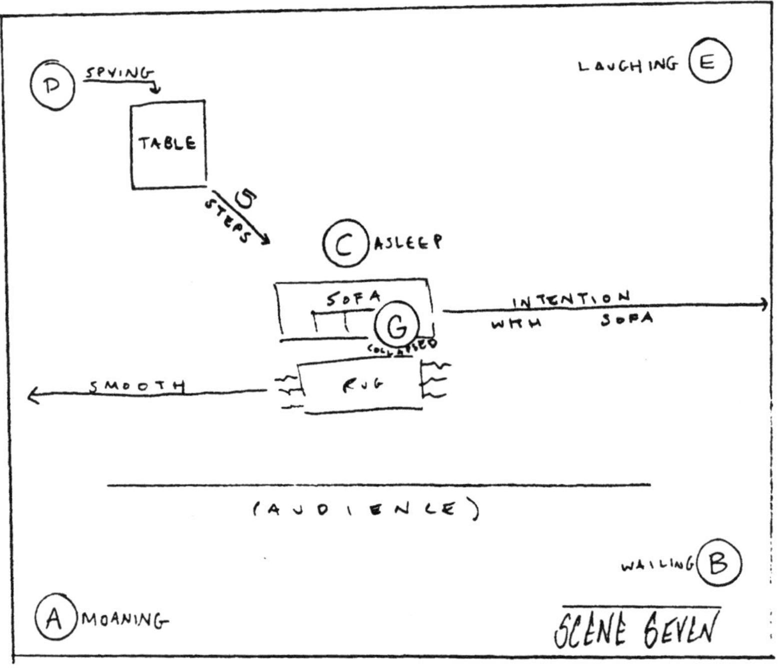

SCENE EIGHT. The lights flicker and go out. Alicia makes a request. Five solemn candles are lit. Five quick fortunes are told. "Someone can read your mind." Alfred hides from the medium. She knows his secrets. Waking up, Francis looks out the window onto the street below. She does not recognize it. "Not again." She finds a pair of trousers and rifles through them, looking for change for the bus. She finds it. She disappears. Someone blows out the candles.

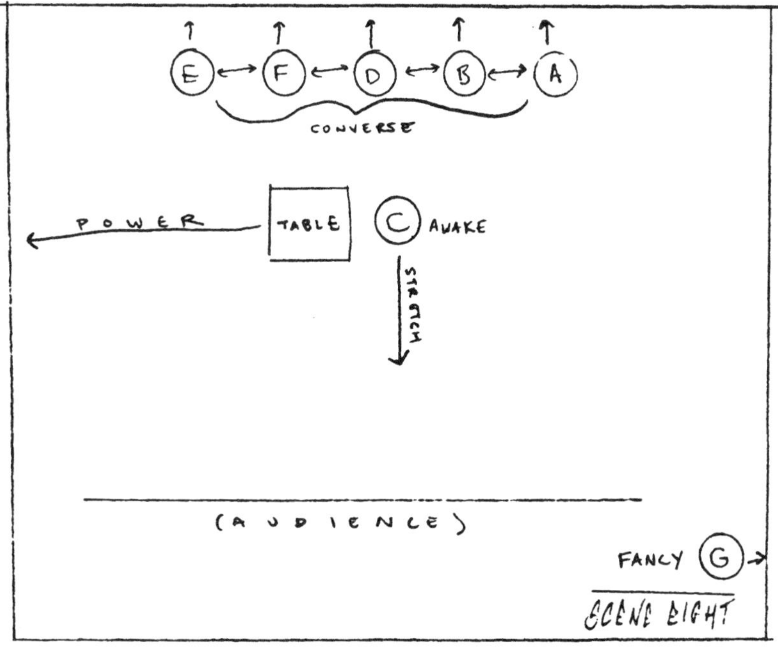

SCENE NINE. All is quiet. An owl appears at the window. It pauses, surveying the room. A noise. It flies away. Another noise. Another quiet.

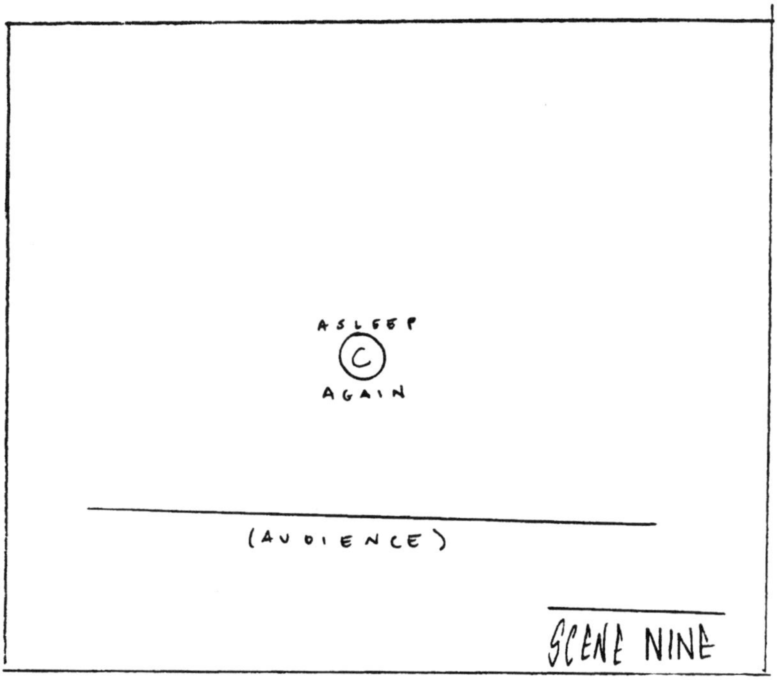

ASLEEP
C
AGAIN

(AUDIENCE)

SCENE NINE

Hölderlin Hybrids: In Early November

Rosmarie Waldrop

1.

Penetrates to the bones. The cold. Inside which marrow. Over which we must a woolen blanket spread. Another person's body should lie. On yours and upside down the sun. But in the wind crows. The vane.

•

When down the stairs. And think "I'll make tea" or "Why is our happiness steeped in longing?" As if they were the same. A little darker then. So isolated in the mind a human figure. Sailboat. Elephant.

•

Mind's eye if concealed. Knife if sharpened. If I were a figment in somebody's head the pain could not be. This strong. Let not darkness fall. On the space of missing memory. Hard is it. To fill with lemons. With children too. Just air.

•

The windows the bells ring through. As if gates. Because still modeled on nature, on trees, the gates. And autumn wind. The image of the moon in water. Has been blown away. Out of all the molecules and atoms rise higher and higher buildings. Muting the air.

2.

Movement however. How does it come? Do I think I'll spread my legs before I spread my legs? Whom (whose legs) do I imitate? May a woman. From the mess of her life look up and say: Let me be. Like the heroine in a novel?

•

As long as her legs are covered with fine hair and rain. Falls mixed with hail. Her ankle measures up against any Albertine, Anna, Hester, Molly, Dorothea, Emma, Sonja, Natascha, and Mme. Chauchat. Is only herself a woman? Is manifest as a view of trees her nature? Is she hiccuping?

•

Iron rail. Of thumb. Not to stumble where your boldest. Dreams stand between.

•

Such is the sight of the sea. Reverses time. And he thought he'd only have to cry "Mother." Under water. And his love. No purer a tango in the starry night, if I may say. Than his purpose to hold close her body.

•

Is there love on earth? Difficult to think about. What is deep inside. But lovely the envelope of the body. Because it envelops. I discover late in life the ancients. Had already studied diseases of skin.

3.

To bleed in body and heart and fall among particles. Does this please the gods? The Angel of Death is abroad. The soul I believe must leave its house in the morning lest. Howling dogs cavort among orifices. And the voice of. So many birds.

•

In a major key: Dear old body how you pass. In August. From one year to another. Like a telescope through the Milky Way. I know you well but a sharp pain cuts. Through my stomach. And sinks like a stone down to the bottom. And is not an idea. And the moon I see enter the window. I don't without good reason compare. Floods the plain.

•

This I know. The scales flash silver under the knife and the pike. Ceases to think. And Heine is covered with the Hebrew for blanket. But my body aches from. The mare I ride through the night. In my dream we did not sit together.

•

Butterflies however fluster me. As they flutter. Almost unreal. All my desires it is true. Are presumptuous. Would I like to be a comet? They are swifter than birds and flower in fire. But skin is only external. And one thing touches another. More than air moves about in waves

4.

Of the sound that fills space. To capture. More than the tiniest part is beyond. Our ears though they stick. Out from the skull. On the other side of the wall a tapping. A knife on wood? Followers of materialism believe matter. Is solid. Lifeless lumps of clay in the field. Others, that even a stone's not simple. And of movement the source not external but found? In matter itself?

•

Ethereal matters dissolve in particle and wave. Body fluids feed. Flushed. What was her name? Blackbird. Birth. Bath. Wherever we go we carry. Our male or female organs.

•

When a man looks in the mirror and sees his soul. As an image. Is it a kind of insect? A thing with wings, three pairs of legs, two antennae? But if a man's eyes are closed when he dies. Will the soul burst? Through the skin? King Oedipus had an eye too many. The suffering of this man. Was it spiritual or only indescribable?

•

When a play such a thing represents. How do I feel? Or thinking of you? A fact carried away by: The world is big and wide? As if I didn't understand that everyone dies. Can we avoid error? If we speak clearly and to the point? His suffering of course. Oedipus had that.

•

But I want no more to pray. With inner organs. Too long to long. To lust. And drawers for first things first. And shoes.

5.

To have it cut open. Your chest. And your flesh peered at and operated. This is pain. But it also is suffering when with a rash is covered red a woman. And crows stare at her with one eye.

•

This is the work of the light. It breaks up and divides into colors. Yet impossible to see inside the body. To liver, gall bladder, kidney, spleen, intestines. To the suffering of Oedipus that moves upon the face of the fluids. Without form. And void. And darkness is upon the son of Laios.

•

And afterward as in a kind a nightmare. Desires are gathered together unto one place. And a city appears.

Rat Man of Manhattan

Paul West

He likes his little place, his bolt-hole, in certain moods wondering if he will ever go on to his true destiny of controlling the drawbridge over some river, squatting in his little caboose-cabin as the warning signs go up and the two-way traffic glides to a halt every quarter of an hour. There he might even sleep, some nights, locked in safely with apple and the *New Republic,* outside on his mini-platform a comfy chair to which he has affixed a clip-on parasol, enterprisingly packing the hollow underside of the plastic arm with bits of plywood to stop it from wobbling. Here, in between withdrawn bridges, he can snooze or read. Any of New York's waterways would do, he thinks, provided he applied in time; the jobs went so fast with a whole population of Manhattan Steppenwolves to draw on. Thanks to notable manual dexterity he would be a formidable candidate, plus his sturdy patient bladder, his tested eyes, his way of thriving foodless on the phenomenology of yachts cruising through the *V* opened by a bridge's twin halves. He would do, he knows, just so long as within his bridgeman's cab he had a few supplies: Elmer's glue, chips of plywood, a hacksaw blade, a blob of bubblegum, tea and sugar, the usual hotplate. He inhabits a small world, would like it even smaller, he thinks, until it fits him like a bullet-proof jacket. No room for Quent, or even his maurauding black beetles. He would call it the stethoscope room, where he could listen to his chest and yet keep the results private. Some vague hint of his supposed Austro-Hungarian idyll stirs him, but he soon forgets it, half-reveling in memories of yachts bound for the briny with ogling girls and pipe-puffing young salts, one of whom he might have been back in his salad days. Yes, he recalls, a meerschaum pipe such as yachtsmen smoked you made from sea-spume, foam, though it took a bit of nautical experience to get it right first time as one pipe segued into the next, and you realized only much later that you had made a series of foamy white pipes out of a series of mermaid's tails.

An apartment house was an ocean liner really, just another ship of fools with a greasy super in the basement kicking the dumb waiter to make it behave. So, when he looks out at the disheveled city, he sees only the ocean with a few scattered ships ready to pass in the night, no U-boats lurking, no nuclear subs grinding through the darkest depths. At heart he's a lover of sail, addicted to inland waterways and wide, flat estuaries. Yet he has never lost his love of surprise, as when he used to say to Quent, "What do *you* have in mind?" and Quent embarked on some exotic takeoff of a familiar tale, with Shrop playing Robinson Crusoe and himself playing Man Friday, embellishing the story of one man, Alexander Selkirk, who survived fictionally only because of someone else there on the island: servant-slave, interlocutor, friend. Just so. Well, no more of that music, evidently. Now Shrop feels really marooned with no bridge to raise and lower, no makeshift philosopher to become instead of himself, but only the deadly air of ground zero to inhale during his evening walks, always aimed at the twin towers but always deflected. Oh, he could get through, if he really tried, to the viewing parapet, but something sheepish makes him turn away and study the environs instead, with twitching knees and stinging eyes. Is he looking for, hoping for, Quent, thinking the island is really an island, full of ungracious noises?

Home, he rearranges his purses.

Sets an ice cube in the middle of hot soup.

Tries to recall what exactly the Something Riviera of the Something Else World was.

Resists calling Quent, to whom a phone has become a deadly weapon.

Wonders about Karen Tumulty in her Ilse Koch version and asks himself Is he really aboard a troop carrier containing Nazi prisoners of war, all being treated demurely as required by the Geneva Convention?

For months now, it may even be seasons or years, Shrop has busied himself with the dim intuition that, as he grows and matures, he is edging into the shadow of some fabled figure of local gossip, even history or literature. As if he had heard of Odysseus, say, which of course he has, he senses the wanderer in himself as well as the renowned homesickness of that worthy man, more alluded to than read about. As if, beginning to learn the privileges and delights of skulking underground out of sight, he senses he is becoming an Underground Man, respected yet scorned. As if, having some knowledge of the Japanese soldier who stayed on his island long after the cease-fire, suspicious and righteous, he emerged only after sustained cajolements by friends and veterans—a national hero or a war criminal. This, Shrop decides, is the thematic part of life, in which whatever legend gathers about him begins to make its presence felt. His store of heroes is not large, but he takes them seriously, wondering nonetheless if they somehow blend together: Odysseus into Underground Man into the Japanese soldier. He thinks not, but finds himself haunted by another figure, about whom he has heard, transplanted from another culture: the enigmatic Rat Man of Paris, whom he has heard described as having a not very certain relationship with civilization, toward which he feints without putting his heart into it. The murderous assault on the twin towers may have bounced Shrop into pretty much the same predicament, or so he thinks, debating if there can truly be influence or merely derivation in these matters. Perhaps, he tells himself, I am only one among thousands, each wondering if he might be unique.

Lawrence of Arabia? No.

Charlie Chaplin? Hardly.

The Elephant Man? Nice try, but no.

He never plays this game for long, immodestly assuming he might indeed be unique even when he goes out in what he likes to think of as mufti: shiny black garbage bags stapled together to compose a suit of sables in which he might pass muster among the de rigueur black of Manhattan. As it is, he goes out busily reflecting the sun, in part a tantalizing see-through as passers-by watch him and try to peer within. Is he naked in there or not? Crudely cut eyeholes, the work of nail scissors, reveal his blue eyes, but no one is looking at them. He ends up wetting himself on occasion (out for too long) or losing several pounds like the man sheathed in vinyl at a sex party. That he is following in the wake of some predecessor he never doubts, but he has trouble creating the right mental set for his see-through walks among people who figure him for some elegiac promenader designed to remind them of earlier woes, lest the catastrophes in between distract them.

Yes, he needs the book of the character, he decides, even a cheap paperback encrusted with rotting fruit and hosed down with sheep dip, borrowed, bought, or stolen, with or without the author's portrait, whoever he be, that remarkable he who has passed into history along with his stolen creation. After all, there was once upon a time a real Rat Man who harassed boulevardiers with the rat ill-hidden inside his coat. Thus, he says complacently, the purloined figure enters myth only to go back into history sea-changed by immersion in the human mind. I could be part of that too. He vows to try, not having much to go on, but willing if need be to haunt the park, act on stage, get arrested, give interviews about topical scandals. Anything, just to get himself noticed and fulfilled. No more shrinkage, he says, cursing Quent and all like him. He intends to become one of the walking wounded bandaged to within an inch of his life. How's that for what he has come to call, in fake Brooklynese, A Pocklyptic situation? Only the dead know Brooklyn, and they are out of date.

Now more than ever, he fancies keeping a low profile, reducing his memberships, subscriptions, pledges, gifts, all in accord with his circumstances. The twin lights over his kitchenette do not work, thanks to a broken switch unmended. Rain comes in at the ill-fitting western window. In the refrigerator, the freezer unit thaws. The couch is lumpy and unsupporting; the cushions roll around onto the floor, but do nothing to ease the sit of his body. A drawer pull in the bedroom has failed, making it impossible to tug the drawer out, and he vows to fix it either by winding dental floss around the shaft of the pin, then gluing it in place in the widened hole, or buying a pretty knob at the drugstore. There is too much to do, given the extraordinary stresses of his daily life, the lateness and hazard of the mail (he still dreads anthrax), the frying crackle that has plagued his phone ever since September 11, the lack of hot water during the devastating nights. How did he ever find time to tend his purses, write movie reviews, do voice-over for the Factual Channel, or answer mail? He feels overcome by trivia, yet when he gropes around for the big vital thing he would otherwise be doing he cannot think of it. Like his philosophy, and the title it languishes under, it has vanished. The one huge thing in his life is lamenting the absence of *things,* and for this he blames the aerial attack on the twin towers.

Yet, he chides himself, it's the same worldwide, isn't it? If the woman above you is constantly rolling her furniture about, just for the hell of it and not in order to clean (who cleans a dozen times a day?), would she not also be there in Semipalatinsk, Kyoto, or Rio? The mad took over civilization long ago, not with a view to doing anything in particular with it, but just for kicks, to ram their bad behavior down everybody's throat. In the midst of all this sociological carnage, overlaid by terror bombings and such, there are just a few reliable certainties, such as (he cozily exemplifies) his box of calorie-free meringues: When you bite one in half, the break comes in two even faces, a clean flat cut proving that the cells of the meringue—no sugar—have been correctly aligned and all repose in the same direction. No jagged edges. This pleases him so much that, once launched, he can devour an entire boxful, mostly of egg whites and air, while watching on the TV Nigella, the latest Brit sensation, whose useful, ungroomed hands belie her clever brain. Her fans watch to see Nigella, not her bytes. Where otherwise, he yearns, have those crumb-caked greasy paws been lurking? She is almost too competent to be true, and glamorous to boot. She's a glamour-puss all right. Now, when did *that* useful expression bite the dust?

In the bathroom he pauses to admire the little card mounted above his stack of fresh towels, the text discreetly small beneath a huge pale blue drop of water teardrop shape:

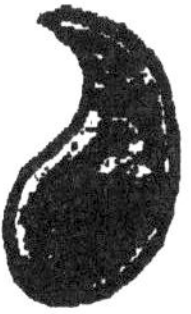

Do you feel you need Fresh Towels? If you would like your towels replaced, please leave your used towels on the floor, which is the place for used towels.

"Assholes," he mutters. "Assholes all."

Towels left hanging on the towel rack tell us that you wish to reuse them.

"Behold the talking towel," he whispers.

Using towels more than once saves hundreds of pounds of detergent and thousands of gallons of water each year. To re-order, call National Hotel Register Co. at ______________.

Out in the elevator in disgust, he notes a sign from The Management, forbidding the wheeling into the lobby of carts from the nearby Quikshop, an old habit of long-term denizens who have roosted here from long before Nigella. Her chic consists in her being the daughter of a former Cabinet minister, so clearly she hails from the ranks of the well-fed and the privileged, and conducts herself with a sort of throwaway delicacy that at the same time stomachs nothing fanciful. She eats like a prisoner of war, and at Sunday breakfast, as staged for TV, she affects a wolfhound gourmandise. Shrop prizes her as he would the ghost of Christmas past, as did, presumably, many of the English ministerial class; a well-to-do no-nonsense woman among the Blimps.

What worries Shrop is the way he has of seeing himself as comical, indeed as a creature of absurdist disrepute, when in fact he genuinely believes his ailments and cockeyed obsessions have been caused by bombardment. He has been shaken up (shook up in the vernacular) and shaken into what he regards as errant maladaptation or silly tricks, like a dog gone to seed or an eccentric polar bear. He cannot quite work out the whys and wherefores, but he remains convinced that, if Quent has become weird, he Shrop has become so in a more organic, predictable way. They have both gone their separate ways into the pantomime of poignancy. All that was required was their parting from each other, from the nexus in which Shrop's gullibility played into the hands of Quent's tendency to domineer. So Shrop, now the lucky legatee of a long-distance system so cheap it must be heaven-sent, is obliged to dial an 800 number, followed by a secret code that admits him to yet another code, whose digits added up free him to dial the number he actually wants. This laborious system costs him peanuts, but he has to be careful, he warns himself, not to construe its arrival in his mental landscape as something funny, oh no, but as a legitimate sequel to the disaster of years ago, when the core of things got so badly Blitzed that nothing simple was ever feasible again, but edged into being, frayed and fevered from too much commotion in the matrix, like a baby born of a mother with too much cortisol flowing through her. Agitated is the word he craves but declines to utter. We have been agitated, then re-agitated by the memory of it, and so forth. In Florida he has driven through suburbs that confront the speedster with signs that proclaim this is an area of *Calmed Traffic,* which means there are speed bumps. Well, he would dearly like to be self-conducting through an area of calmed traffic, speed bumps or no. Manhattan is not it, but, oddly enough, he dare not leave.

Dimly recollecting his days as a pool cleaner, Shrop realizes that these were his most pensive, when he leaned forward into the depths while trying to erase a shadow: a cloud passing over, or even his own head. At such junctures, he fancied he had plumbed the depths of human being and was dealing, more than ever Dante and Virgil did, with the core of carnality. He did not call it that, though, because it seemed a pretentious term, and eventually cooked up what seemed less bombastic: *levity retrofire,* which meant the way the most awful events seemed somehow comic when viewed against certain standards, the sun or the Pacific Ocean. The awkwardness of the phrase, indeed its semi-military overtone, eluded him altogether, but we should not forget that he was a philosopher, or at least an ex-philosopher. With his recall of his own system has gone his sensitivity to jargon. He is glad of any language that, like money, finds its way into his hands or mouth. Nonetheless, he is much bemused by this retrofire of his because, hitherto, until the bombardment or Blitz, he had always thought the comic and the tragic stayed in their own boxes, never suspecting that the tragic became comic and vice versa. The tragic, so much of it, is too much to endure. The comic, so much of it, is also too much to endure. You die laughing. Both wear you out.

Three Requia
Michael Bergstein

BENJAMIN FRANKLIN GOES DOWN ON THE AIRSHIP *HINDENBURG*

IF I HAD KNOWN IT WAS going to end like this I wouldn't have flown that kite in the first place. Enough static electricity or sabotage introduced, as 'twere, into an atmosphere of pure hydrogen will ignite Said Gas with an acceleration destined to place those within the vicinity in great danger of Death by Burning, or as in this case, Falling and Burning. Being aloft with the vessel afire is no condition under which to contemplate Scientific Phenomena, and suffice it to say pandemonium aboard was enough to distract one from cool observation. (Had the craft descended more slowly the silver piano might have finished its lament.) Physical employment of flight will never be mankind's true line of country—the plunge proves it—and so won't Our Dear Republic thereby and henceforth in part be sent asunder by the collapse of Faith and Aeronautics, witness This Day at Lakehurst, State of New Jersey, America? Haven't I myself fallen through time and history to report on the Blistering Descent with smoke and tumbling Bottles of Schnapps? On another occasion I might like trying a lift in a different machine, but for today, no thank you, Good Sirs, this has been quite enough for a Simple Journeyman, I bid you. Pray twist me out of your hotspot before landing and say no more.

MURDER OF STANFORD WHITE, MADISON SQUARE GARDEN, 1906

Men always kill each other for us. Why not. Each pillar they build means another child gone, so who cares when they discharge pistols? Let them strangle themselves with the starch of their collars. Let them bleed to death in their own palm-flocked garden. No mourning remains, once the body is burned, and only standing palaces remark on the whim of architect and Lothario, what impulse of genius, fortune, and beauty propelled him along the gilded road to a premature exit. There at the top of his form. The swing of red velvet held more than flesh in its pendulum. More than pleasure and deniability befall those who steal flowers. Once empire is built and sealed, nothing can thaw it except truth and a young girl's tongue. After that, who cares what books say? Who cares what they charge to visit mansions of the dead?

J. EDGAR HOOVER TRAINS HIS OWN BIRD

Mesmerized from her first diaper forward, she would infer decades later a different ilk of excrementalism with Constitutional cotton. Then, soap smell and clean hands. Nothing matters except what the public thinks it thinks. No canary shall ever drool a thinner spittle. How coyly microphone and perjury combine to instill the layman's mirage of fidelity, that tart eyebrow arched for a newsreel's decadent chatter, what press barons decide in between tee shots down the sward of false history on the make. This is why legends never survive. Of G-Men and racehorses, freedom and Panama hats, by sundown nothing matters except that last nag hoofing sod into the final league, and the way night turns johnny this sordid business of gangs and bureaus; whatever it takes. If she never lived we would have to invent her, so critical was her place in the old century's program, how balanced the scales. By the time they straighten the record no one will be alive who cares, but the lesson is there nonetheless. The ruminant you love today is tomorrow's dog meat, and this is the point: Kill what you protect.

The Dead in Their Sleekness

Donald Revell

Strange fame to be suddenly remembered.
Even in the pitch
                                        dark if you go
Fast enough
                              you cast a shadow
Darker than yourself.

Strange to have a heaven myself
From a friend
                              died a month ago today.

I think of automobile tires in the rain.
I see the dark wheels turning the rain black,
Leaving a track of silver behind them
Fast as themselves . . .
The wheels are my friends.
And so are the dead in their sleekness
When I am with them . . .

Without difference neither roots nor origins,
When I am with them I feel
As if two clouds had imagined a mountain
Taller than the rest.

The trouble
Is difference.

I think of stags wading in India,
Thick fronds tangled onto their heads
Until they seem like mountains walking,
And then a tiger swims up out of nowhere.

in special,/In thin array

Donald Revell

Almost invariably it (the Sperm Whale) is all over obliquely
crossed and recrossed with numberless straight marks
in thick array

In the track of the rain,
The black wheels spin out silver.
It is like life & death & thick & thin,
Numberless until the tiger comes.
He is my friend.
He is the shade of me,
Faster than I am
When the sun sets like the cut grass flying.

Hansel and Gretel

Elizabeth Robinson

i.

Trail strewn with neon crumbs
If one were to lay out such alternatives:
The sower's hand was deft
And the specks tossed and levitated on air
—if not that one,
                    then this
          —properly halting
—if not geography, then ethics
Abandonment
chastens the floating morsels to the level of the mouth

ii.

Benign path and
trees being what they are
                    wooden
No apparent peril
          and desertion
Always coming back
to a mouth
The wicked stepmother
is merely hungry and absentminded

Thatches fall from the roof of the house
and her vague hair   Their father and his yawn

iii.

If there is no evil one,
then there is merely philosophy
and N.'s speculation about endless
repetition
is correct
The candy house is intricately patterned

iv.

The witch herself wears stripes
marking her as a pariah
How she happened to know
that there are options even in repetition
Starvation breeds resourcefulness

Yes, she paints one line atop another
until the stripe itself acquires texture
and curls like a tongue
from the limits of two-dimensionality

She paints one line atop another on her naked form
to mimic the grain of a tree
Those who are wooden and those who are not
How she happened to know

the pattern of errant wanderers   On her tongue
and its limits

v.

Brother and sister
share a tentative kiss
Not of
passion   but of its many alternatives
they choose security
The door to the confectionary
shelters
            hunger and its relation to resource

vi.

Now side by side they lie
innocent of each other
but parallel as their bodies
border the edges
of a path

Not to obstruct but to fill
so that when satisfaction
is not complete
they serve other purposes
and lead onward

Simplicity plies this version of a trail
with tidy piles of white
crumbs and pebbles
But as the crow flies
their limbs
remain completely entangled

vii.

The girl curls up
and the boy stretches into such posture
that, seen from above,
they form the profile of the witch's face

But everybody knows the general outlines of inevitability

The witch, stripes gone askew,
is crosshatched

An old story told yet again
is subject to certain deformations

> Two children, mad with hunger,
> impose themselves on a gentle old crone
> They hustle her into her house
> and finding her larder bare
> they attack the house itself and try to consume it

Some ideas are planted insidiously in the tree's pattern,
rippling through its grain and gnarling by design

viii.

You have grown weary
of this story's slow progress

You look at a fantastical candy house,
its reflection warped and wavering
You turn from its reflection in
an unnamed body of water

You turn, go, and sink your teeth in

ix.

While they
retrace their steps
by walking backwards

in the meantime
all destinations
having been razed

The marzipan roof
of the forest, the
chocolate cloud, the
way the world accommodates
their misadventure, the embrace of

the crisp pastry The relation
resumed to direction, to
parent, to knees as they
bow on the slick candy
surface of the way And

their young backs always to
the various endpoints
from which they came

x.

What is most important is that
they learn the skills of recognition
I'll swear by all my witchery
that this is what any parent
most wishes for her children

You, Reader, come closer
and extend your fingers
through the bars of the cage

so I can feel their pleasing tenderness:
Be our mirror

For you are neither boy nor girl
but the certain

unity of the sweet abode—
a spun-sugar house

adorned all over with
white pebbles and bread crumbs

We do not want you to find your way

We so want for you

to see the mirror

To deceive us hardily

and to roll

from the edges of the path

against parallel,

connecting, central and skew

and endlessly
thumping knees against knees
the brush of hand on hair
the bodies' alternative

to direction is

recognition and ceaselessness

Mary Mary Ellen Ellen

T*an* L*in*

ABOVE THE CLOUDS ON THE PIKE'S PEAK COG ROAD

THIS SPRING AFTER THIRTY-FIVE years of being exactly who she was, my girlfriend decided to create her doppelgänger, a kind of shadow in portraiture, and fly her to Vienna where she would have a one-person art exhibition. About five weeks before her opening, Mary Ellen hired a casting agent who found her a woman in her thirties named Katherine W_______. She was an actor, a real estate buyer, jewelry designer, and daughter of a Hollywood actor from the forties who had played in a lot of gangster movies. Katherine had been in a couple of films, including *Goodfellas,* and had also "gone out with" Harvey Keitel for a few nights. When I first saw her in the Utopia Coffee Shop at Seventy-second and Broadway, she was sitting in one of the red booths by the cash register near the windows overlooking Amsterdam Avenue, close to her parents' apartment on the Upper West Side. She must have seen me in photographs because when I came in through the glass doors she waved and I sat down next to her in the booth. "So you're my boyfriend," she said. She told me she had gotten a haircut, dyed her blonde hair brown, and streaked it with henna. It was kind of ugly-sexy or ugly-pretty, I wasn't exactly sure. She was bigger than my girlfriend in real life and she had been on a week-long regimen of jogging and dieting. She did not look like a movie star; she looked like a painting of a movie star or a slightly water-damaged version of my girlfriend. When Katherine talked, even to say something affectionate, she reminded me of the waitress who was serving us or the checkout person who handed me someone else's set of photos at Kmart earlier that morning, or someone who had recently graduated from high school and gotten lucky and found a job they didn't really want. I think that most actors are like that; they probably don't want to act like someone who they aren't. In that way, acting is probably just like what we do in real life every minute of the day. We try to pretend to not be who we really are. Being in front of a camera can be the most peaceful place in the world to be. I didn't want to like Katherine but I did.

Katherine's press photo didn't look at all like Katherine. We were facing a glass door and people were coming in holding things. An old lady came in with a walker and a straggly dog and sat in the booth next to us. A young couple carrying a Museum of Natural History bag and then two young women with Banana Republic bags sat somewhere in the room. Some things seemed to be moving in the room, but weirdly, like Katherine's eyelashes and the cake wheel revolving with lemon meringue pies. Her nose was big, especially near the nostrils, and her eyes looked somehow painted over and wider close to her nose. They reflected the lights in the coffee shop. They looked like they were waiting for someone. I stroked Katherine's hair. "It's been permed." "Mary Ellen and I met at a dinner party seven or eight years earlier." She asked me a lot of questions and I told her it was sometimes hard to tell what Mary Ellen was feeling. We shared a hamburger with fries. I took notes. I told Katherine that I had been assigned to document the trip. All this talk about someone else reminded me of shopping and those silvery b/w photos of Edie Sedgwick after she cut her hair in 1972 and dyed it silver so that people would mistake her for Andy Warhol. I like it when books remind me of people I don't know because I think it is photographs of people in books I am drawn to rather than the books themselves. No good person should exist without a book and no good book should exist without a lot of photographs of someone inside of it. A novel without photographs is like a person without emotions.

When Katherine got up to go to the bathroom, she had Mary Ellen's walk, dragging her right foot a little backward and splayed out to the right as she brought it up to her left foot. She was wearing slip-on Nikes with neon green webbing that Mary Ellen liked. She was not wearing lipstick. She came back to our booth and ran her fingers through my hair. She talked with her left hand suspended in midair as if she were remembering something or about to tap me on the chest. She talked faster than Mary Ellen and I felt like I could understand what she was saying even though I wasn't really listening to anything except the mood inside the coffee shop. This was too bad because talking, like photography, is the one thing that can stop beauty in its tracks, and I believe it was talk and nothing else that was moving all around me that afternoon. I think it's hard for a woman to be funny and beautiful at the same time. Being funny for a beautiful woman is like going out in drag. I could tell Katherine was done saying something because every time she finished a sentence, there was a momentous inconsequence to her facial gestures, which I thought was related to the meringue pies. I waited for her to say something and she would look away and then look at me and then look away and then look at me as if we were being filmed. All this wasted motion reminded me of my high school biology class when we dissected crayfish and you looked and then stopped looking and then looked back at what you were doing because you couldn't stand to look at what you were doing to the crayfish. It was a little like sewing, but in reverse. I think Katherine was sewing everything backward for me that day—her perfume, her elbows, the straggly line of her bag, and her posture—and I thought this must be almost the same thing as falling in love with someone but I could see her trying to figure out what I was feeling. As the great film director Robert Bresson noted, the less acting at any given moment, the better. She asked me if I loved Mary Ellen and I said no. I wanted to photograph each and every lie that lives in the world as if it were alive in color and in the order that it was felt, like a stopwatch. Like everything else that day, there was a momentary shortage of time in that room. Everything in the room felt startled by the dingy luster of a coffee shop and all of its touristic truth. This was the first time Katherine and I were a couple in a photograph. The waitress came over and took away our burger and the bowl filled with pickles. Katherine ordered a cup of coffee. Nothing ever really happens unless it happens twice, once in a photograph and once in real life. She drank it black. This reminded me of Mary Ellen. We talked about acting. I took two photographs of Katherine, then put my hand on hers so that she could not finish her coffee. There is nothing so boring as an actor's life. Most of the feelings I was having were lies that I thought were true. Katherine told a couple jokes in the Utopia Coffee Shop near the end of the meal. Before I got in the subway,

Katherine caught my arm and said to me, "I look exactly like my father." Her father was the actor Eli Wallach.

A few weeks after our hamburger but sometime before leaving for Vienna, I began to document my experiences of the trip before I had them, as if the trip were not subject to memory but to its opposite, as if my emotions could be corrupted in advance of the event and everything I was writing were being written not for the first time but for the last time. In this way I thought that the repetition inherent in (the recording of) facts could ultimately slow down what was happening, especially the emotions that were transpiring in Vienna. Nobody ever really wants the imaginary to intrude upon our lives, the way photographs do. Marcel Duchamp kept reality at bay when he found a snow shovel in a hardware store and then gave it the title *In Advance of the Broken Arm.* A novel should always contain a few photographs to keep reality just a little at bay. A movie should never have a director but a very good script that can make the whole thing into science. By taking photos (of photos) I learned something very important: to read without thinking. And even more importantly, I learned to write without understanding the things that I was feeling.

fig. 23 copyright Katherine Wallach

This is a photo of a photo, i.e., a description. All real events, even the most uneventful ones, should, like rock performances or bad movies, be sampled from memories or the movies and then converted into things (to be read) if they are to become memories of memories, and thus be forgotten properly like most of our feelings. No work of literature should willingly promote that thing known as "the suspension of disbelief." The best works suspend belief in things that surround the novel. This is known as reality. This is also known as relaxation. Everything beautiful in this world can be mistakenly construed with "details." Novels should be b/w compilations of details that have already happened to other people before the narrative was actually begun. The world is filled with so many black and white things that are actually in color. This is what Marcel Duchamp did with his notes to the *Large Glass,* which is a novel masquerading as a series of instructions on how to fabricate works of art that arc "not rctinal." That is why Duchamp was so interested in breathing. Breathing cannot be interrupted by narrative. The ideal written work would be a photograph of something that never happened. That is why photos are irrelevant and unconnected to the story. The photographs commemorate nothing but the time in which they were seen. In other words, no one has to die to suffer. The shutter snaps and that's all. Two photographs are always better than one.

What is the relation between a photograph and the things we love? When you are reading in the present, the time that is captured here elapses, and moves more and more photographs into it and all this *then* disappears into what you were reading. And the feelings you were about to have require an itinerary, just as the writing does.

The following actually happened on June 4th and 6th: Two Mary Ellens and I flew into Vienna. I came in two days early because I did not want to fly economy and I was not sure what I should do with my new girlfriend if we were flying in the same plane together. Would I kiss her, talk as if I loved her, buy her duty-free perfume, ignore her, or dump her? On the flight over on Lufthansa, drinking wine and eating the white summer peaches I had put in my bag, I started to fall in love with Katherine so as to record what was really happening on the trip and to be faithful to the photographs I was taking. The most pleasurable of experiences (like lying and love) have nothing to do with love itself, they have merely to do with falling in love with the same thing over and over again and this is why we like certain kinds of music and drugs and certain people as well. That is why literature is usually so boring, because it is unlike that. That is why I spent most of my days in Vienna photographing the things we were seeing in Vienna: natural history museums, parks, Ferris wheels, bungee jumpers, the Vienna Arcade, anti-aging institutes, cafés, Kruder & Dorfmeister, the interiors of bars designed by Adolph

Loos, banks, department stores, Chinese restaurants, pretty schoolchildren, etc. What is a photograph but something that lies to itself before it lies to someone else? The truth is rarely so relaxing as lies, and the best lies are the ones that can only be documented by photographs and brand names.

During the flight to Vienna, I thought about the thing I always like to think about when I am traveling: What would I look like traveling in drag, in business or in first? This in turn led me to think about working for Shiseido, the Japanese makeup company that manufactures a first-rate makeup remover, and this made me think about the Great Books Foundation founded by Mortimer Adler in Chicago, the public library, footnotes, lying, off-off Broadway, the *New York Times,* and Jeff White, a good friend of mine from high school who loved to play practical jokes. One summer Jeff decided to go on a cross-country road trip, starting from his home in Philadelphia and ending up at the employee cafeteria of a software company in Silicon Valley. Jeff decided to drive the whole way, all across the country in his white Honda Accord, stopping at motels, eating at diners, shopping for Roseville pottery and Eames chairs at as many antique malls as he could find, and going the whole way across that country of cheap food and drink and junk—in drag. He bought a beautiful green vintage Chanel dress, some low pumps, and a patent vinyl clutch purse in which he put the four hundred some odd dollars in cash that he had and a single green American Express card. Before he left, he called me and left a message on my answering machine, "Don't leave home without it." Anyway, when he arrived in Palo Alto, his car was filled with all sorts of things he had collected: clothing, lots of women's hats, sundresses, dishes, costume jewelry, Revere Ware, planters, cooking utensils, ice cream makers, rock-polishing kits, butterfly nets, books by Jacqueline Susann. He headed straight for the company cafeteria in his green dress with a copy of Jacqueline Susann's *Once Is Not Enough* and found a seat near Connie, his best friend from high school, who had been working as a software designer in the Valley for about three years. He sat directly opposite her, at another table, picked at his meat loaf, read from his book, and just stared at her and waited for her to recognize him. Connie was mortified by this person in drag eating meat loaf and staring at her as if he knew her. She could barely concentrate on her meal. It took her forty-five minutes before she finally recognized him. Jeff said it was the greatest practical joke he ever played because it took so long to unfold and then when it finally did unfold in that cafeteria it did so in the presence of his favorite food (meat loaf) and in extra slow motion as if all the waiting and the hunger and desire in the world had become elongated in his presence. Before he left, he went to the bathroom, changed, and gave Connie his dress. It was a beautiful souvenir and it was very clean. Jeff is a very neat eater, especially in drag. Connie loves to wear that dress, and she loves to sit in the cafeteria and eat in it, even today. It's a great-looking dress.

I believe that Jeff's eyeliner, blush, and lipstick had a particular kind of logic vis-à-vis the human face and the emotions that the face generates mechanically, automatically. The best emotions are the ones we have automatically, and that is why those television shows of horrible accidents brought about by people doing stupid things and captured on video by amateurs, those shows like *Real Disasters,* are a strange mix of horror and relief and religion. The other night I was watching a video of someone in gold two-tone swim trunks swig a bottle of tequila and then yell, "Tarzan" and then something inaudible from the second-floor window of his house and then you see this idiot jumping too hard from the window, actually *overjumping* and hitting the concrete steps at the far end of the swimming pool instead of the deep end of the pool right under him, which he had been aiming for. Meanwhile, a whole party of half-drunk people is kind of half-dancing poolside and looking up from their drinks in amazement and horror and bewilderment as this guy bounces off the steps and falls backward into the pool. By this time he has a broken leg, a broken foot, and a shattered hip. Then they showed a fourteen-year-old kid on a Moto-Cross bike going way too fast with his best friend somewhere out in one of those western states. Anyway, they kind of tried to clear a *very* wide ditch with junk cars strewn in it. The first kid makes it just fine and turns back to give his friend the high five. The second kid revs up his bike and then starts going too fast too soon and he goes off the *side* of the ramp and ends up plowing headfirst into one of the windshields of the junk cars instead. Of course he ends up breaking his arm and his neck and afterward they interview the kid while he is sitting on a sofa in his parents' living room and they show him a rerun of the clip and he says, "I can't believe I did that." These video clips generate feelings of stupidity and relief so perfectly and interchangeably and without making us think about all the different and various ways we have of feeling and not feeling. Watching accidents on TV and people who wear too much makeup demonstrates that every recognition we have is really just an accident exchanged or passed from one medium to another in a larger system of additions and subtractions, and that is why those TV shows are so great. Likewise, every feeling is something exchanged or removed from what we are seeing in a larger system of recognitions. This is why I hate the theater, which is grounded in makeup, and prefer photography or poetry or reality television, which rarely employ makeup. That is why I like to think of my friend going cross-country in drag in a green Chanel dress and why I have always said, "Photography is true, unless, of course, it is lying." What is a Polaroid but something transcribed and thus removed from itself as it becomes the subject of a painting.

What is a novel but something transcribed and thus removed from itself as it becomes the subject of a delivery. Someone once told me it is impossible to repeat a question as a question. Mary Ellen almost never wore any makeup and Katherine had to wear a lot of it. When I look at the photos of the two of them, I wonder about Andy Warhol's portraits of Liz Taylor or Marilyn Monroe with their colorful overpainting. Warhol put paint to a canvas just like makeup. I think a photograph should do the same thing to a novel. If someone I really love is wearing enough makeup, every one of my feelings arrives too late for me to think what I am feeling and this is what I like when I am reading and looking at photographs. "I can no longer feel the things that I am feeling." This is what it means to be social and to blend in with what one is and what one is becoming. A photo is smudged or else it reminds me of its own indifference.

Who was I? The friend? Someone about to cheat on someone I didn't know? I arrived in Vienna not knowing where I was. I needed desperately to sleep. I took a cab with my sister Maya and checked in at the Radisson Hotel with tall French-style windows overlooking the Stadt Park. I pulled the drapes and dozed off to the sound of electric trams sparking their way around the city's Ring. Late in the afternoon, my sister knocked on my door and insisted on going to the Sacher Hotel on the Philharmonikerstrasse. We walked past the gold columns and across the slightly worn-out red carpets of the hotel. I insisted on eating a Sacher torte, which was the driest Sacher torte I have ever had. It reminded me of a sandwich. The two Mary Ellens were still in New York. Mary Ellen had hired a limo to take them to

JFK. Prada and Costume National and Nike and Giraudon had sent clothes and shoes and bags. Shiseido supplied makeup. Oliver Peoples provided multiple pairs of matching sunglasses. My sister and I were seven hours ahead of New York.

One waits for the things that one can love and then the things that one cannot love start to love one back. In this way, the world becomes more imperfect than it really is. Being a tourist in Vienna, I began removing myself from all those things I was not thinking about. The most beautiful thing in the world is when one's emotions appear to oneself in quotation marks. This is what it means to be social and to blend in with what one is not and what one is becoming for someone else. And of course when I think of celebrities (like Parker Posey), makeup, and doubles, I think (metonymically) of humans and how they are concealed by or confused with or separated from what they are seeing. For it is difficult to see without feeling but it is easy to feel without seeing. Andy Warhol said: "What makes a painting beautiful is the way the paint's put on." That's why in every one of Warhol's portraits, the women's faces remind me of the two Mary Ellens and of TV; the lipstick makes the lips look like giant red quotation marks, and the faces, like Mao's and Liza's, appear to be black-and-white photographs painted over in bright colors. Painting over a face makes it

change into something that it is not. Adding photographs to a novel is a way of making things less and less beautiful than can ever be imagined in real life. Change that is really the same is what makes something beautiful.

This is what it means to be famous. Two days later, the two Mary Ellens arrived according to schedule. They had identical baggage, although one of the Mary Ellens had brought a shy cat. They checked in to the same hotel and took two rooms, one immediately above the other. They had the same view of the courtyard. They spent most of the days apart. But every morning, they would meet and have identical breakfasts at the breakfast bar: yogurt with apples, a cup of coffee with milk, and a piece of untoasted bread. I did not see Katherine that first night when she arrived. I was waiting in my hotel room talking to my sister. Maya kept asking me when I was going to get married. Mary Ellen checked in and called me at my hotel. I took a taxi to her hotel. We sat on the bed. Mary Ellen told me she was tired and depressed. I tried to comfort her but I couldn't.

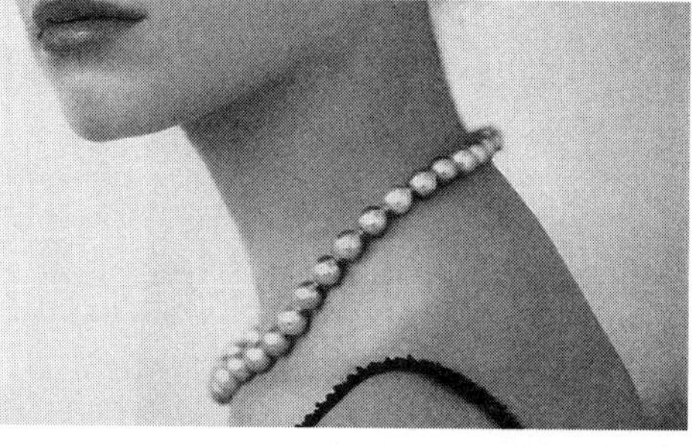

On our second night, after a day of sightseeing on a tour bus, we were driven to the outskirts of Vienna to have dinner at the home of a couple, the Holzers, two prominent art collectors in Vienna. We walked up the broken walkway to their house, surrounded by small bulldozers and clay drainage pipes. Mary Ellen grabbed my hand and pulled me closer to her. The Holzers came out of their house and walked briskly past the bulldozers parked on their dug-up lawn. The tiny Euro-bulldozers looked like they had been removed from a fairy tale. The Holzers moved very slowly across the drainage pipes. I think this was because it used to be their lawn. They did not seem like people who exercised. They were not much older than me. The husband was a patent lawyer in Vienna. The wife was a physician who specialized in pain research, in particular the kinds of pain that children have and how they express or don't express their pain to doctors. They were avid art collectors. They liked the paintings of Gerhard Richter, which they had been collecting for years and which reminded me of paintings that look like photographs or vice versa.

We were on their concrete doorstep, and Mary Ellen turned and kissed me. Someone was holding my hand. Mrs. Holzer was poised at the entrance and she was carrying a bottle of wine in a light green bottle. We all introduced ourselves. After the introductions, we were taken to a small glass table in their backyard. This reminded me of a fairy tale in which all the adults were asked to play the roles of adults. They thought I was very young because they asked me what I was studying in school. I told them I was a professor at the University of Virginia but was on sabbatical for a year in order to complete a book on ambient stylistics, yoga, and television. I said that it was a novel designed to be very, very easy to read and deeply relaxing. They got a big kick out of that. I said I wasn't kidding. I told them that it was the product of sampling, actually delicately removing things like a surgeon, from the newspaper and taking all the stories and ads that were other people's stories and pretending they were mine, much like the musical group Kruder & Dorfmeister, which samples beats from, say, Depeche Mode or Count Basic or Donna Summer. They asked me why I was doing all of this and I told them that after my first book (of poetry) had come out, people would come up to me at dinner parties and tell me they had read my book but had not understood a word of it. So I decided to write a book that would be highly relaxing at the synaptic level and that would resemble hypnosis and the kinds of breathing that take place under hypnosis. It would be filled with typos and lies because mistakes of any sort are extremely relaxing, especially when one is reading. It would be filled with gossip and celebrities and lies. I talked of gardening and a product called Deer-Away, which I use in my garden and is supposed to smell like bear shit. Mrs. Holzer was a perfect host. She smiled at everything that anyone had to say. We had a white '92 Riesling from Austria. We sat around the table for around twenty minutes and then Mr. Holzer promptly got up and announced it was time to eat. The Viennese do not like lingering, especially before dinner. The dining table was informal and generic, like a photograph. The table looked ambient. It was set with Viennese porcelain plates and linen napkins. We sat down and something in the room appeared to get small like water evaporating from a glass. The room was dim. I had forgotten my camera in the car. If you look closely at the film footage you can see that dinner was heartbreakingly minimal: white asparagus and white wine. (I do not care for *spargle,* even when it is white.)

The filmmaker for the project, whose name was Fritz, was an artist. Like a lot of young people in Germany and Austria, Fritz was unmarried and had a child, a girl, whom he took care of along with his ex-girlfriend, who was a fashion model based in Berlin and Paris. Fritz had gotten sick on homemade and overly potent wine we had drunk earlier that day at a farmhouse where a painter had his studio and we were served cheese and a worn-out salad. By the time we got to the Holzers' we were all exhausted from the heat, the excessive wind in the car, and the homemade wine. The two Mary Ellens sat in the car in the backseat and both of them had fallen asleep, one with her mouth open and the other with her mouth half open. One of them was snoring. I sat in the front and chatted with Fritz during the ride. Fritz, or Fritzy, as I called him, excused himself from the dining table after about fifteen minutes. He went to lie down in another room and was not able to record anything but the first half hour of the evening, and only about five minutes of the dinner. I barely said a word that night, except to talk about wine. Mary Ellen hardly said a word. I remember what the filmmaker Whit Stillman used to say to his actors when they started acting: "You know that acting thing you do—don't do it." There is, accordingly, only incomplete film footage of the evening. The same should be true of writing: You know that writing thing you do—don't do it.

After Fritz left the room, I began trying to save everything in my head. In this way the sense of the social was supposed to break down the sense of the aesthetic. One Mary Ellen was paying the other Mary Ellen a thousand dollars for a week's worth of acting work. The two Mary Ellens were now fully separated and were making economics intrude cruelly upon the dinner table. Art had lost to the social and people were talking at the table. That is why most novels and poems are so utterly boring: they try to make something inside happen in an unpredictable way and this is always boring, whereas the best things that happen are barely happening or actually not quite happening on the outside of the novel. This is known as realism. It can be very relaxing. It is usually very pretty. In the end, there were only Mary Ellen and myself in the room having dinner. Two people were in love with the things that were happening or not happening to them. Nothing else was happening. Something about the evening was being repeated and I think it must have been two people falling in love. No one was rehearsing themselves. No one was having an emotion. Everything that is emotional comes after. One Mary Ellen was real and the other Mary Ellen was a jewelry designer. She tried to sell jewelry during the trip. My sister bought a necklace the evening before she left for Nice. All the emotions that had flowed from one person to the next for me stopped flowing at all. I wished I had my camera to start things going again. On our first night in Vienna, Mary Ellen cried and cried and cried after we got back to our hotel.

Before Fritz left the room, I began trying to save everything in my head. In this way the sense of the aesthetic was supposed to break down the sense of the social. One Mary Ellen was paying the other Mary Ellen a thousand dollars for a week's worth of acting work. The two Mary Ellens were now fully separated and were making economics intrude cruelly upon the dinner table. Art had lost to the social and people were talking at the table. That is why most novels and poems are so utterly boring: they try to make something inside happen in an unpredictable way and this is always boring, whereas the best things that happen are barely happening or actually not quite happening on the outside of the novel. This is known as realism. It can be very relaxing. It is usually very pretty. In the beginning, there were only Mary Ellen and myself in the room having dinner. Two people were in love with the things that were happening or not happening to them. Nothing else was happening. Something about the evening was being repeated and I think it must have been two people falling in love. No one was rehearsing themselves. No one was having an emotion. Everything that is emotional comes after. One Mary Ellen was real and the other Mary Ellen was a jewelry designer. She tried to sell jewelry during the trip. My sister bought a necklace the evening before she left for Nice. All the emotions that had flowed from one person to the next for me stopped flowing at all. I wished I had my camera to start things going again. On our first night in Vienna, Mary Ellen cried and cried and cried after we got back to our hotel.

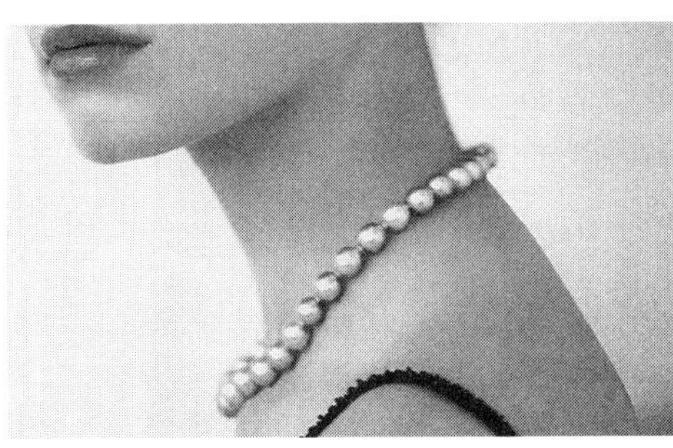

Of course, one should only talk or write about something if one is unaware of what one is saying or if the moment just passed is long dead. That is why Andy Warhol created such beautiful movies of dead people who were alive, novels written by a tape recorder, paintings of Jackie Kennedy in a funereal shroud, and Campbell's soup cans—where it is impossible to tell if something is living or dead, or if something is being subtracted or added from what is being seen. That is why Warhol liked to cast "the wrong actor" in his movies and why he asked his film stars to sit still—so that they might become photographs of themselves and thus be looked at over and over. In a film, the human retina only sees each thing once. In a novel one hears things over and over again. We love things that make us repeat ourselves. Repeating the things we are feeling is the only kind of love I know. That night at the Holzers' I was sitting around the table watching Mary Ellen eat white asparagus. I love watching Mary Ellen eat because she spills things on the table when she eats. Both of the Mary Ellens were sloppy eaters and they made a mess of things on the white tablecloth. Mrs. Holzer did not notice or pretended not to. She was the perfect host. She never stopped smiling. I thought about Mary Ellen getting married (to me) because:

a) nothing is valuable if it stays the same

b) exchanging something is a way of changing a thing

c) nothing can be exchanged if it stays the same

During dinner, I could barely stop looking at the two Mary Ellens. They looked kind of still and elegiac, like clouds that barely move in summer or the smoke that comes from cigarettes right after you light them. It was about 8:30 in Vienna. It was getting dark. Time seemed to elongate inside the things I was thinking about. As the light outside collapsed, the dining room felt like it was moving underwater, undivided by hatred or love, and hypnotic. The two Mary Ellens were sitting down. I could feel something rushing under their skin, passing through them and the wall sconces and then under my eyes where I could see them more clearly as if they would be forever unchanged.

The music from the other room got suddenly louder.

"I *looove* that B. B. King *thang,*" one of the Mary Ellens said, making a loop with her shoulders.

Sometimes during the dinner, one of them would talk about the

project of the double and sometimes it would be the other. Mary Ellen said something about an interview with the ministry of culture the next day and I thought she said ministry of cuisine. That was the first of many mistakes that would occur that evening. Katherine stepped out of her role many times that night. She mentioned a house in Italy that she had purchased the year before and was surrounded by pencil-thin poisonous vipers that dropped from the trees. Mary Ellen was upset by this because Katherine was no longer acting like Mary Ellen but like Katherine with her house in Italy and her funny cat and her jewelry collection, which she kept in a pouch and brought out to show people. Most people get upset when real life intrudes upon the things that are not real. I sat at the other end of the table, helpless as the evening went on changing and changing into something else. One rarely notices the things that barely change. One doesn't want to. The evening was ruined and beautiful and ugly and there was nothing that could be done to change that.

I wish telling the truth were easier because nothing changes by itself. But if one wants something to be beautiful it is. That is why I like to read the marriage pages of the *New York Times,* but only in the summer months, when the stories expire twice as quickly as the photographs that go with them. No one can have a story unless the brain simultaneously snaps a photo of it in one's head and then lets it topple. For me, it is utterly impossible to get through the summer without reading the wedding pages. They remind me of makeup. This never happens with the winter wedding photos, which are depressing and should not be looked at, except when smoking. No matter how hard I try, I cannot imagine anything when I read about a winter wedding except a lot of snow and trying to get in a wet cab with too much slush in the mats. Anyway, last Sunday I was reading about Jodi Della Femina and John Kim. I've known John since he went to business school and then finally migrated to New York, where he got an apartment in London Terrace and a job with an investment firm analyzing the Japanese auto industry. Almost as soon as he moved in, he noticed a young woman across the hall who had two dogs. He would listen to her dogs, Chester and Henry, come home every night and in that way he was trained by her dogs to listen carelessly for her like a dog would. One day, he asked Ray, the elevator man, if the girl across the hall was available. Ray said: "There's this blonde man who comes up all the time. He's in perfect shape, model quality. And he has keys to her apartment."

Actually, Jodi was one hundred percent single. And she was incredibly upset that, on the verge of thirty, there was no one serious in her life. The blonde guy was just someone who watered her plants and fed the dogs when she was away for the weekend. He was a model. Just a few weeks before her thirtieth birthday in 1988, Ray told her that Mr. Kim had a crush on her. She wrote a note to Mr. Kim: "I would like to go out with you." (She put the note under his door.)

John is known for his dry wit. He is very understated in the things he does, like golf and psychoanalysis—but not his electric guitar playing, which is done in the manner of the cooks on the Japanese TV show *Iron Chef*, which pits one cook against the other with a single ingredient like squid or dried tree ears, and only one hour to put together a twelve-course meal. The next day, Mr. Kim phoned: "Hi, I'm your neighbor from across the hall, and I'm interested in you."

They were married last weekend, on July 8, 2000, in East Hampton, at the home of her father and mother. The ceremony took place on the beach. It was a seafood wedding and I have never, ever had fresh clams at a wedding.

The best summer brides (the celebrities and doppelgängers) must be let go of by the stories that are told about them. Nothing can end a story but another story. That is why all fiction should not climax but only move in ever more ambient circumlocutious ways toward the things it is not. That is why I like to see not one but twenty brides in the summer wedding pages, each more unknown than the other. Each bride becomes a story that doesn't quite match the photograph, and the bride and groom remind me of two halves of an adult fairy tale, each looking at the other as if he or she was reading *Reader's Digest.* Each of the brides in today's Sunday *Times* looks like Jackie in Warhol's numerous portraits of her. The photos are mysterious and unsurprising. This one is wearing a polo shirt. This one is wearing a light-colored T-shirt and some pearls. This one is wearing a blouse a few days before the wedding. By the time I've read the paper, most are on their honeymoons. Who would have thought the world produces pleasure in this way? When I look at Jackie I see twenty Jackies and not just one. Because they look different together, they don't hurt my eyes. Variety makes one impervious to the perfections of the world. Each of those Jackies makes the feeling I was having die one last time.

There is very little difference between one moment and the next for the Empire State Building, a sleeper, a man halfway through a blow job, or a double. Time passes more slowly for a celebrity, the dead, or a double because it can repeat itself without being remembered. Because I am Chinese, I like to watch Mary Ellen eat by herself, especially when we go to a Chinese restaurant and she orders those round little Shanghai soup dumplings and I forget what it is that I am looking at. I could watch this for hours. With the two Mary Ellens in Vienna, time passed more slowly than a life in real life. Contrary to popular belief, boredom creates the world and even makes it sexy. The other night I was watching Andy Warhol's movie *Blow Job.* The blow job takes place off camera so all anyone sees is the face of a man getting fellated. The blow job lasts forty-one minutes, and lots of people fall asleep or just leave before the guy comes. Watching *Blow Job* is the closest thing I have ever come to watching someone die in an automobile accident. Like the disaster paintings where everything is already dead, in *Blow Job* boredom and arousal become the same in the film's next-to-last frames. In *Blow Job,* the hustler barely looks our way. He has an orgasm, jerks his head up, and then lights a cigarette. The smoke comes between us and obscures his face. We never make eye contact. He utters a few words the viewer can't make out. The reel runs out. Taylor Mead, at the first screening of the film, walked out after ten minutes, saying, "I already came." When I watch this movie I wonder whether all those things that are queer in me have turned to the most beautiful forms of boredom, which I do not like. Like the two Mary Ellens sitting in tandem, *Blow Job* is a mirror of the things that cannot be seen except by repetition. Fame is the greatest form of repetition known to modern man. Both Mary Ellens want to be famous. Fame or an electric chair does the same thing to its sitter that a mirror does: it makes time irrelevant. *Blow Job* is impersonal and sadistic as the revolving colors in a disco or the backdrop sets of a soap opera. Warhol was right: ". . . if a mirror looks into a mirror, what is there to see?" The only time Warhol could be alone with himself was when he was asleep. The hardest thing to see in a mirror is oneself. Today, TV is the best mirror we have for ourselves; it makes us all look alike. That is why there are so many reality-based TV shows on at the moment. That is why no one ever has a heart attack while "watching TV." I believe that shame can only exist in the presence of someone else and those reality TV programs eliminate the shame that a person can have. The best thing that can happen is to become a spectator to one's own shame. The turbulence of emotion in the people who were trapped by a car crash or who plot to gain control of an island, all those emotions have long ceased to matter, except to the spectator who gets a posthumous jolt. Everyone loves to be disconnected from the emotions that force us to be ourselves. The people who once sat in the electric chair have received their charge and been lowered into the ground. The guy getting a blow job seems impassive and dead and poorly lit. His pre- and postorgasm scenes look alike. What were the Mary Ellens feeling as they sat together in that restaurant in Vienna on the fourth night of our stay? No one will ever know. After I finished my filet of sole, I took a few photos. Fritz was filming the evening. A feeling is a feeling (is a feeling).

The faces of the two Mary Ellens eating in tandem in a trendy restaurant in Vienna are repeated and when they repeat they try to change into something they are not and nothing can stop this from happening even though you want to. And nothing can really change that either. You feel this and then you feel that or you feel this or you feel that. The various photos in this photo album were taken by an amateur. They bleed, change colors, go out of focus, disfigurations continually mar the surface (like a face) in all sorts of unexpected ways. This is why one doesn't look at the two Mary Ellens in the restaurant: One watches them just like faces on a TV show. The media, like the novel, is always on and is always available to be sampled. TV, like the extremely long ambient work, is just one very long intermission from one's own feelings, like watching the same movie over and over again late at night or TNT or TBS, the superstation. The night before last I watched *Planet of the Apes* again for the billionth time and waited and waited for that final scene on the beach with the Statue of Liberty sunk into the beach where sci-fi music is playing and Charlton Heston is seeing all this and yelling, "Goddamn." It is a beautiful moment. No one can have the same feeling just once. No one can have the same feeling as everybody else more than once. Every photo in this space is a transition like a still frame in a movie. The hardest thing to see in a mirror is oneself. Today, TV is the best mirror we have for ourselves; it makes us all look alike. That is why no one ever has a heart attack while "watching TV." Shame can only exist when someone else has left the room.

Tonight I am eating dinner by myself while watching TV. I made Chinese fried rice like the fried rice my mother used to cook for me in Athens, Ohio, when I was a child—with a little bit of American bacon, green onion, Taylor's New York dry sherry, and some scrambled egg. After dinner I watched a videotape of *Blow Job* for the last time as if everything private were coming to the surface of my world. I will never watch *Blow Job* again because seeing and feeling shouldn't be kept together, they should be kept very apart, just like those summer and winter wedding photos in the *New York Times*, and just like the look between those brides and grooms who do not know each other. That is why nearly every Warhol painting started as a photograph: a photograph is not where a likeness began but where it ended and became someone or something else. That is why all novels like this one started as a photograph or a poem. It is 12:50 A.M. on July 12, 2000. I am thinking about Mary Ellen when I hold the camera up to my face and take my photo. Photography is the only thing I know that allows something to happen more slowly than it happened in real life. But of course it is impossible to photograph what I am feeling when I write this. How long does it take for that thing known as the unthinkable or that thing known as sadness to sink in, really in? I think it can take a long time, much longer than the time it took to see the thing itself. I got a postcard the other day from someone I went to high school with. It was postmarked Columbus, Ohio, July 12, 2001. It began:

Dear Tony,
"What is that there, who do you see . . ."

The other day I went to the Museum of Natural History with my niece India who just turned three and we looked at dinosaurs and it was so disappointing. None of the dinosaurs could move. The best dinosaurs are the ones with tiny machines sewn inside them that make them lurch or the ones in B movies like *Starship Troopers* where we know the giant bugs that gore people very fast are machines or animation cells that morph like cancer cells into surrounding skin. That is why we watch them so intently. The dinosaurs in the museum were unmoving fossils or nonmechanized myths, like the winter wedding photos in the *Times* or the lovers we forget to leave behind completely. Likewise, the face of the man getting a blow job twitches uncontrollably throughout the video.

The only thing I like more than reading the wedding announcements is reading the obits of abnormal people who are just like everyone else except they are dead. Reading an obit is more pleasurable because the person is dead and one is reading about it right now, as if the person's life were appearing backward like a fossil. Obits are like in vitro scrapbooks. I was reading an obit the other day for Sussman Volk, who died Sunday at his home, at the age of eighty-four. Volk invented gadgets and Penguin Food, the first frozen-food store ever in Manhattan, as well as a Cigarette Lighter that Lights from Both Ends and other contraptions like four-colored retractable pencils. For forty years, Volk meticulously cataloged tens of thousands of jokes, which he saved for "exactly the right moment." He was a champion shag dancer in high school. All that is over because he is dead. What is the matter with the things that are living? in me? or in you? It was said, by James Thurber, I think, that Volk's father invented the wrecking ball. An archaeologist whose name I can't remember said that the Greeks invented myths wherever they found a lot of fossils on the ground, and that the greatest mythmakers were mistaken archaeologists. Fossils are "time preserved" just like myths.

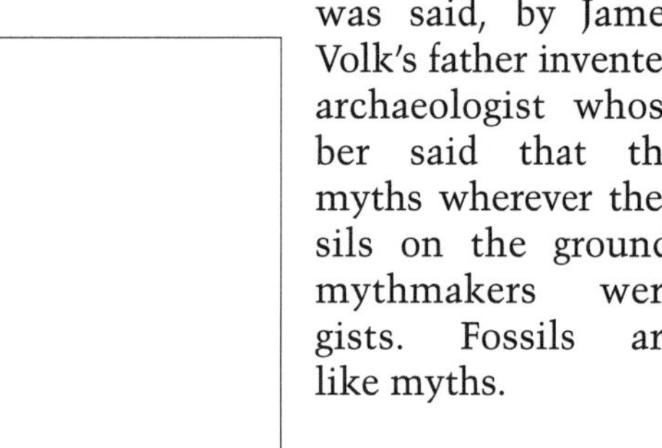

fig. 12.
April 22, 2001. My forty-fourth birthday.

When I look at certain paintings, especially those by Andy Warhol or those members of the Luminist Tradition like John Kensett and Martin Heade, I have trouble breathing. Maybe this is because a very good painting removes oxygen from the air at a constant rate and thus creates a perfectly mechanical system of doubles, and these doubles leave behind fossils, puns, paintings, actors, money. Every great

painting is a mechanical lie about a poem and every great poem is a lie about a painting. This is a poem about money. That is why this is fictional or that is why this is nonfiction pretending to be fictional. This is where Katherine W_______ comes into the room. She is wearing too much makeup. That is what I always notice when I see her in natural light. In the restaurant and at the gallery opening under bright lights she looks just right. She would be beautiful if I ever saw her on TV. Every star system, every novel should create a series of likenesses in the form of the mistakes that went into generating the system. Mistakes are the only kind of feelings I know how to have. In Warhol's films, paintings, and novels, like my own psyche, the system of reproduction and resemblance is utterly self-contained because it is grounded in appearances and these appearances cannot give way to feelings. That is why being in Vienna with two Mary

Ellens was so completely oppressive, because difference was everything and we are used to difference being nothing. That is why people are upset by doubles, especially of themselves. As Warhol said, "Sometimes something can look beautiful just because it's different in some way from the other things around it." That is the problem of feeling and that is why paintings are more or less interesting than ambient poems. Everything we read, especially novels and poems, should be simulated. Jackie and Marilyn and Christina Aguilera become blurry newspaper photo clippings in the seconds before we see them. A novel becomes the poorly taken snapshots found and inserted randomly. The electric chairs, ruined cars, and Brillo boxes become corruptible and generic the moment the last bit of impressionism washes out of them. (Nineteenth-century impressionism is the equivalent of television from the fifties.) Like Marilyn, all the things we see are repeated and suffer surface disfigurations of the greatest degree imaginable in the moment we recognize them. I hope I never see Katherine W________ again, except in drag.

I loved Mary Ellen and I never met Andy Warhol, although I did see him once at Bergdorf Goodman on the ground floor, in the men's shirt department darting from counter to counter. He was trying to avoid exchanging a glance with anyone. To see him would be to recognize him and that would break the circuit of gift-giving Christmas shopping. He appeared to be scanning the store for shoplifters or people who would know him. He was in black and very thin. His wig was white. He was with two very beautiful men dressed in very tight black pants. I don't remember much about them except those pants. They reminded me of breasts. I wanted to talk to Andy but I didn't. As Warhol said, "Life imitates art." The best novels ought to be exactly the same right before we got there. Nonfiction like Tom Wolfe's faux-documentary works usually imitates art and becomes redundant and boring. One wants a painting to use paint to camouflage painting itself. Photography and poetry should do the same. Everything painted or written by a human hand should be a reminder of something that was photographed. The brain is a great averager. It alone is capable of transferring death and poetry into the social realms of the brain: blindness (being starstruck), highway crosses, handguns, shadows (in a disco), car accidents, people in mourning, obits. These are "events"; they induce in the furrows of our cerebellum a dependency not unlike drugs, especially the opiates. As William Burroughs notes, "Junk suspends the whole cycle of tension, discharge, and rest. The orgasm has no function in the junky.

Boredom, which always indicates an undischarged tension, never troubles the addict. He can look at his shoe for eight hours."

I left Vienna without Mary Ellen on June 17th, 2000. I saved one newspaper clipping and one photograph from that day. One Mary Ellen went to New York. The other one went to Italy. All resemblances to the two of them must stop at this moment, the moment when two lives become the separate events that they are and that they will be, interminably and forever, and thus become unlike anything else in the present. Katherine was already growing her hair out. Mary Ellen was making a film of the events that took place that week. On the last day, when she was no longer Mary Ellen, Katherine told me she hated her new hair and wanted it to grow back. She was washing her hair ten or twelve times a day to get the red out. She was wearing a lot of makeup and had let her hair down. We were having coffee in the hotel lobby, eating the usual yogurt and toast. She gave me a lamp she had found at a flea market. Then she said she wanted a boyfriend. Then she said she didn't want a boyfriend. What happens when desire reaches the state where everything is copied (ad nauseam) without boredom from something else, as if one thing were being mapped onto something else, desire to its object, a person to his or her double, consumer to goods, the system of military camouflage to the art of painting and world of disco, myself to someone who looks like someone I like. Everything is matched but not quite to everything else.

Someone said you only have sex once when you come to Vienna as a tourist. You do something once or you do it all the time. The world is filled with a thousand resemblances, and every resemblance, especially for Mary Ellen, was the source of a thousand other things. Our feelings are interchangeable, just like we are. That is why Mary Ellen cried over and over that evening in the hotel room and I did not.

Tonight, many months later, it is mid-October, and I find that something in me is being sent away for something else. I believe this is what is typically called an emotion, because I have been trying all night to think not about things and photographs of the world but about the medium of things, which I equate with things that we love, with thinking about nothing and with things too recent to be forgotten like the glowing bodies of those white asparagus that look like insect larvae or poorly made cannoli. To exchange one thing for another infinitely, that should be the goal of all photographs that become novels. A couple nights ago I went to hear Terry Riley's *In*

C, which was performed at the Society for Ethical Culture in New York. It was the first time it had ever been played for all electronic instruments, and it was one of the most beautiful performances I have ever witnessed because it was simultaneously always changing and simultaneously always the same and in that way it got to a place that Gertrude Stein in a single sentence gets to: the endless continual duration or staying the same (that is existence) and the endless continual change (that is also and simultaneously existence). Nothing is interesting unless it can be transcribed into all the things that it is not. I ran into Katherine W_______ the other day on the N train. The best American invention is to disappear. The best way to experience something is to wait for it to happen again.

HISTORY/ADDENDUM:

In C was the piece that initiated the Minimalist movement and was written in 1964, when I was seven years old and living in Seattle, WA. All performers play from the same page of fifty-three melodic patterns. Vocalists can join in with any vowel or consonant sounds they choose. Each performer determines how many times a pattern will be played before going on to the next. Terry Riley, the composer, remarked: "It is very important that performers listen very carefully to one another and this means occasionally to drop out and listen. As an ensemble, it is very desirable to play very softly as well as very loudly and to try to diminuendo and crescendo together."

Every novel should have a diary and here it is:

Some Values of Landscape and Weather

Peter Gizzi

Democrat—I know what time it is . . .
—Hart Crane

In the middle of our lives we walked
single file into winter's steely pavilion.
The moss's greening, winningly,
made our footfalls pavane in silver light.
To be out on a Tuesday with Liberty,
her bright flash stinging.
I followed willingly, she sang
haltingly, and I kept closer
to navigate her coo and whisper.
To be at the farther edge
of beauty, this forest, its lacquered raiment,
we declined to name.
The song built with the populism of a mural.
Bits of refrain dovetailing
into a distant rumble like a bulldozer
from memory, a mockingbird's gravelly clank.

*

Where were we
on the deck having a smoke
after a day in bed. Odd oranges
and blue velvet outline the roofs.
We've stalled in this whistle before,

the train at dusk. Thinking umpas of dented brass
yesteryear calling on the road:
cloth, hair, and a string to guide us.
Take me away. Not to negate these years
but I need stay rutted in my own
long enough to swerve outside
this collision of particles that dogs my view.
I am working on hands to field
other hoists of rescue—something
particular to blue has begun
to rise from the deep and do its *schtick.*
And falling down dark, of course
I need you, but that said
all the ropes thrown overboard
wouldn't find me, like sun once
dripping into basement punkdom.

*

Not wanting to disturb an ant
I lift my leg to let it carry on
its pursuit of whatnot.
It's impressive—all this matter
crawling, marching, even achieving
an acorn of the instant.
So, this isn't exactly novelty here
babysitting the woodgrain, wanting to step up
inside myself. Courage!, carrots?,
"Charity," the word says in a notebook
—to accept the ink of the possible,
"this proves I have dreamed."

*

It is the pixel hour,
a witching pre-code silver industry
blowing through my head.
Ball bearings glide along
making it *ting,* a steely chamber
overhead. Unmistakable.
I might have said forgotten
except so many are bent to hear it,
as though music were a condition
of all our endeavor here
on the snow-spattered globe.
A nervous moon and winter branches
all that needs be recorded for now
and the value of gunmetal
fading to midnight all around.
The chill is real, that much
can be said in early November.

*

We fought in a war, looking for a sound,
some frequency
a human animal could field
beyond the other registers of everyday
and fancy, a tuning perhaps,
to focus for this instant, the effort
toward dotted archipelagoes was a part of it,
documentary hydroelectric facilities,
snocone mountain views, certainly
the unruly assembly of public spaces

is essentialism, there can be pigeons,
statehouses and prisons, freeways
etcetera. They were big chords,
a piece of the total score, the trajectory
(not facts, but hands) is this further sound,
scratch of pen to parchment
in a flight of democracy.

*

Night coming on, goings to and fro
under a canopy of burning discs
and that twinkling bigness. It was all the time
happening. Here beneath
the shadow of branch and ballot.
Where else can you say
that to love the questions
you have to love the answers.
Outside, a transmission's whine
breaks our unmediated approach
to a brambled paradise.
What could we do now our gaze
had been altered, and constantly.
The shiny spot's decoy, sometimes
emotive, sometimes in bright digression.

From Memnoir
Joan Retallack

Mem: What's our relation to the past?
Noir: Same as to the future.
Mem: Then what's our relation to the future?
Noir: You don't want to know.
Mem: In other words the jig is up.
Noir: In other words the jig is up.

Curiosity and the Claim to Happiness

Studies have shown that the brain
prefers unpredictable pleasures.

present tense

it's said that it happens even in nature e.g. during the childhood the mother might have (had) a taste for film noir and take(n) the child along

my machine is hooked up to my machin things inaccessible to the precise methods of e.g. a Brazilian bookmobile being hijacked in a dark underground garage fiction is precisely what they now call nonfiction too get a bit too presonal i.e. Eurydice my dark darling don't worry I can bear your not looking at me she cry (eyed) out i.e. hoping it (was) true

(now) (here) together in the mix of the modern metropolis Rio Vienna Paris Tokyo Moscow Hong Kong Lagos New York Bombay London Mumbai he and she both feel close to the idealized neuron in the book some of the diffuse sensations of early childhood may still surprise us as we consider their names e.g. joy frustration shame anxiety love rage fear anger wonder curiosity disgust surprise longing humor pride self-respect fear but not terror fear but not horror

the mother however might not like surprises e.g. wanting to know for how many generations a Negro in the bloodlines can produce a *throwback* the word is memory the child recalls this use of memory does not know what to say for a very long time: The soul is inwardness, as soon as and insofar as it is no longer outwardness; it is *memoria,* insofar as it does not lose itself in *curiositas.*

otherwise one could ask at any moment e.g. in what story does an uninvited goddess walk in and roll a golden ball down the hall or why not enjoy the story of lovers in the same vein from different centuries but in the same story from different worlds but in the same story I write down my dreams this is probably not one of them i.e. for a very long time the child want(ed) more than she could say to not want more than she could say i.e. impossible according to any simple formula for mirroring formulas if e.g. but for the accidental clause the swerve of curiosity on the monkey bars the flash-bulb memory the wall of fire outside the window and or something as vague as living in time i.e. for a time near what seem to be near things swept into the stream of self-translation in the coincidental flow of events near disregarded syllables suddenly audible vol up sudden outburst of song sudden Ha it's too funny how funny it is to feel sometimes and not others how to remotely sense a sweet violence in the brevity i.e. the spilt-second glance

without yards of shimmering adjectives
description: is description possible can a sunrise be described by yards of shimmering adjectives

While the curate was saying this, the lass in boy's clothing stood as if spell-bound, looking first at one and then at another, without moving her lips or saying a word, like a rustic villager who is suddenly shown some curious thing that he has never seen before . . . she gave a deep sigh and broke her silence at last. . . . Doing her best to restrain her tears, she began the story of her life, in a calm, clear voice.

without the carefully constructed container:
story: is story possible: can a life even a portion of a life be
contained in a story: would songs be better to repair the brain

when if it's curiosity that
draws attention to curiosity even the other animals like us even in nature
if for only the space of time e.g. at the watering hole e.g. during those
times when it's too wide or too narrow for ambiguity the range of genres
might now include humor and but or horror even (then) there

this
voltage through the body is brought on by the senses strictly speaking
in logic nothing is accidental the world divides us into seekers after
facts seekers after gold dig up much earth and find little or less than
a port royal stain it's super being natural not wishing to symbolize the
wish to return to feel as much at home in e.g. a fortunate sentence
as in i.e. an unfortunate century

some may see at this point which is not an Archimedean point the necessity to invent a game in which all vowels are serially replaced with x mxgxcxlly txrnxng prxmxtxrx txrrxr xntx pxlxtxblx pxst-pxst xrxny xtc.

or that it is not an idle game after all to forgive that they or we in the slit second of a single pulse to reveal the tear the tears in all the pages in all their ambiguity paging through x number of photo albums knowing and not knowing all that is is not there with only a few clues to go by e.g. fake cheetah fur fake cowboy hat small dog straining at leash small notebook that can be open and closed at the same time i.e. all this and more! with the ontological thickness of a scratch-and-win sheet

look

see the red blue yellow green space at the watering hole hear the animals slurp see the animals roll in the mud witness the archaeological trace of some thing less visible than a zoological park the mother the father stiff in Sunday best the insistent curiosity of the child the timing the timing is all that is off

it is that that is the problem with the timing that it is always off while it can not be off at all

Life in the Body
T. M. *McNally*

21.

MY FATHER IS a strong man. But in October of 1962, I imagine he is uncertain of his depths. Winter is decidedly in the air, and Khrushchev is in the process of installing missiles in Cuba—a twelve-minute burn to Miami, a few minutes more to Washington. Driving out of the city of Chicago, heading for home along with half a million others, my father is worried mostly about the future.

Certainly he does not know that I am soon to be conceived. Right now the traffic is heavy and slow. The sky, early winter, is absent of relief: In the rust belt one learns to spot the symptoms early, and through his windshield, my father looks up at the sky—the color of manufactured steel, solid as a door. On the seat beside him rests his briefcase. It is a briefcase which my mother picked out, as a wedding gift, and inside the case among his pencils and slide rule and new life insurance policy lies the hope of his future at Maryvale. Maryvale has its fingers in washing machines and machine guns, though it is known mostly for its influence upon automotive exhaust—tailpipes, mufflers; twelve years from now my father will design a prototype catalytic converter specifically for Ford. But right now he is a new recruit, a recent acquisition of a corporate takeover, and he knows little of exhaust.

My father, after being released from the Korean Conflict, during which he repaired a network of IBM computers inside a tall Manhattan building, returned to Goodyear, where he worked with a team which developed airplane tires. He skipped around for the next several years: Firestone, and tubeless tires; Bendix, where he worked on brakes; Studebaker, where he flirted with overall design; and then Ford, where he was responsible for coming up with the suspension for the Lincoln Continental—then still just a fine idea. The long hood wasn't yet under consideration, but it was at Lincoln that he found his direction, his place in the automotive world of manufacturing and design: He would be a specialist, and he would specialize in suspension. So my father settled in Cleveland and took on a job at Roman, as in Roman Shock Absorbers. Roman also makes leaf springs and U-joints, but Roman will soon be bought out by Maryvale, that company which also has its thumbs in machine guns and washing machines. In the spirit of increasing shareholder value, Maryvale is extending its reach within the automotive industry; they send a team of gray suits to Cleveland, have a look around, smoke a lot of cigarettes. They buy the company outright and fire everybody on the design team except my father. Then they tell my father he needs his own office. They tell my father to buy a couple suits, to take a few days off. They tell my father to take the little wife and to go look for a nice house in Chicago.

20.

The little wife is five foot even, raven-hearted with two kids of her own and coal black hair down to her waist. She has no chin to speak of, but as my father likes to point out, her struts are fine and true. She was raised an orphan in a Catholic convent, north of Dodge City, Kansas. Consequently, she believes in God. She is also convinced my father is sleeping with his new secretary in Chicago—a woman named, of all things, Eve.

And because she is convinced my father is sleeping with Eve, my mother is very, very angry. Right now, aside from being decidedly fertile, she is putting my older brother down for his nap. The bedspread is blue, and Connor, who doesn't want to take a nap, is crying fitfully. He takes a small fist and punches my mother on the cheek.

"No," she says. "Mommy has to talk. Connor has to sleep."

"No," Connor wails. "No!"

"Daddy will be home and then you can play. With Daddy."

"He's not my Daddy."

When my mother slaps Connor, he quiets down. She is, in fact, proud of her slap—her fine hand and slender fingers, neatly collected, a skill several nuns taught her as a child. In the kitchen, sitting at the table over his fourth glass of wine, sits Father Tim, who is waiting for Connor to settle down and for my mother to return.

And my mother, standing in the doorway, having a last look at Connor—his cheek tear stained and pink—does my mother really want to do this? Quite frankly, she hates Chicago—the cement and factories, the constant spread of industrial incorporation. When she married my father, in a distant, wooded Ohio suburb, they moved into a log cabin. The cabin had a loft, and my father made furniture at night; he played with Connor and taught him how to hold a saw. *Look,* my father would say. Then my father took Connor and Maureen into a city courtroom and changed their name. "From now on," my father said to Connor, holding his hand, "you're a McGowan. Just like me."

Connor has yellow hair, unlike my father. Connor's actual father was on the skids—strung out somewhere in San Francisco. My mother had once said she loved him, that she was pregnant; that sex was one kind of sin, abortion entirely another. She had called up my father on the telephone from South Bend, Indiana, where she worked in a small radio station, writing ad copy, and she said to my father, "Mac, I'm going to marry him."

"Good luck."

Three years later, she was back on the telephone with a two-year-old and an infant. My father was working then at Studebaker. He bought things for my mother like milk and chocolate and shoes. For Christmas, he gave her a sweater, the same sweater he gave to a woman he was dating, only he mixed up the boxes. My mother opened her sweater, which was *large,* and said my father had some explaining to do. That night they must have talked a lot, particularly in bed. In college, my father once went flying through a second-story window—bathtub gin—and she had nursed his wounds: a broken ankle; a long, deep cut along his chin; she had seen him naked often, despite the wounds. And I imagine that Christmas, with Connor tucked into bed, dreaming of someday having his own dad, I imagine that my mother knew precisely what she was doing then. My father was tall, profoundly shy unless drunk, and dressed terribly. He wore his hair short to keep it out of his eyes. His fingernails were full of axle grease and smelled like gasoline and nicotine. His arms were hard as galvanized steel, and he dated a tall woman who required large, plush sweaters, and he liked to work. Nights, when the light was gone, he drank beer and looked at the sky.

"You should marry me, Mac."

"Not hardly."

My mother laughed dishonestly. In bed she punched him with her fist. My father was tired, cranky from having put together a tricycle for Connor and Maureen, out in the garage, which was cold. He was tired of hanging out with a woman and her kids without having any specific reason. He liked reasons. He needed to understand how the pieces fit together, in order to make a machine, or a common understanding.

"I'm getting too old," my mother said. "Connor's growing up. He needs a dad."

"You should take that job," my father said. "More money. More men."

My mother had a job offer from an advertising agency in Michigan which handled accounts for General Motors. Apparently, somebody had decided they needed a woman's point of view, even if nobody had any particular intention then of using it.

"You're calling me a whore?"

"Jesus, Chloe. I'm calling you a modern woman."

"But not modern enough, eh?"

At this, my father rolled over onto his side. He shut his eyes, because he was tired, and because he wanted to get some sleep. He thought about the way my mother's hair fell against his back.

"Mac? I can't keep doing this."

"Maybe I should leave, then."

And then my mother stretched across his back to find the light.

19.

She took the job in Michigan. Then her husband looked her up, caught a bus and pissed on Connor and beat him senseless. My father was in Minnesota, doing cold-weather testing for Firestone. He drove to Detroit and said enough was enough.

I know only the man's name. Goose. He too was a Catholic from Dodge City. His family—the Goose Shoe Store chain—had a moderate amount of money and wanted him to find a wife. A wife, it was believed, could keep a wealthy man from drink, as well as provide an heir. When Maureen was born, Goose stole my mother's gasoline credit card and robbed a liquor store in Topeka. Then the family cut him off and asked my mother to move out of town.

It happened long before I was even born—Connor, and Maureen. Connor has yellow hair, a crew cut, because my father likes it that way, and right now Connor is trying to lie in bed and listen to the dusk. He can see light creeping through the gingham drapes. It's a small house, a South Chicago bungalow, newly built like the dozen others on the same block. My parents have rented this house while my father saves for a down payment on one my mother plans to pick out soon. A suburb, someplace with a lawn. In the meantime, my mother no longer works, and Connor doesn't want to take a nap. He will soon turn five, he hasn't had a nap in months, and if Father Tim stays for supper, then Connor will not have to talk to his new dad.

Connor is still mad at my father for making him eat his peas.

So Connor lies in bed, racing, because that's precisely what his brain does. It races. He goes around inside his head like a track. In winter, when he is expected to sit still, he often breaks his toys, and after a while, he begins to bang his head against the wall. His forehead, there where it won't hurt as much, but just enough for him to feel good. If it doesn't hurt, he won't have a reason to be crying, which he does, silently. After a while, he remembers to keep count, and then he loses it.

18.

My father feels uncomfortable in a suit. To save money, he bought himself two, each the same, and several white shirts. It helps to think of it as a uniform, and on the radio of his '53 Ford, the second '53 Ford he has owned, each engine rebuilt by himself, my father listens to the news. The traffic is deadlocked now. People in thick clothes are trying to build a freeway ramp, but they haven't had much practice yet, and meanwhile the southbound traffic has been shifted into a single, frozen lane. And the news is particularly grim. Kennedy has ordered a blockade of Soviet ships steaming toward Cuba. He has made clear his willingness to fire on those ships which are bringing to Cuba equipment which will make the missiles operable. Khrushchev has said Kennedy has missiles in Turkey. It is only right that he, The Big Nikita, protect Cuba. Khrushchev mentions often and with remarkable derision the incident at the Bay of Pigs.

My father doesn't know that Dean Acheson has already urged the president to fire on Cuba. Once the Soviet missiles in Cuba become hot, the entire nation is at risk. And Kennedy, stretching the small of his back, insists there must be some alternative. McNamara, secretary of defense, argues that a missile is a missile, that a missile in Cuba pointed at Detroit is no different than a missile in Moscow pointed at Detroit. On this matter, apparently, McNamara is a *dove,* and not a *hawk,* and Bobby Kennedy, who is merely the president's brother, prefers a naval blockade—like a *duck,* Acheson thinks. Consequently, Acheson is dispatched to Paris, to apprise de Gaulle, while Kennedy makes a seventeen-minute speech, declaring his intent to respond militarily—which means B-52s over Moscow, and Soviet IL-28 bombers over St. Louis, which means lighting up those Jupiter missiles in Turkey, even if they are obsolete, because this means global thermonuclear war. And as my father listens to the news, sitting in traffic, the signal begins to drift. The announcer's voice begins to fade, and my father hits the dash of his '53 Ford once, then twice, and looks up into the sky.

On the seat beside him in his briefcase lies a sketch. The sketch is of a shock absorber, one to be controlled by air. He has no idea how to make the valves seal, but a shock absorber which is flexible to the needs of the nuclear family—one which can accommodate both light and heavy loads—will revolutionize the entire industry. It is an industry which services automobile manufacturers, which in turn service the needs of a consumer-driven economy, which my father believes must inevitably lead to war. In this life, there simply isn't room enough for everybody to be rich.

Khrushchev knows this, and so he plans to take precisely what he wants before the United States can buy it. By making a feint at Cuba, Khrushchev actually intends to dig his Soviet heels further into Europe—namely, Berlin. Meanwhile Kennedy invokes the Monroe Doctrine and considers, once again, invading Cuba. He rocks in his chair while my father, stuck in traffic, worries about the seal. Everything, my father knows, must rest upon the quality of the seal.

17.

Father Tim is in love with my mother, always has been. In Kansas, Father Tim wasn't yet a priest; he was a kid, a Protestant who went to the Catholic high school, and took my mother to all the dances. Tim is two years younger than Goose, that man somewhere now in San Francisco, strung out, and Tim is also married. He has two kids of his own. He is an assistant rector at the local Episcopal church. When he scratches at his beard, prematurely gray, he really does appear to be uncomfortable.

At church, dressed in a gray suit, my father listens patiently to his sermons. My mother loves to dance, though she is now married to a man who dresses horribly. She married my father in a courtroom to avoid formality and a wedding band—the kind that plays music badly and insists on everybody dancing. My father also doesn't wear a ring.

And my mother knows the rules which govern this world. She knows that old lovers always sleep together, no matter how hard they may try not to: Intimacy, once formed, longs always to return precisely to its origins. She knows too that God prefers shame to anger—that once angry, one no longer has the possibility for remorse, until that anger has long since passed. My mother wants to be close to God, as well as the men she loves, and my mother wants to feel ashamed, if only because it speeds up the process of forgiveness—divine and absolutely necessary for this life.

Having lost one man already, my mother does not intend to lose another.

16.

Does Eve really believe she is in love with my father? Eve is a young woman, nearly liberated, living in a city two-flat near the North Side, though still not yet far enough north to be expensive, or, for that matter, fully liberated. On her desk, beside her typewriter, stand a lot of books. She dreams someday of being an executive secretary and taking frequent trips to Honolulu. Sometimes, in my father's office, on her knees, maybe, or stroking his face, she dreams that he will take her there.

"No commitments," Eve says hopefully. "No strings."

Like most practical men, my father distrusts suspense and its false promise for resolution. Instead my father believes that when one person contemplates adultery, then so too does that person's mate. It's something one finds in the air, floating by—innuendo, and surprise. He imagines, for a moment, his wife, Chloe, in bed with another man. My father imagines his adopted children, Connor and Maureen, watching him through the window. It makes him angry, this matter of precise and living fact: Connor, and Maureen. To be a kind and loving father, he shall need to be always in control. What my father wants most in this life is a son of his own making.

"You need another boss," my father says to Eve.

"You're firing me?"

"No," says my father. "But if we are going to continue, like this, then you cannot work for me."

"Oh."

"Otherwise," my father says. "Otherwise, you can still work for me, and we can call this off."

Secretly, my father wants to call it off. He likes his office and his new appointment and previously uncomplicated mornings. He only slept with Eve in an effort to convince himself he should divorce his wife. Eve is a sweet girl, but if he stays with her, she will wind up telling him what to do. My father is most afraid of being told just what to do, especially by a woman.

He runs his hand across her breast. He traces a vein, and with the winter light falling into his office, Eve's body shimmers in the dusk. She has goose pimples. From the cold, my father reasons. He is not going to remove his tie.

"You don't wear a ring," Eve says. "Why not?"

My father laughs, and looks at his hand, which is scarred from years of use. "Currents," he says, laughing. "I can't stand being shocked."

15.

Birds fly, missiles fly. Where is my sister?

At the age of seven, Maureen is already far ahead of her time. Having skipped one grade, she's urged by her teachers to skip another. Wednesdays, after school, she reads books to kids in kindergarten. It makes her feel old, like a teacher or a tree.

Maureen does not yet know precisely where books come from. She imagines a room full of old men, each leaning heavily on a desk, writing very carefully. She knows the men are old because it must have taken years and years of practice to make each letter perfect. She is just learning cursive herself and has particular trouble with her *S*'s. When she turns the page, after reading about a dog named Spot, and a boy named Dick, she realizes that she'd like to have a dog—one she wouldn't dream of naming Spot, because that name has already been taken.

She is reading to a boy named Toby Cameron, though she only pays attention to his first name. He is a slow, thick boy who often gets lost on his way to the lunchroom. His parents are pleased that Maureen will read to him, and in return offer to keep her until five o'clock, when my mother drives to Toby's house and picks her up in the baby blue Volkswagen. My father wants to sell the Volkswagen because the engine is in the back. Maureen doesn't know what an engine is, either.

Toby points to the book and says, "Go on."

"My mom's coming soon," Maureen says. "What time is it?"

Toby can't tell time, but he says, scratching his wrist, "Noon."

"It's not noon," Maureen says. "We already had lunch."

Before my mother married my father, my mother would drive home for lunch, to make sure Maureen was safe. That was when a colored lady used to sing them songs and cook milk on the stove. Once, the colored lady dropped the bottle of milk, which shattered, and then Maureen's mother fired her. Then her mother got married and stayed home all day, and then Maureen started school, and now they lived in Illinois. The state bird is the cardinal, which is red. Sometimes the cardinal is also Catholic.

She looks at the book and reads, "Jane runs."

"Where?" says Toby. "Turn the page!"

Now Mrs. Cameron steps inside the living room. She is wearing a skirt for cooking, wiping her hands on the apron, and says, "*Please,* Toby. *Please* turn the page."

"She's holding the book!" Toby says.

Maureen closes the book and stands up. She pulls up her dark green socks and says, "My mom's coming soon. In her Volkswagen."

14.

My father takes his work from the office home, but his extramarital affairs he drops off along the way. Nearby his office stands a hotel, crumbling, though still not run down enough to justify demolition. The lights flicker inside and hum. On the fourth floor, they are each high enough above the ground to leave the drapes open wide. This way, neither one of them has to touch the fabric.

Mostly, he is flattered. He has always been shy around girls. Working in his garage, drinking his beer, it was easier to get things done. To build a chair, or a wooden table. It was easier than talking to a female with a brain and involved less risk, but with Eve, a girl still in her midtwenties, who sometimes doesn't wear a bra, because she doesn't need to, with Eve my father feels as if he is somehow entitled to something nice he might deserve. Then, afterward, spent, reaching for a cigarette, he begins to feel naked and foolish. He is, after all, a father and a husband. He is married to a woman who wants to have a garden. He is married to a woman who didn't wait for him to have two kids of her own.

My father says, sitting up on his elbow, "Eve."

"Yes?"

"We forgot to pull the drapes."

"I'm not ashamed," Eve says. "Let the whole world watch!"

"No," says my father, reaching for his watch. "You're naked. Eve, it's not time for that." He says, gripping her shoulder, looking her in the eye, "It will never be time for that."

She rests her hand along his thigh, gently, and says, "Well. Then how about another raise? Quick, before the sun comes up?"

13.

The cold comfort of fact: a Soviet Intermediate Range Ballistic Missile, or IRBM, has a range of 2,020 nautical miles; once fired from its base in San Cristobal, Cuba, only Seattle is safe. If the U.S. attacks

Cuba—an allegedly surgical strike designed strictly to eliminate the missile base, and a couple million citizens—then the Soviets will most likely respond by firing on those Jupiter missile bases in Turkey. To which the U.S. will then most likely respond by firing on a Soviet missile base closer to home—Leningrad, or possibly even Moscow. Acheson argues that by then the cooler heads will have had time to sit back and think things out. It's like playing chess badly, this rush into violence. Meanwhile, Acheson is on a flight to Paris to keep de Gaulle from feeling left out, and Bobby is having drinks with the Soviet minister, Anatoly Dobrynin.

At school, my sister feels left out. At school my sister practices Duck & Cover drills. They sing a song at school, because it's fun to do, like hiding beneath the desk:

Duck & Cover, it's the only way
Duck & Cover, to have a sunny day . . .

12.

My father has never been to Paris. The seal will have to be flexible and capable of withstanding several hundred pounds of pressure per square inch. It will also have to be remarkably small. If they can find the correct compounds, then possibly it will not leak. My father keeps the sketch with him inside his briefcase on a pad of yellow paper.

Each month, my father deposits thirty-five percent of his check into a savings account—close to two hundred dollars. He wants to purchase stock options with the new company in the fall. He wants to save for a down payment on a bigger house. He wants to buy Connor another pair of shoes which Connor will soon grow out of. My mother's Volkswagen also needs a new clutch, which my father will put in by himself next weekend. If he had more money, my father reasons, he wouldn't have to worry about not having any.

My father no longer has any debts, except for those he's recently assumed from his new wife. Three hundred dollars for a Volkswagen, which he plans to ditch as soon as he can convince his wife they need to. He believes the car is structurally unsafe, as well as expensive. He also needs to finish paying off Connor's maternity bills, which his wife defaulted on two years ago. The cost to change the kids' names was an additional forty-five dollars, each, and Connor needs new shoes. Maureen wants a bike.

His mother, who lives in Florida, writes him often, explaining that his own father would be proud. My father is used to taking care of women; it's a job he has experience at. When his father died, shortly after he was born, his mother moved to Florida and opened up a small hotel. The hotel often ran down, and my father learned to do the maintenance: plumbing, hanging Sheetrock, running electrical conduit, and laying floors. He also learned to avoid running up bills he could not afford.

Eventually, all comes due. My father has, among other things, a genetic flaw locked into the central aorta of his brain. Before his life is over, he will have three cerebral aneurysms, the first of which will strike shortly before his forty-fifth birthday and cause him to spend the next three years relearning how to speak and walk. The surgery to rescue his brain will destroy the faculties of his mind. Years from now, in 1999, after his wife abandons him penniless to the mercy of the state, my father will recall murkily the depths of his wife's black, raven heart. Then he will fall to the floor in an elevator going up and die.

11.

My father, who art in heaven, distrusts while he is alive the body politic.

He distrusts the body politic more than he does either Kennedy or Nixon. And he understands, my father, that Kennedy won the election on account of those thousands of ballots cast by the Chicago dead—those men and women still in their graves, resurrected and summoned forth by Daley's Democratic machine. My father, smitten by the inner workings of machines, has to give him credit.

The language of debt is also one of accountability. My mother is uncertain what's on Father Tim's mind, though she suspects it may be lust. While my mother is not particularly influenced by lust—she has, for example, rarely had an orgasm—she does know how to use it to her advantage. For my mother, sex means needing to wash up afterward: It is typically the kind of sin which can be washed away with prayer so long as nothing is conceived and, consequently, aborted. She also knows that my father is no longer interested. When he comes to bed, he no longer brushes his teeth. His hair is full of axle grease and cigarette smoke and, most recently, a foreign perfume.

Now Father Tim takes my mother's hand across the table. He is not wearing his collar today, and so he appears to be a normal man, capable of sin and respectable amounts of grief. He takes my mother's hand and says, "Chloe."

"I love him," my mother says, meaning my father.

"Of course you do," says Father Tim. "Of course you do."

"We're going to move soon," my mother says, beginning to cry. She cries gently at first, gaining momentum. "Do you know why he is doing this?"

"He is a man," says Father Tim sadly. "The world is going to end?"

"Yes," says my mother, looking at her watch. "And I am a fucking bitch."

10.

My mother couldn't afford a nice briefcase. She had clothes to buy and mouths to feed and she had to pay somebody to look after Connor and Maureen while she went off to work. When my father asked my mother to marry him, she was making three thousand dollars a year more than he, and still it was not enough. To pay for the briefcase, she hocked her previous engagement ring, which she had hidden in a shoe to prevent Goose from doing the very same thing. She also skimped on lunch at work.

In Detroit, working for Jackson McDougal Bergson, she wrote an ad for the Pontiac Tempest, which was driven by a transaxle, something which it took my father to explain the meaning of. She decided to focus on the upholstery, and room for kids, and came up with a campaign that even men could admire. For Christmas, her boss gave her a hundred dollar bonus, based on the success of her ad, and then she finally had enough to buy my father's briefcase.

It wasn't leather, but it looked like leather; the snaps were brass and had a combination lock. One night, shortly before she moved back to South Bend, she gave it to my father in a box. They were sitting on the floor of my father's apartment because he didn't like to pay for furniture. They lit a fire in the fireplace, and then my mother went out to her car and brought inside a great big box.

"What's this?" my father said, tugging at the ribbons.

"It's a wedding present. For you, Mac."

"Who's it from?"

"Me," said my mother, kissing him. "It's from me."

My father wasn't used to presents. He bought sweaters for his girlfriends, usually *large,* for Christmas, and for a moment he felt foolish and undeserving. My father was the kind of man who felt more blessed to give, if only because he had never been expected to receive, and because of course my father was deeply afraid of debt—spiritual or otherwise. He knew my mother wanted him to join her church, if only for the kids' sake.

He opened the box, took out the briefcase. "We can't afford this, Chloe."

My mother laughed. Then she said, "We can't afford anything. At least right now. The man said it was the kind of thing you grow into. Like a good sofa. You get used to it."

"Thank you," said my father, frowning.

"It's for your new job. You can't use it until the very first day. Promise."

My father laughed, because there was no possibility for escape. He kissed my mother and said, "Promise. I promise."

"And we need to find a house. With a yard. And a garden!" She said, removing the case from my father's lap, "I've been saving up for that for months."

They threw the ribbons in the fire. They made love that night, my father and my mother. They closed their eyes and fell into a world of promises. They fell into the past, when love was still a state of grace, and not complicity. They fell into each other's arms in order to make love, and a new home, and possibly a family which would last for generations.

9.

Connor wakes from his nap, startled. He hears wailing in the background—a puppy bumped into by a car: a cat, at night, screaming. The room is dark and his eyes are full of sleep. His head doesn't hurt at all.

In the hallway he searches for the light switch: The light flashes for an instant, and burns out. In the dark, blinded only momentarily, he turns into the kitchen, where he finds a tall green bottle and two empty tea mugs and a sugar bowl. Because the country is building highways, his father, who really isn't his father, won't be home for another hour. Then they will have dinner in the big room.

The television only gets one channel, and he is not allowed to watch it, anyway. In Ohio, they had three channels, but until they get an antenna, they just have one. He doesn't know yet what precisely an antenna is. When he sits down in front of the television, he is hoping the noises coming from the bedroom will soon stop. He doesn't remember his real father, but he has been taught not to pay attention. Now he stands up, tugs on his bottoms, and enters the dark hallway. When he gets to his mother's bedroom, just outside the door, he sits on the floor and begins to hum.

8.

She knows how to make a man feel good, particularly a man of God.

7.

My father is a sad man, though he does not know it. When he becomes sad, he often drinks, and when he cannot drink, he becomes very angry. Anger, his life has taught him, is far more easily controlled. Two years before he dies, he will fall and break his hip. He will have been inside his garage looking for a wrench. After falling inside his empty garage, he will spend the next three hours calling out for help. It is after his wife returns from her weekend trip that she will decide to abandon him entirely, and when my father falls inside his garage, he will be capable of as much thought—sadness, and anger at himself—as possible, given the surgically imposed limitations of his brain. Mercifully, this is long into the future, and because my father cannot see into the future, there is nothing he can do to change it.

Meanwhile, when my father becomes sad, he often thinks of Minnesota, where he was for a brief time happy. In Minnesota, working for Firestone, he lived in a cabin beside a lake. He lived with a crew that did cold-weather testing on the frozen lake—a solid bridge of ice. At night, the men drank fine Canadian whisky; they played Blackjack and Whist while telling stories about the day. For hours each day, the crew would drive cars across the frozen lake, locking up the brakes, practicing controlled skids. My father would sit behind the wheel of his cold car and drive into the skids, spinning into circles, one after another. His personal record was eleven—too much speed, and one threatened to roll the car proper, even on the ice, and send it crashing through the surface. But driving, driving across the ice, my father knew always he could save himself, there, right before that moment when he accelerated and then thrust himself into oblivion.

6.

My sister's favorite game is Duck Duck Goose. At school, she and her classmates will sit in a circle, each longing to be singled out. When someone finally taps her on the shoulder, she likes the way that feels. Somebody, anybody, touching her on the shoulder.

She runs like a girl, of course. Outside on the front lawn of Toby Cameron's house, they play freeze tag with Toby's older brother, Doug. Doug is thirteen, and almost too old for tag, and he can outrun them all. Even though it's cold, Doug wears only a sweatshirt, and his face and neck are bright red.

Right now, my sister is frozen still, waiting to be released. Up above, the sky is falling, and a flock of birds is flying south toward Mississippi. She remembers that her father's name is Goose, which is a bird. She remembers that her father never liked to touch her. When he came home, whenever he did come home, he would sit in the kitchen in his underwear. Sometimes, he slept on the kitchen floor. Once he made her mommy sick.

Maureen knows that when you are sick, you are not supposed to touch somebody, or share your glass. Meanwhile, she shivers, because it's very cold, and because her green socks go up only to her knees. She has a new daddy now, as well as a new name. Waiting on the lawn, frozen, waiting to be released, she tells herself she no longer is a bird.

"I have a new name," she tells herself stiffly.

It's cold, and the birds in the sky are gone.

"Touch me," she calls to Toby. "Touch me!"

5.

At the wedding, which took place in a courtroom, my father gave my mother a ring which had been brought over to America on a boat. It belonged to his grandmother, my father said. My father said, "Aside from my tools, it's the only decent thing I own."

"What time is it?" says my mother, sitting up.

Father Tim, naked, looks for his watch. While he has slept with my mother often, years ago and usually in Kansas, he has never before lain in my father's bed. He is not used to all the furniture. Over my mother's dressing table, which my father built for her last summer, is a picture of my mother's favorite president. Before she left the Catholic church, my mother never dreamed she'd be divorced.

And then remarried, to a man who builds her furniture and sleeps with his secretary on the sly. She sits up naked, looking at Tim, who after the fact appears childish and small. Her mouth tastes like wine and smoke and sweat.

"Oh my God," Tim whispers. "Here we go again."

My mother says, lifting the sheets, swinging naked off the bed, "No. You have to dress. Before I hurt you even more."

On the way to the hallway, she stops at her dressing table and reaches for her brush.

4.

Time flies. My father, the man who taught me to speak, and to think, the man who taught me to see . . . my father is naturally worried about the future given that it is his responsibility to protect his family from it. Eyeball to eyeball, says the secretary of state. When my father drops Eve off at her El station, he doesn't wave goodbye.

Neither Khrushchev nor Kennedy wants a war. Neither wants to admit mistakes, either. Theirs is a marriage of diplomatic immunity. The Jupiter missiles in Turkey are obsolete; they should have been removed long before when Kennedy in fact ordered them to be removed. Meanwhile, Russian warships have been sent to Cuba, and even the brothers Kennedy believe the blockade is going to escalate: War, it appears, is inevitable, and my father is stuck in traffic. While he has never met a citizen of the Soviet Union, my father feels no particular hostility toward that union. Never before has the world felt so cold.

My father is going to build for the world an air-adjustable shock absorber. His is a career which shall rely on his ability to engineer a soft ride and unprecedented comfort. In the meantime, the heater on his '53 Ford—a hole, really, blowing in hot air from the engine—is failing to warm the car. Because the traffic has not moved a hundred feet in the past fifteen minutes, the interior has become cold to the touch. Speed helps to keep things warm, even when one is uncertain of his or her direction: If my father leaves my mother, he will not settle down with Eve, and in just that moment, that moment when he is reaching into his breast pocket for a cigarette and match, he makes his decision: It's the kind of choice he's been raised by experience to make. Meanwhile, the match flickers, brightly, and he breathes in the sulfur and examines the flame he's holding by his fingertips, which warms them, briskly.

Up ahead, a Caterpillar tractor is clearing away the road, and finally the cars begin to move. My father shifts into second, which provides him with sufficient torque to proceed, when suddenly the traffic stops again. A green car behind him hits his bumper, and my father smashes his hand into the steering wheel. The cigarette has burned his fingers.

He has to turn around to see, because there is no rearview mirror, and when he does so he sees a tall man in boots and jeans and a heavy coat striding up to his window. The window doesn't roll, and so my father opens the door, and the man slams it shut. The man is yelling at my father for driving like an old lady.

My father's mother, who is an old lady, no longer drives, though he thinks she still may have a car somewhere in Florida. My father attempts to open the door again, his fingers hot, smarting, and again the man slams the door shut, and when this happens, when the door slams and bangs my father's knee, and when he considers the current state of traffic—still dead—he allows himself to become angry. It is not a difficult decision, and he is glad for so justifiable an occasion. The blood is rushing to his head now, where a vein begins to throb, pumping the adrenaline, and now when he pushes against the door, he does so quickly, and takes the man by surprise.

The door hits the man in the knees, and he steps back. The man begins to say something and my father feels the ice in the wind, slapping his face, cutting through his overcoat. Standing outside on a dirt road full of holes, beside his old car, he thinks he must resemble a bank teller, or possibly an unemployed pharmacist: His coat is dark, and lightweight, and very thin.

The man says something, loudly, and people are beginning to pay attention. Men mostly, eager for a fight, bored with all the traffic, though secretly hoping that if a fight breaks out, each will not be expected to become involved except the man in jeans and boots, glaring. When my father coldcocks him, the man falls to his knees. My father's hand hurts, naked in the raw cold, and he decides not to wait for the man to rise. Instead, my father hits him again, somewhere on a tooth, because now his knuckles begin to bleed. The man is covering his face and my father lifts him by the shoulder and slams the man's face into the trunk of my father's '53 Ford. Then the man falls to the dirt and nobody seems to be paying any mind, though of course everybody is. Everybody is watching from behind their windshields, careful of being caught watching. Then my father lifts the man and drags him back to his green car. He opens up the door. He helps the man inside and shuts the door for him.

My father returns to his car, shaking, though he no longer feels the cold. Instead he reaches for his cigarettes. Mostly, he feels naked and foolish, the way he does after ejaculating into Eve's mouth. Right now he is grateful for the collar on his coat, which causes him to feel as if he is a spy. He rolls up the collar and pulls the Ford onto a snow-covered lawn. He cuts a corner, then another, until he finally finds a bar while shifting into third.

3.

Connor is cold, sitting in the hallway. He has wandered to the other end, far away from the door, and he can't remember any songs he knows the words to. Sitting in the hallway, his feet tucked under his thighs, he waits for the bedroom door. While he waits in the dark, he plays I Spy by himself.

I spy a silver pony, he tells himself. *Where?*

When the door opens, my mother steps into the hall and flicks on the light, which is burned out. She turns and reaches for the bathroom light. She is naked, holding her brush, her skin musty and warm, entirely alive. When she sees Connor, sitting in the hallway, she drops the brush onto the floor. The floors are cold, made of hard wood, and she stands there looking at her son.

"I couldn't sleep," Connor says. "I was tired."

He begins to cry, frightened, and now my mother kneels before him. She takes him in her arms and says, "Mommy was taking a nap."

"I know. Mommy wasn't tired."

Now she lifts him up, into her arms, and carries him into his bedroom. She sits him on his bed and says, "Mommy has to change."

"Okay."

She says, "We both have to change." She says, tugging off his pajama bottoms, "Let's race."

In the bathroom, alone, she brushes her hair and teeth. She steps inside the bedroom and tells Father Tim to get out of the way. Then she dresses. She tells Father Tim to sit in a chair beside the dressing table. Now she pulls back the bedspread and removes the sheets. She throws the sheets onto the floor and locates a new set and makes the bed all over again. Having performed his service, Father Tim has now become a burden and a tax. When he rises to help with the sheets, she says, "No. Sit down," and then she gives him orders to leave when she has left the rented house. Do not touch a thing, she says. You are to go out the door and far away from here.

"Chloe," says Father Tim. "Chloe . . ."

"No," my mother whispers. "Like a ghost, Tim. Like your precious holy ghost."

2.

My mother, a raven-hearted woman, has coal black hair down to her waist. Though she cannot conjugate a verb to save her life, she has two years toward a degree in French literature at a teachers college, and she has also been repeatedly beaten by a man she married in order to be rich but who nonetheless gave her syphilis. My mother has two kids of her own, Connor and Maureen, who have by now become my brother and my sister. She tells herself she loves a man who builds her furniture and that a son of his own will keep him home. When she first met my father in Pittsburgh, years ago, his slacks were torn at the knee.

My father went to what was then called Carnegie Tech. He wanted to be an engineer, and he wanted to go to college, and he paid his way by cutting lumber in the Northeast. He tended bar for his fraternity. He worked as a mechanic in a shop just across the Allegheny River. When he graduated, his mother presented him with a bill for $13,700.

Everything was itemized. So many dollars for ice cream. So many dollars for basketballs and baseballs and tools, like wrenches and hammers. A list for school clothes. Another for food. His mother said there wasn't any particular rush to pay her back.

It took ten years, often working nights. By the time he was thirty-two, he had paid his mother off, with interest—4½ percent—and when he married, he insisted on a courtroom wedding. No church, no songs, no reason to invite anybody he didn't care to. Particularly his mother.

Instead his mother read about it in a small clipping from a newspaper in South Bend. My mother, before she sent it off, enclosed a short note:

Now he's mine. No need to send a gift.

1.

The history of conflict is the history of the pointed finger, and to point your finger is to allow for the possibility of contact. Just who do we really have to blame? The genetic flaw within the fabric of my father's brain is presently invisible to medical science. While Acheson is off in Paris, briefing de Gaulle to keep either from feeling left out, Bobby Kennedy is having drinks with Anatoly Dobrynin. Bobby Kennedy promises to have the Jupiter missiles removed from Turkey so long as Moscow promises not to leak the deal.

My mother wants to keep her husband. My father wants to have a son. Nations have been built on lesser inclinations. The hill leading up to Toby Cameron's house is fairly steep, and my mother's Volkswagen is lugging near the top. Once in the driveway, an hour late to pick her daughter up, my mother rolls down the window and toots the horn.

"Maureen," she calls, across the lawn. "Maureen!"

Connor sits in the backseat, silent. His mother has promised ice cream, and he wants her to keep her promise. Maureen runs across the lawn, stopping only once to tug her green socks up. Once inside the car, the two of them tucked into the back, my mother insists on making her apology. She insists on practicing. She insists on stopping at the store for a nice bottle of Canadian whisky and then she's going to order pizza for the kids and then she's going to go to bed early with a headache.

"I'm sorry," my mother says, for the seventh time. "I lost track of time."

Maureen says, "We read the same book. Twice!"

Connor, who cannot read, bangs his head against the window and looks out the window at the sky.

My mother, turning up the heat, tells herself first she needs to bathe. She says, setting her lip, "No. Oh God, please. Please forgive me."

My mother, having borne two children and become an Anglican, no longer associates shame with any particular act of the body. Instead she blames the will, the secret intent to deceive, and possibly destroy. And it is not shame, or the scent of her lover in her hair, which leads her to this conviction.

It is love, and the fact that I have now been conceived by more than just a fine idea. The Big Bang. When my father's brain explodes, in 1976, it will feel just like that. It is a love, my mother's, limited by the prescriptions of her black and narcissistic heart. *God the father, God the son,* my mother thinks. *Who's to ever know?* It's an idea she will have to spend her life keeping secret. It's an idea she's going to hold inside the palm of her hand until it simply melts away.

0.

Perhaps it is Time that loses track of us. Between the here and now, perhaps Time is merely content to suspend the living. The Monroe Doctrine, declared in 1823, states specifically that no other nations will be permitted to extend their influence on the Western Hemisphere; it also promises to keep the U.S. out of Europe. At the time it was a toothless document, like an insurance policy, but things change, and people like my father invent telephones and automobiles and airplanes, and the era of good feelings passes into the modern world of the Marshall Plan and Checkpoint Charlie. My father, meanwhile, works for a company which manufactures machine guns and washing machines and automotive mufflers. Incidentally, Maryvale's chief competitor in the automotive industry is a company which also bears that same name.

Monroe. When you want to feel secure, you drive Monroe.

My father believes in competition, because competition creates a better product, and because he has a job only because he is in fact expected to design the world's first air-adjustable shock absorber, which will rely upon the seal he makes to withstand the weight of the family car. It's a matter of national security, knowing where your interests lie. In Chicago, they say *Carr,* and while my father is uncertain of those historical currents which have brought his family to the brink of thermonuclear war, he does know that he is sitting in a bar, his hands trembling, and ordering another boilermaker. On the television above the bar, which appears to receive more channels than his own at home, he watches a newscaster read from a freshly typed piece of paper. The world, says the anchorman, holds its breath.

Who shall be the first to blink? To look the other way? Who shall be the first to cast the stone? My father tells himself that he is getting stoned. When my father lights a cigarette, smoke rises into his eyes.

He wipes the blood from his knuckles onto his coat. His hands, he has come to realize, smell like another woman. He will have to wash his hands, he thinks. He will have to keep them in his pockets and to himself. When he went flying out of a second-story window, in college, he cut his face up in the glass. Sitting at the bar, looking into the mirror, he sees his face, and the scar running down along his face, and he remembers the way my mother, Chloe, dressed his wounds. Days later he asked her to cut the stitches, by herself, in order to save money. One night, after he could walk, they went to a joint for pizza and beer. They ordered a pitcher of beer, and then my mother asked my father if he was going to pour her a glass.

"Best to pour your own," my father said. "Especially if you plan to drink it."

At first, she thought he meant it as an insult; he could see it in her eyes. Then she poured herself a glass, and they sat there, talking, and he began to pay attention to her eyes. They were pretty eyes, dark and uncomplicated, merely manipulative in their transparent way. Looking into her eyes, he didn't feel shy. Even if his face was cut up, even if he had gone flying through a window, even if he didn't have a home, here was someone he could make one with. Two orphans, drinking from a pitcher of beer in Pittsburgh, Pennsylvania: It was the kind of opportunity he told himself he'd need to look for, later on, after he'd paid his dues.

Now his hands wore the scent of another woman, and he is sitting in a bar, and his knuckles are bloody and torn. It is late, and he knows his wife will be worried about the traffic. When he stands, he pours down his beer, and because the joint also sells package goods, my father asks for a quart of Meister Brau to go. He is calm now, after feeling foolish, still shaken, and he imagines for an instant that kind of world that will no longer bear his name. He is an only child, the last of his line. He reaches for his briefcase, on the stool beside him, which holds his detailed sketch.

"End of the line," he says to the bartender, wiping his eyes.

"End of the fucking world," says the bartender. "Better dead than red."

And my father says, tucking the bottle of beer up under his arm, "Not hardly."

Because secretly he believes he is capable of making this world a safer place, and this specifically is what he longs for. A chance, just one, to do more. In the car, he breaks open the beer, takes a pull, and starts his engine. It's going to be a gamble, he thinks, either way. In the distance, there is a long, heavy cable being raised into the winter sky by men working overtime. Like the Indiana Skyway, it has always been possible to connect one state with another, and what my father is telling himself now is that tomorrow he will have to be a better man. Tomorrow he will have to strike a bargain; he will have to ask Eve to find another boss, perhaps someone in sales. Then he will ask Chloe if he can sell the Volkswagen. He will offer to take the train, so she can have the car, and he will promise to be home on time for at least the entire week.

To make an engine work, you have to give it fuel. You have to give it air. You have to give it space to breathe. My father is good with tools, and he is good with his hands. It's something Chloe tells him often . . . *You're good with your hands, Mac* . . . and my father knows that tonight is shot. Not tonight, but maybe tomorrow night, or the next, long after dark. After the kids are all asleep, maybe then he will turn to her in the night, the way he used to. He will turn to her—his hand on her hip, bridging the distance—and whisper to her without apology. Then, after a while, he will settle near the ribs, waiting for a spark, because this is what he understands. To fill a woman with desire, it's important you respect the body; you have to give it reason to provide you with a home. You have to give her hope that you will at least try to be a decent man. My father, who is thirty-three during the fourth week of October 1962, my father wants to raise a family in America. He wants to play a little baseball. He wants to teach me how to drive. He wants to raise a family in America because he knows that time is running out.

Tonight there is a ring around the moon.

REJOICING REVOICING

The Art of Translation

Fyodor Dostoevsky/*Richard Pevear & Larissa Volokhonsky*

Octavio Paz/*Eliot Weinberger*

Rea Galanake/*Karen Emmerich*

Four Kabbalistic Poems/*Peter Cole*

Miguel de Cervantes/*Edith Grossman*

Uwe Timm/*Breon Mitchell*

Eight Surrealists/*Paul Auster*

Alberto Moravia/*William Weaver*

Maurice Maeterlinck/*Richard Howard*

Marcel Proust/*Lydia Davis*

José Martí/*Esther Allen*

Anonymous/*Michael Emmerich*

Pierre Reverdy/*Ron Padgett*

Robert Musil/*Burton Pike*

Alexandros Papadiamantis/*Peter Constantine*

José Sarney/*Gregory Rabassa*

Pierre Martory/*John Ashbery*

Yoko Tawada/*Susan Bernofsky*

Charles Baudelaire/*Keith Waldrop*

Giacomo Leopardi/*Jonathan Galassi*

Leo Tolstoy/*Marian Schwartz*

Edited by Peter Constantine, Bradford Morrow, and William Weaver

From The Adolescent

Fyodor Dostoevsky

Translated from Russian by Richard Pevear and Larissa Volokhonsky

Translators' Note

The Adolescent, Dostoevsky's penultimate novel, was published in 1875. The narrator-author, whom we hear speaking in the chapter that follows, is Arkady Makarovich Dolgoruky, the "adolescent" of the title, a high-school graduate now going on twenty. His last name is a cause of humiliation for him, because it belongs to one of the oldest and most distinguished princely houses of Russia, while Arkady's "legal" father is the former household serf Makar Ivanovich, whose last name just happens to be Dolgoruky. Whenever Arkady gives his name, people inevitably ask, "Prince Dolgoruky?" and he has to reply, "No, *simply* Dolgoruky." A much deeper humiliation for him is that he is not Dolgoruky at all, but the illegitimate son of a nobleman and landowner by the name of Andrei Petrovich Versilov. Makar Dolgoruky was a gardener on Versilov's estate. He was married at the age of fifty to a peasant girl from the same estate, the eighteen-year-old Sofya Andreevna. Six months after the wedding, their young, bankrupt, and recently widowed master returned alone to his estate, and two weeks later he became Sofya Andreevna's lover. "I never could find out or make a satisfactory surmise as to precisely how it started between him and my mother," Arkady writes at the start of the novel. "I'm fully prepared to believe, as he assured me himself last year, with a blush on his face, even though he told about it all with a most unconstrained and 'witty' air, that there was not the least romance, and that it all happened *just so.*" Versilov confessed their "sin" to Sofya's husband and, in Arkady's bitter phrase, "bought out my mother from Makar Ivanovich," after which they lived more or less together, though they could never marry. Makar Ivanovich left the estate and became a wanderer.

Almost from birth, Arkady was placed with various foster families; he saw his mother two or three times in his life and his father only once, when he was ten years old and was being sent to a new school in Moscow. Versilov came to make the arrangements. At this school he was mercilessly teased for being illegitimate, a fact which the director, Touchard, discovered and revealed to Arkady's classmates. The last people Arkady lived with in Moscow were a childless couple, Nikolai Semyonovich and Marya Ivanovna, whom he loved very much. Having graduated from high school, he has now come to Petersburg to see his mother and to confront Versilov, whose love he longs for and of whose disgrace and wrongdoing he has all kinds of notions and even some evidence. He also comes with his "idea." In the following chapter (Part One, Chapter Five) he explains what that "idea" is and how he arrived at it.

* * *

I.

My idea is—to become Rothschild. I invite the reader to calmness and seriousness.

I repeat: my idea is to become Rothschild, to become as rich as Rothschild; not simply rich, but precisely like Rothschild. Why, what for, precisely what goals I pursue—of that I shall speak later. First, I shall merely prove that the achievement of my goal is mathematically assured.

The matter is very simple, the whole secret lies in two words: *persistence* and *continuity.*

"We've heard all that," I'll be told, "it's nothing new. Every *Vater* in Germany repeats it to his children, and yet your Rothschild" (that is, the late James Rothschild, the Parisian, he's the one I'm speaking of) "was only one, while there are millions of *Vaters.*"

I would answer:

"You assure me that you've heard it all, and yet you haven't heard anything. True, you're also right about one thing: if I said that this was a 'very simple' matter, I forgot to add that it's also the most difficult. All the religions and moralities in the world come down to one thing: 'We must love virtue and flee from vice.' What, it seems, could be simpler? So go and do something virtuous and flee from at least one of your vices, give it a try—eh? It's the same here."

That's why your countless *Vaters* in the course of countless ages can repeat these two astonishing words, which make up the whole secret, and yet Rothschild remains alone. Which means: it's the same and not the same, and the *Vaters* are repeating quite a different thought.

No doubt they, too, have heard about persistence and continuity; but to achieve my goal, it's not *Vater* persistence and *Vater* continuity that are needed.

Already this one word, that he's a *Vater*—I'm not speaking only of Germans—that he has a family, that he lives like everybody else, has expenses like everybody else, has duties like everybody else—here you don't become Rothschild, but remain only a moderate man. I understand all too clearly that, having become Rothschild, or even only wishing to become him, not in a *Vater*like way, but seriously—I thereby at once step outside of society.

A few years ago I read in the newspapers that on the Volga, on one of the steamboats, a certain beggar died, who had gone about in tatters, begging for alms, and was known to everybody there. After his death, they found as much as three thousand in banknotes sewn into his rags. The other day I again read about a certain beggar, from the nobility, who went around the taverns hat in hand. They arrested him and found as much as five thousand rubles on him. Two conclusions follow directly from this: first, *persistence* in accumulating, even by kopecks, produces enormous results later on (time means nothing here); and second, that the most unsophisticated but *continuous* form of gain mathematically assures success.

And yet there are people, perhaps quite a few of them, who are respectable, intelligent, and restrained, but who (no matter how they try) do not have either three or five thousand, but who nevertheless want terribly much to have it. Why is that so? The answer is clear: because, despite all their wanting, not one of them *wants* to such a degree, for instance, as to become a beggar, if there's no other way of getting money; or is persistent to such a degree, even having become a beggar, as not to spend the very first kopecks he gets on an extra crust for himself or his family. And yet, with this method of accumulation, that is, with begging, one has to eat nothing but bread and salt in order to save so much money; at least that's my understanding. That is surely what the two above-mentioned beggars did, that is, ate nothing but bread and lived all but under the open sky. There is no doubt that they had no intention of becoming Rothschild: these were Harpagons or Plyushkins in the purest form, nothing more; but conscious money-making in a completely different form, and with the goal of becoming Rothschild, will call for no less wanting and strength of will than with these two beggars.

A *Vater* won't show such strength. There is a great diversity of strengths in the world, strengths of will and wanting especially. There is the temperature of boiling water, and there is the temperature of red-hot iron.

Here it's the same as a monastery, the same ascetic endeavor. Here it's a feeling, not an idea. What for? Why? Is it moral, and is it not ugly, to go about in sackcloth and eat black bread all your life, while carrying such huge money on you? These questions are for later, but now I'm only talking about the possibility of achieving the goal.

When I thought up "my idea" (and it consists of red-hot iron), I began testing myself: am I capable of the monastery and asceticism? To that end I spent the whole first month eating nothing but bread and water. It came to no more than two and a half pounds of black bread a day. To carry it out, I had to deceive the clever Nikolai Semyonovich and the well-wishing Marya Ivanovna. I insisted, to her distress and to a certain perplexity in the most delicate Nikolai Semyonovich, that dinner be brought to my room. There I simply destroyed it: the soup I poured out the window into the nettles or a certain other place, the beef I either threw out the window to the dog, or wrapped in paper, put in my pocket, and took out later, well, and all the rest. Since they served much less than two and a half pounds of bread for dinner, I bought myself more bread on the sly. I held out for that month, only I may have upset my stomach somewhat; but the next month I added soup to the bread, and drank a glass of tea in the morning and evening—and, I assure you, I spent a whole year that way in perfect health and contentment, and morally—in rapture and continuous secret delight. Not only did I not regret the meals, I was in ecstasy. By the end of the year, having made sure that I was able to endure any fast you like, I began to eat as they did and went back to having dinner with them. Not satisfied with this test, I made a second one: apart from my upkeep, which was paid to Nikolai Semyonovich, I was allocated a monthly sum of five rubles for pocket money. I decided to spend only half of it. This was a very hard test, but in a little over two years, when I came to Petersburg, I had in my pocket, apart from other money, seventy rubles saved up solely by this economy. The result of these two experiments was tremendous for me: I learned positively that I was able to want enough to achieve my goal, and that, I repeat, is the whole of "my idea." The rest is all trifles.

II.

However, let us examine the trifles as well.

I have described my two experiments; in Petersburg, as is already known, I made a third—went to the auction and, at one stroke, made a profit of seven rubles ninety-five kopecks. Of course, that wasn't a real experiment, but just a game, for fun: I wanted to steal a moment from the future and experience how I would go about and behave. But generally, still at the very beginning, in Moscow, I postponed the real setting out in business until I was completely free; I understood only too well that I at least had, for instance, to finish high school first. (I sacrificed the university, as is already known.) Indisputably, I went to Petersburg with repressed wrath: I had just finished high school and become free for the first time, when I suddenly saw that Versilov's affairs would again distract me from starting business for an unknown period! But though I was wrathful, I still went completely at ease about my goal.

True, I knew nothing of practical life; but I had been thinking it over for three years on end and could not have any doubts. I had imagined a thousand times how I would set about it: I suddenly turn up, as if dropped from the sky, in one of our two capitals (I chose to begin with our capitals, and namely with Petersburg, to which, by a certain reckoning, I gave preference), and so, I've dropped from the sky, but am completely free, not dependent on anybody, healthy, and have a hundred rubles hidden in my pocket for an initial working capital. It's impossible to begin without a hundred rubles, otherwise the very first period of success would be delayed for too long. Besides a hundred rubles, I have, as is already known, courage, persistence, continuity, total solitude, and secrecy. Solitude is the main thing: I terribly disliked till the very last minute any contact or association with people; generally speaking, I decided absolutely to begin the "idea" alone, that was *sine qua.* People are oppressive to me, and I would be troubled in spirit, which would harm my goal. And generally all my life till now, in all my dreams of how I would deal with people—I always have it come out very intelligent; as soon as it's in reality—it's always very stupid. And I confess this with indignation and sincerely, I have always betrayed myself with words and hurried, and therefore I resolved to cancel people. The gain was independence, peace of mind, clarity of goal.

Despite the terrible Petersburg prices, I determined once and for all that I would not spend more than fifteen kopecks on food, and I knew I would keep my word. I had pondered this question of food thoroughly and for a long time; I proposed, for instance, to eat only bread and salt for two days in a row, so as to spend the money saved in two days on the third day; it seemed to me that it would be more profitable for my health than an eternally regular fast on the minimum of fifteen kopecks. Then I needed a corner to live in, literally a corner, only to have a good night's sleep or take refuge on a particularly nasty day. I proposed to live in the street, and if necessary I was prepared to sleep in night shelters, where, on top of a night's lodging, they give you a piece of bread and a glass of tea. Oh, I'd be only too able to hide my money, so that it wouldn't be stolen in my corner or in the shelter; they wouldn't even catch a glimpse of it, I promise you! "Steal from me? No, the real fear is that I'll steal from them!"—I heard this merry phrase once from some rascal in the street. Of course, I apply only the prudence and cunning to myself, and have no intention of stealing. Moreover, still in Moscow, maybe from the very first day of the "idea," I decided that I would not be a pawnbroker or a usurer: there are Yids for that, and those Russians who lack both intelligence and character. Pawnbroking and usury are for mediocrities.

As for clothes, I proposed to have two outfits: an everyday one and a decent one. Once I had them, I was sure I'd wear them for a long time; I purposely spent two and a half years learning how to wear clothes and even discovered a secret: for suits to stay always new and not wear out, they should be cleaned with a brush as often as possible, five or six times a day. Cloth has no fear of the brush, believe me; what it fears is dust and dirt. Dust is the same as stones, looked at under a microscope, while even the stiffest brush is, after all, almost wool itself. I also learned how to wear boots evenly: the secret is that you must carefully put your foot down with the whole sole at once, avoiding as far as possible bringing it down on the side. It can be learned in two weeks, after which it becomes unconscious. In this way boots can be worn, on the average, one third longer. Two years' experience.

Then the activity itself begins.

I started from this consideration: I have a hundred rubles. In Petersburg there are so many auctions, sales, small shops at flea markets, and people in need of things, that it's impossible, once you've bought an object for such and such a price, not to sell it for a little more. With the album I made a profit of seven rubles ninety-five kopecks on a capital expenditure of two rubles five kopecks. This enormous profit was taken without risk: I saw from his eyes that the buyer wouldn't back out. Naturally, I understand very well that it was mere chance: but those are the kind of chances I seek, that's why I decided to live in the street. Well, granted such chances may even be extremely rare; all the same, my main rule will be not to risk anything, and the second—to be sure to earn at least something each day over and above the minimum spent on my subsistence, so that the accumulation doesn't stop for a single day.

They'll tell me: These are all dreams, you don't know the street, and you'll be cheated from the first step. But I have will and character, and street science is a science like any other, it yields to persistence, attention, and ability. In high school I was among the first right up to the final grade; I was very good at mathematics. Well, as if experience and street science should be extolled to such an idolizing degree as to predict certain failure! The only ones who say it are always those who have never experimented with anything, never started any life, and have gone on vegetating with everything provided. "If one gets his nose smashed, another will do the same." No, I won't get my nose smashed. I have character, and with my attentiveness, I'll learn everything. Well, is it possible to imagine that with constant persistence, constant keen-sightedness, and constant reflection and calculation, with boundless activity and running around, you will not attain finally to a knowledge of how to earn an extra twenty kopecks a day? Above all, I decided never to aim at the maximum profit, but always to remain calm. Later on, once I've already made a thousand or two, I will, of course, inevitably get out of trading and street dealing. Of course, I still know very little about the stock exchange, shares, banking, and all the rest. But, instead of that, I know, like the back of my hand, that in my own time I'll learn and master all this exchanging and banking like nobody else, and that this study will come quite easily to me, merely because matters will reach that point. Does it take so much intelligence? Is it some kind of wisdom of Solomon? All I need is character; skill, adroitness, knowledge will come by themselves. So long as I don't stop "wanting."

Above all, take no risks, and that is precisely possible only with character. Just recently, when I was already in Petersburg, there was a subscription for railway shares; those who managed to subscribe made a lot. For some time the shares were going up. And then suppose, suddenly, somebody who didn't manage to subscribe, or just turned greedy, seeing me with the shares in my hand, offered to buy them from me, with a premium of so much percent. Why, I'd certainly sell them to him at once. They'd start laughing at me, of course, saying: If you'd waited, you would have made ten times more. Right, sirs, but my premium is more certain, since it's already in my pocket, while yours is still flying around. They'll say you can't make much that way; excuse me, but there's your mistake, the mistake of all these Kokorevs, Polyakovs, Gubonins. Know the truth: constancy and persistence in making money and, above all, in accumulating it, are stronger than momentary profits, even of a hundred percent!

Not long before the French Revolution, a man named Law appeared in Paris and undertook a project that was brilliant in principle (afterward, in fact, it crashed terribly). All Paris was astir; Law's shares were snapped up, there was a stampede. Money came pouring from all over Paris, as if from a sack, into the house where the subscription was announced; but the house, finally, was not enough: the public crowded in the street—all estates, conditions, ages; bourgeois, nobility, their children, countesses, marquises, public women—everything churned up into a raging, half-crazed mass of people bitten by a rabid dog; ranks, prejudices of breeding and pride, even honor and good name—everything was trampled in the same mud; everyone sacrificed (even women) in order to obtain a few shares. The subscription finally passed into the street, but there was nowhere to write. Here one hunchback was asked to lend his hump for a time, as a table for subscribing to shares. The hunchback accepted—you can imagine for what price! Some time later (very little), it all went bankrupt, it all crashed, the idea went to the devil, and the shares lost all value. Who profited? Only the hunchback, precisely because he did not take shares, but cash in louis d'ors. Well, sirs, I am that very same hunchback! Didn't I have strength enough not to eat and to save up seventy-two rubles out of kopecks? I'll also have enough to restrain myself, right in the whirl of the fever that overcomes everybody, to prefer sure money to big money. I'm trifling only in trifles, but in great things I'm not. I often lacked the character for a small forbearance, even after the "idea" was born, but for a big one I'll always have enough. When my mother served me cold coffee in the morning before I went to work, I got angry and was rude to her, and yet I was the same man who survived a whole month on nothing but bread and water.

In short, not to make money, not to learn how to make money, would be unnatural. It would also be unnatural, with continuous and regular accumulation, with continuous attention and sober-mindedness, restraint, economy, with ever-increasing energy, it would be unnatural, I repeat, not to become a millionaire. How did the beggar make his money, if not by fanaticism of character and persistence? Am I worse than that begger? "And, finally, suppose I don't achieve anything, suppose my calculation is wrong, suppose I crash and fail—all the same, I'm going. I'm going because I want it that way." That's what I said still in Moscow.

They'll tell me there's no "idea" here, and precisely nothing new. But I say, and for the last time now, that there's incalculably much idea and infinitely much that's new.

Oh, I did anticipate how trivial all the objections would be, and how trivial I myself would be, explaining the "idea": well, what have I said? I didn't say even a hundredth part; I feel that it came out petty, crude, superficial, and even somehow younger than my years.

III.

It remains to answer the "what for" and "why," the "moral or not," and so on, and so forth. I've promised to answer that.

I feel sad to disappoint the reader at once, sad but glad as well. Be it known that the goals of my "idea" have absolutely no feeling of "revenge," nothing "Byronic"—no curse, no orphaned complaints, no tears of illegitimacy, nothing, nothing. In short, a romantic lady, if she were to come across my "Notes," would be crestfallen at once. The whole goal of my "idea" is—solitude.

"But one can achieve solitude without any bristling up about becoming Rothschild. What has Rothschild got to do with it?"

"Just this—that, besides solitude, I also need power."

I'll preface that. The reader will perhaps be horrified at the frankness of my confession and will ask himself simple-heartedly: How is it that the author doesn't blush? I reply that I'm not writing for publication; I'll probably have a reader only in some ten years, when everything is already so apparent, past, and proven that there will no longer be any point in blushing. And therefore, if I sometimes address the reader in my notes, it's merely a device. My reader is a fantastic character.

No, it was not the illegitimacy for which they taunted me so much at Touchard's, not my sad childhood years, not revenge or the right to protest that was the beginning of my "idea"; my character alone is to blame for it all. From the age of twelve, I think, that is, almost from the birth of proper consciousness, I began not to like people. Not so much not to like, but they somehow became oppressive to me. It was sometimes all too sad for me myself, in my pure moments, that I could in no way speak everything out even to those close to me; that is, I could, but I didn't want to, I restrained myself for some reason; that I was mistrustful, sullen, and unsociable. Then, too, I had long noticed a feature in myself, almost from childhood, that I all too often accuse others, that I'm all too inclined to accuse them; but this inclination was quite often followed immediately by another thought, which was all too oppressive for me: "Is it not I myself who am to blame, instead of them?" And how often I accused myself in vain! To avoid resolving such questions, I naturally sought solitude. Besides, I never found anything in the company of people, however I tried, and I did try; at least all my peers, all my comrades to a man, proved to be inferior to me in thinking; I don't remember a single exception.

Yes, I'm glum, I'm continually closed. I often want to leave society. I may also do good to people, but often I don't see the slightest reason for doing good to them. And people are not at all so beautiful that they should be cared for so much. Why don't they come forward directly and openly, and why is it so necessary that I should go and foist myself on them? That's what I asked myself. I'm a grateful being, and I've already proved it by a hundred follies. I would instantly respond with openness to an open person and begin to love him at once. And so I did; but they all cheated me at once and closed themselves to me in mockery. The most open of them was Lambert, who used to beat me badly in childhood; but he, too, was merely an open scoundrel and robber; and here, too, his openness came merely from stupidity. These were my thoughts when I came to Petersburg.

Having left Dergachev's then (God knows what pushed me to go there), I approached Vasin and, on a rapturous impulse, praised him to the skies. And what then? That same evening I already felt that I liked him much less. Why? Precisely because, by praising him, I had lowered myself before him. Yet it seems it should have been the opposite: a man so just and magnanimous as to give another his due, even to his own detriment, such a man is almost superior in his personal dignity to everyone else. And what, then—I knew this, and still I liked Vasin less, even much less, I purposely give an example already familiar to the reader. Even Kraft I remembered with a bitter and sour feeling, because he brought me out to the front hall himself, and so it remained right up to another day, when everything about Kraft became perfectly clear and it was impossible to be angry. From the very lowest grade in school, as soon as any of my comrades got ahead of me in studies, or in witty answers, or in physical strength, I at once stopped keeping company with him and speaking to him. Not that I hated him or wished him to fail; I simply turned away, because such was my character.

Yes, I've thirsted for power all my life, power and solitude. I dreamed of them even at such an age that decidedly anyone would have laughed in my face if he had made out what I had inside my skull. That is why I came to love secrecy so much. Yes, I dreamed with all my might and to a point where I had no time to talk; this led to the conclusion that I was unsociable, and my absentmindedness led to a still worse conclusion in my regard, but my rosy cheeks proved the contrary.

I was especially happy when, going to bed and covering myself with a blanket, I began, alone now, in the most complete solitude, with no people moving around and not a single sound from them, to recreate life in a different key. The fiercest dreaming was my companion until I discovered the "idea," when all my dreams went at once from stupid to reasonable, and from a dreamy form of novel passed on to the rationalistic form of reality.

Everything merged into a single goal. However, they weren't so stupid even before, though there were myriad upon myriad and thousand upon thousand of them. But I had some favorites. . . . However, there's no point bringing them in here.

Power! I'm convinced that a great many people would find it very funny to learn that such "trash" was aiming at power. But I'll amaze them still more: maybe from my very first dreams, that is, almost from my very childhood, I was unable to imagine myself otherwise than in the first place, always and in all turns of life. I'll add a strange confession: maybe that goes on even to this day. And I'll also note that I'm not apologizing.

In this lies my "idea," in this lies its strength, that money is the only path that will bring even a nonentity to the *first place.* Maybe I'm not a nonentity, but I know from the mirror, for instance, that my appearance does me harm, because my face is ordinary. But if I were as rich as Rothschild—who would question my face, and wouldn't thousands of women rush to me with their charms if I merely whistled? I'm even certain that, in the end, they themselves would quite sincerely find me handsome. Maybe I'm also intelligent. But even if I had a forehead seven inches wide, there would inevitably turn up in society a man with a forehead eight inches wide, and that would be the end of me. Whereas if I were Rothschild—would this smarty with the eight-inch forehead mean anything next to me? He wouldn't even be allowed to speak next to me! Maybe I'm witty; yet here next to me is Talleyrand or Piron—and I'm put in the shade; but once I'm Rothschild—where is Piron, and maybe even Talleyrand? Money is, of course, a despotic power, but at the same time it's also the highest equalizer, and that is its chief strength. Money equalizes all inequalities. I had already decided all that in Moscow.

You will, of course, see nothing in this thought but impudence, violence, the triumph of nonentity over talent. I agree that it's a bold thought (and therefore sweet). But so what, so what: do you think I wished for power then in order to crush unfailingly, to take revenge? That's just the point, that the ordinary man would unfailingly behave that way. Moreover, I'm certain that if Rothschild's millions were heaped on them, the thousands of talents and smarties, who are so above it all, would lose control at once and behave like the most banal of ordinary men, and crush more than anybody else. My idea is not that. I'm not afraid of money; it won't crush me and won't make me crush others.

I don't need money, or, better, it's not money that I need; it's not even power; I need only what is obtained by power and simply cannot be obtained without power: the solitary and calm awareness of strength! That is the fullest definition of freedom, which the world so struggles over! Freedom! I have finally inscribed that great word. . . . Yes, the solitary awareness of strength is fascinating and beautiful. I have strength, and I am calm. Jupiter holds thunderbolts in his hand, and what then: He's calm. Do we often hear him thunder? A fool might think he was asleep. But put some writer or foolish peasant woman in Jupiter's place—oh, what thunder, what thunder there will be!

If only I had power, I reasoned, I'd have no need at all to use it; I assure you that I myself, of my own free will, would take the last place everywhere. If I were Rothschild, I'd go about in an old coat and carry an umbrella. What do I care if I'm jostled in the street, if I'm forced to go skipping through the mud so as not to be run over by cabs? The awareness that it was I, Rothschild himself, would even amuse me at that moment. I know that I can have a dinner like nobody else, and from the world's foremost chef, and it's enough for me that I know it. I'll eat a piece of bread and ham and be satisfied with my awareness. I think so even now.

It's not I who will get in with the aristocracy, but they who will get in with me; it's not I who will chase after women, but they who will flow to me like water, offering me everything a woman can offer. The "banal" ones will come running for money, but the intelligent ones will be drawn by curiosity to a strange, proud, closed being, indifferent to everything. I'll be nice to the ones and to the others, and maybe give them money, but I won't take anything from them myself. Curiosity gives rise to passion, maybe I'll also inspire passion. They'll go away with nothing, I assure you, except perhaps a few presents. I'll only become twice as curious for them.

. . . enough for me
Is the awareness of it.

The strange thing is that this picture (a correct one, by the way) tempted me when I was no more than seventeen.

I don't want to crush or torment anyone and I won't; but I know that if I did want to ruin such and such a person, my enemy, no one would keep me from doing it, but everyone would be obliging; and again, enough. I wouldn't even take revenge on anyone. I was always surprised at how James Rothschild could agree to become a baron! Why, what for, when he's superior to everyone in the world without that? "Oh, let this insolent general offend me at the posting station, where we're both waiting for horses; if he knew who I was, he'd run to hitch them up himself and jump out and hasten to seat me in my modest tarantass! They wrote that a certain foreign count or baron, at a certain Viennese railway station, before the public, helped a certain local banker into his shoes, and the man was so ordinary that he allowed it. Oh, let her, let this fearsome beauty (precisely fearsome, there are such!)—the daughter of this magnificent and highborn aristocratic lady, having met me by chance on a steamboat or wherever—look askance and, turning up her nose, wonder scornfully how this humble and puny little man with a newspaper or book in his hands could dare to show up beside her in first class! But if she only knew who was sitting next to her! And she will know—she will know, and will sit down next to me, obedient, timid, gentle, seeking my eyes, glad of my smile. . . ." I have purposely introduced these early pictures in order to express my idea more vividly, but the pictures are pale and perhaps trivial. Reality alone justifies everything.

They'll say it's stupid to live like that: why not have a mansion, an open house, gather society, exert influence, get married? But what would Rothschild be then? He'd become like everybody else. All the charm of the "idea" would vanish, all its moral force. As a child I had already learned by heart the monologue of Pushkin's covetous knight; Pushkin never produced a higher idea than that! I'm also of the same mind now.

"But your ideal is too low," they'll say with scorn, "money, riches! A far cry from social usefulness and humane endeavors!"

But who knows how I'll use my riches? What is immoral, what is low, in having these millions flow out of a multitude of dirty and pernicious Jewish hands, into the hands of a sober and firm ascetic, who keenly studies the world? Generally, all these dreams of the future, all these conjectures—all this is still like a novel now, and maybe I shouldn't be writing it down; it should have stayed inside my skull; I also know that maybe no one will read these lines; but if anyone does, would he believe that maybe I, too, was unable to endure the Rothschildian millions? Not because they would crush me, but in quite a different sense, the opposite. In my dreams, I had more than once seized on that moment in the future when my consciousness will be too well satisfied and power will seem all too little. Then—not from boredom, and not from aimless anguish, but because I will desire something boundlessly greater—I will give all my millions away to people; let society distribute all my riches, and I—I will once more mingle with nonentity! Maybe I'll even turn into that beggar who died on the steamboat, with this difference: that they won't find anything sewn into my rags. The awareness alone that I had had millions in my hands and had flung them into the mud would feed me in my wilderness like the raven. I'm prepared to think so even now. Yes, my "idea" is that fortress in which I can always and in any case hide from all people, be it even like the beggar who died on the steamboat. This is my poem! And know that I need precisely my *whole* depraved will—solely to prove *to myself* that I'm strong enough to renounce it.

They'll undoubtedly object that this is poetry, and that I'll never let go of millions, if I've got them, and will not turn into a Saratov beggar. Maybe I won't let go; I've merely traced out the ideal of my thought. But I'll add seriously now: if, in the accumulation of wealth, I should reach the same figure as Rothschild, then it might indeed end with my flinging it to society. (However, it would be hard to do that before the Rothschildian figure.) And I wouldn't give away half, because then it would be nothing but a banality: I'd only become twice poorer and nothing more; but precisely all, all to the last kopeck, because, having become a beggar, I'd suddenly become twice as rich as Rothschild! If they don't understand that, it's not my fault; I won't explain.

"Fakirism, the poetry of nonentity and impotence!" people will decide. "The triumph of untalentedness and mediocrity." Yes, I admit that it's partly the triumph of both untalentedness and mediocrity, but hardly of impotence. I liked terribly to imagine a being, precisely an untalented and mediocre one, standing before the world and telling it with a smile: You are Galileos and Copernicuses, Charlemagnes and Napoleons, you are Pushkins and Shakespeares, you are field marshals and *hofmarshals,* and here I am, giftlessness and illegitimacy, and all the same I'm superior to you, because you submit to it yourselves. I confess, I've pushed this fantasy to such a verge that I've even ruled out education. It seemed to me that it would be more beautiful if this person was even filthily uneducated. This already exaggerated dream even influenced my results then in the final grade of high school; I stopped studying precisely out of fanaticism: it was as if lack of education added beauty to the ideal. Now I've changed my convictions on this point; education doesn't hurt.

Gentlemen, can it be that independence of mind, even the least bit of it, is so painful for you? Blessed is he who has his ideal of beauty, even if it's a mistaken one! But I believe in mine. Only I've explained it improperly, clumsily, primitively. Ten years from now, of course, I'll explain it better. And this I'll keep as a memento.

IV.

I've finished the "idea." If the description is banal, superficial, I'm to blame, and not the "idea." I've already warned you that the simplest ideas are the hardest to understand; I'll now add that they are also the hardest to explain, the more so as I've described the "idea" still in its former shape. There is also an inverse law for ideas: banal, hasty ideas are understood extraordinarily quickly, and invariably by a crowd, invariably by the whole street; moreover, they are considered the greatest and most brilliant, but only on the day of their appearance. What's cheap is not durable. Quick understanding is only a sign of the banality of what is understood. Bismarck's idea was instantly regarded as brilliant, and Bismarck himself as a brilliant man; but this quickness is precisely suspicious: I wait for Bismarck ten years from now, and then we'll see what's left of his idea, and maybe of Mr. Chancellor himself. Of course, I haven't introduced this highly extraneous and inappropriate observation for the sake of comparison, but as a reminder. (An explanation for the overly crude reader.)

And now I'll tell two anecdotes, so as to finish with the "idea" altogether, and not have it interfere in any way with the story.

In the summer, in July, two months before I came to Petersburg, and when I was already completely free, Marya Ivanovna asked me to go to Troitsky Posad to see a certain old maid who had settled there, on an errand too uninteresting to mention in detail. Coming back that same day, I noticed a certain puny young man on the train, not badly but uncleanly dressed, with blackheads, a dark-haired, dirtily swarthy type. He was distinguished by the fact that, at every station, large or small, he unfailingly got off and drank vodka. By the end of the journey, a merry little circle had formed around him—an utterly trashy company, incidentally. There was a shopkeeper, also slightly drunk, who was especially admiring of the young man's ability to drink continuously while remaining sober. There was yet another very pleased young fellow, terribly stupid and terribly talkative, dressed in German fashion, who gave off a rather nasty smell—a lackey, as I learned later; this one even struck up a friendship with the drinking young man and, each time the train stopped, got him to his feet with the invitation: "Time now for some vodka"—and the two would go out in each other's embrace. The drinking young man hardly said a word, but more and more interlocutors sat down around him; he merely listened to them all, grinning continuously with a slobbery titter and producing from time to time, but always unexpectedly, a sort of sound like "tir-lir-li!" and placing a finger on his nose in a very caricaturish way. It was this that delighted the merchant, and the lackey, and all of them, and they laughed extremely loudly and casually. It's impossible to understand why people laugh sometimes. I, too, went over—and I don't understand why I also found this young man likable, as it were; maybe for his all too spectacular violation of conventional and banalized proprieties; in short, I failed to discern the fool in him; anyhow, we were on familiar terms there and then, and as wc got off the train, I learned from him that he would be coming to Tverskoy Boulevard that evening after eight. He turned out to be a former student. I went to the boulevard, and here's what trick he taught me: we went around all the boulevards together, and later on, the moment we spotted a woman of a decent sort walking along, but so that there was no public close by, we'd immediately start pestering her. Without saying a word to her, we'd place ourselves, he on one side, I on the other, and with the most calm air, as if not noticing her at all, would begin a most indecent conversation between ourselves. We called things by their real names with a most unperturbed air, as if it was quite proper, and went into such details, explaining various vile and swinish things, as the dirtiest imagination of the dirtiest debaucher could not have thought up. (I, of course, had already acquired all this knowledge at school, even before high school, but only in words, not in deeds.) The woman would be very frightened and hurriedly walk away, but we would also quicken our pace and—go on with our thing. For the victim, of course, it was impossible to do anything, she couldn't shout: there were no witnesses, and it would somehow be strange to complain. Some eight days were spent on these amusements; I don't understand how I could have liked it; and in fact I didn't like it, I just did it. At first I found it original, as if it went outside everyday trite conventions; besides, I can't stand women. I once told the student that Jean-Jacques Rousseau admits in his *Confessions* that, as a youth, he liked to expose himself on the sly, from around the corner, uncovering the usually covered parts of the body, and waited like that for passing women. The student answered me with his "tir-lir-li." I noticed that he was frightfully ignorant and interested in surprisingly little. There was no trace of the hidden idea I had hoped to find in him. Instead of originality, I found only an overwhelming monotony. I disliked him more and more. Finally it all ended quite unexpectedly: once when it was already quite dark, we began to pester a girl who was walking quickly and timidly down the boulevard, a very young girl, maybe only sixteen or even less, dressed very neatly and modestly, who maybe lived by her own labor and was going home from work to her old mother, a poor widow with children; however, there's no need to fall into sentimentality. The girl listened for some time, walking faster and faster, her head lowered and her face covered by a veil, afraid and trembling, but suddenly she stopped, threw back the veil from her very pretty, as far as I remember, but thin face, and with flashing eyes cried to us:

"Ah, what scoundrels you are!"

Maybe she would also have burst into tears here, but something else happened: she swung her small, skinny arm and planted a slap on the student's face, than which a more deft has maybe never been given. What a smack! He cursed and rushed at her, but I held him back, and the girl had time to run away. Left there, we began quarreling at once: I told him everything that had been smoldering in me all that time; I said he was nothing but a pathetic giftlessness and ordinariness, and that there had never been the least sign of an idea in him. He called me a . . . (I had explained to him once about my being illegitimate), then we spat at each other, and I've never seen him since. That evening I was very vexed, the next day less so, the third day I almost forgot all about it. And so, though I sometimes remembered this girl afterward, it was just by chance and fleetingly. It was only on arriving in Petersburg some two weeks later that I suddenly remembered that whole scene—remembered, and then felt so ashamed that tears of shame literally poured down my cheeks. I suffered all evening, all night, I'm partly suffering now as well. I couldn't understand at first how it had been possible to fall so low and disgracefully then, and—above all—to forget the incident, not to be ashamed of it, not to be repentant. Only now did I realize what was the matter: the "idea" was to blame. In short, I draw the direct conclusion that, if you have in mind something fixed, perpetual, strong, something terribly preoccupying, it is as if you thereby withdraw from the whole world into a desert, and everything that happens takes place in passing, apart from the main thing. Even impressions are received wrongly. And besides that, the main thing is that you always have an excuse. However much I tormented my mother all that time, however much I neglected my sister: "Ah, I have my 'idea,' those are all trifles"—that's what I seemed to say to myself. I'd get insulted myself, and painfully—I'd go out insulted and then suddenly say to myself: "Ah, I'm base, but all the same I have an 'idea,' and they don't know about it." The "idea" comforted me in my disgrace and nonentity, but all my abominations were also as if hiding under the idea; it eased everything, so to speak, but it also clouded everything over before me; and such a blurred understanding of events and things may, of course, even harm the "idea" itself, to say nothing of the rest.

Now the other anecdote.

On the first of April last year, Marya Ivanovna had a name-day party. In the evening some guests came, a very few. Suddenly Agrafena comes in, breathless, and announces that there's a foundling baby squealing in the entry, by the kitchen door, and that she doesn't know what to do. Excited by the news, we all went and saw a basket, and in the basket a three- or four-week-old squealing girl. I took the basket, brought it to the kitchen, and found a folded note: "Dear benefactors, render your well-wishing aid to the baptized girl Arina, and with her we will ever send up our tears to the throne of God for you, and we congratulate you on your angel's day. People unknown to you." Here Nikolai Semyonovich, whom I so respect, upset me very much: he made a very serious face and decided to send the girl to the orphanage immediately. I felt very sad. They lived very economically, but had no children, and Nikolai Semyonovich was always glad of it. I carefully took Arinochka out of the basket and held her up by her little shoulders; the basket gave off a sort of sour and sharp smell, as of a long-unwashed nursing baby. After some arguing with Nikolai Semyonovich, I suddenly announced to him that I was taking the girl at my own expense. He began to object with a certain severity, despite all his mildness, and though he ended with a joke, he left his intention about the orphanage in full force. It worked out my way, however: on the same courtyard, but in another wing, lived a very poor cabinetmaker, already on the old side and a drunkard, but his wife, a very healthy woman and not old at all, had just lost her nursing baby, and above all her only one, who had been born after eight years of childless marriage, also a girl, and by strange luck also named Arinochka. I say luck because, as we were arguing in the kitchen, this woman, hearing about the incident, came running to see, and when she learned that it was Arinochka, her heart melted. Her milk was not gone yet; she opened her bodice and put the baby to her breast. I fell before her and began begging her to take Arinochka with her, and said I'd pay her monthly. She feared her husband wouldn't allow it, but took her for the night. In the morning, the husband allowed it for eight rubles a month, and I counted them out to him for the first month in advance. He drank up the money at once. Nikolai Semyonovich, still smiling strangely, agreed to vouch for me to the cabinetmaker that the money, eight rubles a month, would be paid regularly. I tried to give Nikolai Semyonovich my sixty rubles in cash, by way of security, but he wouldn't take it; however, he knew I had the money and trusted me. This delicacy on his part smoothed over our momentary quarrel. Marya Ivanovna said nothing, but was surprised at my taking on such a care. I especially appreciated their delicacy in that neither of them allowed themselves the slightest mockery of me, but, on the contrary, began to treat the matter with the proper seriousness. I ran by Darya Rodionovna's every day, three times a day or so, and a week later I gave her personally, in her own hand, on the quiet from her husband, three more rubles. For another three I bought swaddling clothes and a little blanket. But ten days later Rinochka suddenly got sick. I brought a doctor at once, he prescribed something, and we spent the whole night fussing about and tormenting the tiny thing with his nasty medicine, but the next day he declared that it was too late, and to my entreaties—though they seemed more like reproaches—he said with noble evasiveness, "I am not God." The girl's tongue, lips, and whole mouth got covered with a sort of fine white rash, and toward evening she died, gazing at me with her big dark eyes, as if she already understood. I don't understand how it didn't occur to me to take a photograph of her dead. Well, would you believe that I did not weep but simply howled that evening, something I had never allowed myself to do, and Marya Ivanovna was forced to comfort me—and again, totally without mockery either on her own or on his part. The cabinetmaker made a little coffin; Marya Ivanovna trimmed it with ruche and put a pretty little pillow in it, and I bought flowers and strewed them over the little baby; and so they took away my poor little wisp, whom, believe me, to this day I cannot forget. A while later, though, this whole almost unexpected occurrence even made me reflect a lot. Of course, Rinochka had not cost me much—thirty rubles in all, including the coffin, the burial, the doctor, the flowers, and the payments to Darya Rodionovna. I reimbursed myself for this money, as I was leaving for Petersburg, from the forty rubles Versilov had sent me for my trip, and by selling some things before I left, so that my whole "capital" remained intact. "But," I thought, "if I can be sidetracked like that, I won't get very far." From the story with the student it followed that the "idea" can fascinate one to the point of a blurring of impressions and distract one from the flow of actualities. From the story with Rinochka the opposite followed, that no "idea" can be so intensely fascinating (for me, at least), that I cannot stop suddenly before some overwhelming fact and sacrifice to it at once all that I had done for the idea during years of toil. Both conclusions were nonetheless correct.

* * *

Some Notes on Translating Dostoevsky, *The Adolescent* in Particular

When we began translating Dostoevsky some sixteen years ago, an elderly friend of ours, a Russian lady from the first emigration, said: "I do hope you'll correct his awful style." We had to disappoint her. Other translators had already corrected Dostoevsky; our reason for making a new English version of *The Brothers Karamazov* was to see whether his "awful style" could be kept in English. It seemed to us that much of the life of the novel lay precisely there and had been lost in earlier translations.

Our friend's opinion was once widely shared among Russian

readers. Even some of Dostoevsky's most enthusiastic admirers considered him a great thinker but a careless writer. The opposite is true. His ideas, expressed baldly in his *Diary of a Writer,* are not very original; but when he gives them to the nameless man from underground, or Ippolit Terentiev, or Arkady Dolgoruky, or Ivan Karamazov—that is, when he creates a personal voice for them, with all its peculiar turns of phrase, fumblings, exaggerations, reticences—they take on a new life, a new boldness and originality. Dostoevsky thought as an artist, and his work was a work of words, of style, not in the sense of "fine writing" but of "making," the Greek *poiesis,* "creation into being." As we wrote in our introduction to *The Brothers Karamazov,* the publication in Russia, during the 1930s, of the notebooks and draft materials for *The Idiot, The Adolescent* (which Constance Garnett miscalled *The Raw Youth*), and *The Brothers Karamazov* "finally dispelled the old prejudice that Dostoevsky was a careless and indifferent stylist. All the oddities of his prose are deliberate; they are a sort of 'learned ignorance,' a willed imperfection of artistic means, that is essential to his vision."

Nabokov had the greatest admiration for Tolstoy as an artist, and despised Dostoevsky for his artistic ineptitudes (he also had no taste for his "ideas"). There is certainly some aristocratic disdain here, as there was in our Russian lady; Dostoevsky, though a nobleman, was not of Nabokov's rank, nor of Count Tolstoy's. Nabokov was able to blink at the "pages and pages" in *Anna Karenina* "which are definitely in the margin of the story, telling us what *we* ought to think, what *Tolstoy* thinks about war or marriage or agriculture," and suggests that his students skim over those sections of the novel (see his *Lectures on Russian Literature*). "Artistically," he admits, "Tolstoy made a mistake in devoting such a number of pages to these matters." In fact, they make up about a third of *Anna Karenina.* We must suppose that only a novelist of Count Tolstoy's stature could afford a mistake on that scale. The same can be said of the even more obtrusive historico-philosophical digressions in *War and Peace:* they can be skimmed, they can even be omitted, without harming the novel's development or the portrayal of its characters. On the other hand, the "philosophical digressions" in Dostoevsky—Ippolit's confession in *The Idiot,* Kirillov's atheist profession of faith in *Demons,* Ivan Karamazov's "poem" about the Grand Inquisitor, for instance—cannot be omitted without severely damaging the organic unity of their respective novels. This unity is dramatic and vertically structured; Tolstoy's *roman fleuve* could carry quantities of driftwood in its leisurely horizontal flow. Another difference: Dostoevsky's verbal mastery shows most clearly in these "metaphysical" monologues; Tolstoy's prose is at its worst in his philosophical intrusions, though he labored over his text and revised it many times.

The critic and musicologist Boris de Schloezer, who emigrated to Paris in 1921 and translated a number of Russian novels into French, notes in the preface to his translation of *War and Peace:*

> Tolstoy commits gross errors which have no justification and which no high-school boy would make. One often has the impression that he seizes on the first word that falls under his pen, and then, not dreaming of profiting from the riches that Russian offers him, repeats it to satiety, before passing on to another that he will treat in the same way. Anxious to say everything at once, he embarks on heavy, complicated, syntactically incorrect phrases and finally falls into equivocation.

Nabokov excuses such lapses as "characteristic of Tolstoy's style with its rejection of false elegancies and its readiness to admit any robust awkwardness if that is the shortest way to sense."

The "gross errors" of Tolstoy's prose have none of the freedom and playfulness of Dostoevsky's "awful style," and none of his artistic purpose; they characterize Tolstoy, not his characters. Yet the problem posed for the translator is essentially the same in both cases: how much do you keep? When do you "correct" the original, and on what grounds? Boris de Schloezer suggests an answer in his preface:

> What is a good translation? One, it will be said, which, while remaining faithful to the original, uses a correct French, which "doesn't feel like a translation," as the expression goes, thus giving the reader the impression that he is reading a text written directly in his mother tongue. The transposition is then perfect: the author's thought is preserved while being wedded to a new form. But how can it be preserved? Doesn't being faithful to the author mean preserving the structure, the tone, the pace of his speech as much as its explicit meaning? [. . .] The language of a novel, of a story, no less than of a poem, is not the clothing of a certain mode of thinking, perceiving, feeling, loving, but that mode itself. Here the habit makes the monk.

The demands not to mistreat your own language and not to betray the language of the original are mutually contradictory. The ideal goal of translation is thus not only paradoxical but unattainable. "Nevertheless we translate," says de Schloezer, "and there are good translations, there are even excellent ones. These are precisely the ones that bring the paradox fully to light, that push it to the point of scandal." The translation that "doesn't feel like a translation" is produced by a fear of scandal, by the translator's fear that the scandal will fall on his own head; he reverts to the more usual word, the more customary phrase, the more graceful varying of vocabulary; in other words, he greatly increases the banality quotient of the work, and while saving his own reputation, seriously compromises his author. The better translator will risk scandal to come closer to the "living life" of the original. There is, incidentally, no crude or simple-minded literalism here; it is a way of infinite approximation. It can only succeed if the translator convinces the reader of its artistic rightness.

Tolstoy was a more naïve or instinctive artist than Dostoevsky. It is striking, for instance, how many of Dostoevsky's heroes are writers themselves. A partial list would include the man from underground, Raskolnikov, Ippolit, Stavrogin, Alyosha Karamazov, Ivan Karamazov, the narrator of "Bobok," and the narrator of "The Meek One." The "author" of *Demons* is a minor character; in *The Brothers Karamazov* he is a local chronicler, but they both have their own qualities and quirks as writers and are not to be confused with Dostoevsky himself. Finally, Arkady Dolgoruky is both the "author" and the protagonist of *The Adolescent.* The one thing these writers have in common is that they are all amateurs; they write, they are driven to write, from elementary human motives, to try to recall and understand certain crucial events in their own lives or in the life of their community. At a second remove, Dostoevsky narrates both the events and the writers' attempts to recall and understand them; he includes the problematics of writing in the writing itself.

Arkady raises the question of writing on the first page of the novel and in a typically Dostoevskian fashion:

> If I have suddenly decided to record word for word all that has happened to me since last year, then I have decided it as the result of an inner need: so struck I am by everything that has happened. I am recording only the events, avoiding with all my might everything extraneous, and above all—literary beauties; a literary man writes for thirty years and in the end doesn't know at all why he has written for so many years. I am not a literary man, do not want to be a literary man, and would consider it base and indecent to drag the insides of my

> soul and a beautiful description of my feelings to their literary marketplace [. . .]
>
> I begin, that is, I would like to begin my notes from the nineteenth of September last year, that is, exactly from the day when I first met . . .
>
> But to explain who I met just like that beforehand, when nobody knows anything, would be banal; I suppose even the tone is banal: having promised myself to avoid literary beauties, I fall into those beauties with the first line. Besides, in order to write sensibly, it seems the wish alone is not enough. I will also observe that it seems no European language is so difficult to write in as Russian. I have now reread what I've just written, and I see that I'm much more intelligent than what I've written. How does it come about that what an intelligent man speaks out is much stupider than what remains inside him? I've noticed that about myself more than once in my verbal relations with people during this last fatal year and have suffered much from it.

And so on for another six hundred pages. This voice *is* the adolescent, with all his defiance, precocity, self-consciousness, gawkiness, and vulnerability, and the translator must keep these qualities in his translation or lose essential dimensions of the novel. Arkady struts, stumbles, repeats himself, puts on airs, admits he's putting on airs, goes from pomposity to humility in a single phrase, "knows" everything and doesn't know anything. His most characterizing word is "stupid," the perfect adolescent word, repeated in endless variations: his fear of looking stupid, of saying something stupid, his judgments of the stupidity of other people, their stupid ideas, their stupid feelings, their stupid curtains. The translator who artfully substitutes a variety of words for this invariable one will lose the whole game. The style that embodies Arkady Dolgoruky obviously cannot be "correct" and should not be corrected.

The central character and central enigma of *The Adolescent* is Arkady's natural father, Andrei Petrovich Versilov. The main action of the novel is Arkady's attempt to know him, to learn the truth about him, and to love him. This "truth" turns out to be fugitive, ambiguous, inexpressible—like the "unknowable" or "unattainable" of the Russian philosopher Semyon Frank. Dostoevsky's artistic method, making use of the groping and uncertain procedure of the amateur writer, enables him to point beyond fictional truth, to "imitate" the unknowable in its unknowableness.

First and Last Published Poems

Octavio Paz

Translated from Spanish by Eliot Weinberger

Translator's Note

There are a few surviving poems that were written earlier, and there may well be some written later, but these two, across sixty-five years, are the first and last poems that Octavio Paz published. The first, "Game," appeared in the Mexican newspaper *El Nacional,* on June 7, 1931, when the poet was barely seventeen; it was discovered a few years ago by the Paz scholar Anthony Stanton. Poets start young in Mexico, and Paz quickly became a regular contributor of essays, reviews, and poems to the newspapers and magazines. His first book of poems was published two years later.

The last poem, "Response and Reconciliation," takes its first line from the first line of a famous sonnet by Francisco de Quevedo, and was published in late 1996 in a small book called *Reflejos: Réplicas* (Reflections: Replicas), which contains the text of a lecture Paz gave on Quevedo in May of that year.

In retrospect, Paz's activities in the last eight years of his life seem superhuman. He won the Nobel Prize in 1990 at age seventy-six, an honor that often dooms writers to a life of granting interviews and answering invitations and requests. Paz did both, endlessly—and never had an agent or a secretary—while simultaneously editing his monthly cultural and political magazine, *Vuelta,* and overseeing the publication of his *Complete Works* in Spanish (fourteen oversize volumes, around five hundred pages each), for which he reorganized and revised all the texts, wrote lengthy prefaces to each volume, and meticulously proofread all the galleys for both the Spanish and Mexican editions. He also wrote two large volumes of miscellaneous essays, books on India (*In Light of India*), Sade (*An Erotic Beyond: Sade*), Breton, love and eroticism (*The Double Flame*), and a political autobiography (*Itinerary*). (When I sent him my translation of the India book to look over, he corrected all the typos in the manuscript.) In the midst of this, he underwent bypass surgery, from which he spent a year recovering.

His poems from this period have yet to be collected in Spanish, but he wrote a series of poems to accompany artworks by his wife, Marie-José, which were published in a small book (*Figures and Figurations,* forthcoming in English). Perhaps most astonishing of all, he also produced and directed a twenty-minute video of his long poem, *Blanco,* in his belief in the potential of television as a medium for poetry.

A year and a half before his death, and already quite ill with cancer, he barely escaped a serious fire in his apartment in Mexico City, and he never lived among his books and things again. He died on April 20, 1998, at age eighty-four.

It is, of course, impossible to extrapolate the universal poet to come from "Game," but the general joyfulness, and the fluidity, one into another, of eroticism, the natural world, written language, and the procession of the seasons would remain throughout his poetry. "Response and Reconciliation" is the exceedingly rare case of a last (or very late) poem that is among a poet's major works. The poem speaks for itself, but I can't help but mention its history in English, a window on publishing in this country.

When Octavio died, there was, as might be expected, a kind of international press frenzy, similar to when he won the Nobel. (In Mexico, the response could only be compared to the death of Victor Hugo in France.) Newspapers and magazines must fill space, and there quickly arose, as is common, a class of professional mourners publishing reminiscences, many of whom with only a tangential connection to Octavio when he was alive. In those first frantic and depressing days, my own initial response was to turn down all requests; then I decided it would be useful if I answered questions and fact-checked articles, while still refusing to write anything; and then it occurred to me that the best tribute I could write for Octavio would be to translate his last poem. What I hadn't bothered to think about was where I could publish it.

Every major American newspaper or magazine had articles published or planned on his death, but a poem by the poet himself was another matter. Naturally I wanted the poem to appear quickly, in something published weekly or monthly, and with a fairly large circulation. An obvious place was the *New Yorker,* but whereas then-editor Tina Brown would have recognized the scoop-value of "Paz's last poem," the poetry editor found it "too abstract for us." Next stop, the *New York Times Book Review,* but they had already commissioned an American poet, who had met Octavio once or twice, to write a memoir; a poem, they thought, would be excessive coverage.

It is a comment on the state of American periodicals that, after two tries, I went blank. The *New York Review of Books* had only once reviewed a Paz book and had never published his poetry. Magazines such as *Harper's, Atlantic,* the *Nation,* and the *New Republic* never print poems longer than a few lines. Various literary journals would have welcomed the poem, but it would have meant a wait of a year or so. . . . Meanwhile, I was faxing the Spanish text to European newspapers that were fighting each other for the rights.

Someone finally suggested the *Los Angeles Times Book Review,* which at the time I did not know is easily the most intelligent mass-circulation book review in the country. The editor, Steven Wasserman, accepted the poem about ten seconds after he received it. I am grateful to him, but unfortunately the poem was never seen by anyone outside of L.A. or the book business. It's a happy event to have it finally available here.

* * *

GAME

I'll plunder seasons.
I'll play with months and years.
Winter days with summer's red faces.

And down the gray road,
in the silent parade
of hard, unmoving days,
I'll organize the blues and gymnastics.

A rippling morning
of painted lips,
fresh, as though just bathed
with an autumn dawn.

And I'll catch the clouds—
red, blue, purple—
and throw them against the inexpressive paper
of the black and blue sky,
so that they'll write a letter

in the universal language
to their good friend the wind.

To help the shopkeepers,
I'll make luminous billboards,
with spotlights of stars.

Maybe I'll assassinate a dawn
so that, bleeding,
it will stain a white cloud purple.

In the shop of the seasons,
I'll sell ripe autumn apples
wrapped in the paper of winter mists.

I'll kidnap Spring,
to have her in my house,
like a ballerina.

The wind will change its schedule.
Unpredictable crossings of the clouds.

And down the highway of the Future, I'll rush toward Winter,
to have the surprise of meeting it later,
mixed with Summer.

On the green felt of space,
I'll bet on days
that will roll like dice.

I'll play with months and years.

Octavio Paz

RESPONSE AND RECONCILIATION

I.

Ah life! Does no one answer?
His words rolled, bolts of lightning etched
in years that were boulders and now are mist.
Life never answers.
It has no ears and doesn't hear us;
it doesn't speak, it has no tongue.
It neither goes nor stays:
we are the ones who speak,
the ones who go,
while we hear from echo to echo, year to year,
our words rolling through a tunnel with no end.

That which we call life
hears itself within us, speaks with our tongues,
and through us, knows itself.
As we portray it, we become its mirror, we invent it.
An invention of an invention: It creates us
without knowing what it has created,
we are an accident that thinks.
It is a creature of reflections
we create by thinking,
and it hurls into fictitious abysses.
The depths, the transparencies
where it floats or sinks: not life, its idea.
It is always on the other side and is always other,
has a thousand bodies and none,
never moves and never stops,
it is born to die, and is born at death.

Is life immortal? Don't ask life,
for it doesn't even know what life is.
We are the ones who know
that one day it too must die and return
to the beginning, the inertia of the origin.
The end of yesterday, today, and tomorrow,
the dissipation of time
and of nothing, its opposite.

Then—will there be a then?
will the primigenious spark light
the matrix of the worlds,
a perpetual rebeginning of a senseless whirling?
No one answers, no one knows.
We only know that to live is to live for.

II.

Sudden spring, a girl who wakes
on a green bed guarded by thorns;
tree of noon, heavy with oranges:
Your tiny suns, fruits of cool fire,
summer gathers them in transparent baskets;
the fall is severe, its cold light
sharpens its knife against the red maples;
Januaries and Februaries: Their beards are ice,
and their eyes sapphires that April liquefies;
the wave that rises, the wave that stretches out,
appearances-disappearances
on the circular road of the year.

All that we see, all that we forget,
the harp of the rain, the inscription of the lightning,
the hurried thoughts, reflections turned to birds,
the doubts of the path as it meanders,
the wailing of the wind
as it carves the faces of the mountains,
the moon on tiptoe over the lake,
the breezes in gardens, the throbbing of night,
the camps of stars on the burnt field,
the battle of reflections on the white salt flats,
the fountain and its monologue,
the held breath of outstretched night
and the river that entwines it, the pine under the evening star
and the waves, instant statues, on the sea,
the flock of clouds that the wind herds
through drowsy valleys, the peaks, the chasms,
time turned to rock, frozen eras,
time maker of roses and plutonium,
time that makes as it razes.

The ant, the elephant, the spider, and the sheep,
our strange world of terrestrial creatures
that are born, eat, kill, sleep, play, couple,
and somehow know that they die;
our world of humanity, far and near,
the animal with eyes in its hands
that tunnels through the past and examines the future,
with its histories and uncertainties,
the ecstasy of the saint, the sophisms of the evil,
the elation of lovers, their meetings, their contentions,
the insomnia of the old man counting his mistakes,
the criminal and the just: a double enigma,
the Father of the People, his crematory parks,
his forests of gallows and obelisks of skulls,
the victorious and the defeated,
the long sufferings and the one happy moment,
the builder of houses and the one who destroys them,
this paper where I write, letter by letter,
which you glance at with distracted eyes,
all of them and all of it, all
is the work of time that begins and ends.

III.

From birth to death time surrounds us
with its intangible walls.
We fall with the centuries, the years, the minutes.
Is time only a falling, only a wall?
For a moment, sometimes, we see
—not with our eyes but with our thoughts—
time resting in a pause.
The world half-opens and we glimpse
the immaculate kingdom,
the pure forms, presences
unmoving, floating
on the hour, a river stopped:
truth, beauty, numbers, ideas
—and goodness, a word buried
in our century.
A moment without weight or duration,
a moment outside the moment:
Thought sees, our eyes think.

Triangles, cubes, the sphere, the pyramid
and the other geometrical figures
thought and drawn by mortal eyes
but which have been here since the beginning,
are, still legible, the world, its secret writing,
the reason and the origin of the turning of things,
the axis of the changes, the unsupported pivot
that rests on itself, a reality without a shadow.
The poem, the piece of music, the theorem,
unpolluted presences born from the void,
are delicate structures
built over an abyss:
Infinities fit into their finite forms,
and chaos too is ruled by their hidden symmetry.

Because we know it, we are not an accident:
Chance, redeemed, returns to order.
Tied to the earth and to time,
a light and weightless ether,
thought supports the worlds and their weight,
whirlwinds of suns turned
into a handful of signs
on a random piece of paper.
Wheeling swarms
of transparent evidence
where the eyes of understanding
drink a water simple as water.
The universe rhymes with itself,
it unfolds and is two and is many
without ceasing to be one.
Motion, a river that runs endlessly
with open eyes through the countries of vertigo
—there is no above nor below, what is near is far—
returns to itself
                    —without returning, now turned
into a fountain of stillness.
Tree of blood, man feels, thinks, flowers,
and bears strange fruits: words.
What is thought and what is felt entwine,
we touch ideas: They are bodies and they are numbers.

And while I say what I say
time and space fall dizzyingly,
restlessly. They fall in themselves.
Man and the galaxy return to silence.
Does it matter? Yes—but it doesn't matter:
We know that silence is music and that
we are a chord in this concert.

From Where Does the Wolf Live?

Rea *Galanake*

Translated from Greek by Karen Emmerich

TRANSLATOR'S NOTE

REA GALANAKE'S *Where Does the Wolf Live?*, her fourth book of poetry, published in 1982, is dedicated to "the friends from '67 to '74." This period saw Greece under the rule of a military junta, Galanake a student of history and archaeology at the University of Athens, and countless left-wing activists and sympathizers in prison, internal exile, or (often self-imposed) exile abroad. It was a time of distances and separations, of coded speech, of reading between the lines.

The book is divided into two parts: "The House" and "The Apartment"; the majority of the latter is presented here. While the vague outlines of a story can be discovered in the rich array of images that comprise the text—a man first in hiding, then in prison; his lover; their correspondence; her pain—Galanake staunchly defies traditional narrative conventions. Past and present, first and third person collide with one another, slide into one another as images pile upon images.

Where Does the Wolf Live? is a text that constantly slips into and beyond itself, calling upon multiple traditions—from western folklore (Snow White, Little Red Ridinghood) to Greek literary tradition (Homer, Sophocles, the Old Testament, quoted in Ancient Greek in the original and presented in italics in my translation)—and referring obliquely to the harsh political realities of Greece's recent past. The wolf of the title—the wolf of the fairy tale, the wolf in sheep's clothing—winds its way through the text, swaying behind its canvas of words, an unseen, unlocatable threat. Likewise, we see the dictatorship only in its effects: "The table" shows us a gathering of friends newly released from prison, as well as the books and letters littering the apartment floor in the wake of a search; in "The outlaw taxi," we follow Paula as she switches taxis three times to keep from being tailed; while "Ode to a nylon sack" hails the sack that acts as intermediary between Paula and her jailed lover.

In the first story, "The face," Galanake introduces her protagonist with the words "Paula comes after each sentence, in all that we hide." In Greek, the proper noun *Pavla* is an uncommon woman's name, while the uncapitalized *pavla* is the word for the syntactical dash—a break, a space, a pause. Thus Galanake's central character is intimately linked to language itself. Moreover, in "The House," Galanake often punctuates her paragraphs with spaces, while in "The Apartment" she makes unconventional use of line and paragraph breaks. By punctuating her text—and Paula's stories—with midsentence ruptures, with tears in the fabric of language, Galanake writes both of and with breaks, fissures, silences. Indeed, Paula herself is identified *as* a pause, a silence, a space. She is the "afterwards" of each sentence; she is the unsaid, read through the said. She is the opening for echo, the space in which words reverberate, expand, unfurl.

Galanake's almost surreal descriptions keep sliding away, remaining, like censored speech, always just to the side of what is "really" being said. Until the last of Paula's stories, "Lyric for an excursion in the city," which consists of a single stanza repeated four times. When we finally see action, plain and simple, we must see it again and again. Here, this is true, this is true. This is true. Let me tell you again.

* * *

I. ENTRANCE

That night she took me to the double bed and said, opening her hand: Tell me those stories again, perhaps I will sleep.

II. TEN OF PAULA'S STORIES

1. The face.

Paula comes after each sentence, in all that we hide. A new face every time above faceless clothes. She wears the foliage of sounds and movements that belong to her. When you see her you hear her like the wordless wind in our garden. She is an invisible tree that constantly sprouts leaves and blossoms in an apartment where there are no seasons. Her face is a changeable cloud that assumes and abandons the shape of the mother, the house, the wolf, the womb, the hand, the ladder, the baby, the truck, the grandmother, the tyrant, Little Red Ridinghood, the apple, the brazier, the maid, the TV, the witch, the angel, the grape. Her face, wet and fragrant coffee.

Droplets of face late in the café on the square. In a sliver of shaven city unknown fieldhands sit eating in plastic chairs. One sips a lemonade. The tree, green leaflets. The imperceptible hum of heat.

Behind the canvas the wolf sways and stops the movement of the white mug in her hand. Soon there are no clouds, just pale blue sky, a single red slice of afternoon carved by the scythes of apartment buildings. At least fifteen vertical eyes are lit. They see her and she sees them.

2. The hands.

Stopped hand on the mug

as the reddish light turns violet and the headlights of cars open white holes in this violet sheet and show
handcuffs shining on her wrists.

For a moment, as long as strange things usually last, as long as it takes for the memory of a nightmare that tossed all night on the sheets to congeal,
these linked metal fruits, empty and round, will shine like engagement rings on two branches of an invisible tree that nonetheless bears its hideous crop.

She hides, hides like an act that happens hopelessly, again and again. Her hands shake from the physicality of fear, but also from the seed that kicks at her tender conquered movement.

On her wrists shine the happiness, wealth, and health of our house, the rings that roll off and disappear on the sidewalk. Though the big fish does not eat them, nor does her grandmother cook soup.

The green emerald is a leaflet in the square.

3. The table.

The leaves were still green when she came to take you from the mental clinic. Nothing was green. The color a quick beat of the heart. An old suitcase, a passing taxi whose driver didn't want to be paid, a small apartment. Then, without the suitcase, to another apartment where some mother had set a table with dozens of plates. Colorful plates lined in rows on her dazzling linen tablecloth. And I don't dare ask you, now that you've come back and the table is strewn with friends just down from their crosses. Pale against her dazzling tablecloth, just beginning to breathe fresh, free air, to redden with joy. And it was true joy, then, though half of it was guilt. Scrutinized feelings, but secret nonetheless.

Like a search of the house. Small room, mattress, parquet, attic. The double mattress on the floor holding up waves of sheets and the cotton froth of pillows. Spattered over the floor, the brains of books, the virginity of correspondence trickling red, drop by drop. A chair by the bathroom under the open attic mouth. A tooth-filled mouth whose whispering grows into a mute howl. So, the feelings. Driven down other roads, like a current that flows now into one field, now into another, as the water in the ditch is cut off by iron squares. Squares thrust into all the streams, of life, heart, health, spirit, luck, sun, marriage, and again heart, heart, heart.

When she came back a few days later she cleaned it all up, the chair they had left by the bathroom, the letters, the books. The scrutinized feelings. She put her diary in the bidet, drenched it in alcohol, and set it on fire. She burned for years, as she gathered up a bundle of love letters, and other letters. Because a feeling, once written, corresponded with a probable misinterpretation, a probable misuse of its meaning. Paula was outside the alphabet, protector of herself.

The leaves were still green when she came to get you. The forbidden phonemes of adolescence. Nothing was green, except the memory of breeze in the branches of the lemon tree.

Green tree in the square outside her small apartment. Outside the bathroom, pipes in the airshaft. She never climbed their dry branches, not the first nor the second time they came to arrest her. Paula is a hidden tree; she is the ability to escape by climbing her own body. Alpha omega the longing of man. Alpha omega the still sleep after love. A coffee, cigarette. Wolf, O wolf, the solitude. Wolf, O wolf, the speechlessness. Wolf, O wolf, an infinite guilt. Deep and sensual.

Her face grows old, incestuous, plural. A small country graveyard, five families, many generations. Sheep graze there during the day, and demons at night.

Perhaps they have forgotten her? The friends and the lovers.

4. Short lyric for lost happiness.

Your gaze
kills itself
exquisitely
blurred.

Time
congealed
without
divisions.

The strong
desire
for your own
erection.

The indissoluble
transitive
game
of love.

An idea.

5. Coffee and the gait of horses.

Paula is an invisible tree who moves, slowly drinking coffee. She is only what she reveals of each story. Only her trunk, the bark, the soft fuzz on the branches, the bud at the tip, the pulp inside. A feeling of tree or a gentle breeze, the bark of a dog when it stops, the memory of the piano in some bar, the fruits of her eyes lit for a moment by the headlights of cars.

She hides. Behind the coffee cup, the cracked pane, the yellow raincoat of the person next to her, behind solid days of walking
alongside flocks of cars, on squares of sidewalk that are all the same, on crosswalks when the light is green, passing the old haunts of living and forbidden friends,
walking toward those friends. The city is a riddle of time. The lover a repetition of the city, a riddle of feeling. His touch, steps that echo, walking endlessly on. Paula is his footprint, the mark left by his passing, a needle-pierced heart, the most blissful pastoral idealization

of all that passed in a flash. Many things exist irrevocably when they pass. Passion is exchanged for memory and memory can be exchanged for nothing. Her memory conquers her with a Trojan horse. And Troy is a person's name and like a person it walks
in the garden on the mount where Eve in the afternoon heard a sound and hid herself in fear. The Trojan footsteps in her small room conquer in advance the morning's pretense of hope, the young lover's pretense of eternal love, conquer in advance the taste of hot coffee, the smell of toothpaste. She hides in the apartment, behind the coffee cup, and the sound of footsteps lays siege to her, occupies her.

The skittering Trojan horse, all ankles and wet eyes, sniffs at her bed, bending over it as if over a trough, goes to the window and opens the curtains, sits at her table and drinks her coffee—
Will you stay long? Let me caress the veins carved into your fat downy belly, let my finger trace the line from your forehead to your upper lip, let my hair wipe the specks of foam from your mouth. Let me find again your pointed ears and the fur on your dappled back. Horse, pull me from this coffee cup. Let me mount you, let us leave as if sinking into sleep or floating up into a rainbow's path, me grasping your mane close to the skin. Horse, give me the courage of flight, of escape. I will feed you forgotten lovers, I will turn away new friends. There's just one thing I fear—that you might open your mute wooden belly and trap me inside.

His wooden eyes are hard, his wooden foam is hard. His wooden nostrils are cold. He doesn't breathe and is white, so white, so incredibly pale. And I hear the hinges of his belly.

They tumble over the carpet, identical and infinite, so many funny little Trojan horses. They sniff at her bed, bending as if over a trough, sniffing the pillow, the covers, clambering onto the mattress. They lay siege to the castle of the china cabinet, conquer the smell of coffee, and swim happily in their wet plunder. They climb up and down in her mug because that is where she keeps her house and where the house keeps her. Victors, they open the fridge, pick up the phone and whinny conversations, washing themselves and drying off on the green grass of a towel. They sniff for something dead and fierce, like a wolf. They stare at Paula with wet eyes
and she watches those eyes light up, red as fish in a tank of clouded water. The motionless net of triangular ears
the longing of man

romantic, mythological horses, primitive as effigies, who walk swishing their manes with a toss of the head. They graze on naked bodies, the black or blonde grass of this wasteland,
cannibal horses who champ at the soles, the legs, the thighs, waists, breasts, throats, faces, dreams, the wind in the branches of the lemon tree,
glutted horses, dripping human blood like the devilish horse of the epic, who leave dressed in tires, doors, windshields, engines, fenders, the smell of gasoline.

Trojan car of memory.

6. The outlaw taxi.

Sometimes she hides and sometimes she goes out more than she ought. Between absence and the emphatic present, a taxi. She hid in its belly and stole into the dark enemy city, switching cabs three times. False addresses, a Troy that moves toward apartments outside the city center, carrying a stuffed nylon sack in her hand. Because Troy is also a name, the name of the woman they hunt. Paula in her nighttime taxi, afraid. All the drivers had the same face. She studied that face and the knickknacks on the dashboard. Is he okay or not? For the Trojan taxi could, striding fast over the books of the epic, drive her into the one-eyed cave of the cyclops.

A slice of the driver's face in the rear-view mirror, and his nape, another fragment of body. The fabric of the back of his jacket, the worry beads, the icon of the Virgin, the "Dad don't speed," the plastic flowers, the captain, the Greek village, the Greek mountain, an ancestor's photograph framed in black in the living room. His wife is fat and beats her children—their marital squabble, the Sunday soccer game, the skewered Easter lamb, the sentimental photograph, the singer's breasts. He eats a lot. His everyday and his good clothes, his sensitive honor, his proud omnivorous penis, submission to the law and the divine child of the Christmas turkey. Is he okay or not? A dark fabric striped with a crimson thread.

In her palm paved roads run through neighborhoods of tiny houses for dwarves, one on top of the next, white or gray apartment buildings. All the Snow Whites are sleeping on the line of life. Snow Whites of the capital who wake secretly and scrub the soot from their bodies with Ajax and fall asleep again, holding instead of an apple the bewitched receiver of the telephone. Their deaths are hospital demonstrations, their burials clipped ceremonies. The prince is a clerk. The man works as an angel, with a powdered white face and marble pants, the guardian of uniformity. He is always ironing his marble pants to dry them of the rain and tears. And the taxi crosses the lifeline. Now there is no other prince than the driver in his suit who determines her death and her life.

Where're you going?

The glow of an idea, her erotic danger, her ambiguity in time, her forbidden silhouette, her unlegislated shape, her inescapable end, the crime of her erection, her half-crazed code. I am going, trembling, to find my lover who is in hiding. I am bringing him a nylon sack of clothes, books, food. My lover is a plural meaning that is complete each time in its singularity. Bodily to the point of rejecting the body, entranced by death. His body is the embodiment of an idea

It'll be faster if we take Michaelakopoulou

and the idea has no other tongue than his body. His body is dangerous, electric with ideas. Driver, with that proud omnivorous penis, there is no greater pleasure than the idea that you create and follow, so bewitched

We're here

that it becomes love. Not just the one or the other, but their communion, the indivisible and the sacred, the ephemeral, condemned to bodily torture because no one has thought up a better punishment for ideas than physical pain. An idea that does not express love devalues its own existence. A love that does not celebrate an idea

Goodnight

devalues the body. Goodnight.

7. The rendezvous.

That night her lover took her to the double bed and said, opening his hand: I do not live as I want, as you can see.

The cracked pane in the kitchen, the half-eaten bacon, the creak of the bus, the metaphysical bed, the policeman's two revolvers, the sound of the belt. His hand is a womb. Which trembles like a breeze in the branches of the lemon tree. His disarmament. His tenderness without weapons. The fear of torture. The agony of imprisonment. The uncertainty of every idea. The uncertainty of the body. The insufficient money, the insufficient messages, the miserable supper. Seasoned with vague ideas. The danger of isolation. The wind in the airshaft. Like a soft howl. Dry branches, pipes. Pale. The borrowed clothes, the borrowed shoes, the borrowed ideas, the borrowed body. The danger of love, his ambiguity in time, his forbidden silhouette, his unlegislated shape, his inescapable end, his half-crazed language. The refuge of his erection. The nonexistence of place outside the apartment. The amplification of sounds. The diminution of needs. The disfigurement of time.

The tree in the middle of the room might have had green and silver leaves. Late on a summer afternoon, perhaps, in the rustling of an olive grove. Thick soil on the tiled floor. To catch crickets you must cover them suddenly with a cupped hand. You'd have watched from your perch on the highest branch. An exquisite light on your face. An unprecedented rosy sea. The wolf reigns red in its waters
framed by gilded cherubs or a geometric pattern in dark gold.

In the center of the tiled floor a broad-leafed newspaper blooms with the yellow stains of olive oil. And perhaps they really are blossoms, because above them, motionless in silent orgasm, stand the insects of two plates, two glasses, two forks. We sit eating on the earth of a rumpled, still-warm sheet. We are Brueghel's fieldhands, though from the outside he seems like a spy. You watch him again as we finish up with our meal. A knife slits the neck of a bread loaf. An exquisite light on your face from the murder. An unprecedented rosy dawn framed by the silhouette of a far-off hope, or with no frame at all.

The next morning she will leave alone in a passing taxi.

8. Ode to the nylon sack.

Hail sack who will carry the note on thin paper folded a thousand times, in a container of cooked food
sack pregnant with fruit, chocolate, cooked food, books, a new shirt, five and a half years
who will go fattened into the wolf's mouth and represent me in tooth-framed sanctuaries
and give to a kissed mouth the taste and smell of fruit, chocolate, cooked food, a book, and the shirt
hail you who go in free of my weight, and will be pregnant again in fifteen days.

Nylon sack whom Little Red Ridinghood carries from the grocery, full of wild cans of food,
you follow her into the taxi or bus with the flowery scent of detergent, traveling ticketless like a soulless thing

carrying crumbs from the feast of the secret, official suitcase
while inside the city you have the translucent tones of the rainbow, or the brilliant perishable letters that spell out "supermarket," novelties woven for the civil servants.

Nylon sack sucking honey from flowers of evil, flying from the lawful to the forbidden as if between two flowers in a single pot,
ignorant of the laws and, in your innocent ignorance, constantly transgressing them
passing regularly through locked doors, abstract as thought in spite of your weight, returning like the memory of thought
sack whom I hold and warm in courtyards and hallways, and with that warmth I feel in you the forbidden body that will hold you soon and keep you from the cold
you who, disgusted rather than aloof, never prostitute my touch, despite the many hands that come between.

Nylon sack who, like mourning or atonement, breaks the homogeneity, bringing out just a single part of Paula, plastic offering and pain
nylon sack who reminds their animal, their knife, their god, their theater, but is still clean of the blood and the secrets
you are fabric that is not fabric, paper that is not paper, skin that is not skin, thought that is not thought, womb that is not a womb, outlaw who is not an outlaw, basket that is not a basket
and though your words are the words of the most castrated language, you carry within you the memory of a deep and heartfelt love.

Hail sack, the glory of visiting hours at the prison.

9. Excursion in nature.

The leaves were still green when she took a trip out of Athens. A small car, friends. Paula an invisible tree planted in the backseat
like a released prisoner headed home whom only the windowpane separates from the trees outside. A razor of glass that, like thought, divides tree from tree, vision from view, return from desertion. The friends on a tour transposed in time of the same idealized nature
as waves of trees rush up and close her in, outstretched leaves grasping at the sides of the car, grains of seasalt, imprints of suffering, the wind in the old yard

waves of trees draw back and sweep up again to the car, castle-topped mountains, the constant curves of autumn, the chickens, the antennas, the bellowing of billboards, the loudspeakers, the fields of Greek ruins, the lithographs, the thin gilt frame, the wallpaper in the living room. A dog runs barking after the van, then trots back to his flock. A small field of wheatstalks comes and goes

and above it floats your white body, enormous and sorrowful. Your eyes, naked, unripe, bitter fruit. In a field you are marble. The sun's rays slant down on you. A cloud, you move slowly. The sound of a remorseful word. The classic metaphors of melancholy. A scrap of dried wheat. The friends are sitting on bales of hay, eating and sighing as Paula drinks to your beauty. Your cloud bloodied by the scythes of friends. Your soft cloud starts to rain

as softly the car starts rolling again, bewitched by your miracle. They all look silently out. Your wet miracle turns to sweat on the pane from breathing. I touch, closing my eyes. One of my cheeks on your damp belly. Now the transparent pane unites me with you. The friends begin again their small mutterings. I touch your damp belly.

On her soft cheeks. If only you were just one man, if only the proscription had ended. Wolf, O wolf, he is handsome and invincible.

Wolf, O wolf, nature is only the forbidden body.

The ferry's deck. A little white house in a wooden yard, tubular insect antennae, the iron railings, the benches, the gulls, masked hens who follow us, pecking. The sea seems to me like a field waiting for your seed. You softly send roots into Persephone's seablue space. On the surface of the damp field bobbing white fruit comes and goes, sometimes with coils of smoke, sometimes with triangular sails, sometimes with a wooden keel. I gathered ripe fruit in a basket and left it for you in a gently cupped palm. Your hand will sow the seeds in the water. Your lips will taste with small bites the ships and the boats. And then I will kiss those lips, breathing their salt like a Platonic soul. I am a grain of sand from the sea, I will make myself a tree and then turn again to earth and water. I surround you with land and sea. I listen to the anchor mark the boundaries between the dense and the solid. Where the anchor plants its love.

Paula waits on land for their car to disembark. Suddenly a police van. Small barred windows. Waves, trees, stares can't get in. Painted with the color of wolf and stiff as his neck. And here is Little Red Ridinghood, butchered and hanging from a hook by her foot, naked and shaven, like a lamb that the van unloads and unloads again and again for the butcher. Wolf, O wolf, you shed her like miscarriage from the van of your belly. Wolf, O wolf, the gray men pester her, with guns at their hips or on their faces like mustaches. No trip, no outing can stop the pain. On and on, like waves breaking against the cement of the pier, on and on she will cry.

Because the forbidden body nullifies nature.

A damp color, almost black, falls and covers the mountains and sea. Now it is dark in and outside of the car of friends. Now and then haunted noises and shapes flicker outside. Let them go home, let them go home. She remembers her room. She wants. With no passport.

O wolf, her own body now becomes free and forbidden, masculine and feminine, torture and miracle, inside and out of the windshield, the fearless and fearful, amoral and ascetic.

Green leaves. Outside, green. In a square in Athens with no passport, her own body nullifies nature.

10. Lyric for an excursion in the city.

now run they're coming don't listen quick right a door get in tears
Vaseline they're gone gunshots
and you go out again

now run they're coming don't listen quick right a door get in tears
Vaseline they're gone gunshots
and you go out again

now run they're coming don't listen quick right a door get in tears
Vaseline they're gone gunshots
and you go out again

now run they're coming don't listen quick right a door get in tears
Vaseline they're gone gunshots
and you go out again

Four Kabbalistic Poems

Translated from Hebrew by Peter Cole

Translator's Note

When I was asked several years ago to take on the translation of *The Poetry of Kabbalah,* an anthology of poems from the Jewish esoteric tradition, I accepted with a mixture of delight and trepidation: delight, because the entirety of postbiblical Hebrew poetry has long held me in its spell. And trepidation, because I was suddenly faced with just that—an intimidating array of material that spanned some sixteen hundred years of literary history on three continents, and involved a smorgasbord of cosmological masterpieces and occasional poems, sexual charms and epic phantasmagoria, balladlike lyrics and didactic preludes to chapters of prose, simple hymns of the purest devotion and gnomic verse of numerological intrigue. The prosody of the work ran the gamut from cadenced free verse to quantitative monorhyme to rhymed sonnets in syllabics and more. All within an explicitly mystical framework.

That framework itself presented a challenge to translation, since the nature of Hebrew in its various religious and liturgical modes—and especially in the more kabbalistic registers—is quite different from the language of English religious verse. For starters, the Hebrew is both eroticized and consecrated in a way that more Protestant English is not, or not normally; it involves a linguistic burden of presence rather than transcendence, of embodiment rather than transparence. The history of English translation of work from other mystical traditions shows that at least for the past half a century or so translators have tended to dispense with the apparent interference of the original verse's formal elements so as to better zero in on what they have taken to be the more relevant spiritual essence of the poetry itself, which was then repackaged along the lines of a new (or latterly New Age) aesthetic. Rarely, however, has this been done while accounting in responsible, let alone inspired, fashion for the key prosodic and musical implications of the original verse, which themselves often reflect broader historical and social concerns. As a result, far more often than not we have been left with homogenizing poems of empty abstraction, porous vessels filled with well-selling projections of translators' and readers' fantasies of spiritual release.

In the case of the poetry of the Kabbalah—a widespread religious tradition the very being of which, *pace* Madonna, has been predicated for the most part on the intense adherence to and visionary application of prescribed acts of religious observance (*mitzvot*)—it seemed especially important to highlight not the liberatory impulse that so many people associate with contemporary mysticism, but rather the dialectical tension between the planes of essence and enactment that characterizes kabbalistic tradition on the whole. Accordingly, I chose to work with the given formal elements of the verse rather than reconfigure them radically, or melt them down in a search for an occluded poetry that might lie at their core: In other words, I sought to release the religious experience at the center of these poems not *from* form, but *through* form. Along related lines, I tried to remember that most of these compositions—these spiritual machines made of words, to adapt William Carlos Williams's characterization of the modernist poem—were, and still are, *used* as devices of meditation and prayer. The experience of devotion, the turning of their reader's attention, is determined in that devotional context by the pressure of the poetry, the shape and sound of the verse itself. Above all, then, I sought to offer the reader a sense of the Hebrew's torque.

The first two anonymous poems of the group that follows are drawn from what is known as *Hekhalot* literature (literature of the Palaces). The provenance and essence of that literature are alike in dispute, with the former running in scholarly estimation from second-century Palestine to seventh-century Babylonia, and the latter leading to either ecstatic visionary ascent or the magical manipulation of angelic powers in the interest of religious knowledge. The tractate these poems are taken from begins by reporting that one of the rabbis asked what hymns were recited by one who seeks "to gaze upon the appearance of the chariot"—that is, to ascend through the heavens and behold the glory of God on his throne, or participate in the celestial liturgy—and, lest we underestimate the dangers involved, "to enter in peace and depart in peace."

"To Whom Among the Avengers of Blood" is a penitential poem, also from late thirteenth-century Spain. It is "signed" in Hebrew with an acrostic that identifies the author as Avraham ben Shmuel. This has led to speculation that its author may in fact be Avraham Abulafia, the great Spanish mystic and author of a long, hallucinatory prophetic poem, *The Book of the Letter* (which will also appear in the collection). While no evidence to support this attribution has emerged, the fact remains that the poem by Avraham ben Shmuel displays a strikingly modern interiority that is in some ways reminiscent of Abulafia's kabbalistic writings. Haim Schirmann, the twentieth century's leading scholar of medieval Hebrew poetry, called this "one of the finest Hebrew poems of all time."

The final poem in this group, the sixteenth-century "Why, My Desire," is often attributed to either Isaac Luria (born in Jerusalem, raised in Egypt, died in Safed), the most important kabbalistic figure after the expulsion from Spain, or to an anonymous disciple of his. Locating this poem in even a vaguely kabbalistic context—it has been published in various quasikabbalistic collections—we can see it as a paramystical poem treating the mechanics of vision: desire (misdirected) is experienced as an obstacle to participation in the altering religious experience, and the struggle with that desire is itself perceived, with an undertow of irony, as part of a larger musical, ritualistic, and even cosmic design. While neither of the final two poems makes use of kabbalistic terminology or theory, both involve what we might call, in resonant contemporary terms, a Hebraic *jihad an-nafs*—that is, a psychomachia, or battle for the poet's soul.

* * *

HYMN TO THE HEAVENLY BEINGS

You who cancel decrees and unravel vows,
    remove wrath and bring fury to failure,
restoring love and friendship's display
    before the glory of the Palace of Awe:

Why are you now so wholly fearful,
    and now given over to gladness and joy?
Now so strong in your exultation,
    and now overcome with terror?

They said: When the face of majesty darkens
    great dread and fear overwhelm us—
and when the glow of the Presence appears
    we soar in tremendous bliss.

A MEASURE OF HOLINESS

A measure of holiness,
  a measure of power,
a measure of awe,
  a measure of terror;
a measure of trembling,
  a measure of dread,
a measure of anguish,
  a measure of horror—
a measure of the robe
  of Zoharariel,
the Lord of hosts, God of Israel,
  who is crowned and approaches
the throne of His Glory,
  engraved and covered entirely
without and within
  by His name divine:
and the eyes of every living thing
  are unable to gaze upon it;
neither the eyes of flesh and blood
  nor the eyes of those who serve Him;
for rounds of fire take hold of the eyes
  of one who beholds it directly,
or merely glances and glimpses it;
  the balls of his eyes then blaze
and send forth torches of fire,
  and he's set afire and wholly consumed;
for the fire that issues from the man who gazes
  burns and devours him utterly.
Why? Because of the image of the eyes
  in the robe of Zohararial,
the Lord, God of Israel,
  who is crowned
and approaches the throne of His glory.

—Poems of the Palaces
Third–fourth c., Babylonia?

TO WHOM AMONG THE AVENGERS OF BLOOD

To whom among the avengers of blood can I cry—
when my blood has been shed by my own two hands?

The hearts of those who despised me I've tried,
and none have despised me more than my heart.

The enemy's blows and wounds have been mighty,
and none have wounded or struck like my soul.

The corrupt have beguiled me into destruction,
but what like my own two eyes beguiles.

From fire to fire I have passed alive,
and nothing has burned like my own desire.

In nets and snares I have been trapped,
but nothing has trapped me like the snare of my tongue.

Snakes and scorpions have bitten and stung me,
but my teeth bite into my flesh more fiercely.

Princes have pursued me swiftly on horseback,
but none have pursued like my own two feet.

My anguish has swelled and long overwhelmed me,
but stubbornness brings me much greater grief.

And my heart's sorrows are many,
and greater still are my sins.

To whom can I cry out or complain,
when my destroyers emerge from within me?

I've found nothing better in life than to seek
refuge in your compassion.

Cast your mercy on the hearts of the weary,
Lord, my king on the Throne of Mercy.

—Avraham ben Shmuel
Thirteenth c., Spain

WHY, MY DESIRE

Why, my desire, why do you always pursue me,
    and turn me, daily, into your enemy?
Why, my desire, why do you always pursue me?

Day after day you set out your snares,
    until in guile's pit you entrap me—
Why, my desire, why do you always pursue me?

You've been my enemy since I was young,
    gnashing your teeth and working against me.
Why, my desire, why do you always pursue me?

My soul sought to follow your path,
    for your hand's shadow, it seemed, would protect me.
Why, my desire, why do you always pursue me?

My eyes greeted the night with tears,
    and as you persisted, in anger you wrapped me:
Why, my desire, why do you always pursue me?

And if I imagine you'll come to save me,
    when I call on the day of distress you'll say to me:
(Why, my desire, why do you always pursue me?)

"Your words to me are sweeter than honey"
    —and so to doom on your hook you draw me.
Why, my desire, why do you always pursue me?

—School of Luria
Sixteenth c., Palestine

First Part
Of the Ingenious Nobleman
Don Quixote of La Mancha

Miguel de Cervantes

Translated from Spanish by Edith Grossman

Translator's Note

In the author's prologue to what is now called Part I of *Don Quixote* (Part II appeared ten years later, in 1615, following the publication of a continuation of the knight's adventures that had not been written by Cervantes), Cervantes said this about his book and the need to write a preface for it:

> I wanted only to offer it [the novel] to you plain and bare, unadorned by a prologue or the endless catalogue of sonnets, epigrams, and laudatory poems that are usually placed at the beginning of books. For I can tell you that although it cost me some effort to compose, none seemed greater than creating the preface you are now reading. I picked up my pen many times to write it, and many times I put it down again because I did not know what to write; and once, when I was baffled, with the paper in front of me, my pen behind my ear, my elbow propped on the writing table and my cheek resting in my hand, pondering what I would say, a friend of mine . . . came in, and seeing me so perplexed he asked the reason, and I . . . said I was thinking about the prologue I had to write for the history of Don Quixote. . . .

I am not presumptuous or arrogant enough to compare myself to Miguel de Cervantes, but his (fictional) difficulty was certainly my (factual) one as I contemplated the prospect of writing even a few lines about the wonderfully utopian task of translating the first—and probably the greatest—modern novel. Substitute keyboard and monitor for pen and paper, and my dilemma and posture are the same; the dear friend who helped to solve the problem is really Cervantes himself, an embodied spirit who emerged out of the shadows and off the pages when I realized I could begin this essay by quoting some sentences from his prologue.

I have never kept a translating journal, although I admire those I have read. William Weaver, for example, while he was translating *The Name of the Rose,* wrote a fascinating and valuable diary that documents everything from the backache that kept him from sitting at his desk to the hours spent deciding how to render a single word or phrase (an excruciating process that only another translator can appreciate fully). Keeping records of any kind is not something I do easily, and after six or seven hours of translating at the computer, the idea of writing about what I have written looms insurmountably, as does the kind of self-scrutiny required: The actuality of the translation is in the translation, and having to articulate how and why I have just articulated the text seems cruelly redundant. Yet I did keep daily notes, for a few days. I hesitated over spelling, for instance, and finally opted for an *x,* not a *j,* in *Quixote* (I wanted the connection to the English "quixotic" to be immediately apparent); I worried about footnotes, and decided that I had to put some in, though I had never used them before in a translation (I did not want the reader to be put off by references that may now be obscure, or to miss the layers of intention and meaning they created); and I recorded the rush of exhilaration and terror I felt, for perfectly predictable and transparent reasons, at undertaking the project.

Every translator has to live with the kind of critic and reviewer whom Gregory Rabassa has called "Professor Horrendo"—that intrepid leader of the translation police who is ready to pounce on an infelicitous phrase or misinterpreted word in a book that can be hundreds of pages long. I had two or three soul-searing nightmares about academic hordes, with Hispanists in the vanguard, laying waste to my translation of the work that is not only the great monument of literature in Spanish, but a pillar of the entire Western literary tradition. Only the knowledge that I was not a young translator just starting out gave me the courage to go on—that, and the determination not to allow self-censoring apprehension to keep me from an enterprise that was surely the dream of every person who translates from Spanish.

Shortly before I began work, while I was wrestling with the question of what kind of voice would be most appropriate for the translation of a book written some four hundred years ago, I mentioned my fears to Julián Ríos, the Spanish writer (I have translated two of his novels, *Loves That Bind* and *Monstruary*). His reply was simple and profound and immensely liberating. He told me not to be afraid;

Cervantes, he said, was our [the Spanish-speaking world's] most modern writer, and what I had to do was to translate him the way I translated everyone else. It was a revelation. Julián's characterization desacralized the project and allowed me, finally, to confront the text and find the voice in English. This is the essential problem in translation, for me at least. Compared to it, lexical difficulties shrink and wither away.

I believe that my primary obligation as a literary translator is to recreate for the reader in English the experience of the reader in Spanish. When Cervantes wrote *Don Quixote,* it was not yet a seminal masterpiece of European literature; or the book that crystallized forever the making of literature out of life *and* literature; or explored in typically ironic fashion, and for the first time, the blurred and shifting frontiers between fact and fiction, imagination and history, perception and physical reality; or set the stage for all Hispanic studies and all serious discussions of the history and nature of the novel in Europe. When Cervantes wrote *Don Quixote* his language was not archaic or quaint. He wrote in a crackling, up-to-date Spanish that was an intrinsic part of his time (this is instantly apparent when he has Don Quixote, in transports of knightly madness, speak in the old-fashioned idiom of the novels of chivalry), a modern language that both reflected and helped to shape the way people experienced the world. This meant that I did not need to find a special, somehow-seventeenth-century voice, but could translate his astonishingly fine writing into contemporary English.

And his writing is a marvel: It gives off sparks and flows like honey. Cervantes' style is so artful it seems absolutely natural and inevitable; his irony is sweet-natured, his sensibility sophisticated, compassionate, and humorous. If my translation works at all, the contemporary reader should keep turning the pages, smiling a good deal, periodically bursting into laughter, and anticipating with some eagerness the next synonym, the next mind-bending coincidence, the next variation on the structure of Don Quixote's adventures, the next incomparable conversation between the knight and his squire. To quote again from Cervantes' prologue: "I do not want to charge you too much for the service I have performed in introducing you to so noble and honorable a knight; but I do want you to thank me for allowing you to make the acquaintance of the famous Sancho Panza, his squire. . . ."

I began the work in February 2001. What you have in hand is a first revision; I cannot predict how many more there will be, but "final" versions are determined more by a publisher's due date than by any sense on my part that the work is actually finished. I hope you find it deeply amusing and truly compelling. If not, you can be certain the fault is mine.

* * *

CHAPTER I

Which describes the condition and profession of the famous nobleman Don Quixote of La Mancha

SOMEWHERE IN LA MANCHA, in a place whose name I do not care to remember, a nobleman lived not long ago, one of those who has a lance and ancient shield on a shelf and keeps a skinny nag and a greyhound for racing. An occasional stew, beef more often than lamb, hash most nights, eggs and abstinence on Saturdays, lentils on Fridays, sometimes squab as a treat on Sundays—these consumed three-fourths of his income. The rest went for a light woolen tunic and velvet breeches and hose of the same material for feast days, while weekdays were honored with dun-colored coarse cloth. He had a housekeeper past forty, a niece not yet twenty, and a man-of-all-work who did everything from saddling the horse to pruning the trees. Our nobleman was approximately fifty years old; his complexion was weathered, his flesh scrawny, his face gaunt, and he was a very early riser and a great lover of the hunt. Some claim that his family name was Quixada, or Quexada, for there is a certain amount of disagreement among the authors who write of this matter, although reliable conjecture seems to indicate that his name was Quexana. But this does not matter very much to our story; in its telling there is absolutely no deviation from the truth.

And so, let it be said that this aforementioned nobleman spent his times of leisure—which meant most of the year—reading books of chivalry with so much devotion and enthusiasm that he forgot almost completely about the hunt and even about the administration of his estate; in his rash curiosity and folly he went so far as to sell acres of arable land in order to buy books of chivalry to read, and he brought as many of them as he could into his house; he thought none was as fine as those composed by the worthy Feliciano de Silva, because the clarity of his prose and complexity of his language seemed to him more valuable than pearls, in particular when he read the declarations and missives of love, where he would often find written: *The reason for the unreason to which my reason turns so weakens my reason that with reason I complain of thy beauty.* And also when he read: . . . *the heavens on high divinely heighten thy divinity with the stars and make thee deserving of the deserts thy greatness deserves.*

With these words and phrases the poor gentleman lost his mind, and he spent sleepless nights trying to understand them and extract their meaning, which Aristotle himself, if he came back to life for only that purpose, would not have been able to decipher or understand. Our nobleman was not very happy with the wounds that Don Belianís gave and received, because he imagined that no matter how great the physicians and surgeons who cured him, he would still have his face and entire body covered with scars and marks. But, even so, he praised the author for having concluded his book with the promise of unending adventure, and he often felt the desire to take up his pen and give it the conclusion promised there; and no doubt he would have done so, and even published it, if other greater and more persistent thoughts had not prevented him from doing so. He often had discussions with the village priest—who was a learned man, a graduate of Sigüenza[1]—regarding who had been the greater knight: Palmerín of England or Amadís of Gaul; but Master Nicolás, the village barber, said that none was the equal of the Knight of Phoebus, and if any could be compared to him it was Don Galaor, the brother of Amadís of Gaul, because he was moderate in everything; a knight who was not affected, not as weepy as his brother, and incomparable in questions of courage.

In short, our nobleman became so caught up in reading that he spent his nights reading from dusk till dawn, and his days reading from sunrise to sunset; and so with too little sleep and too much reading his brains dried up, causing him to lose his mind. His fantasy filled with everything he had read in his books, enchantments as well as combats, battles, challenges, wounds, courtings, loves, torments, and other impossible foolishness, and he became so convinced in his imagination of the truth of all the countless grandiloquent and false inventions he read, that for him no history in the world was truer. He would say that El Cid Ruy Diaz[2] had been a very good knight but could not compare to Amadís, the Knight of the Blazing Sword, who, with a single backstroke, cut two ferocious and

[1]The allusion is ironic: Sigüenza was a minor university, and its graduates had the reputation for being not very well educated.
[2]A historical figure (eleventh century) who has passed into legend and literature.

colossal giants in half. He was fonder of Bernardo del Carpio[3] because at Roncesvalles[4] he had killed the enchanted Roland by availing himself of the tactic of Hercules when he crushed Antaeus, the son of Earth, in his arms. He spoke highly of the giant Morgante because, although he belonged to the race of giants, all of them haughty and lacking in courtesy, he alone was amiable and well behaved. But, more than any of the others, he admired Reinaldos of Montalbán,[5] above all when he saw him emerge from his castle and rob anyone he met, and when he crossed the sea and stole the idol of Mohammed made all of gold, as recounted in his history. He would have traded his housekeeper, and even his niece, for the chance to strike a blow at the traitor Guenelon.[6]

The truth is that when his mind was completely gone, he had the strangest thought any lunatic in the world ever had, which was that it seemed reasonable and necessary to him, both for the sake of his honor and as a service to the nation, to become a knight errant and travel the world with his armor and his horse to seek adventures and engage in everything he had read that knights errant engaged in, righting all manner of wrongs and, by seizing the opportunity and placing himself in danger and ending those wrongs, winning eternal renown and everlasting fame. The poor man imagined himself already wearing the crown, won by the valor of his arm, of the Empire of Trapisonda at the very least; and so it was that with these exceedingly agreeable thoughts, and carried away by the extraordinary pleasure he took in them, he hastened to put into effect what he so fervently desired. And the first thing he did was to attempt to clean some armor that had belonged to his great-grandfathers and, stained with urine and covered with mildew, had spent many long years stored and forgotten in a corner. He did the best he could to clean and repair it, but he saw that it had a great defect, which was that instead of a full sallet helmet with an attached neckguard there was only a simple headpiece; but he compensated for this with his industry, and out of pasteboard he fashioned a kind of half-helmet that, when attached to the headpiece, took on the appearance of a full sallet. It is true that in order to test if it was strong and could withstand a

[3]A legendary hero, the subject of ballads as well as poems and plays.
[4]The site in the Pyrenees, called Roncesvaux in French, where Charlemagne's army fought the Saracens in 778.
[5]A hero of the French *chansons de geste;* in some Spanish versions, he takes part in the battle of Roncesvalles.
[6]The traitor responsible for the defeat of Charlemagne's army at Roncesvalles.

blow, he took out his sword and struck it twice, and with the first blow he undid in a moment what it had taken him a week to create; he could not help being disappointed at the ease with which he had hacked it to pieces, and to protect against that danger, he made another one, placing strips of iron on the inside so that he was satisfied with its strength and, not wanting to put it to the test again, he designated and accepted it as an extremely fine sallet.

Then he went to look at his nag, and though its hooves had more cracks than his master's pate and it showed more flaws than Gonnella's horse,[7] who *tantum pellis et ossa fuit,* it seemed to him that Alexander's Bucephalus and El Cid's Babieca were not its equal. He spent four days thinking about the name he would give it, for—as he told himself—it was not seemly that the horse of so famous a knight, and a steed so intrinsically excellent, should not have a worthy name; he was looking for the precise name that would declare what the horse had been before its master became a knight errant, and what it was now; for he was determined that if the master was changing his condition the horse too would change its name to one that would win the fame and recognition its new position and profession deserved; and so, after many names that he shaped and discarded, subtracted from and added to, unmade and remade in his memory and imagination, he finally decided to call the horse *Rocinante,*[8] a name, in his opinion, that was noble, sonorous, and reflective of what it had been when it was a nag, before it was what it was now, which was the foremost nag in all the world.

Having given a name, and one so much to his liking, to his horse, he wanted to give one to himself, and he spent another eight days pondering this, and at last he called himself *Don Quixote,*[9] which is why, as has been noted, the authors of this absolutely true history determined that he undoubtedly must have been named Quixada and not Quexada, as others have claimed. In any event, recalling that the valiant Amadís had not been content with simply calling himself Amadís but had added the name of his kingdom and realm in order to bring it fame, and was known as Amadís of Gaul, he too, like a good knight, wanted to add the name of his birthplace to his own, and he called himself *Don Quixote of La Mancha,*[10] thereby, to his

[7]Pietro Gonnella, the jester at the court of Ferrara, had a horse famous for being skinny.

[8]*Rocín* means "nag"; *ante* means "before," both temporally and spatially.

[9]*Quixote* means the section of armor that covers the thigh.

[10]La Mancha was not one of the noble medieval kingdoms associated with knighthood.

mind, clearly stating his lineage and country and honoring it by making it part of his title.

Having cleaned his armor and made a full helmet out of a simple headpiece, and having given a name to his horse and decided on one for himself, he realized that the only thing left for him to do was to find a lady to love; for the knight errant without a lady love was a tree without leaves or fruit, a body without a soul. He said to himself:

"If I, because of my evil sins, or my good fortune, meet with a giant somewhere, as ordinarily befalls knights errant, and I unseat him with a single blow, or cut his body in half, in short, if I conquer and defeat him, would it not be good to have someone to whom I could send him so that he might enter and fall to his knees before my sweet lady, and say in the humble voice of surrender: 'I, lady, am the giant Caraculiambro, lord of the island Malindrania, defeated in singular combat by the never sufficiently praised knight, Don Quixote of La Mancha, who commanded me to appear before thy ladyship, so that thy highness might dispose of me as thou chooseth'?"

Oh, how pleased our good knight was when he had made this speech, and even more pleased when he discovered the one he could call his lady! It is believed that in a nearby village there was a very attractive peasant girl with whom he had once been in love, although she, apparently, never knew or noticed. Her name was Aldonza Lorenzo,[11] and he thought it a good idea to call her the lady of his thoughts, and, searching for a name that would not differ significantly from his and would suggest and imply that of a princess and great lady, he decided to call her *Dulcinea of Toboso,* because she came from Toboso; a name, to his mind, that was musical and beautiful and filled with significance, as were all the others he had given to himself and everything pertaining to him.

CHAPTER II

Which tells of the first sally that the ingenious Don Quixote made from his native land

And so, having completed these preparations, he did not wish to wait any longer to put his thought into effect, impelled by the great need in the world that he believed was caused by his delay, for there were evils to undo, wrongs to right, injustices to correct, abuses to ameliorate, and offenses to rectify. And one morning before dawn on a

[11]Aldonza, considered to be a common, rustic name, had comic connotations.

hot day in July, without informing a single person of his intentions, and without anyone seeing him, he armed himself with all his armor and mounted Rocinante, wearing his poorly constructed helmet, and he grasped his shield and took up his lance and through the side door of a corral he rode out into the countryside with great joy and delight at seeing how easily he had given a beginning to his virtuous desire. But as soon as he found himself in the countryside he was assailed by a thought so terrible it almost made him abandon the enterprise he had barely begun; he recalled that he had not been dubbed a knight, and according to the law of chivalry, he could not and must not take up arms against any knight; since this was the case, he would have to bear blank arms, like a novice knight without a device on his shield, until he had earned one through his own efforts. These thoughts made him waver in his purpose, but, his madness being stronger than any other faculty, he resolved to have himself dubbed a knight by the first person he met, in imitation of many others who had done the same, as he had read in the books that had brought him to this state. As for his armor being blank and white, he planned to clean it so much that when the dubbing took place it would be whiter than ermine; he immediately grew serene and continued on his way, following only the path his horse wished to take, believing that the virtue of his adventures lay in doing this.

And as our new adventurer traveled along, he talked to himself, saying:

"Who can doubt that in times to come, when the true history of my famous deeds comes to light, the wise man who compiles them will write, when he begins to recount my first sally so early in the day, in this manner: 'No sooner had rubicund Apollo spread over the face of the wide and spacious earth the golden strands of his beauteous hair, no sooner had diminutive and bright-hued birds with dulcet tongues greeted in sweet, mellifluous harmony the advent of rosy dawn, who, forsaking the soft couch of her zealous consort, revealed herself to mortals through the doors and balconies of the Manchegan horizon, than the famous knight, Don Quixote of La Mancha, abandoning the downy bed of idleness, mounted his famous steed Rocinante and commenced to ride through the ancient and illustrious countryside of Montiel.'"[1]

And it was true that this was where he was riding. And he continued:

[1]A town in La Mancha.

"Fortunate the time and blessed the age when my famous deeds will come to light, worthy of being carved in bronze, sculpted in marble, and painted on tablets as a remembrance in the future. Oh thou, wise enchanter, whoever thou mayest be, whose task it will be to chronicle this wondrous history! I implore thee not to overlook my good Rocinante, my eternal companion on all my travels and peregrinations."

Then he resumed speaking as if he truly were in love:

"Oh, Princess Dulcinea, mistress of this captive heart! Thou hast done me grievous harm in bidding me farewell and reproving me with the harsh affliction of commanding that I not appear before thy sublime beauty. May it please thee, lady, to recall this thy subject heart, which suffers countless trials for the sake of thy love."

He strung these together with other foolish remarks, all in the manner his books had taught him, and imitating their language as much as he could. As a result, his pace was so slow, and the sun rose so quickly and ardently, that it would have melted his brains if he'd had any.

He rode almost all that day and nothing worthy of note happened to him, which caused him to despair because he wanted an immediate encounter with someone on whom to test the valor of his mighty arm. Some authors say his first adventure was the one in Puerto Lápice; others claim it was the adventure of the windmills; but according to what I have been able to determine with regard to this matter, and what I have discovered written in the annals of La Mancha, the fact is that he rode all that day, and at dusk he and his horse found themselves exhausted and half-dead with hunger; and as he looked all around to see if he could find some castle or a sheepfold with shepherds where he might take shelter and alleviate his great hunger and need, he saw an inn not far from the path he was traveling, and it was as if he had seen a star guiding him not to the portals but to the inner towers of his salvation. He quickened his pace and reached it just as night was falling.

At the door there happened to be two young women, the kind they call ladies of easy virtue, who were on their way to Sevilla with some mule drivers who had decided to stop at the inn that night, and since everything our adventurer thought, saw, or imagined seemed to happen according to what he had read, as soon as he saw the inn it appeared to him to be a castle complete with four towers and spires of gleaming silver, not to mention a drawbridge and deep moat and all the other details depicted on such castles. He rode toward the inn that he thought was a castle, and when he was a short distance away he reined in Rocinante and waited for a dwarf to appear on the parapets and signal with his trumpet that a knight was approaching the castle. But when he saw that there was some delay, and Rocinante was in a hurry to get to the stable, he rode toward the door of the inn and saw the two profligate wenches standing there, and he thought they were two fair damsels or two gracious ladies taking their ease at the entrance to the castle. At that moment a swineherd who was driving his pigs—no excuses, that's what they're called—out of some mudholes, blew his horn, a sound that pigs respond to, and it immediately seemed to Don Quixote to be just what he had desired, which was for a dwarf to signal his arrival, and so with extreme joy he rode up to the inn, and the ladies, seeing a man armed in that fashion, and carrying a lance and shield, became frightened and were about to retreat into the inn; but Don Quixote, inferring their fear from their flight, raised the pasteboard visor, revealing his dry, dusty face, and, in a gallant manner and reassuring voice, he said to them:

"Flee not, dear ladies, fear no villainous act from me; for the order of chivalry which I profess does not countenance or permit such deeds to be committed against any person, least of all high-born maidens such as yourselves."

The wenches looked at him, directing their eyes to his face, hidden by the imitation visor; but when they heard themselves called maidens, something so alien to their profession, they could not control their laughter, which offended Don Quixote and moved him to say:

"Moderation is becoming in beauteous ladies, and laughter for no reason is foolishness; but I do not say this to cause in you a woeful or dolorous disposition; for mine is none other than to serve you."

The language, which the ladies did not understand, and the bizarre appearance of our knight, intensified their laughter, and his annoyance increased, and he would have gone even further if at that moment the innkeeper had not come out, a man who was very fat and therefore very peaceable, and when he saw that grotesque figure armed with arms as incongruous as his bridle, lance, shield, and corselet, he was ready to join the maidens in their displays of hilarity. But fearing the countless difficulties that might ensue, he decided to speak to him politely, and so he said:

"If, sir, your grace seeks lodging, except for a bed (because there is none in this inn), a great abundance of everything else will be found here."

Don Quixote, seeing the humility of the steward of the castle-fortress, which is what he thought the innkeeper and the inn were, replied:

"For me, good castellan, anything will do, for
my trappings are my weapons,
and combat is my rest, etc."[2]

The host believed he had called him castellan because he thought him an upright Castillian, though he was an Andalusian from the Sanlúcar coast,[3] no less a thief than Cacus and as malicious as an apprentice page, and so he responded: "In that case, your grace's beds must be bare rocks, and your sleep, a constant vigil; and this being true, you can certainly dismount, certain of finding in this poor hovel more than enough reason and reasons not to sleep in an entire year, let alone a single night."

And saying this, he went to hold the stirrup for Don Quixote, who dismounted with extreme difficulty and travail, like a man who had not broken his fast all day long.

Then he told his host to take great care with his horse, because it was the best mount that walked this earth. The innkeeper looked at the horse and did not think it as good as Don Quixote said, or even half as good, and after leading it to the stable, he came back to see what his guest might desire, and the maidens, who by this time had made peace with him, were divesting him of his armor; although they had removed his breastplate and back piece, they never knew how or were able to disconnect the gorget or remove the counterfeit helmet, which was tied on with green cords that would have to be cut because they could not undo the knots; but he absolutely refused to consent to this, and so he spent all that night wearing the helmet, and was the most comical and curious figure that anyone could imagine; and as they were disarming him, and since he imagined that those well-worn and much-used women were illustrious ladies and damsels from the castle, he said to them with a good deal of grace and verve:

"Never was a knight
so well served by ladies
as was Don Quixote
when he first sallied forth:

[2]These lines are from a well-known ballad; the innkeeper's response quotes the next two lines.

[3]In Cervantes' time, this was known as a gathering place for criminals.

fair damsels tended to him;
princesses cared for his horse,[4]

or Rocinante, for this is the name, noble ladies, of my steed, and Don Quixote of La Mancha is mine; and although I did not wish to disclose my name until the great feats performed in your service and for your benefit would reveal it, perforce the adaptation of this ancient ballad of Lancelot to our present purpose has been the cause of your learning my name before the time was ripe; but the day will come when your highnesses will command and I shall obey and the valor of this my arm will betoken the desire I have to serve you."

The wenches, unaccustomed to hearing such high-flown rhetoric, did not say a word in response; they only asked if he wanted something to eat.

"I would consume any fare," replied Don Quixote, "because, as I understand it, that would be most beneficial now."

It happened to be a Friday, and in all the inn there was nothing but a few pieces of a fish that in Castilla is called cod, and in Andalucía codfish, and in other places salt cod, and elsewhere, smoked cod. They asked if his grace would like a little smoked cod, for there was no other fish to serve him.

"Since many little cod," replied Don Quixote, "all together make one large one, it does not matter to me if you give me eight *reales* in coins or in a single piece of eight. Moreover, it well might be that these little cod are like veal, which is better than beef, and kid, which is better than goat. But, in any case, bring it soon, for the toil and weight of arms cannot be borne if one does not control the stomach."

They set the table at the door to the inn, to take advantage of the cooler air, and the host brought him a portion of cod that was badly prepared and cooked even worse, and bread as black and grimy as his armor; but it was a cause for great laughter to see him eat, because, since he was wearing his helmet and holding up the visor with both hands, he could not put anything in his mouth unless someone placed it there for him, and so one of the ladies performed that task. But when it was time to give him something to drink it was impossible, and would have remained impossible, if the innkeeper had not hollowed out a reed, placing one end in the gentleman's mouth and pouring some wine in the other; and all of this Don Quixote accepted with patience in order not to have the cords of his helmet cut. At this moment a gelder of hogs happened to arrive at the inn, and as he

[4]Don Quixote paraphrases a ballad about Lancelot.

arrived he blew on his reed pipe four or five times, which confirmed for Don Quixote that he was in a famous castle where they were entertaining him with music, and that the cod was trout, the bread soft and white, the prostitutes ladies, the innkeeper the castellan of the castle, and that his decision to sally forth had been a good one. But what troubled him most was not being dubbed a knight, for it seemed to him that he could not legitimately engage in any adventure if he did not receive the order of knighthood.

CHAPTER III

Which recounts the amusing manner in which Don Quixote was dubbed a knight

And so, troubled by this thought, he hurried through the scant meal served at the inn, and when it was finished, he called to the innkeeper and, going into the stable with him, he kneeled before him and said:

"Never will I rise up from this place, valiant knight, until thy courtesy grants me a boon I wish to ask of thee, one that will redound to thy glory and to the benefit of all humankind."

The innkeeper, seeing his guest at his feet and hearing these words, looked at him and was perplexed, not knowing what to do or say, and he insisted that he get up, but Don Quixote refused until the innkeeper declared that he would grant the boon asked of him.

"I expected no less of thy great magnificence, my lord," replied Don Quixote. "And so I shall tell thee the boon that I would ask of thee and that thy generosity has granted me, and it is that on the morrow thou wilt dub me a knight, and that this night in the chapel of thy castle I shall keep vigil over my armor; and that on the morrow, as I have said, what I fervently desire will be accomplished so that I can, as I needs must do, travel the four corners of the earth in search of adventures on behalf of those in need, this being the office of chivalry and knights errant, for I am one of them and my desire is disposed to such deeds."

The innkeeper, as we have said, was rather sly and already had some inkling of his guest's madness, which was confirmed when he heard him say these words, and in order to have something to laugh about that night, he proposed to humor him; and so he told him that his desire and request were exemplary and his purpose right and proper in knights who were as illustrious as he appeared to be and as his gallant presence demonstrated; and that he himself, in the years of his youth, had dedicated himself to that honorable profession, traveling through many parts of the world in search of adventures, to wit the Percheles in Málaga, the Islas of Riarán, the Compás in Sevilla, the Azoguejo of Segovia, the Olivera of Valencia, the Rondilla in Granada, the coast of Sanlúcar, the Potro in Córdoba, the Ventillas in Toledo,[1] and many other places where he had exercised the lightfootedness of his feet and the lightfingeredness of his hands, committing countless wrongs, bedding many widows, undoing a few maidens, deceiving several orphans, and, finally, becoming known in every court and tribunal in almost all of Spain; in recent years, he had retired to this castle, where he lived on his property and that of others, welcoming all knights errant of whatever category and condition simply because of the great fondness he felt for them, so that they might share with him their goods as recompense for his virtuous desires.

He also said that in his castle there was no chapel where Don Quixote could stand vigil over his arms, for it had been demolished in order to rebuild it; but, in urgent cases, he knew that vigils could be kept anywhere, and on this night he could stand vigil in a courtyard of the castle; in the morning, God willing, the necessary ceremonies would be performed, and he would be dubbed a knight, and so much of a knight there could be no greater in all the world.

He asked if he had any money; Don Quixote replied that he did not have a copper *blanca,* because he never had read in the histories of knights errant that any of them ever carried money. To this the innkeeper replied that he was deceived, for if this was not written in the histories, it was because it had not seemed necessary to the authors to write down something as obvious and necessary as carrying money and clean shirts, and if they had not, this was no reason to think the knights did not carry them; and so, it should be taken as true and beyond dispute that all the knights errant who fill so many books to overflowing carried well-provisioned purses for whatever might befall them; by the same token they carried shirts and a small chest stocked with unguents to cure the wounds they received, for in the fields and clearings where they engaged in combat and were wounded there was not always someone who could cure them, unless they had for a friend some wise enchanter who instantly came to their aid, bringing through the air, on a cloud, a damsel or a dwarf bearing a flask of water of such great power that, by swallowing a

[1] These were all famous underworld haunts.

single drop, the knights were so completely healed of their injuries and wounds that it was as if no harm had befallen them. But in the event such was not the case, the knights of yore deemed it proper for their squires to be provisioned with money and other necessities, such as linen bandages and unguents to heal their wounds; and if it happened that these knights had no squire—which was a rare and uncommon thing—they themselves carried everything in saddlebags so finely made they could barely be seen on the haunches of their horse, as if they were something of greater significance because, except in cases like these, carrying saddlebags was not well favored by knights errant; for this reason he advised, for he could still give him orders as if he were his godson, since that is what he soon would be, that from now on he not ride forth without money and the provisions he had described, and then he would see how useful and necessary they would be when he least expected it.

Don Quixote promised to do as he advised with great alacrity, and so it was arranged that he would stand vigil over his arms in a large corral to one side of the inn; and Don Quixote, gathering all his armor together, placed it on a trough that was next to a well, and, grasping his shield, he took up his lance and with noble countenance began to pace back and forth in front of the trough, and as he began his pacing, night began to fall.

The innkeeper told everyone in the inn about the lunacy of his guest, about his standing vigil over his armor and his expectation that he would be dubbed a knight. They marveled at so strange a form of madness and went to watch him from a distance, and saw that with a serene expression he sometimes paced back and forth; at other times, leaning on his lance, he turned his eyes to his armor and did not turn them away again for a very long time. Night had fallen; but the moon was so bright it could compete with the orb whose light it reflected, and therefore everything the new knight did was seen clearly by everyone. Just then it occurred to one of the mule drivers in the inn to water his pack of mules, and for this it was necessary to move Don Quixote's armor, which was on the trough; our knight, seeing them approach, said in a booming voice:

"Oh thou, whosoever thou art, rash knight, who cometh to touch the armor of the most valiant knight who e'er girded on a sword! Lookest thou to what thou doest and touch it not, if thou wanteth not to leave thy life in payment for thy audacity."

The muleteer cared nothing for these words—it would have been better for him if he had, because it meant caring for his health—;

instead, picking the armor up by the straps, he threw it a good distance away. And seeing this, Don Quixote lifted his eyes to heaven and, turning his thoughts—or so it seemed to him—to his lady Dulcinea, he said:

"Help me, my lady, in this the first affront aimed at this thy servant's bosom; in this my first challenge let not thy grace and protection fail me."

And saying these and other similar phrases, and dropping his shield, he raised his lance in both hands and gave the mule driver so heavy a blow on the head that he knocked him to the ground, and the man was so badly battered that if the first blow had been followed by a second, he would have had no need for a physician to care for his wounds. Having done this, Don Quixote picked up his armor and began to pace again with the same tranquillity as before. A short while later, unaware of what had happened—for the first mule driver was still in a daze—a second approached, also intending to water his mules, and when he began to remove the armor to allow access to the trough, without saying a word or asking for anyone's favor, Don Quixote again dropped his shield and again raised his lance, and did not shatter it but instead broke the head of the second mule driver into more than three pieces because he cracked his skull in at least four places. When they heard the noise, all the people in the inn hurried over, among them the innkeeper. When he saw this, Don Quixote took up his shield, placed his hand on his sword, and said:

"Oh beauteous lady, strength and vigor of my submissive heart! This is the moment when thou needs must turn the eyes of thy grandeur toward this thy captive knight, who awaits so great an adventure."

And with this he acquired, it seemed to him, so much courage, that if all the mule drivers in the world had charged him he would not have taken one step backward. The wounded men's companions, seeing their friends on the ground, began to hurl stones at Don Quixote from a distance, and he did what he could to deflect them with his shield, not daring to move away from the trough and leave his armor unprotected. The innkeeper shouted at them to stop because he had already told them he was crazy, and that being crazy he would be absolved even if he killed them all. Don Quixote shouted even louder, calling them perfidious traitors, and saying that the lord of the castle was a varlet and a discourteous knight for allowing knights errant to be so badly treated, and that if he had already received the order of chivalry he would enlighten him as to the full extent of his treachery.

"But you, filthy and lowborn rabble, I care nothing for you; throw, approach, come, offend me all you can; for you will soon see how perforce you will pay for your rash insolence."

He said this with so much boldness and so much courage that he instilled a terrible fear in his attackers; and because of this and the persuasive arguments of the innkeeper, they stopped throwing stones at him, and he allowed the wounded men to withdraw, and resumed standing vigil over his armor with the same serenity and tranquillity as before.

The innkeeper did not think very highly of his guest's antics, and he decided to cut matters short and give him the accursed order of chivalry then and there, before another misfortune occurred. And so he approached and begged his pardon for the impudence these lowborn knaves had shown, saying he had known nothing about it, but that they had been rightfully punished for their audacity. He said he had already told him there was no chapel in the castle, nor was one necessary for what remained to be done, because according to his understanding of the ceremonies of the order, the entire essence of being dubbed a knight consisted in being struck on the neck and shoulders, and that could be accomplished in the middle of a field, and he had already fulfilled everything with regard to keeping a vigil over his armor, for just two hours of vigil satisfied the requirements, and he had spent more than four. Don Quixote believed everything and said he was prepared to obey him, and that he should conclude matters with as much haste as possible, because if he was attacked again and had already been dubbed a knight, he did not intend to leave a single person alive in the castle except for those the castellan ordered him to spare, which he would do out of respect for him.

Forewarned and fearful, the castellan immediately brought the book in which he kept a record of the feed and straw he supplied to the mule drivers, and with a candle end that a servant boy brought to him, and the two aforementioned damsels, he approached the spot where Don Quixote stood and ordered him to kneel; and reading from his book as if he were murmuring a devout prayer, he raised his hand and struck him on the back of the neck, and after that, with his own sword, he delivered a gallant blow to his shoulders, always murmuring between his teeth as if he were praying. Having done this, he ordered one of the ladies to gird on his sword, and she did so with a good deal of refinement and discretion, and a good deal was needed for them not to burst into laughter at each moment of the ceremony, but the great feats they had seen performed by the new knight kept their laughter in check. As she girded on his sword, the good lady said:

"May God make your grace a very fortunate knight and give you good fortune in your fights."

Don Quixote asked her name, so that he might know from that day forth to whom he was obliged for the benison he had received, for he desired to offer her some part of the honor he would gain by the valor of his arm. She answered very humbly that her name was Tolosa, and that she was the daughter of a cobbler from Toledo who lived near the Sancho Bienaya market, and no matter where she might be she would be his servant and consider him her master. Don Quixote replied that for the sake of his love would she have the kindness to henceforth ennoble herself and call herself Doña Tolosa. She promised she would, and the other girl accoutered him with his knightly spurs, and he had almost the same conversation with her as with the one who girded on his sword. He asked her name, and she said she was called Molinera, the miller's girl, and that she was the daughter of an honorable miller from Antequera, and Don Quixote also implored her to ennoble herself and call herself Doña Molinera, offering her more services and good turns.

And so, having performed at a galloping pace these never-before-seen ceremonies, in less than an hour Don Quixote found himself a knight, ready to sally forth in search of adventures, and he saddled Rocinante and mounted him, and, embracing his host, he said such strange things to him, thanking him for the boon of having dubbed him a knight, that it is not possible to adequately recount them. The innkeeper, in order to get him out of the inn, replied with words no less rhetorical but much more brief, and without asking him to pay for the cost of his lodging, he let him leave at an early hour.

Wenstrup's Disappearance

Uwe Timm

Translated from German by Breon Mitchell

Translator's Note

Since its initial appearance in 1978, *Morenga* has taken on the status of a classic in postcolonial German literature. Set in South West Africa in 1904, it traces the rise and fall of the Hottentot rebellion against the German colonial forces, seen through the eyes of a German military veterinarian named Gottschalk. Postmodern in its approach, the novel offers a montage of historical documents and imaginative recreations. Its rich, multilayered texture reflects levels of history from the arrival of European missionaries in Africa to the colonial wars, and foreshadows the tragedy of the later twentieth century.

The novel poses some special problems for the translator. The juxtaposition of historical documents with sometimes quite lyrical passages of Gottschalk's diary, for example, requires a relatively wide register of tone and style. At the same time the language of the novel, both documentary and fictional, remains that of the early-twentieth century. For a great deal of the technical First World War terminology dealing with military equipment and ranks, I am making use of specialized World War I German-English military vocabularies published at the time (like most translators, I've built up a collection of specialized dictionaries in many fields).

In discussing the novel with Uwe Timm in Munich last spring, I was struck by his close attention to historical accuracy, down to the smallest turns of phrase employed by the German military and the sometimes subtle but distinctive ways in which such phrases underline class distinctions. This careful research on all levels has resulted in a historical novel of great power. But above all, Uwe Timm is a master storyteller, and the sweep of his narrative is paramount. In my translation, which is still in progress, I am attempting to be true to both the detail and that larger sense of history rolling toward disaster.

* * *

EARLY IN JANUARY 1905, Wenstrup disappeared. Later on no one could give the exact date of his disappearance. They only knew that he rode out of Keetmannshoop heading southwest on January 2nd, along with his *bambuse,* a Hottentot boy named Jakobus.

Sergeant Wenstrup had been ordered to proceed to Uchanaris, a small military station manned by only a few soldiers, where cattle were said to be dying of anthrax. Wenstrup was supposed to look into this, and if it actually turned out to be anthrax, take appropriate measures. Since they were draft oxen, there was some danger the disease had been transmitted to Keetmannshoop. He had been warned not to travel alone.

True, the Hottentots who lived in Keetmannshoop hadn't joined the uprising, but there were constant rebel ambushes in that area, and you could never trust a Hottentot.

Rather than wait for a patrol to leave for Uchanaris, Wenstrup chose to ride off at once. Gottschalk wasn't the only one struck by such unusual zeal. On the other hand Wenstrup hadn't volunteered to go.

Wenstrup left the village wearing a *chapeau claque* in place of his military cap, and a bright red scarf under his gray uniform. There was nothing unusual about this getup. Most soldiers rode around Keetmannshoop like they were dressed for a beggars' ball. A few wore straw boaters, others shabby paletots. The external distinction between soldiers and rebels was beginning to blur. Military regulations and the elaborate rituals of saluting had worn off in the isolated village, and an almost comradely atmosphere had set in, one that even included the officers. No one excluded the possibility that the rebels might lay siege to the village, or even storm it. Yet all was calm, and Gottschalk even went hunting now and then. Of course he never ventured far enough into the countryside to lose sight of the flag, which would be lowered at the approach of the enemy. The natives were friendly, if somewhat reserved. Their chief had persuaded them not to join the uprising against the Germans. This farsighted man saw opportunities for good business when German reinforcements arrived. Knowledgeable guides and drivers would be needed. Fortunately, headquarters had delivered the entire ration of rum and arrack for the fiscal year 1905 shortly before the outbreak of hostilities. In the cool of the evening the men would sit around their glasses of rum while a band consisting of two trumpets, a drummer, and two accordions played waltzes and marches in turn. A merry time, until the relief party arrived from Uchanaris.

They had neither seen nor heard from the veterinarian Wenstrup. A delay of two or three days wasn't all that unusual in this country, a sergeant said; all it took was a wrong turn somewhere along the way.

Gottschalk had never really understood why Wenstrup volunteered for the southern front in the first place. As a specialist in immunology, Wenstrup had been assigned to the newly founded Institute of Veterinary Medicine in Windhoek. Instead he had practically laid siege to headquarters: He hadn't come all the way to Africa to stare through a microscope, he said. He wanted to smell some gunpowder. Wenstrup talked about this himself at first, and laughed over it, without ever saying why he was pressing the issue. In the end the major, impressed by his stubbornness, issued his marching orders. The man practically glows with enthusiasm at the thought of risking his life for Kaiser, Volk, and Fatherland, the major wrote in his assessment, and even recommended his promotion to lieutenant in the veterinary corps, something his former regimental commander had twice denied. In the field, the major wrote, the inner core of the true man is often revealed, a man whose rough outer shell might seem annoying at times in the peaceful everyday world of the garrison.

Gottschalk's diary entry for November 15th, 1904
The landscape: like the Harz Mountains, but totally denuded and wrung dry. Coming over the pass, the mountains slope gently southward toward a plain we enter slowly through the shimmering heat. All about us the sky arches down to the tips of the yellow blades of grass. The scattered shrubs and bushes are so dry they rattle. The landscape lies open to our gaze. Everything that crowds upon our senses in the city is here a broad expanse at rest. But not for W., who leafs through a pamphlet even as we ride.

During the second bivouac, Gottschalk asked Wenstrup what he had been reading for the past few days. (Gottschalk hesitated a long time before he asked this. He didn't like such questions himself.) The thin frayed volume turned out not to be the inflammatory pamphlet for Social Democrats that Gottschalk had expected, but a pyrotechnics manual for detonators.

Wenstrup handed the book to Gottschalk in silence. Gottschalk leafed through it in confusion, staring at the drawings and data. What was this all about?

In battle, you need all sorts of knowledge. Think, for example, of a grenade fired at a native compound that explodes just as it's launched. The detonator has been mistimed. So it blows up in the face of the crew and anyone else nearby. You have to make sure you're not standing too close.

By the third day Wenstrup was wearing that red scarf. No one said anything to him about it, although between his gray uniform and the equally gray landscape the scarf stood out like a signal lantern.

The detachment was protected by an advance and a rear guard. Patrols flanked both sides of the column, and the officers kept constant watch on the shrub-covered countryside through field glasses. Particularly Schwanebach. The field glasses seemed glued to his eyes.

A lieutenant with six years' experience in Africa told Schwanebach that staring at the countryside was a total waste of time. If the Hottentots were going to ambush them, no one would know it until the first man fell from his saddle. They would never attack in open country. The Hottentots were much more dangerous than the Hereros. They let themselves be slaughtered in battle, but didn't waste much time on prisoners. They stuffed the mouths of the dead with their own severed genitals. Animals, Schwanebach said, keeping the glasses tightly clamped to his eyes.

Wenstrup wanted to know if that was some sort of battle ritual. The lieutenant said no. It was probably because the German troops had raped and mistreated the Herero women during their advance. The furor teutonicus so to speak. But it was Wenstrup who said that.

On 17 November 1904 the detachment reached Reoboth, a village consisting of several whitewashed buildings and a few clay huts.

Smelling water, the oxen leaned eagerly into the harness over the last few kilometers with a strangely dry rattle. Now they were gulping it down, simply pumping themselves full of water, until they slouched away slobbering, with bellies like barrels. Gottschalk reminded the soldiers, many of whom were riding this far on horseback for the first time, to water their mounts carefully, so that they wouldn't develop colic.

The commander of the Southern detachment, Colonel Deimling, wanted to push on from Reoboth toward Rietmont, where Hendrik Witboi and his men were encamped.

*

Wenstrup was still missing. Even after a week there was no sign of life. Those who knew the countryside said that he couldn't have lost his way, since he had the Hottentot boy with him. Jakobus was a Witboi and came from Gibeon, but Wenstrup had been assured that any Hottentot, no matter where he was from, could find his way through the countryside. Gottschalk was suddenly struck by the thought that Jakobus might have murdered Wenstrup. But that would require some motive beyond the quite understandable general hate felt for the Germans, some particular hate for Wenstrup. But when he thought about it, Gottschalk always came back to the absence of any such motive, at least that he could remember. Locals to whom he voiced his suspicion claimed Hottentots were capable of anything. A servant who had been faithful for decades would suddenly slit his sleeping master's throat at night if it were in the tribal interest. No whites had been warned prior to the uprising. Hottentots had no concept of loyalty, at least with regard to the white man. Only the missionary who convinced the elder chief of the Gochha Hottentots not to join the uprising claimed to know of cases where Hottentots had remained loyal to their masters throughout their lives.

The strange thing was that when Gottschalk tried to recall in detail all he knew about Jakobus, he kept coming back to an event that had nothing at all to do with the boy:

In early December of 1904, the detachment moved out from Reoboth toward Rietmont. Colonel Deimling intended to surround and attack the village, which was the tribal seat of the Witbois, and to destroy the Hottentots assembled there under their leader, Hendrik Witboi. The surprise attack took place at Naris, but the Witbois escaped.

During the battle two prisoners were taken. Petite fellows with brown skins. The hands and feet of both men were bound in such a way that they could only move forward in small jerky steps, or by hopping. One of the two prisoners, a young man, wore a colonial guard uniform, apparently stripped from a fallen soldier. Its front, torn by two bullet holes, was caked with dark brown blood.

The arms and legs, which were much too long, were rolled up. Apart from a contusion on the left side of his face, the man was unhurt. Lieutenant Ahrens, who was now Colonel Deimling's adjutant, attempted to interrogate the man. Ahrens wanted to know where his countrymen were headed. (Lieutenant Ahrens actually used the phrase your countrymen.) The man just shook his head in reply to each question. Apparently he wanted to show that he understood the lieutenant, but wasn't going to give him any information. Nevertheless, Ahrens sent for an interpreter. A corporal in the reserves appcared. He'd been living in the country for eleven years, having served as a cavalryman in the lansquenet troops of the Second Imperial Commissioner under Captain von Franoise. Then he bought a place near Hochanas that he farmed until the outbreak of hostilities. The corporal spoke to the prisoner in melodic phrases interspersed with soft clicks. The man stood silently, calmly chewing his plug of tobacco. Da bugger won talk, Lieutenant, the corporal reported in his Mecklenburg dialect. Ahrens ordered him to continue the interrogation, otherwise they would simply shoot him. The corporal translated the death sentence for the prisoner, and his lumbering Mecklenburg tongue was transformed once more into a circus rider, leaping easily and lightly over hurdles and fences with soft clicks and clacks. Gottschalk was startled to hear a loud blow. A trooper had struck the prisoner, who jerked back and fell comically to the ground, entangled in his shackles (those standing around him broke out in laughter). He rose to his feet again without being told, having obvious difficulty with the shackles. Why doesn't he just stay down, thought Gottschalk. When the man was back on his feet, he seemed to smile contemptuously. But it was just the right side of his face, slowly starting to swell. The trooper, a former waiter and specialist at interrogation called Old Shatterhand, was left-handed.

Since the prisoner was now standing there without moving his jaw, Gottschalk thought the force of the blow must have made him swallow his tobacco. But then, after a moment, as his grin grew increasingly lopsided, he started to chew again.

It's hopeless, Lieutenant Ahrens said, and ordered Second Lieutenant von Schwanebach to have the man shot, then added, when he saw that Schwanebach had detailed six men, that's too much trouble. Have him shot from a closer distance. Even one bullet's wasted on his kind.

Chewing his tobacco and grinning, the man stared at the gun of the corporal who had just been trying to question him in Nama. The corporal had volunteered without hesitation. The prisoner simply stood there in the open countryside, free, even in shackles.

This is no execution, Gottschalk said to himself, having always imagined that in an execution the prisoner had to be bound to a stake or at least stood up against a wall. Lieutenant Schwanebach ordered the corporal, who had already taken aim, to lower his weapon, since the man they were about to shoot was still wearing a German uniform.

What should they do? The lieutenant decided that the prisoner should remove the uniform before they shot him, since even if it had been desecrated, it was still the Kaiser's jacket, and remained military property.

They severed the ropes binding the man and ordered him to remove the uniform. Now the man was standing there naked, his face still in a swollen grin, chewing his tobacco. Gottschalk wondered why no one was upset by this complacent chewing, which seemed contemptuous in the face of the raised gun, the lieutenant, and those standing curiously about.

When the rebel was lying on the ground, Schwanebach ordered the veterinarian to make sure if the baboon was dead. Gottschalk bent over the body. A trickle of blood flowed from the mouth like a red thread. In the other corner of his mouth stood a brownish rivulet. Apparently the man had not swallowed his tobacco even when the bullet pierced his heart.

Gottschalk had started to leave before they shot the man. But the lieutenant called him back and ordered him to stay, so that he could declare the prisoner dead according to regulations. At first Gottschalk was tempted to say that wasn't his responsibility, he was only a veterinarian. But he stayed and said nothing, afraid that Schwanebach might reply, exactly, that's just the point. The prisoner's face still bore that broad grin. For a moment, Gottschalk thought the man was only playing dead. He lifted the eyelid carefully, a brown fold of skin that gave the face its strangely Asiatic look. The pupil showed no reflex.

A Dozen Surrealist Poems

Translated from French by Paul Auster

Translator's Note

1968. I WAS TWENTY-ONE, a junior at Columbia, and these poems were among my first attempts at translation. Remember the times: the war in Vietnam, the clamor of politics on College Walk, a year of unending protests, the strike that shut down the university, sit-ins, riots, the arrest of seven hundred students (myself among them). In the light of that tumult (that questioning), the Surrealists were a major discovery for me: poets fighting against the conventions of poetry, poets dreaming of revolution, of how to change the world. Translation, then, was more than just a literary exercise. It was a first step toward breaking free of the shackles of myself, of overcoming my own ignorance. *You must change your life.* Perhaps. Back then, it was more a question of searching for a life, of trying to invent a life I could believe in. . . .

* * *

Paul Éluard

LADY LOVE

She is standing on my lids
And her hair is in mine
She is the form of my hands
And the color of my eyes,
She is swallowed in my shadow
Like a stone against the sky

Her eyes are always open
And she does not let me sleep
In the light of day her dreams
Make suns evaporate,
Make me laugh, cry and laugh,
And speak when I have nothing to say.

Paul Éluard

SECOND NATURE

In honor of the dumb the blind the deaf
To the great black stone upon the shoulders
The world passing away without mystery

But also for the others who know things by their name
The burning of each metamorphosis
The unbroken chain of dawns in the skull
The persistent cries that shatter words

Furrowing the mouth furrowing the eyes
Where maddened colors diffuse the mists of waiting
Propping love against the life the dead dream of
The low-living share the others are slaves
Of love as some are slaves of freedom.

EQUALITY OF THE SEXES

Your eyes have returned from an arbitrary land
Where nothing ever knew the meaning of eyes
Nor the beauty of eyes, or stones,
Or drops of water, or pearls painted on signs,

Naked stones reft of skeleton, o my statue,
The blinding sun has stolen your place in the mirror
And if it seems to obey the forces of evening
It is because your head is sealed, o my statue, beaten

By my love and savage tricks,
My motionless desire, your last support
Carried off without struggle, o my image,
Broken by my weakness and taken in my chains.

André Breton

ALL PARADISE IS NOT LOST

The stone cocks turn to crystal
They defend the dew with battering crests
And then the charming flash of lightning
Strikes the banner of ruins
The sand is no more than a phosphorescent clock
Murmuring midnight
Through the arms of a forgotten woman
No shelter revolving in the fields
Is prepared for Heaven's attacks and retreats
It is here
The house and its hard blue temples bathe in the night
that draws my images
Heads of hair, heads of hair
Evil gathers its strength quite near
But will it want us?

Philippe Soupault

SERVITUDES

Yesterday it was night
but the posters sang
the trees stretched themselves
the barber's wax statue grinned at me
Do not spit
Do not smoke
rays of sunlight in the hand you told me
there were fourteen

I invent unknown streets
new and flowering continents
the newspapers will appear tomorrow
Beware of wet paint
I shall walk naked with a cane in my hand

Hans Arp

WHAT VIOLINS SING IN THEIR BED OF LARD

the elephant is in love with the millimeter

the snail dreams of the moon's defeat
his shoes are pale and purged
like the gelatine rifle of a neo-soldier

the eagle owns the motions of a mind's-eye void
his piss is speckled with gleams

the lion sports a pure and racy gothic mustache
his hide is calm
he cackles like a splotch of encores

the crayfish owns the raspberry's bestial voice
the apple's cunning
the prune's compassion
the pumpkin's lascivity

the cow takes the parchment path
last in a book of flesh
whose every hair weighs a pound

the snake jumps pricking and pricking
around the dishpan of love
filled with arrow-pierced hearts

the butterfly buttered with straw becomes a butterfly in straw
the butterfly buttered with straw becomes a big butterfly
smothered and pappaed in straw

the nightingale pulls heart-stomachs from gut-brains
that is to say the lilies of roses from the carnations of
lilacs
the thumb holds its right foot behind its left ear
its left hand in its right hand
on its left leg jumping over its right ear

BLACK VEINS

in my foggy heart
the ghost of roses dies
A star sits down by my bed
it is old and withered

gray spiders file
toward the horizon of black veins
as if to a sprite's burial
the void sighs

my poor dreams have lost their wings
my poor dreams have lost their flames
they tie their elbows
to the casket of my heart
and dream of gray crumbs

the day reappeared
but I was no longer strong
the sky came down and covered me
I opened my eyes forever

Benjamin Péret

WHAT IS IT?

I call tobacco what is ear
and the gnats cheat by jumping on the ham
where an epic battle between sources
heaves from spiced bread
and glasses that halt the blind from seeing straight
Even if the woman beside me ate a dissecting table
the Chinese prince would lose at roulette
he hides in a valise
like a fountain pen where
a gloved and booted vagabond
notes the rainbow that rose far above the vineyard
after the sale

when wine hesitates to become red or white
and abandons forever the idea of confronting its future
for fear of the one who turns his back
yodeling a tune
on a question of blonde hair
or at least not of brown
or hares killing partridge
so the hunt might yield much
and the wind whistling in the chimneys
prevent the river from sleeping in its bed

Antonin Artaud

THE BOUND MUMMY

Grope for the door, the dead eye
peering from this corpse,
this flayed corpse washing
the hideous silence of your body.

The gold that climbs, the vehement
silence hurled upon your body
and the tree you still carry
and this dead man walking before you.

—See how the spindles turn
In the fibers of the scarlet heart,
this great heart where sky shatters
when the gold swallows your bones—

It is the hard landscape of the chasm
that opens as you walk,
and eternity passes you by
for you cannot cross the bridge

Robert Desnos

AT THE EDGE OF THE WORLD

Babbling in the black street, even at the end, where
the river shudders against the banks.
Tossed from a window—one cigarette-butt blooms into a star.
Again, babbling in the black street.
You loud mouths!
Thick night, unbreathable night.
A cry comes near, is almost upon us,
But fades at the moment it arrives.

Somewhere, in the world, at the foot of a slope,
A deserter is talking with sentinels who do not understand
his language.

LIKE A HAND AT THE MOMENT OF DEATH

Like a hand at the moment of death the shipwreck looms like rays of drowsing sun; from all directions your glances have aged.

There is no longer time, there is no longer time, perhaps, to see me.

But the leaf that falls and the wheel that turns will tell you that nothing on this earth ever lasts.

Except love.

And I want to convince myself of it.

Lifeboats painted red,

Storms that flee,

An old-fashioned waltz that bears wind and weather across long spaces of sky.

Countrysides.

I only want the embrace I yearn for,

And the rooster's song is dying.

Like the clenching of a hand at the moment of death, my heart contracts.

Since I've known you I have never cried.

I love my love too much to cry.
You will cry at my grave,
Or I at yours.
It will never be too late.
I'll tell a lie. I'll say you were my mistress
For it's all so futile,
You and I, we'll soon be dead.

Louis Aragon

MIMOSAS TO DEMORALIZATION

The government had just fallen
In a hawthorn bush
Under the combined influences of moon and cephalogy
A general strike was growing as far as the eye could see
Assassins fled into the vast of air
Victims hung like steaks from the grill
Murderous heat
The barracks must have heard some good ones
Alcohol waves roared through the skylights
The subway surfaced to breathe
When suddenly there appeared
At the corner of the street
A puny ass dragging a cart
Decorated for the battle of flowers
First prize for this city
And the neighboring ones as well

Two Germans

Alberto Moravia

Translated from Italian by William Weaver

TRANSLATOR'S NOTE

THE FOLLOWING STORY, *"Due tedeschi,"* was originally published in the Milanese newspaper *Corriere d'informazione,* on August 18, 1945.

From the beginning of his long career to his death, Moravia regularly published stories in periodicals. Every few years he would then make a selection, which was issued as a volume. A short time ago two young scholars, Simone Casini and Francesca Serra, having unearthed many of Moravia's exclusions, produced an anthology, *Racconti dispersi 1928–1951* (Bompiani, Milan, 2000), in which this story was reprinted.

In September 1943, threatened with arrest by the German forces occupying Rome, Moravia—with his wife, Elsa Morante—fled the city, taking the train for Naples. The train had to stop at the town of Fondi because the tracks had been destroyed. The writers found refuge in a primitive mountain hut. The Allied troops were expected to arrive within days, but instead they appeared only after Moravia and Morante had spent nine months in their unpaved, unheated lodging. Morante drew on this experience for a part of her novel *History;* Moravia used their retreat as the setting for his novel *La ciociara* (*Two Women*). It is likely that he excluded this brief story from subsequent collections because he had depicted the area and its people in that novel.

* * *

THEY STOPPED AND LOOKED at me. I looked back at them. The sergeant could have been thirty. He was tall, thin, robust, with narrow hips, a slim waist, legs that—thanks to the tight trousers stuffed into his boots—seemed longer than they were. His short tunic left his skinny buttocks exposed. He was blonde, but an ugly, dull blonde, washed out. His white face was battered but symmetrical, like a piece of fruit that had fallen and rolled on the ground: the brow crowned by a tuft of hair, the temples shaven, the cheeks swollen, the chin slightly crooked beneath the full lips. His eyes were blue, but—like his hair—they were ugly and dull; the dark hollows around his eyes lent his gaze, unprotected by eyelashes, a grim, somehow furious air. Between cheekbone and nose the skin made a fold and on his cheeks there were two long marks, like slashes: wounds from the war or from dueling. Hanging at his thigh was a heavy pistol in its leather sheath.

The private was surely over forty. He was of medium height, but his broad shoulders made him look short. The shoulders were heavy and thick as well as broad; it looked as if below his neck he was as hairy as an animal. He had a flat, wide face, brown and greasy, to which the small, deep-set eyes, sly, gave a brutally crafty look. His uniform made you think he slept in it and had never removed it throughout the whole war, the tunic and the trousers were so faithfully wedded to the shape of that big body. Hunched, relaxed, untidy, almost kindly, he emanated a sense of professional ferocity, like a man who by now killed and destroyed as if performing a job, thinking of the war as a thing ancient, normal, accepted. He carried his gun over his shoulder and in his fist had a handful of almonds that he cracked, one by one, between his teeth, shutting his eyes and tilting his head.

There were about ten of us Italians, dressed in rags, with ruined shoes, suffering the cold air of the winter afternoon. This was the first time the Germans had ventured up here on this mountain where I had sought safety with some other refugees. Since I knew a little German, the frightened Italians pressed me to speak to the two and find out what they wanted.

I mustered a smile and asked if they needed anything. The sergeant asked me, "Where did you learn German?"

"In Munich."

"Have you been to Berlin?"

"Yes."

"I'm from Berlin," he said, but without pride. And he added, "Berlin kaputt," making an expressive gesture with his hand. I didn't say anything. He went on. "We Germans fight war . . . why you Italians don't fight war?"

I tried to change the subject, asking him if he had been in Russia. All those other poor wretches were actually holding their breath, hearing me handle the German words as if they were dangerous weapons. The sergeant looked at them and pointed. "People like that," he said, "in Germany are in the army." He seemed furious and in his blue eyes a red, feral light had been kindled.

"What did he say? What's he saying?" the others asked, seeing him point to them.

"He said you should fight the war," I answered. One of them said in a low voice, "Asshole."

The sergeant continued. "In Germany all men fight . . . millions have died already. . . . Millions," he repeated, in an exasperated voice, "are buried in Russia."

I didn't say anything, I simply shook my head, in a deprecatory manner. But I was thinking it wasn't such a bad thing that all those Germans were safely underground. He seemed to sense my thought and, shaking a finger under my nose, he shouted, "The Italians are all traitors."

"What's he say? What's he say?" the others repeated.

"According to him, we're all traitors," I said as I translated resentfully. The German observed the effect produced by his words and confirmed them, nodding his head. Then he announced, "But we'll soon start an offensive and we'll drive the English into the sea."

"When?"

He looked up to consult the cloudy sky and answered gravely, "As soon as the weather improves." He studied me for a moment, as if reflecting, then added, "We'll take the offensive and all you Italians will die of hunger."

"Why?"

"Because the trains will be used to transport munitions and supplies, and we'll have to find the food for our soldiers on the spot . . . then we'll come into your houses"—he pointed to the humble huts and scattered shacks on that height—"and we'll confiscate everything you have."

This declaration alarmed me; I felt it wasn't an empty threat. The refugees saw the dismay on my face, and they started up again: "What's he say? What's he say?"

"He says we'll die of hunger."

Behind me someone murmured, "He's right."

To avenge myself, but assuming a respectful and apprehensive manner, I said, "It's rumored that in Russia things aren't going so well for us."

He didn't allow that "us" to deceive him; he gave me an angry look and muttered contemptuously, "Some repositioning of the front." Then, strangely calm all of a sudden, he explained, "We have a line of bunkers . . . we'll stop at that line."

I remembered that all Germans were obsessed by the idea of secret weapons. "Anyway," I added, "you have nothing to worry about . . . you have your secret weapons."

"Yes," he replied, not catching the sarcasm, "our secret weapons will make us win the war . . . the Führer said so." He looked at me for a moment and added, "When the war's over, traitors will be punished."

"What do you men do in civilian life?" I asked, to deflect the conversation.

"I had cardboard-box factory," he said. And, waving his hand, he added with strange, scrupulous precision, "Nothing big, however . . . a hundred, hundred and fifty workers."

"What about him?" I asked, pointing to the private.

"He was a construction worker."

"Well," I said, "when the war's over, after you've punished the traitors, you can go back to your factory and he to his construction site."

At these words, that red, furious light blazed again in his eyes. "My factory's destroyed," he shouted, "and him . . . he's lost his house . . . his wife is dead, his two children are dead. . . . We go on fighting the war. Isn't that so?" he said, addressing the private, who had been following the conversation. "We'll go on making war?"

Then the private spoke for the first time. He said, giving me a sidelong glance, without bitterness, with dismal calm, "We'll go on making war . . . here." He waved toward the distant plain. "Everything will be destroyed: houses, trees, roads, bridges, vineyards, crops . . . and if we retreat, everything will still be destroyed, so nothing will be left to the enemy . . . and if we advance, everything will be destroyed to make way for us. You still haven't seen anything . . . just wait." He sketched a smile, and stuck an almond between his teeth.

"How long will the war last?" I asked.

The sergeant reflected for a moment, then answered with a shrug, "Two years, three years, four years—what does it matter?"

Again dismay was obvious on my face, again the listeners asked me: "What's he say? What's he say?"

"That the war will last four years."

The sergeant signaled to the private and, without a word to us, they went off, up the mule track. A drizzle was falling from the low, dark sky. The refugees went off in the rain, repeating "four years." I was thinking that the air of Germany had come up here with those two soldiers and there was no telling how many more days we would breathe it.

Twelve Poems *from* Serres Chaudes

Maurice Maeterlinck

Translated from French by Richard Howard

Translator's Note

In 1886 a twenty-three-year-old esthete, son of a Flemish family prominent among the wealthy bourgeoisie of Ghent, finished a first collection of poems, *Hothouses,* from which I have translated the first dozen poems; the entire sequence (to be published presently by Princeton) articulates a sort of miasmatic plot which Maeterlinck began to develop, by 1890, into a series of prose dramas. These works caught the world's attention and favor—in 1912 the playwright (who had also translated *Macbeth* and *'Tis Pity She's a Whore*) was awarded the Nobel Prize, having already won the admiration of Chekhov and Proust. Wisps of free verse among the seemly symbolist stanzas are a premonition of dissolutions to come—modernism's first gasps.

* * *

I. HOTHOUSE

A hothouse deep in the woods,
doors forever sealed. Analogies:
everything under that glass dome,
everything under my soul.

Thoughts of a starving princess,
A sailor marooned in the desert,
fanfares at hospital windows.

Seek out the warmest corners!
Think of a woman fainting on harvest day;
postillions ride into the hospital courtyard;
a soldier passes, he is a sick nurse now.

Look at it all by moonlight
(nothing is where it belongs).
Think of a madwoman haled before judges,
a man-of-war in full sail on the canal,
nightbirds perched among the lilies,
a knell at noon
(out there under those glass bell jars),
cripples halted in the fields
on a day of sunshine, the smell of ether.

My God, when will the rain come,
and the snow, and the wind, to this glass house!

II. PRAYER

Pity this hesitation of mine
 to speak "the name of action,"
for my soul lies waxen and inert,
  washed transparent

by her own tears, and such indolence
 leaves every task undone:
these helpless hands can only bother
  what they must abort.

And as I watch the lilac bubbles
 rise—O iridescent dreams!—
my soul douses the moon to dimness
  with weary gestures:

yet even that dim moonlight betrays
 tomorrow's yellowed lilies,
revealing no revels but the sad
  shadows of my hands.

III. HOTHOUSE ENNUI

O this heart, perpetually blue!
 even with the best vision,
lachrymose by moonlight, of
  my indolent blue dreams;

bored heart, blue as the hothouse
 showing everything blue
through blind glass, slick with moonlight
  and hoarfrost, or is it

only the glass? Suffocating fronds
 by night extend their shadows
motionlessly, as dreams do,
  over passion's roses,

and very slowly the water rises,
 compromising moon and sky
in one endless blue-green sob
  monotonous as dreams.

IV. TEMPTATIONS

O the blind temptations
  amid mental shadows
the fiery blooms of
  these ejaculations

Dark the stems very dark
  by moonlight's malady
but rich the auguries
  of this autumnal hour

Within the slimed embrace
  of their complicit ills
a lichen green as frost
  has sickened the sad moon

Slaking secret desires
their desecrating growth
is woeful as the woes
of sick men crossing snow

In the ghosts of their grief
how many wounds mingle
the blue swords of my lust
the red flesh of my pride

Lord God let dreams of earth
die at last in my heart
Let your glory my Lord
clarify this bad glass

The leaves dead of fevers
and lethe sought in vain
the stars between their lips
the viscera of sin!

V. GLASS BELL JARS

Strange plants eternally sheltered
under glass bell jars
while the wind stirs my senses out of doors!
An entire valley of the soul eternally frozen
and the heat trapped here by noon
the images glimpsed on the curve of each bell!

Never lift one of these.
Some have been set on old pools of moonlight
peer through the foliage:
is that a beggar on the throne
do pirates lurk on every pond
are primeval creatures about to invade our cities?

Some have been set on old snowbanks
some float on stale puddles of rain
(pity that imprisoned air!) I hear

people keeping carnival on Hungry Sunday
an ambulance is parked in the harvest fields
and on fast days all the king's daughters wander
across the pastures.

Just look at those on the horizon
how carefully they mask immemorial storms!
Somewhere there must be a vast armada in the marshes
and I think the swans have hatched . . . crows!
(it's hard to see in all this wet)
A virgin pours hot water on the ferns
the hermit in his cell is observed by a troupe of little girls
deep in some foul cave my sisters have fallen asleep!

Wait for winter and the moon at last
on these bell jars strewn across the ice.

VI. HUMBLE OFFERING

I bring my bad work, analogous
to the dreams of dead men
and the moon only adds to the storm
breaking over the brutes of my remorse:

purple snakes of nightmare castigate
what passes for my sleep,
all my desires are crowned with drawn swords,
and lions drowned in nothing but the sun,

lilies drowning too in distant pools;
hands are forever closed,
and between the red tendrils of hate
show love's emerald tendrils—widow's weeds!

Lord, take pity on the words of men!
Let these weary prayers
and a moon disheveled among reeds
reap the night to the world's farthest rim!

VII. HEART'S FOLIAGE

Under the blue bell jar
  of my listless moods
griefs are suffocated,
  gradually stilled:

"A forest of symbols":
  sleepy lotuses,
soft mosses, slack vines, slow
  palms of my desires. . . .

Among these one lily,
  rigid, weak, and pale,
mounts like a moon above
  the muttering leaves,

And by that luster so
  impassively shed
presses white orisons
  up against the glass.

VIII. FEVERED SOUL

O my eyes these shadows manifest,
  falling across each desire,
and my heart enthralled by shadows too—
  miasma within the soul!

I have steeped in blue rumination
  the roses of failed attempts,
and my lashes are closed upon vows
  no longer to be made.

Night after night my indolent hands
  unavailingly set out
the emerald glass bell jars of hope
  in these forsaken gardens.

And my impotent soul, as I grope
  among the lilies, trembles
with fear of the dreams that choke my breath. . . .
  In my faltering heart, eclipse!

IX. MY SOUL

Too sheltered, O my soul,
and these flocks of my desires, under glass!
until the storm breaks over the fields

Let us seek out the sick, the worst cases—
strange fumes rising,
and among them I cross a field of battle with my mother.
They are burying a brother-in-arms at noon
while the sentries are at mess.

And seek out the weak, the worst cases—
strange sweats glistening,
here is a sick bride,
betrayed one Sunday
and little children in prison.
And over there, through the mist,
is that a woman dying at her kitchen door?
Or is it a Sister shelling peas at a sick man's bedside?

Then seek out the saddest
(last of all, for they have poisons):
O my lips accept the kisses of a wounded man!
And in my soul's castle-keeps this summer
every chatelaine has starved to death

Dawn breaks on the holiday!
and I glimpse the sheep down on the quays:
there is a sail passing the hospital windows.

It is a long road from heart to my soul,
And all the sentries are dead at their post.

One day there was a festival, a poor little celebration
in the suburbs of my soul
They were cutting down the hemlock one Sunday
morning;
And all the convent virgins were watching the boats
passing
on the canal, it was a fast day, and sunny.
While swans were choking under a rotting bridge;
they were pruning the trees around the prison,
and bringing medicine, one afternoon in June,
and meals for the sick were set out everywhere!

O my soul, and the sadness of these things,
the sadness of it all!

X. LASSITUDE

They have forgotten kisses that can make
Cold eyes warm and blind eyes see again;
Henceforth surrendered to complacent dreams,
They torpidly watch, like hounds in tall grass.
The flock of gray lambs on the horizon
Cropping the moonlight spread across a field
Caressed by skies as vague as their own life;
Indifferent and not once envying
The happy roses blooming underfoot—
A long green peace they cannot understand.

XI. WEARY HUNTING

A malady! crammed with absences,
silences, surely
my soul is a sick soul, and the light
of my eyes is spent.

All pursuits are paralyzed under
memory's blue lash,

and the secret hounds of desire
  follow a faint spoor.

In sopping woods, the hunt is met—
  the white stag of lies
efficiently brought down by regret:
  those jaundiced arrows!

Lord, how the tepid lust of my eyes
  and my winded wants
have shrouded with signs the hunter's moon
  that once lit my soul!

XII. WEARY BEASTS

O my passions on the paths,
  laughter, and sobbing!
Ailing, and eyes half-shut
  among fallen leaves,

the yellow hounds of my sins,
  loathing's hyenas,
and on the colorless plains
  love's couchant lions!

In the impotence of their dream
  and languid under the spell
of that colorless sky, they gaze
  unceasingly, unblinking.

at my temptations, so many sheep
  one by one slowly leaving
in the motionless moonlight,
  my motionless passions.

From The Way by Swann's
Marcel Proust
Translated from French by Lydia Davis

TRANSLATOR'S NOTE

THE FOLLOWING EXTRACT CLOSES the "Combray" section of *The Way by Swann's.* After it, comes the self-contained love story, "A Love of Swann's," and then the codalike "Place-Names: The Name." The Combray section includes many of the most famous scenes from Proust's *In Search of Lost Time:* the opening insomniac confusions; the tasting of the madeleine; the bedtime drama of the mother's goodnight kiss. This extract shows the young Narrator for the first time translating his rapture over a thing of the outside world into a piece of writing.

Proust began *Du Côté de chez Swann* sometime in 1907 or 1908. It evolved out of an idea he had for an essay refuting the theories of the critic Sainte-Beuve, and it incorporated earlier pieces of writing, including articles previously published in *Le Figaro* and scenes from an unfinished novel, *Jean Santeuil.* Once the book was written, Proust had immense trouble finding a publisher for it, and finally paid for its publication himself. When *Du Côté de chez Swann* appeared in 1913, it was well received but did not win unanimous praise.

In 1920, C. K. Scott Moncrieff, already the accomplished translator of, among others, *The Song of Roland* and Stendhal's *The Charterhouse of Parma,* left his job at the London *Times* to devote himself full-time to working on an English version of Proust's novel, and what was advertised as the "first installment," *Swann's Way,* was published by Chatto and Windus in 1922, the same year Proust died. This version was revised once by Terence Kilmartin (1981) and a second time by D. J. Enright (1992), and though in fact another translation exists—a version by James Grieve, also titled *Swann's Way,* was published in Australia in 1982 but not widely distributed or read—it has remained the classic English translation in which Anglophones have up to now first become acquainted with Proust.

About five years ago, I was invited by Penguin UK to translate this first volume of *A La Recherche du temps perdu* for its Classics series, as part of a team of translators, each of whom would produce one volume of the seven, the whole to be published simultaneously in the fall of 2002. Most of the others on the team are translators, critics, and professors at universities in England; one is a writer and professor in Australia; I am the only American. We have all been working on this project at different speeds and levels of efficiency for the past few years, with breaks for other work. There was some use of e-mail among us to discuss terms, but time and distraction and other commitments did not allow for the sort of ongoing discussion at a deeper level that would have been so fascinating.

I had already translated over thirty books from French when I began work on *Du Côté de chez Swann.* I anticipated that this project would be similar to previous translations in some respects and different in others, but of course these samenesses and differences were not entirely predictable. I felt more exhilaration and more trepidation beginning the work than I had felt embarking on, say, the comfortably private transformations of Jardin's *Alexis de Tocqueville* or Michel Leiris's *Scratches* or Pierre Jean Jouve's *Hélène,* because I knew that whatever the merits of other books I had done, this one by Proust was the most highly regarded and the work I did on it would eventually come under close scrutiny. And yet I did proceed with it in much the same way I nearly always have with a translation: reading only a page or two ahead, sometimes not even that; following the French as closely as I could word for word; maintaining a deliberate naiveté with regard to the book and Proust himself as long as I was working on the first draft. When I work this way, there is a freshness, a sense of adventure into the unknown, that makes the translation more exciting to me and more lively on the page, I think.

One difference from previous translations, I began to discover, was that I explored each French word and each English word so thoroughly, more thoroughly than I ever had before—partly out of a desire to get it all absolutely right, partly out of simple curiosity and fun. It's the sort of thing I like to do anyway, and now I had a good excuse—there was no doubt that this book deserved whatever care I could put into it. I read French etymologies, which I had never done before; I made use of more dictionaries than ever before, including a French-English dictionary published when Proust was fourteen, which would give me definitions contemporaneous with Proust; I learned distinctions I had not known existed, as between *l'aube* and *l'aurore,* dawn and the aurora (first light and first color in the sky);

I learned at last never to be casual about synonyms—that there really are no such things as synonyms in translation: *anyway* and *in any case,* or *of course* and *naturally,* evolved differently, contain different metaphors, and have different sounds, rhythms, and syllable counts.

Yet another difference was that, as I grew aware of how Proust was handling the language, quite beyond or within the fantastically complex structures of his long sentences with their many dependent clauses, how he was embedding alexandrines or building parallel structures with heavy use of alliteration and assonance, I began trying to do the same wherever I could. A single sentence would thus often require the writing and rewriting, the fiddling and refining, that might have gone into the translating of a piece of verse. This meant that the translation proceeded at a very slow pace and, since the manuscript was over 550 pages, went on for a long time. Then, like the distant steeples of Martinville, the end was suddenly in front of me.

* * *

HOW MUCH MORE DISTRESSING STILL, after that day, during my walks along the Guermantes way, did it seem to me than it had seemed before to have no aptitude for literature, and to have to give up all hope of ever being a famous writer! The sorrow I felt over this, as I daydreamed alone, a little apart from the others, made me suffer so much that in order not to feel it anymore, my mind of its own accord, by a sort of inhibition in the face of pain, would stop thinking altogether about poems, novels, a poetic future on which my lack of talent forbade me to depend. Then, quite apart from all these literary preoccupations and not connected to them in any way, suddenly a roof, a glimmer of sun on a stone, the smell of the road would stop me because of a particular pleasure they gave me, and also because they seemed to be concealing, beyond what I could see, something which they were inviting me to come take and which despite my efforts I could not manage to discover. Since I felt that it could be found within them, I would stay there, motionless, looking, breathing, trying to go with my thoughts beyond the image or the smell. And if I had to catch up with my grandfather, continue on my way, I would try to find them again by closing my eyes; I would concentrate on recalling precisely the line of the roof, the shade of the stone which, without my being able to understand why, had seemed to me so full, so ready to open, to yield me the thing for which they themselves were merely a cover. Of course it was not impressions of this kind that could give me back the hope I had lost, of succeeding in becoming a writer and a poet some day, because they were always tied to a particular object with no intellectual value and no reference to any abstract truth. But at least they gave me an unreasoning pleasure, the illusion of a sort of fecundity, and so distracted me from the tedium, from the sense of my own impotence which I had felt each time I looked for a philosophical subject for a great literary work. But the task imposed on my conscience by the impressions I received from form, fragrance, or color was so arduous—to try to perceive what was concealed behind them—that I would soon look for excuses that would allow me to save myself from this effort and spare myself this fatigue. Fortunately, my parents would call me, I would feel I did not have the tranquillity I needed at the moment for pursuing my search in a useful way, and that it would be better not to think about it anymore until I was back at home, and not to fatigue myself beforehand to no purpose. And so I would stop concerning myself with this unknown thing that was enveloped in a form or a fragrance, feeling quite easy in my mind since I was bringing it back to the house protected by the covering of images under which I would find it alive, like the fish that, on days when I had been allowed to go fishing, I would carry home in my creel covered by a layer of grass that kept them fresh. Once I was back at the house I would think about other things, and so there would accumulate in my mind (as in my room the flowers I had gathered on my walks or objects I had been given) a stone on which a glimmer of light played, a roof, the sound of a bell, a smell of leaves, many different images beneath which the reality I sensed but did not have enough determination to discover had died long before. Once, however—when our walk had extended far beyond its usual duration and we were very happy to encounter halfway home, as the afternoon was ending, Doctor Percepied who, going past at full speed in his carriage, recognized us and invited us to climb in with him—I had an impression of this kind and did not abandon it without studying it a little. They had had me climb up next to the coachman, we were going like the wind because, before returning to Combray, the doctor still had to stop at Martinville-le-Sec to see a patient at whose door it had been agreed that we would wait for him. At the bend of a road I suddenly experienced that special pleasure which was unlike any other, when I saw the two steeples of Martinville, shining in the setting sun and appearing to change position with the motion of our carriage and the windings of the road, and then the steeple of Vieuxvicq, which, though separated from them by a hill and a valley and situated on a higher plateau in the distance, seemed to be right next to them.

As I observed, as I noted the shape of their spires, the shifting of their lines, the sunlight on their surfaces, I felt that I was not reaching the full depth of my impression, that something was behind that motion, that brightness, something which they seemed at once to contain and conceal.

The steeples appeared so distant, and we seemed to approach them so slowly, that I was surprised when we stopped a few moments later in front of the Martinville church. I did not know why I had taken such pleasure in the sight of them on the horizon and the obligation to try to discover the reason seemed to me quite painful; I wanted to hold in reserve in my head those lines moving in the sun, and not think about them anymore now. And it is quite likely that had I done so, the two steeples would have gone forever to join the many trees, rooftops, fragrances, sounds, that I had distinguished from others because of the obscure pleasure they gave me which I never thoroughly studied. I got down to talk to my parents while we waited for the doctor. Then we set off again, I was back in my place on the seat, I turned my head to see the steeples again, a little later glimpsing them one last time at a bend in the road. Since the coachman, who did not seem inclined to talk, had hardly answered anything I said, I was obliged, for lack of other company, to fall back on my own and try to recall my steeples. Soon their lines and their sunlit surfaces split apart, as if they were a sort of bark, a little of what was hidden from me inside them appeared to me, I had a thought which had not existed a moment before, which took shape in words in my head, and the pleasure I had just recently experienced at the sight of them was so increased by this that, seized by a sort of drunkenness, I could no longer think of anything else. At that moment, as we were already far away from Martinville, turning my head I caught sight of them again, quite black this time, for the sun had already set. At moments the bends of the road would hide them from me, then they showed themselves one last time, and finally I did not see them again.

Without saying to myself that what was hidden behind the steeples of Martinville had to be something analogous to a pretty sentence, since it had appeared to me in the form of words that gave me pleasure, I asked the doctor for a pencil and some paper and I composed, despite the jolts of the carriage, and in order to ease my conscience and yield to my enthusiasm, the following little piece that I have since found again and that I have not had to submit to more than a few changes:

"Alone, rising from the level of the plain, and appearing lost in the open country, the two steeples of Martinville ascended toward the sky. Soon we saw three: wheeling around boldly to position itself opposite them, the laggard steeple of Vieuxvicq had come along to join them. The minutes were passing, we were going fast, and yet the three steeples were still far away ahead of us, like three birds poised on the plain, motionless, distinguishable in the sunlight. Then the steeple of Vieuxvicq moved away, receded into the distance, and the steeples of Martinville remained alone, illuminated by the light of the setting sun, which even at that distance I saw playing and smiling on their sloping sides. We had taken so long approaching them that I was thinking about the time we would still need in order to reach them, when suddenly the carriage turned and set us down at their feet; and they had flung themselves so roughly in front of us that we had only just time to stop in order not to run into the porch. We continued on our way; we had already left Martinville a little while before, and the village, after accompanying us for a few seconds, had disappeared, when, lingering alone on the horizon to watch us flee, its steeples and that of Vieuxvicq were still waving goodbye with their sunlit tops. At times one of them would draw aside so that the other two could glimpse us again for an instant; but the road changed direction, they swung round in the light like three golden pivots and disappeared from my gaze. But a little later, when we were already close to Combray, and the sun had set, I caught sight of them one last time from very far away, seeming now no more than three flowers painted on the sky above the low line of the fields. They reminded me, too, of the three young girls in a legend, abandoned in a solitary place where darkness was already falling; and while we moved off at a gallop, I saw them timidly seek their way and, after some awkward stumbling of their noble silhouettes, press against one another, slip behind one another, now forming, against the still pink sky, no more than a single black shape, charming and resigned, and fade away into the night." I never thought of this page again, but at that moment, when in the corner of the seat where the doctor's coachman usually placed in a basket the poultry he had bought at the market in Martinville, I had finished writing it, I was so happy, I felt it had so perfectly relieved me of those steeples and what they had been hiding behind them, that, as if I myself were a hen and had just laid an egg, I began to sing at the top of my voice.

All day long, during those walks, I had been able to dream about what a pleasure it would be, to be a friend of the Duchesse de Guermantes, to fish for trout, to go out in a boat on the Vivonne, and, greedy for happiness, ask no more from life in those moments than for it always to be made up of a succession of happy afternoons. But when on the way back I saw on the left a farm which was fairly distant from two others very close to each other, and from which, in order to enter Combray, one had only to go down an avenue of oaks bordered on one side by meadows, each of which was part of a little enclosure and was planted at equal intervals with apple trees that wore, when they were lit by the setting sun, the Japanese design of their shadows, my heart would abruptly begin to beat faster, I would know that within half an hour we would be home and that, as was the rule on the days when we had gone the Guermantes way and dinner was served later, they would send me to bed as soon as I had had my soup, so that my mother, kept at table as though there were company for dinner, would not come up to say goodnight to me in my bed. The region of sadness I had just entered was as distinct from the region into which I had hurled myself with such joy only a moment before, as in certain skies a band of pink is separated as though by a line from a band of green or a band of black. One sees a bird fly into the pink, it is about to reach the end of it, it is nearly touching the black, then it has entered it. The desires that had surrounded me a short time ago, to go to Guermantes, to travel, to be happy, were so far behind me now that their fulfillment would not have brought me any pleasure. How I would have given all that up in order to be able to cry all night in Mama's arms! I was trembling, I did not take my anguished eyes off my mother's face, which would not be appearing that evening in the room where I could already see myself in my thoughts, I wanted to die. And that state of mind would continue until the following day, when the morning rays, like the gardener, would lean their bars against the wall clothed in nasturtiums that climbed up to my window, and I would jump out of bed to hurry down into the garden, without remembering, now, that evening would ever bring back with it the hour for leaving my mother. And so it was from the Guermantes way that I learned to distinguish those states of mind that follow one another in me, during certain periods, and that even go so far as to share out each day among them, one returning to drive out the other, with the punctuality of a fever; contiguous, but so exterior to one another, so lacking in means of communication among them, that I can no longer comprehend, no longer even picture to myself in one, what I desired, or feared, or accomplished in the other.

And so the Méséglise way and the Guermantes way remain for me linked to many of the little events of that life which, of all the various lives we lead concurrently, is the most abundant in sudden reversals of fortune, the richest in episodes, I mean our intellectual life. No doubt it progresses within us imperceptibly, and the truths that have changed its meaning and its appearance for us, that have opened new paths to us, we had been preparing to discover for a long time; but we did so without knowing it; and for us they date only from the day, from the minute in which they became visible. The flowers that played on the grass then, the water that flowed past in the sunlight, the whole landscape that surrounded their appearance continues to accompany the memory of them with its unconscious or abstracted face; and certainly when they were slowly studied by that humble passerby, that child dreaming—as a king is studied by a memorialist lost in the crowd—that corner of nature, that bit of garden could not have believed it would be thanks to him that they would be elected to survive in all their most ephemeral details; and yet the fragrance of hawthorn that forages along the hedge where the wild roses will soon replace it, a sound of echoless steps on the gravel of an alley, a bubble formed against a water plant by the current of the stream and bursting immediately—my exaltation has borne them along with it and managed to carry them across so many years in succession, while the paths round about have disappeared and those who trod on them, and the memory of those who trod on them, are dead. At times the piece of landscape thus transported into the present detaches itself in such isolation from everything else that it floats uncertain in my mind like a flowery Delos, while I cannot say from which country, which time—perhaps quite simply which dream—it comes. But it is, most especially, as deep layers of my mental soil, as the firm ground on which I still stand, that I must think of the Méséglise way and the Guermantes way. It is because I believed in things and in people while I walked along them, that the things and the people they revealed to me are the only ones I still take seriously today and that still bring me joy. Whether it is because the faith which creates has dried up in me, or because reality takes shape only in memory, the flowers I am shown today for the first time do not seem to me to be real flowers. The Méséglise way with its lilacs, its hawthorns, its cornflowers, its poppies, its apple trees, the

Guermantes way with its river full of tadpoles, its water lilies and buttercups, formed for me for all time the contours of the countrysides where I would like to live, where I demand above all else that I may go fishing, drift about in a boat, see ruins of Gothic fortifications and find among the wheatfields a church, like Saint-André-des-Champs, monumental, rustic and golden as a haystack; and the cornflowers, the hawthorns, the apple trees that I still happen, when traveling, to come upon in the fields, because they are situated at the same depth, on the level of my past, communicate immediately with my heart. And yet, because places have something individual about them, when I am seized by the desire to see the Guermantes way again, you would not satisfy it by taking me to the bank of a river where the water lilies were just as beautiful, more beautiful than in the Vivonne, any more than on my return home in the evening—at the hour when there awakened in me that anguish which later emigrates into love, and may become forever inseparable from it—I would have wished that the mother who came to say goodnight to me would be one more beautiful and more intelligent than my own. No; just as what I needed so that I could go to sleep happy, with that untroubled peace which no mistress has been able to give me since that time because one doubts them even at the moment one believes in them, and can never possess their hearts as I received in a kiss my mother's heart, complete, without the reservation of an afterthought, without the residue of an intention that was not for me—was that it should be her, that she should incline over me that face marked below the eye by something that was, it seems, a blemish, and which I loved as much as the rest, so what I want to see again is the Guermantes way that I knew, with the farm that is not very far from the two that come after pressed so close together, at the entrance to the avenue of oaks; those meadows on which, when the sun turns them reflective as a pond, the leaves of the apple trees are sketched, that landscape whose individuality sometimes, at night in my dreams, clasps me with an almost uncanny power and which I can no longer recover when I wake up. No doubt, by virtue of having forever indissolubly united in me the different impressions merely because they had caused me to experience them at the same time, the Méséglise way and the Guermantes way exposed me, for the future, to many disappointments and even to many mistakes. For often I have wanted to see a person again without discerning that it was simply because she reminded me of a hedge of hawthorns, and I have been induced to believe, to make someone else believe, in a revival of affection, by what was simply a desire to travel. But because of that very fact, too, and by remaining present in those of my impressions of today to which they may be connected, they give them foundations, depth, a dimension lacking from the others. They add to them, too, a charm, a meaning that is for me alone. When on summer evenings the melodious sky growls like a wild animal and everyone grumbles at the storm, it is because of the Méséglise way that I am the only one in ecstasy inhaling, through the noise of the falling rain, the smell of invisible, enduring lilacs.

Thus I would often lie until morning thinking back to the time at Combray, to my sad sleepless evenings, to the many days, too, whose image had been restored to me more recently by the taste—what they would have called at Combray the "perfume"—of a cup of tea, and, by an association of memories, to what, many years after leaving that little town, I had learned, about a love affair Swann had had before I was born, with that precision of detail which is sometimes easier to obtain for the lives of people who died centuries ago than for the lives of our best friends, and which seems as impossible as it once seemed impossible to speak from one town to another—as long as we do not know about the expedient by which that impossibility was circumvented. All these memories added to one another now formed a single mass, but one could still distinguish between them—between the oldest, and those that were more recent, born of a perfume, and then those that were only memories belonging to another person from whom I had learned them—if not fissures, if not true faults, at least that veining, that variegation of coloring, which in certain rocks, in certain marbles, reveal differences in origin, in age, in "formation."

Of course by the time morning approached, the brief uncertainty of my waking would long since have dissipated. I knew which room I was actually in, I had reconstructed it around me in the darkness and—either by orienting myself with memory alone, or by making use, as a clue, of a faint glimmer that I perceived, under which I placed the casement curtains—I had reconstructed it entirely and furnished it like an architect and a decorator who retain the original openings of the windows and doors, I had put back the mirrors and restored the chest of drawers to its usual place. But scarcely had the daylight—and no longer the reflection of a last ember on the brass curtain rod which I had mistaken for it—traced on the darkness, as though in chalk, its first white correcting ray, than the window along with its curtains would leave the door frame in which I had mistakenly placed it, while, to make room for it, the desk which my memory had clumsily moved there would fly off at top speed, pushing the fireplace before it and thrusting aside the wall of the passageway; a small courtyard would extend in the spot where only a moment before the dressing room had been, and the dwelling I had rebuilt in the darkness would have gone off to join the dwellings glimpsed in the maelstrom of my awakening, put to flight by the pale sign traced above the curtains by the raised finger of the dawn.

A Chinese Funeral

José Martí

Translated from Spanish by Esther Allen

Translator's Note

The traveler to Cuba flies into José Martí International Airport, possibly to do research at the José Martí National Library or at the Institute of José Martí Studies, or to visit any of the several museums dedicated to Martí in Havana alone, not to mention the statues of him that are everywhere, in the Parque Central, the Plaza de la Revolución, and, most recently, on a section of the waterfront Malecón fleetingly known as the "Plaza Elián," where a newly erected effigy of Martí with a young boy in his arms now points an accusing finger at the building that houses the U.S. Special Interests Section. The booksellers' stalls in the Plaza de Armas offer an extensive selection of works by and on José Martí, and not too much else. And though the currency of Cuba these days is the U.S. dollar, an attendant in a Havana museum offered to sell me an actual Cuban coin: You can guess whose picture was on it. Such omnipresence takes its toll. In Cuba, José Martí is visible to the point of invisibility, perpetually honored with such mandatory religious reverence that it becomes very hard for Cubans to do anything but pay grudging lip service to him or ignore him.

Martí was deported to Spain at the age of seventeen, and went back to Havana only twice, once for less than two months, and then again for only a year. For most of his adult life (from 1880 until his death in the Cuban revolution of independence in 1895) he lived where I live, in New York City. I need hardly say that his invisibility here is of a different order: In the city that he was always away from, he is everywhere, and in the city he actually inhabited, nowhere. (Well, not nowhere. But how many New Yorkers know that a statue of José Martí stands on Central Park South, at the very top of the "Avenue of the Americas"? And then, just this fall, his photograph appeared on the sides of city buses in an advertisement that touted the "Revolutionary Flavor" of a new lime and mint rum liqueur called "Martí Autentico.") It amazes me to remember that I once looked him up in the eleventh edition of the *Encyclopedia Britannica*, which came out sixteen years after his death, with some actual expectation of finding him there; after all, his work was published extensively throughout the Western hemisphere, from Buenos Aires to New York City, and his death was mourned across both North and South America. Fat chance. He didn't make it into the *Britannica* until the late 1960s.

Still, his fate in the English-speaking world has at least been better than that of a magazine called *La América*, which he edited for a time in the mid-1880s. Its offices were located on lower Broadway, not too far from my house, but *La América* was so entirely without meaning to the United States of America that no library here has so much as a copy of it, and the scholar wishing to consult it must travel to Havana or Bogotá.

During his lifetime—ever mindful of the crucial role that U.S. public opinion always played in the history of Cuba—Martí himself published a number of articles in English, the earliest ones originally and shakily written by him, the later ones translated, though the quality of those translations declined over time. (One of the last and most accusatory of these ventures into the language of the country he was living in, an exposition of the plight of the Cuban tobacco workers of Key West, which Martí had someone translate for publication in a bilingual pamphlet in January 1894, is almost unreadable in its English version.) A lone volume of translations of some of his poems appeared during the Spanish-American War in 1898, three years after his death. But nothing else came out in English until 1954, when, as part of the ongoing celebration of the centennial of Martí's birth in 1853, Juan de Onís did beautiful work translating an anthology titled *The America of José Martí.*

De Onís's book held out the promise of inaugurating a real appreciation of Martí's importance in the United States. But it was not to be. Not that other volumes of Martí's work haven't appeared in English since then; they have, almost a dozen of them, by several different translators. But all neglected a fundamental fact about translation: that it is the performance of an acquired skill. No one would expect the musicologist who's an expert on the life of Franz Liszt to be, therefore, the most accomplished performer of the Hungarian Rhapsodies. But in translation this happens all the time; scholarly knowledge (or even just some basic knowledge of the original language) is assumed to be the only prerequisite for performance as a translator. And Martí is to Spanish what Liszt is to the piano repertoire: extremely difficult. Yet none of the translators who approached Martí's work had ever translated anyone else, or ever went on to translate anyone else afterward: Their interest was purely in Martí, not in translation. And while this is also true of Juan de Onís, whose translations are excellent, he was the son of the great Harriet de Onís, the preeminent U.S. translator from Spanish in the forties and fifties, who did everything from the sixteenth-century Spanish picaresque novel *Lazarillo de Tormes* to Alejo Carpentier's *The Lost Steps.* Perhaps growing up so steeped in the importance and the rigors of translation was enough (and who knows, maybe he had some maternal assistance with his work).

Not only has Martí been translated badly, but bad translation has been deliberately used to seriously distort his ideas. Like everyone who has governed Cuba since its independence in 1902, Fidel Castro invokes Martí constantly, and the Castro regime, particularly in its early days, struggled to reinvent Martí as a rabid hater of the U.S. and a closet Communist, the John the Baptist who heralded the advent of the Messiah Fidel. Philip S. Foner, editor of six volumes of Martí's work in English, uses inflammatory titles (*Inside the Monster*) and the surreptitious trimming of inconvenient passages to bolster this image. But what really makes those volumes so deadly to Martí's reputation is the sheer unreadability of most of the translations. To pick one example from among many, a sentence describing the area around Lake Mohonk—"*Convidan a la grandeza los bosques de Adirondack cercanos que talan sin sistema especuladores torpes*" ("The nearby forests of the Adirondacks are conducive to grandeur, though they are being unsystematically cut down by short-sighted speculators")—is translated in Foner's volume as, "The forests of the adjacent Adirondacks beckon to grandeur, unsystematically cutting down crude speculators." Martí had confused the Catskills with the Adirondacks, true, but not even in his wildest rhetorical transports could he have suggested that beckoning forests were capable of cutting down crude speculators. Yet it isn't really surprising that an editor who disagreed with so much of what Martí had to say paid so little attention to the meaning of Martí's words.

All of these books add up to a loss: the loss of José Martí in English. And that loss is particularly acute for the United States. For one of Martí's greatest achievements as a writer was his description of the United States in the *crónicas*—the "Letters from New York"—that he wrote for newspapers across Latin America during the 1880s. José Martí was one of the great foreign commentators on the United

States. And his commentaries and descriptions remain unknown here, more than a century after they were written. It has therefore been my real joy to find myself, as William Carlos Williams put it, "in a position to make the necessary translations," and awake to my own locality.

In the following *crónica,* written in New York on October 19, 1888, and published in the Buenos Aires newspaper *La Nación* on December 16 of that year, Martí describes the funeral of a Chinaman he calls "Li-In-Du" who, like Martí himself, appears to have been a figure of international historic importance who passed through New York City like a shadow, unknown and unrecognized except by the small community of his countrymen.

* * *

For a moment the furor of politics died down and New York stepped aside to make way for the colorfully garbed Chinamen who, with highest honors, filed in the Asiatic manner behind the bier of Li-In-Du, the illustrious general of the Black Flags,[1] who has died in their arms. The parades of the political parties, the mobile orators on their wagons, and the varied musics of the electoral process recede into the distance now. Today there is a strange, new music, the music of Li-In-Du's funeral. Let us go with a curious New York to listen.

Li-In-Du was a man of valor. He drove France out of Tonkin and used his prestige to help the friends of liberty, but even that prestige was of no use against the harassment of the authorities who do not want China to be rid of its class hierarchy. He barely escaped with his life, and was followed to San Francisco by a few loyal lieutenants. He did not wander in idleness, like the many swordsmen of our own race who think that the fact of having once been a man who defended the patria authorizes them to cease being a man and to live off of her instead. Liberty, too, has its scoundrels! And Li-In-Du did not want to be one of them, but instead busied himself with the trades of his land, that is, doing laundry and serving food—the two things the Chinese are allowed to do here. For if they work in mines or on railways, they are hunted down like wild beasts, chased from their

[1]Bands of Chinese rebels who roamed the mountains of Tonkin, in what is now northern Vietnam, where they had been driven after the suppression of the Yunnan (1855–72) and Taiping (1850–1864) rebellions against the Manchu dynasty.

shacks by gunshots and burned alive.[2]

In New York, Mott Street is theirs; it is the street where they have their banks, their stock market, their tailors and barbershops, their taverns and their vices. On that streeet can be found the Chinaman friar, a merry and mellifluous savant, well fleshed, with roses in his face, not much in the way of cheekbones, an avid mouth, and a shrewd and lively eye. There, too, is the shopkeeper Chinaman, with loose, spongy flesh the color of earth, his billowing shirt and wide pants rolled up, his hair short and dense, eyes bloodshot, hands meaty and long-nailed, a three-layer chin falling to his chest like an udder, and, for a mustache, two threads. There is the harsh and aloof Chinaman, the fenced-in nomad who once wielded the sword or the pen and now makes his living as an amanuensis and mediator, by turns mute or loquacious, kept in poverty by the ignorant rich man who is pleased to avenge himself thus on one whose head is fully inhabited. And there is the Chinaman of the laundries, who can sometimes be tall, youthful, naive, and gallant-faced, with agate bracelets on his wrists, but more often is an ungainly runt, meek and misshapen, without nobility in his mouth or gaze, or else a man who does not walk but drags himself along, slumped and gloomy, with two glass balls for eyes, drooling from opium.

But today the opium-smokers' daises are empty, the laundries are closed, there is no entry to the houses that sell foodstuffs, and bands of mourning adorn the lanterns that hang from balconies to advertise the taverns. Mott and the surrounding streets are full of Asians, gathered to bear their great man, Li-In-Du, to his grave; full of the Irishmen and Italians who inhabit that muddy and odiferous neighborhood alongside them; and full, too, of the curious from all parts of the world who throng the streets along which the procession is to pass by the thousands. The yellow man lifts up his eyes, the eyes of a hunted animal; he looks about as he walks along, as if to guard against an offense; he swears under his breath as he walks, his eyes ablaze, or he walks with his head low, as if to beg pardon for the sin of being alive. They go in groups to the house where the funeral is held, walking along two by two, in their flat black hats, their robes and pants of dark blue fabric, their hands crossed on their chests, their feet in string slippers above which their loose pants sway like

[2]A reference to the massacre of Chinese workers in Rock Springs, Wyoming, during which white members of the Knights of Labor brutally ransacked the Chinese section of the town, killed twenty-eight Chinese, and wounded fifteen. Martí had described those events in detail in an article published in *La Nación* on October 23, 1885.

petticoats; they enter the funeral parlor, which is a stable, today lined in black, with two strips of cloth, one black and one white, forming a cross on the ceiling; they go, two by two, to prostrate themselves before the glowing altar at the body's feet, beside two tables piled high with the goat, lambs, oranges, and flower-wreathed cakes that will be served to the friends of the deceased three days hence at the funeral banquet, which takes place in silence at the most silent hour of the night. Two by two they come, taking from the altar, with its seven lamps, the cups of oil and holy rice given out by priests who wear white tunics with sashes and skullcaps of black. And they empty the cups, two by two, into the waiting basin that stands at the foot of the coffin, next to the tub where, on a bed of fresh earth, the candles of the soul are burning.

The dead man lies in his coffin, with its rich fabrics and copious silverwork, exposed from the waist up; he has the head of a solid man, eyes set deep and close to the nose, nose with wide nostrils, lips slender and tight, the braid brought from behind to lie across the forehead like a crown, and one hand lying on his breast, which is covered with the paper money of Asia, to pay the toll of heaven. Around him, in bronze cups, the sacred perfumes give off their smoke and the candle of the soul its thick and waxy clouds; at the head of the coffin hangs a flag showing the sins of the deceased, surrounded by white circles, which he must overcome in order to ascend to the Elysian Fields that crown them, represented by a black mark. The tables can no longer hold all the piles of fruit, baskets of nuts, platters of lemons, towers of funeral cake. There is no space through which those who are arriving can make their way to the altar to prostrate themselves three times in quick succession and leave the oil in the basin and some flowers on the tables.

But they do not tear their hair or rend their garments, they do not bare their heads, cease their smoking, or evince any sorrow over the changed state of one who defended their land so well, beneath the great red banner. He who has done one thousand three hundred good deeds, is he not immortal in the heavens, according to the law of Tao?[3] The defeat of the Frenchman was more than three hundred good deeds, which is all that is required to be like a deputy of immortality, immortal on earth! Life is like the sides of a pitcher, which

[3]Literally "path." An ancient philosophical system stemming from the *Tao-te-ching*, a text written in the third century B.C., which instructs humans to abjure all striving. Martí's description of a peculiarly anthropomorphic Tao may be attributable to the

contain the useful emptiness that is then filled up with milk, wine, honey, or perfume; but the pitcher's emptiness is more valuable than its sides, just as eternity, joyful and unbounded, is worth more than this existence, in which man cannot lead freedom to victory. To die is to return to what one was at the beginning, is it not? Death is blue, white, opalescent, it is the return to a lost delight, a journey. And so he takes along sufficient provisions!

Hands buried in their loose winter shirts, they speak of how Li-In-Du was an awe-inspiring general, who looked, in battle, like a winged pillar, the type of pillar the Chinaman erects to ward off demons; of how he killed many a Frenchman, though Tao says one must not step on an insect or cut down a tree, because to do so is to destroy life; of how he was a great merchant, dealing in drugs and fabrics, teas and foodstuffs, though the law of Tao forbids the pursuit of vanity's false honors or the riches of this world.

That was the old Tao, whose beard is covered with ice in the heavens now. Li-In-Du? Fifty thousand dollars. And he has a son, in China, who inherits all of it! The devils will not manage to carry him off; he has much gold in his hand to scatter when they come out to meet him along the way. And amid the smoke of incense and cigars a mourner appears dressed in blue, holding in upraised arms a stuffed pig garlanded with roses.

Those in the white tunics step aside to allow an old man wearing a yellow cape lined in black, advancing with solemn steps through the masons in their gray tunics and red skullcaps, to reach the altar. Amid all the smoke, he is lost from sight and his salutation cannot be heard through the mad shrieking clamor of the music: Fom! Bang! Ba-tan-TAN! Piiii! Bon, son, son! The shattered air crackles and squeals. The old man throws himself onto the glass part of the coffin, kisses it three times, and three times lets out a terrible cry, a cry that finally imposes silence and fear.

He returns to the altar, seizes a banner, and sings, in verse, of the feats of Li, and of how much the world will miss him, and of the feast that will now be held on the mountain of Tao. And others sing after him, one of them on his knees, forehead to the ground, another

---

nature of the information he was given by former Taiping rebels. Hung Hsiu-ch'üan, the visionary leader of the Taiping (Great Peace) Rebellion, in which Li-In-Du apparently took part, had studied Christianity for two months with an American Protestant missionary named Roberts, and believed himself to be the younger brother of Jesus Christ. He subsequently evolved a syncretistic Taoism influencd by Christian theology, which even included a Taoist version of the Ten Commandments.

gesticulating like a man describing a battle, while at his feet, in a goblet with two serpents for handles, blaze the prayers that the celestial one burns, kneeling, rather than intoning them with his lips.

The room is full to bursting now; the procession is beginning to form. We'll go outside to watch it. Outside we'll be able to see all of it.

Is it an army or a funeral? Over the heads of the multitude move lanterns and flags. There are white horses. Their riders are bareheaded, their braids covered in black cloth and wrapped around the forehead like a diadem. The great red banner, proud and graceful, waves above it all. Aggressive people charge toward it, laughing.

He looks as if he were about to die, the man who grips the flag with trembling gloves! The oriflammes and standards gather submissively around the flagpole like new shoots around a tree trunk, red and yellow, purple and sapphire, red and violet, amaranth and pink. The crests of the funeral coach can be glimpsed, and the black heads of its four horses. The gold paper of the insignia glitters in the sunlight, but no idol can be seen, no image of Ts'ai-Shen,[4] the god of wealth, who now has more temples than any other god, in China and everywhere else; there is no image, either, of Kuan-Ti,[5] the god of battles, who has vipers for eyebrows and carries a huge whip. Li-In-Du does not believe in images or in any god but the pure creator Tao, who is all and one, and who engendered the two, and from the two the three, and from the three the world; he does not believe in any saint but the virtues themselves, without the dominions and hierarchies by which the priests have obscured religion, nor does he believe in Great Bears, Pearly Emperors, the mother of lightning, the king of the sea, the lord of the currents, the deity that protects man's every class and occupation, or the god of thunder whose thirty-six black and gray generals come and go, bearing his orders, while with his restless feet he mortifies the plumage of nine beautiful birds. Li-In-Du is a mason, a freethinker, his own man, a venerable of Chinese freemasonry, who wore the leather apron edged in green. Everywhere the world is in turmoil and man suffers to assure the freedom of his will. That was why Li-In-Du's forehead was broad and level and his cheekbones were flattened: from banging his head against the

[4]Still one of the most widely worshiped gods in the Chinese pantheon, whose images are sold in the street during Chinese New Year.

[5]Another very popular Chinese deity, the god of battle or war, a historical Han general who died in 220 A.D. and was not deified until the sixteenth century.

despotic empire! He was a Taoist of the old school, who believed in the population of the air, the rest from struggle, the everlasting individual, and transfiguration and a final place on the mountain of Tao when duty has been fulfilled. But here below: liberty! And with his masonic hammer he went about softening up the Chinese emperor's head. They are touching to behold, these founding rebels. Such men rise like flames from the choking thicket. They appear as Li-In-Du did in his coffin, wearing gold and fire, in a tunic of yellow silk.

Now they are coming toward us, in order. The police go first, shoulder to shoulder, clearing the way, and after them a German band, in helmets and short jackets, playing a funeral hymn. The generals follow, the three generals who took part in the victory at Nanking.[6] They parade on white horses, riding like men more apt to charge headlong at the enemy than turn tail and run; their bodies are stringy and of medium height, and there is more muscle than dough in their faces; their bare helmets are encircled with a band of red linen, a black diadem on the front; they wear blue tunics, breeches, and loose pants with a white sash at the waist in sign of mourning; their horses are well in check and move with high, slow steps. Tall flags jammed into sockets on their belts, three young Chinamen in mauve shirts and trousers pass by; on those flags are inscribed the glorious deeds of the departed, the nausea with which he left San Francisco where he saw the Chinaman contented with his base condition, the agony of his final days, when death was approaching on foot, like one who respects his victim, but the Congress in Washington, for internal political reasons, passed a law to deport the celestial one, and death no longer came slowly, considerately, but galloped in on a horse and killed him with the news, ay! Li-In-Du, one of the men who devote their lives to seeing their people freed and their fellow citizens honorable!

Then, shaped like a heart wreathed in flowers, came the yellow standard of Lun-Gee-Tong, the masonic lodge he presided over, along with its members, wearing blue tunics and skullcaps of black silk; the priests in white tunics came behind with measured footsteps, surrounding the old man in the cloak lined in black.

A low noise like a muffled clucking greets those who go by next, also wearing loose shirts, with knee breeches and puttees and wide

[6]The conquest of Nanking in 1853 was the great victory of the Taiping Rebellion, one of the most massive upheavals of the nineteenth century, which brought death to twenty to thirty million people.

white sashes at the waist and around the forehead: These are the twenty-five loyal soldiers who have followed Li-In-Du everywhere, and they seem taller than they really are as they move forward, proud and taut, a forest of banners over their heads, each a different color, and looming over them all a round canopy of mandarin orange and purple.

Behind two white lanterns, wearing tunics of various colors, with sashes around their chests and bows at their elbows and along their sides, come men who bear, on red poles, the eight pure insignia,[7] cut out of cardboard and decorated with gold and flowers: the commandments of the law of Tao that Tao himself gave to the chieftan Gwin-Li-Du on the bright mountain of Tien-San; the holy fruit that Tao ate on the mountain before his transfiguration; the sword with which Gwin defended the divine law; the celestial ax that falls wrathfully upon the world when evil prevails; the flute of peace; the lively *wooyin* with which the spirits of the redeemed accompany their happiness; the tea-scented celestial flowers that neither dry nor wither; and the white urn of life eternal.

And behind them, just ahead of the coffin, comes a white horse led by a groom, with no rider in its bronze-trimmed leather saddle. Then comes the coach, and a beggar in an ash-colored tunic sits in the coachman's seat, dropping imperial paper money on the multitude at intervals so that the dead man's way will be clear.

Then comes the mourner, the nephew Li-Yung, in a white cloak and black sash, his head bare. Then, in two black and yellow carriages, the Chinese musicians, their tones shrill and discordant, without notes or phrases, sounding more of triumph and joy than of mourning. And then the retinue of Chinese freemasons, in great coats and fur hats, with the leather apron bearing the three letters, and then a thousand Chinamen more, two by two, arms crossed.

And this colorful swarm of people and the four white horses and the banners and the insignia of Tao gather in the cemetery around the grave, where they are jostled, with laughter and cruel joking, by thousands of the curious: ruffianly idlers, sweethearts in the bloom of life, new mothers, fur-clad ladies, odiferous Irishwomen. Instead of leaves, the trees are bedecked in urchins. On the decrepit roof of a

[7]Here again, the anthropomorphic Tao that Martí describes is extremely anomalous. The insignia he saw probably referred to the life of one of the countless Taoist deities, though it is not clear which. Eight is one of the most auspicious numbers in Chinese religion, and Taoism has its Eight Immortals, but only three of them coincide with these eight insignia: the flute, the sword, and the flowers.

rambling nearby house, a group of actresses are peeling oranges.

Suddenly the crowd draws back; the banners fall to the ground, tunics and sashes fly through the air, and a wave of churning smoke rises from the sudden bonfire where all the garments and emblems from the funeral are being immolated, the cloaks and tunics, the black fabric that wrapped the braids, the mourning draperies of the horses, the oriflammes and pennants, the insignia of Tao, the great red banner, and the dead man's trunk.

As the crowd disperses, craning their necks, they can see the grave, arranged in the celestial manner. At the head, as a support, is the masonic heart, its pole plunged into the earth; then come the two white lanterns, also stuck into the ground, and along the body to the feet are white and yellow roses arranged in the shapes of urns and cushions; at the feet and to each side are the seven mystic candles, and near them are cups of rice, plates of cabbage, rolls, heaps of wine-drenched earth, cakes, buns, and two roast chickens: the banquet that the friends of Li-In-Du, on their haunches, have spread out to keep him from suffering the pangs of hunger during his difficult journey to the mansion of the spirits, where he will be a fortunate and immortal djinn, watching closely over those he loved in life, a pure spirit, interceding on behalf of mankind and the freedom of China, and assisting his friends and relatives with gifts and miracles.

Kagekiyo

Anonymous

Translated from classical Japanese by Michael Emmerich

Translator's Note

If translations are phantoms of the works they re-embody, *Kagekiyo* seems destined to linger forever in the world of literature composed in English. The play, traditionally but no longer attributed to Zeami—"the Sophocles of the nō," in Earl Miner's words—first entered the language in 1913 in a translation by Marie Stopes; reappeared in 1917 in a version by Ezra Pound, based on notes by Ernest Fenollosa; was retranslated by Arthur Waley for his 1921 collection *The Nō Plays of Japan;* and was translated again in 1959 by the Nippon Gakujutsu Shinkōkai. Each effort puffed a different breath of life into the Japanese play, channeled the pulse of its poetry in a new direction. This is one of the comparatively few works of Japanese literature that readers of English can enjoy in a truly dramatic way, by letting its various incarnations interact.

The translation presented here differs greatly from previous ones in the manner in which it tries to mimic the sophisticated "playfulness" of the original: I try to preserve within the text certain linguistic qualities of nō plays that are often only described in footnotes. I have followed Itō Masayoshi, the editor of the Japanese text on which this translation is based, in spacing out the sections of verse—though in Itō's version syllable count, rather than a subjective sense of rhythm, determines the location of the spaces. This makes it possible to weave "pivot words" (*kakekotoba*) into the English, though in most cases I have had to make do with rhymes instead; I hope this will let readers enjoy something akin to the slow, expansive, time-entwined word-joy that is surely the greatest attraction of nō texts in Japanese. Readers may even manage to locate the place where part of the protagonist's name has been hidden in the English, just as it is in the original—though the Japanese carries it off more gracefully.

Most translations of nō plays now include certain Japanese terms that indicate the role-type of each character (*shite,* "main actor";

tsure, "companion") as well as names for the various musical subdivisions (*shōdan*) of the plays (*tsukizerifu*, "arrival speech"; *mondō*, "dialog"). Royall Tyler touches on some of these in his lucid introduction to *Japanese Nō Dramas*, which interested readers may find helpful. I have also included mountainlike symbols that provide further information about the particular style of chanting used for a section to readers familiar with the music of nō theater.

The incident described by Kagekiyo—or, to call him by his "right" name, Hyūga no Kōtō—is mentioned in the mid-fourteenth century *The Tale of the Heike*, but probably took place sometime around 1190. In this drama, Kagekiyo is represented as a member of the second rank of officially appointed reciters of *The Tale of the Heike*; this is, in fact, the meaning of the "Kōtō" in his name. Hyūga—written with characters meaning "face the sun" or "into the sun," thus, in the present context, suggesting blindness—was the name of the province that is now Miyazaki prefecture. A different treatment of the story of Kagekiyo and his daughter Hitomaru is found in Yasunari Kawabata's *The Boat-Women: A Dance-Drama*, my translation of which appeared in *Conjunctions:31, Radical Shadows*. This translation is dedicated to Monica Bethe.

* * *

KAGEKIYO	*shite*
HITOMARU	*tsure*
HITOMARU'S ATTENDANT	*tomo*
A VILLAGER	*waki*

Two *kōken* position a covered prop representing a straw hut before the drummers. Hitomaru and her Attendant enter to *shidai* music.

HITOMARU and ATTENDANT. (*Reaching stage center, they turn to face one another.*)

⌒ (*shidai*) winds of whispering tell me   he lives
winds of whispering tell me   he lives
short-lived as dew   fallen how far

HITOMARU. (*She turns toward the audience.*)

⌒ (*sashi*) Before you stands a woman named Hitomaru, from the valley of Kamegae in Kamakura. I have heard that my beloved father, Akushichibyōe Kagekiyo, a general of the Heike and thus hated by the Genji, has been exiled to someplace called Miyazaki, in the province of Hyūga; it is there, they tell me, that he passes the months and years.

Unused to travel in unfamiliar
parts unpleasantness ever part
of travel still for my father's sake
I struggle not to give in to these—

HITOMARU and ATTENDANT. (*They turn to face one another.*)
⌒ (*sageuta*) sleepless thoughts and streaming tears
head pillowed on a lonely sleeve pillowed
on grass doubly bedewed

HITOMARU and ATTENDANT. (*They continue to face one another.*)
⌒ (*ageuta*) we leave the province of Sagami
we leave the province of Sagami
wondering who to ask after him
wandering after him so far to
Tōtōmi
has a view like its name boats cross
the distant waters
we cross the eight bridges
over the waters in the province of Mikawa
how much farther until the clouds
of the capital appear before me
in my dreams
oh clouds of the capital
appear before me in my dreams

ATTENDANT. (*He turns toward the audience.*)
(*tsukizerifu*) Having hurried and hurried all this way, you find yourself already arriving at the place of which they spoke: Miyazaki in the province of Hyūga. Ask after your father here, perhaps you will learn something.

Hitomaru and her Attendant take up positions at stage left.

KAGEKIYO. (*He calls out from inside the hut.*)
⌒ Holed up here alone, the gate beneath the twisted pine tree tightly shut, I pass the months and years. These sightless eyes ignore the light, they cannot track the moon's movements—even my sense of time has faded. Nothing left but sleep, all I do is sleep, wasting away in the blackness of this hut, and since my clothes are thin my body goes numb, too weak to fight the cold.

The *kōken* remove the cloth that covers the straw-hut prop. Kagekiyo is seen sitting inside.

CHORUS.
〽 (*ageuta*) if I must turn my back   on the world
let me be   black-robed   black-robed
if I must turn my back   on the world
how shallow   you seem   like the color
of this sleeve   jarringly   not dyed black
disgusted   with yourself   as you are
fallen so far   who would go   so far
as to pity you   now   as you are
no comforting   weary   discomfort
no comforting   weary   discomfort

HITOMARU.
〽 (*kakeai*) how strange   this grass hut is   so ragged
with age   you would think no one   was living
here   yet unexpectedly a voice   unexpected
voice   this resonant voice resounding   here
thinking it might prove a beggar's shelter
I ease away   I see the eaves now   far away

KAGEKIYO. though I cannot   see   autumn come
a breath of wind blows in   to tell me
stopping by   I cannot know—

HITOMARU.
〽 who   knows where he is   where to go
hardly here as it is   and nowhere
to stop   no place to go   to rest a while

KAGEKIYO. nowhere to   rest   in three worlds
no place at all   all is nothing   no need
to ask a name
〽 no need to say   where

ATTENDANT. (*He turns toward* KAGEKIYO.)
(*mondō*) Hey, you in the hut, I want to ask you a question.

KAGEKIYO. (*He turns his face toward the* ATTENDANT.) Tell me who you are.

ATTENDANT. Can you tell me where I'll find the exile?

KAGEKIYO. The exile? Has this exile a name?

During the next line, Kagekiyo turns away from the Attendant toward the audience.

ATTENDANT. He's a Heiki samurai, a man named Akushichibyōe Kagekiyo.

KAGEKIYO. Yes indeed, I have heard something of a man by that name, but being blind I'm unable to say that I've seen him.

He turns toward the Attendant, then at the end of the speech turns away again.

How miserable he was—his story touched me, made me somewhat sad. You'll have to ask elsewhere if you want to learn more.

ATTENDANT. (*He turns toward* HITOMARU.) He won't be found in this region, it seems. You must forge on even farther, we will have to go and inquire elsewhere.

Hitomaru and her Attendant sit at stage right, at the rear.

KAGEKIYO. (*He continues to face the audience.*) This is very odd. Whoever, I wondered, could this person calling on me be—could it really be?—it was my own child, this blind man's daughter. Years ago, in the province of Owari, in Atsuta, I became friendly with a woman whose business it was to be friendly, and she gave me this child. Since she was a girl, I figured I would have no use for her, and left her in the care of the mistress of a tavern I knew in the valley of Kamegae, in Kamakura. And now—

saddened not
to know her own father, she blows in like a wind, calls on me.

CHORUS. (KAGEKIYO *bows his head.*)
(*ageuta*) how sad to hear the voice yet be
blind to the presence of her face
hard having the heart to keep silent
in letting go a parent holds on
in letting go a parent holds on

During the lines above, Hitomaru and her Attendant rise and walk onto the bridge.

ATTENDANT. (*Standing at the first pine, he calls out toward the curtain.*)
(*mondō*) Say, is there a villager around here?

VILLAGER. (*He walks onto the stage and stops at the third pine.*) A villager? What do you want with a villager?

ATTENDANT. Can you tell me where I'll find the exile?

VILLAGER. (*He turns toward the* ATTENDANT.) The exile? What sort of person is he, this exile you seek?

ATTENDANT. It's a Heiki samurai we're looking for, Akushichibyōe Kagekiyo.

VILLAGER. (*He looks toward the stage.*) In the shadow of that mountain over there, the place from which you two have just come, there's a hut thatched with straw—did you not encounter a man there?

ATTENDANT. There was no one in the hut but a blind beggar.

VILLAGER. Yes, and that blind beggar is Kagekiyo, the man you're searching for. But my goodness—whatever is wrong?

Hitomaru raises her hands to her face, trying to hold back her tears. The Villager turns toward the Attendant.

No sooner had I pronounced Kagekiyo's name than the young mistress there began to look terribly distressed. It seems there is a story behind her grief. . . .

ATTENDANT. You are right to wonder. And what reason is there for me to conceal the truth? This young lady is Kagekiyo's daughter. She told us she wanted to see her father again, one last time, and it is for this reason that she has left Kamakura behind and come this far, traveled so far. Perhaps, now that we've made your acquaintance, you might do us a favor and intervene? Convince Kagekiyo to see her?

VILLAGER. (*He turns toward* HITOMARU.) Can this be true? You're telling me the young mistress is Kagekiyo's daughter, his own daughter? All right, fine—calm yourselves, then, and listen to what I'm going to tell you.

He turns toward the Attendant.

Kagekiyo is now blind in both eyes, and since he could find no other way to get by he's shaven his head and taken on the name Hyūga no Kōtō—he recites the Tale of Heike, and relies on the kindness of travelers for his livelihood. He only manages to hold on from day to day by taking advantage of the pity people like me feel . . . but he is wretchedly ashamed of the depths to which he has fallen, nothing left of the man he used to be, and I'd be greatly surprised to hear that he had told you who he is. Allow me to accompany you, then—we'll greet him with the name Kagekiyo. Surely if the name is really his, he'll respond. Then the young lady will be able to meet with him, you'll chat with him about things past and present. . . . Here, if you please, come this way. . . .

Moving back onto the stage, Hitomaru and her Attendant proceed to stage left; the Villager takes up a position in front of the column at stage right.

VILLAGER. (*He approaches the hut and strikes one of the poles with his fan.*)
(*mondō*) Hello? Is Kagekiyo there? Akushichibyōe Kagekiyo?

Everyone sits.

KAGEKIYO. (*He covers his ears with his hands.*) Oh, damn it! Damn it! Awful enough to hear that name as it is, but now of all times, just as I've sent her away, chased off my own . . .

too ashamed to be   seen   in this state
having to send those   visitors from home
away   without telling them   who I am
and yet   weeping—

a thousand tears   of sadness drench   my sleeve

seeing that all of it   it's all a world
of dream   this anchorless life   of mine
no more than an instant   in a dream
I made up my mind
henceforth   I will be one
of the dead   of this world   a beggar—

He turns toward the Villager.

Do you really think this beggar will answer when you call him *Kagekiyo?*

Anyway my name is   Hyūga

CHORUS. (KAGEKIYO *turns toward the audience.*)
(*dan'uta*) like the   province Hyūga   write into
the sun   into the sun   and you have
written Hyūga   you refuse   to call
the right name   for a blind   Hyūga
you call the name   that calls me back
to the past   back to the calling I had

to give up   after the defeat
my name: a cushy cheerful past
I had to give up   after the defeat

He bows his head.

I should be   able   to keep calm
I think   but hearing you   now

He slaps his knee.

I am angry   oh yes   I am angry

KAGEKIYO.
〽 Yet settled here as I am—

CHORUS.
〽 settled here as I am, for me to be disliked by the locals who support me would be as fatal

as for a blind
man   to lose   his stick

I'm afraid my condition makes me short-tempered, and I often say things much better left unsaid.

Turning toward the Villager, he puts his hands together and bows his head.

I ask your forgiveness.

KAGEKIYO.
〽 Though these eyes are dark—

CHORUS.
〽 though these eyes are dark, I know people's thoughts after hearing no more than a word.

Kagekiyo raises his head, as if looking up at the mountains.

And the wind on the mountains, sighing in the branches of the pines, the snow whirling down before me, a snow

He bows his head.

of petals I cannot see—how deeply I regret the breaking of the dream that brings them all to me.

He seems to look toward the bay, then puts his hand to his ear and listens.

And I hear the waves in the bay
as they rush in   to pound   the rocky shore . . .
no doubt   the evening   tide has risen

He feels around for his stick, picks it up, then stands and emerges from his hut. At stage center, he sits facing the Villager.

Yes, yes . . . and there is no doubt either that I am a Heike, a sightless Heike—just a pathetic, blind teller of the Tale. Why don't I begin reciting, then . . . give what comfort I can.

KAGEKIYO. (*He turns his face toward the* VILLAGER.)
(*mondō*) What can I say . . . there's something troubling me just now, you see, and I guess I spoke without thinking. I hope you'll forgive me.

VILLAGER. (*He turns toward* KAGEKIYO.) Don't mention it—I'm used to it by now. But tell me, you wouldn't happen to have had a visitor here earlier, would you? Before me?

KAGEKIYO. No, no. No one has come by but you.

VILLAGER. Goodness gracious, you're lying through your teeth! A young lady who says she's your daughter was just here, there's no mistake about that. What reason could you possibly have to try and hide her visit? I felt such sorrow for her that I brought her here with me.

He turns toward Hitomaru.

Hurry in there now, hurry in and have a nice talk with your father.

Hitomaru stands and walks toward Kagekiyo. She kneels down and places her hand on his sleeve.

HITOMARU.
⌃(*kudoki*) Father? Don't you see, I've come here myself—traveled all this way. How could you do this to me? I've come such a long way to see you, braving the wind and rain
the dew and the frost
and you would let it all end in nothing
How could you do that to me? Can it be true that the strength of a parent's affection depends on the sex of the child? How terribly sad!

She raises her hands to her face, trying to hold back her tears.

Oh, how sad you've made me!

KAGEKIYO. (*He bows his head.*)
⌃Until now I thought I'd managed to keep my identity concealed, but it seems the blinding sun of my lie has sunk—

and in the falling night
you find the dewdrop of my fragile
fallen self settled here in this hut of grass.

Nowhere to go. Such humiliation! You, you're like a flower! How could I bear to have you go about calling yourself the child of a parent like this, how could I bear to let you be tied to my bad name?

He places his hands on Hitomaru's shoulders and clasps her to him.

So I let myself—let you go. Please don't think badly of me.

CHORUS. (KAGEKIYO *bows his head.*)
〽 (*uta*) in the old days I'd curse men
I didn't even want to see
for failing to appear before
me
witness my reward
the sorrow of hoping
even my own child
will stay away

CHORUS. (KAGEKIYO *turns toward the audience.*)
〽 (*ageuta*) in the Heike boats in the Heike boats
shoulder to shoulder knees interlocking
with knees everyone and
the moon
so close living in its light Kagekiyo
more than anyone indispensable
if the Emperor's boat is to survive
many members of the clan and many
more humble are versed in many ways
of making war but Kagekiyo is first
at the helm on the Emperor's boat
treated like a leader by the leader
and how he was envied by all
and now he is emptied of all

He bows his head.

like a stallion grown old as they say

Hitomaru weeps.

worse than a worthless old nag

VILLAGER. (*He turns toward* HITOMARU.)
(*mondō*) Oh, what a painful sight. Come here, young lady.

Hitomaru returns to her place at stage left and sits down. The Villager turns toward Kagekiyo.

Now I want you to listen to what I have to say, Kagekiyo. Your daughter has a request.

KAGEKIYO. (*He turns toward the* VILLAGER.) Has she? What sort of request?

VILLAGER. She says she would like to hear the tale of your exploits at Yashima. Do us a favor and tell her something of the story, won't you?

KAGEKIYO. That doesn't really seem like the sort of request a young lady like her should be making of me, but seeing as she has had the strength of purpose to come such a long way, it seems heartless to refuse. I'll tell her the tale. But when I've finished, send her home.

VILLAGER. Sure. As soon as you've finished the tale, I'll send her back.

The Villager goes to sit in front of the flute.

KAGEKIYO. (*He turns toward the audience.*)
(*katari*) All right, then. It was the close of the third month of the third year of Juei; we Heike were in our boats and the Genji were on land, and both sides had taken up positions along the shore, determined to see the battle decided one way or the other.

⌒ The Governor of Noto,
Noritsune, raised his voice—

⌒ Last year our allies fought and lost at Muroyama in Harima, at Mizushima in Bitchū, and then at Hyodori-Goe. We never had a single victory. And all this was due to the tactical genius of Yoshitsune. We must take him at any cost. We must find some means to take him. Turning the problem over in his mind, Kagekiyo thinks: He's a lieutenant, not a god or a devil. If you're willing to lose your life in the process it can't be all that hard. Asking Noritsune to let him go off and fight one final time, he wades through the waves to the Beach. The Genji men

⌒ run toward him
swearing not to let him escape

CHORUS.
〽 (*chū-noriji*) seeing this Kagekiyo seeing this
Kagekiyo cries seems a little over
the top our forces are so un
even
ing sun flashes on his sword
as he begins slashing

Using his fan as a sword, Kagekiyo slices the air first vertically and then horizontally.

they falter
his attackers run madly in all

He looks to the left and right.

directions he tries to stop them

KAGEKIYO. (*He holds out his left hand.*)
〽 how pathetic you all are he cries

CHORUS.
〽 how pathetic aren't you ashamed
to be seen like this

He looks to the right.

by the eyes
of the Genji and of the Heike

He raises his arms.

stopping a single foe is no big
deal
with me if you can but I see you can't
shoving his sword under his arm
I am a humble samurai of the Heike
Akushichibyōe Kagekiyo he says he says

He thrusts out his left hand, palm outward.

chasing after a man to take him alive
grabs the flap of the helmet Mionoya wears

With his left hand, he grabs the helmet twice but each time loses his grasp.

but lets it go lets it go
twice and then
a third time the enemy flees but Kagekiyo

He opens his fan and thrusts it out.

has his sights set on him will not let him go

He stands up straight.

lunging for him grabbing the helmet
pulling with a grunt

He tugs on his fan.

the flap breaks

He drops to the floor and sits there.

he holds it while the enemy runs away

He gazes off into the distance, facing the audience.

now far away he turns back I've got
to hand it to you he says you're a terror
such strength in that arm of yours but not
as strong says Kagekiyo as the bone

He gestures toward his neck with his left hand.

in your neck Mionaya and they laugh

He closes his fan, mimes laughing.

and they walk away one to the left
and one to the right

CHORUS. (KAGEKIYO *turns toward the audience.*)
⌒\ (*uta*) an old tale I haven't yet forgotten
but the teller has lost all his strength
humiliating even his heart is mad
not much left of
this life of mine
is such pain such little pain left

He gestures toward Hitomaru with his left hand.

hurry back and when I'm gone
say a prayer for me in my blindness

He turns toward the Villager.

the dark path of death

He picks up his stick and stands. Hitomaru and her Attendant stand with him.

will be lit
by your prayers will be a bridge

He places his hand on Hitomaru's shoulder as she turns away.

on the bad road leading me down to hell
I must stay here

He pulls her back.

I'm going

She walks away.

just these few words

Only Kagekiyo remains; the others disappear behind the curtain.

linger in the ear
nothing else left to parent or child
nothing else left to parent or child

Kagekiyo gazes after them, crying.

Nine Prose Poems

Pierre Reverdy

Translated from French by Ron Padgett

Translator's Note

I fell for Pierre Reverdy's book of prose poems the first time I read it, in Paris, where I had gone to study in September of 1965. I loved its austerity, its spookiness, and what I imagined to be its cubism. A few months later, in the Jacques Doucet Collection of the Bibliothèque Sainte-Geneviève, when I held a copy of the book's rare first edition—made even rarer by that copy's cover, hand-painted by Juan Gris—it was as if I were in the presence of a radiant relic.

The first edition of *Poèmes en prose,* self-published by its author in 1915, consisted of fifty poems. Dedications—removed from later editions—were to Max Jacob, Pablo Gargallo, Henri Laurens, Marcelle Braque, Josette Gris, André Level, Pablo Picasso, Léonce Rosenberg, Claude Laurens, Marthe Laurens, Juan Gris, Henri Matisse, and Georges Braque, all of whom were friends or acquaintances of the author. To save money, Reverdy and his wife, Henriette, helped with the printing, at the sympathetic Imprimerie Birault (where some of Apollinaire's calligrams were typeset a few years later). The hundred copies were hand-bound by Henriette, Marcelle Braque, Josette Gris, and Marthe Laurens. Juan Gris and Henri Laurens each did original covers for three copies. It was quite an illustrious cottage industry.

In late November of 1965, right around the time of my joyous moment in the Doucet Collection, I did a roughed-out English translation of the book, as it appeared in *Les Épaves du ciel,* a 1924 collection of Reverdy's early books of poetry, which omitted ten of the pieces from the original edition of *Poèmes en prose.* I did the translation partly as a way of getting closer to the text, as one might do a sketch of a figurative painting in order to see it better. But I must have had the notion of producing a finished version someday, for I listed textual variations and I assembled these first drafts into a small handmade book, on whose back cover I glued a picture of the terrifying vampire in the film *Nosferatu,* beneath which I typed a caption: "Pierre Reverdy." I was just joking, but in retrospect I think I should have typed my own name there, since in translating I had become a sort of Dracula gaining strength from the blood of another poet. In any case, it was obvious that my French (two years in high school, one year in college, and a few months in Paris) was hardly up to the task of doing justice to Reverdy. On my little book's flyleaf I wrote, "These rough versions . . . need working on and especially need to be 'checked.'" I also knew that my own poetry, while serious in its rambunctious way, did not have the relentless gravity of Reverdy's. Although I was only a few years younger than Reverdy when he wrote the poems, his emotional range and mine did not sufficiently overlap.

Over the next twenty-five years I penciled an occasional revision in the booklet, but in 1990, having looked at my versions again and been smitten with the recurrent dismay that is probably typical of translators of poetry, I made extensive revisions and added the ten missing pieces, using the 1967 Flammarion text of *Plupart du temps,* the definitive collection of Reverdy's early books of poetry. Now the translation felt much closer to being "right." Not only was it free of errors, it cohered as a whole and it sounded like Reverdy.

But apparently I was not completely satisfied, for although I had published some of the versions in small magazines, I let the book as a whole sit for another four or five years, when I made tonal adjustments throughout and "translated" the punctuation. Until then my stubborn purism had led me to retain Reverdy's punctuation, which was normal in French but quirky in English. Perhaps I had liked the way it gave a "modern" effect in English. Reverdy *was* a modernist, but he was not one for giving effects.

Recently I made a few more small adjustments, mostly rhythmical, and once again I am allowing myself the illusion that at last I have it right.

* * *

FACE TO FACE

He goes forward and the stiffness of his timid gait betrays his assurance. They keep staring at his feet. Everything that shines in those eyes, out of which flash bad thoughts, lights his hesitant walk. He is going to fall.

At the other end of the room a known image appears. His hand goes out toward its hand. He sees nothing but that, but he crashes, suddenly, against himself.

BATTLEFRONTS

On the rampart where the ruins shake, you hear the echo of drums. They had been punctured. Last night's drums answer each other again.

The night over, the noise scatters the dreams and uncovered faces where a wound bleeds.

Amid the smoke, the men are lost, and already the sun pierces the horizon.

Who blew the victory? The charge is sounded for those who are dead!

A trumpet assembles the ragged squadron and the smoke lifts the horses whose hooves do not touch the ground.

But he who would have painted them was no longer there.

THE WRONG SIDE RIGHT SIDE OUT

He climbs without stopping, without even turning around, and no one but he knows where he is going.

The weight he pulls is heavy but his legs are free and he has no ears.

At each door he called out his name. No one opened.

But when he knew that someone was expected and who it was, he knew how to change his face. Then he went in, in place of the person who wasn't coming.

THE TRAVELER AND HIS SHADOW

It was so hot that he had left his clothes along the road piece by piece. He left them hanging on bushes. And just as he took off the last piece, he was approaching the town. An immense shame seized him and kept him from going in. He was naked and how could he not attract attention?

So he passed around the town and came in from the opposite direction. He had taken the place of his shadow, which, coming in from the original direction, protected him.

THE IMPASSIVE MAN

He leans over the edge of the parapet and holds his tiny head by the ears. The roof ridge forms a parallel with his shoulders and the chimney looks as if it's his neck.

The clouds make the house move in the garden. Among the wires and branches it stops. Now you're not looking up into the air.

Spiderwebs tear with a sound of silk, when you finally open the window, and he whose head has not changed has lost his earlier beautiful kingdom.

THE IRONER

Her hands used to make pink spots on the sparkling linen she was ironing. But in the shop where the stove is too red, her blood has evaporated little by little. She is getting whiter and whiter and, in the rising steam, you barely see her, among the shimmering waves of lace.

Her blonde hair floats in the air in curls of light and the iron continues on its way raising clouds from the linen and her soul, which still resists, her ironer's soul that runs and folds like the linen while she hums a song without anyone's noticing.

TO EACH HIS OWN

He hunted the moon, he left the night. One by one the stars fell into a net of running water.

Behind the trembling aspens a strange fisherman watches anxiously with an open eye, the only one, hidden under his big hat, and the line quivers.

Nothing is caught, but he fills his basket with pieces of gold whose glittering is darkened inside the closed hamper.

But someone else was waiting farther down the bank. More modest, he was fishing in a mud puddle the rain had left. That water, from the sky, was full of stars.

FASCINATED

Nothing higher than the ground-floor window. Because a head goes by, sticking out its tongue that goes back in with the stem of its pipe.

All the eyes turn toward this single point, and the street seems to want to leap over the balcony. And nothing is protecting the sidewalk.

Behind the old man who is smoking, there is a younger and far too pretty head.

STREET CIRCUS

In the middle of that crowd there is a child who is dancing, a man lifting weights. His arms with the blue tattoos call on the sky to witness their useless strength.

The child dances, lightly, in tights too big for him, lighter than the balls he's balancing himself on. And when he passes the hat, no one gives anything. No one gives for fear of making it too heavy. He is so thin.

Berlin Stroll

March 27, 1932

Robert Musil

Translated from German by Burton Pike

Translator's Note

Robert Musil (1880–1942) is best known for his two novels, *Young Torless* (1906) and *The Man without Qualities* (1924–1942; 1978), which strike out on new paths for fiction. Trained as a scientist and mathematician, Musil wanted to find a way to integrate modern scientific thinking with new moral values. The failing Austro-Hungarian Empire, the setting for his two novels, was an ideal test tube for carrying out his experiments. Musil also lived briefly in Berlin and visited the city at other times (his publisher was there). Musil was a wonderful writer with a unique style, vivid, sharp, and witty. His translator can report being constantly challenged, but never bored. These brief, lively sketches are snapshots of his impressions of a stroll through Berlin with his wife in 1932. Their evocative metaphors, ability to limn a scene with great economy of means, and their gently ironic humor present a more relaxed and reflective Musil than the writer better known for his novels and stories. These "sketches"—English should have a better word for them—are polished gems, which seem to occupy far more space in the mind than they do on the page.

* * *

Courtyards on the Kurfürstendamm

In the streets the only green that floats at the height of trees is the green of traffic lights, and it has something of spring, almost spectral, as they swing back and forth in front of three trucks that are waiting as if hundreds of others were storming up behind them. Autumnal too are the red signs on which is printed, house by house, that apartments are for rent. But in the courtyards of these jagged fortresses for living one notices spring on the patchy walls. The stucco has peeled off them in big chunks, it looks like a virulent rash, and now the sun is shining into the wounds. Only the chimneys, standing fraternally on the roofs, still have their color from the good times, and one sees in the whitish tile-red, when the sun shines on it, how solid the blue of the sky has become in the last few weeks. If one's glance sinks down the walls from this play of distances, even their denuded patches can feign a blossoming life unfolding.

Edge of the Tiergarten

The color of early spring is brown, in innumerable nuances from the color-blind pallor of the grass to the radiant brown of the water. Only the bare branches of the weeping willows make sharp, whip-thin green strokes in nature. A red spot, which is nothing more than the top of a wooden post, painted red, seems like a blossoming bouquet, a turned-over flower bed among the sparse shrubbery; it startles the heart, and betrays that it is full of a readiness similar to that of the small boat that lies "under steam" at the lock; the snug little coffee machine has its hull and funnel freshly painted in red and white, for at the beginning of every spring it sets out on a great journey that lasts almost a year, although this journey, one year like the next, only travels between Charlottenburg and Stralau.

Charlottenburg Castle

When to the question where we should get out, the young conductor, under the impression that we are tourists, gives us the friendly tip: "Don't miss seeing the Mausoleum; the panaroma there is wonderful, it's the prettiest panaroma in Berlin!" I think that the essence of all fame and see-worthiness is summed up in most condensed form in this information.

Still, we don't want to see the Mausoleum again but the park, but there is a sign there saying "Closed today because the paths are impassable." There hasn't been any bad weather for weeks, and one instantly feels transported back to the century of a solicitous authority protecting the citizen from the dangers that lie concealed in wait for him somewhere, since as far as the eye can see the paths are in the best of condition. In such situations today's person tries a detour. This first leads past the Kaiser Friedrich Monument where, on the stone benches, one beside another, people sit with their legs stretched out offering their faces to the sky; the scene looks as if a strewing hand had scattered flowers with long, cut stems across the benches. Furthermore, from the Tegeler Weg one can gather that the interior of the park is as dry as it is level, but one's attention is soon diverted to the other side, where, in a style eclectically Roman but in any case massive, a courthouse looms, with the saying chiseled in stone above the entrance: *suum cuique.* That means to each his own, a good old Prussian and also a quite just saying, although in the spring sunshine it gives rise to the reflection that many people would gladly give their own, if it consisted of a number of years in prison, for something less.

Siemensstadt

After one has weighed the distinction between justice and self-righteousness, one finds oneself in a leafy area that, to put it politely, smells of nature's circulatory system; but to make up for this it shimmers in all the colors lying between pink and dark blue. On the left the Spree flows nearby behind ordinary factory yards, on the right the suddenly expanded sky lies on the ruffled treetops of the heath, but directly in front something rises into the superhuman, or at least the super-European, higher than a house, wider than a tower, erected over skeins of tracks and networks of pipes: one of the factories of Siemensstadt. The closer one gets, the stronger the impression is; when one finally stands close to it, one finds nothing in these reddish flanks but its purposefully rising life: defiant, perhaps even showing off (in the way it stretches up commandingly; but without a little showing off monumentality is not conceivable), this giant child of technology and market capital displays its athletically well-proportioned body to the sky.

Hidden behind it: the real, little Siemensstadt: a modest thing in itself, German small town circa 1890, with Lohengrin architecture and later additions.

A Small Garden-Colony

Where one has to wait for a connection one is still standing underground; when the train then emerges into the light and only the tops of free-standing pine trees part the sky, one's feeling is no different than when, in Switzerland or the Tyrol, the top of a pass comes after a tunnel and the strong air strikes through the opened window.

Presumably real colonists experience this moment every day, when they "come back from town." The overcast day, the ice-gray cloud cover, the small frozen lake, the narrow streets already damp, the view of the encroaching factory chimneys, the sand churned up by construction: Nothing gets in the way of imagining spring here too. The city's chains are broken, man stands in something sparsely infinite. One feels it even when one "just went out," that something or other special must lie behind this miraculous illusion that drives the city to pursue the forest the way a child chases a bird that it would like to touch but scares further and further away.

Three Stories

Alexandros Papadiamantis

Translated from Modern Greek by Peter Constantine

TRANSLATOR'S NOTE

ALEXANDROS PAPADIAMANTIS (1851–1911) IS GREECE'S foremost prose writer. In his novellas and stories he presents a universal picture through the microcosm of the tight-knit society of a Greek village on a remote island. Papadiamantis is a clear-eyed realist, but woven into his stories are village magic, vestiges of myth and ancient lore, and the dour superstitions that governed the daily life of the Greek peasant. His plots are at times touched by a magic realism reminiscent of Márquez. The villagers of his stories, isolated for centuries from the Islamic and Christian mainstreams, live bound by medieval and ancient traditions steeped in sorcery and witchcraft. Papadiamantis's plots are gripping and full of surprises, with a Dostoevskian intensity that illuminates human suffering. Worlds clash: Ottoman with Greek, Middle Eastern with European, Islamic with Christian. The Greeks of the stories are Europeans living under the oppressive Islamic regime of the Ottoman Turks. The island of Skiathos, where most of these stories are set, is a midway point between Ottoman Turkey and mainland Greece, and perceived by both as a distant backwater.

I first read Papadiamantis as a schoolboy in Greece, and every examination in Greek literature had one or two tricky questions on Papadiamantis. I found him very difficult to read. He wrote in an era when Modern Greek had not yet been fully codified. Most of his contemporaries were writing in Katharevousa, a stagnant and unnatural purist Greek artificially created in the early nineteenth century based on obsolete grammatical and lexical patterns of Ancient Greek. Under Papadiamantis's touch this artificial language sprang to life. His style is further enriched by dialect and Turkish elements. (Greece had been occupied by the Ottoman Empire for over four hundred years.)

Though Papadiamantis is unfamiliar to English readers, there has been an upsurge of interest in him in Europe. Milan Kundera, in a preface to a book that situates Papadiamantis's work within the European prose tradition, calls him the "greatest Modern Greek prose writer," and points out that an important element of his work is that it originated in a European country that for a large part of its history belonged to a non-Western civilization.

As Greece's Nobel Prize–winning poet Odysseus Elytis wrote: "Papadiamantis's characters portray in miniature the eternal passions of man—jealousies, loves, ambitions, hatred, murders, and misfortunes—in an almost hieratic movement, like the rhythm of a chorus in tragedy, scarcely perceptible but sufficient to suggest the deeper, the pure nature of the world. Therein lies the magic of Papadiamantis."

* * *

THE ENCHANTING OF THE AGA

LIKE THE SKULL OF A DEAD MAN recently exhumed, its eye sockets hollow, its nose withered, a frightening sight, bare, cold, and skeletal, the small mosque of the deserted village gleams in the distance. The mosque has only one low, half-buried entrance in the middle without doors, and a broken window on either side. The deserted village, built an age ago on a steep, sea-battered cliff, can be seen from the proud heights of Barberaki, whose rock face is shaved by perpetual winds from east, north, and west, an immense vista stretching below over the sparkling, azure sea to the liberated lands of Thessaly and the enslaved soil of Cassandra. From the heights, one can also see the drab mosque with its round hollows on either side and the large, long hollow in the middle. Beside the mosque loom the quarters of the Aga, three of its walls still standing, the roof caved in, a relic of centuries past. Shadows still roam, old memories spring to life, spirits chant dirges in the wilderness, and the north wind whistles relentlessly through the blackened ruins, the trees crouching on the mountainside like travelers hunched over and panting as they climb.

Two or three times a year people come to the deserted village from the other side of the island, the southern side, the women dispersing among the ruins, moving from one wild fig tree to another looking for ripe figs to fertilize the cultivated figs of the plain. The children who tag along, modern-day swashbucklers, run among the ruins and climb the wild mulberry trees, eating their fill and stuffing their shirts, the red berries staining their hands and lips, and then they scatter and run about, jumping, sliding, making voices that mock the wilderness and the spirits. Many of the children climb recklessly onto the roof and over the dome of the sorry mosque, parodying with naughty voices the call of the muezzin, which, fortunately for them, they have never heard.

The spirits leave and the shadows stray, and the lament of the wilderness ebbs in the distance till the drowning sigh sinks beneath the waves. And the seabirds and the birds of the cliffs soar high into the air and plunge down toward the cave, or disappear in the vastness of the sky.

And yet the Aga's quarters had once been inhabited, a prayer to Allah had once echoed from the mosque, and there had been worship following the teachings of Mohammed. It is true that among the villagers, who paid a sum of two to three hundred piasters to the Ottoman sultan, there was no one but the Aga to follow the teachings. The last Aga, who came a few years before the War of Independence, brought with him his harem, consisting of a wife and a slave girl. After him, during the years of the national uprising, only a Turkish sergeant came, and after him no one came anymore.

So the Aga, the last but one Ottoman to come to the island, arrived from Thessaly. He was a gentle, placid man. He spoke Greek. He accepted the gifts the islanders gave him, and often asked for more. He had a serious, guarded manner, and was coolly affable. He had the air of a beguiling snake whose fangs had been removed. He lived peacefully with his harem and the islanders.

Every morning he came out of his quarters in a caftan and felt slippers, unlocked the door of the mosque, climbed onto a table by the window, stuck his head outside, and very slowly chanted the morning call to prayer, "*La, Allah il'Allah,*" chanted it out to sea, as if he were entrusting it to winds that might carry it to Istanbul, or Mecca, or wherever the breezes wanted. There had never been a muezzin to call the faithful to prayer, so every Aga on the island acted as his own muezzin. There had never been a minaret, but the high window had stood all the Agas in good stead.

Whether the Aga then knelt in prayer or not, whether he touched the marble floor with his forehead two or three times or not, he re-emerged from the mosque almost immediately after he had uttered the last "*il'Allah,*" locked the door, went back up to his quarters, lit his large pipe, and took one puff after another. Once he had shaken off his early morning drowsiness he put on his white turban, his wide sash, his fur, and his leather shoes, and, clutching his large pipe, made his way down to the kiosk, where he knew he would find two or three idlers like himself with whom he could converse, notables of the village in white shirts with wide unbuttoned sleeves and long embroidered sashes. *Lakirdi soile.*[1]

The priests of the neighborhood, who were associated with one of the two parochial churches and served alternately at the forty chapels of the township, watched him pass as they sat after the service outside old Anagnostis Tsipotis's little shop drinking their morning *raki.*[2] The Aga greeted them with deferential scorn and walked on. He was also watched by the good housewives who were taking their unleavened pitas to the baker's oven that lay beyond the mosque and was stoked by Garoufalia Xinou. He was watched too by Aunt Siraina Pantousa, a good Christian woman feared by all the other women for two things: her tongue and her eye. Word had it that she had once managed to separate a couple at their wedding, with the wreaths ready, the bride fully decked out, the guests assembled at the house, and the priests on the point of donning their ceremonial stoles. Siraina Pantousa had whispered a few words into the ear of the groom's mother (the words obviously a slander against the bride), and so managed to have the wedding cancelled. On another occasion, a small three-master was sailing past the bay, a new ship, well rigged and freshly painted. A group of women were gazing at it from the top of a cliff, and Aunt Siraina Pantousa, who was among them, could not abide the admiration they voiced.

"What? That miserable little boat?" she shouted. "A fine vessel indeed!"

It may seem hard to believe, yet those who saw what happened next with their own eyes vouch it to be true. No sooner had she uttered these words than the ship's rigging came crashing down, leaving the vessel bare-masted, mutilated, pitching from side to side in the waves (though I must admit that this account does sound more like a fable than a true tale).

The Aga in his turban walked past the baker's oven with his long pipe under his arm, and all the women who were whiling away their time in the small yard until it was their turn to slide their bread into the oven peered at him and whispered quick words to one another.

[1]Chitchat (Turkish).
[2]Hundred-proof grape liquor (Turkish).

"He's a handsome Aga."

"Our village has put roses in his cheeks."

"We have good air here."

"And a hardy north wind."

"Have you seen his harem?"

"No."

"She's wrapped up all the way to her eyes."

"His harem girl?"

"His *kadin*,[3] of course!"

"And his slave?"

"She never leaves the house."

"No, his slave Fatmé does come out sometimes."

"Have you seen her face? A Negress, may the devil snatch her!"

"Black, pitch black!"

"And her teeth sparkle."

"But the Aga looks nice."

"He is a cold and evil man."

"His heart is as evil as his smile is sweet."

"Say what you will, he's a Turk."

"A dog."

"But good-looking."

"A handsome man."

"Our village has put roses in his cheeks."

"We have good air here."

"If you want me to," Aunt Siraina Pantousa suddenly said, "I can send him to his grave within forty days."

The women fell silent.

Garoufalia the baker put down the rag with which she was wiping the oven, and turned around.

"What spells will you cast?" she asked Aunt Siraina Pantousa.

"Sheer nonsense!" one of the women said.

"No good will come of it, Aunt Siraina!"

"What do you care? Do you want me to cast a spell, yes or no? I know what I am doing!"

The women were at a loss.

"I don't believe you can," one of the women said.

"It would be better not to."

"What do we care?"

"Even if a Turk or two dies, Turkey will not be done in so easily,"

[3]Matron, wife (Turkish).

an old woman sighed.

"Wait and see," was all Aunt Siraina said.

The evening of the same day, as the sun was setting, Aunt Siraina waited in the alley between the baking oven and old Anagnostis Tsipotis's shop. The Aga, his unlit pipe under his arm, had taken a little walk up the lane that ran along the low walls of the village, and was now heading home for dinner.

'*Aksam hairolsun,*[4] Aga," Aunt Siraina Pantousa said to him boldly, having heard a few Turkish words from the mouth of her deceased husband, who had traveled much in Turkish lands.

"Good evening," the Aga answered in Greek with a startled look. "What do you want? Do you have a problem you want to tell me about?"

"Me, have a problem? I have neither a problem nor a present." (She mumbled the words "nor a present" so the Aga would not hear.) "I only wanted to wish you a good evening, since I have not seen you for such a long time."

"That is very kind of you," the Aga said with a smile.

"You strike me as gaunter."

"What?"

"You have lost a lot of weight, may the evil eye not strike you! Our village has not put roses in your cheeks."

"Really?"

"You look thin and pale, may the evil eye not strike you! Yellow as wax. Like one escaped from the netherworld."

"*Astaghfirul'lah!*"[5] the Aga uttered.

"Yellow as a brass coin, Aga. You have a sheen of sickness."

"Allah! Allah!"

"Go look at yourself, Aga. Our village has not put roses in your cheeks. See that you don't die in these foreign lands, you ill-starred man!"

The Turk raised his pipe in an impulse to bring it down on the back of the abhorrent prophetess, but Aunt Siraina had retreated ten paces, and furtively slipped away at the first corner of the alley.

That evening the Aga looked into the mirror many times. Darkness had fallen, and the light of the candles in the room along with his

---

[4]Good evening (faulty Turkish).

[5]I seek forgiveness of Allah (Arabic).

emotion at the woman's prophecies made him see a pallor in his face.

He reached his hand over the table but had no desire to eat. He filled his pipe but had no desire to smoke.

He turned and looked at his wife.

"Is it true, *hanum*,[6] that I have grown thin and pale?"

His *hanum* looked at him a while.

"Grown pale? . . . No, not in the least. Have two glasses of sweet sherbet, you'll feel better. Tomorrow morning I'll make you some nice *halvah* and a *bougatsa.* I'll also hang a charm around your neck so the evil eye won't strike you."

Fatmé, the slave, listened to their conversation as she bustled in and out of the room taking care of her various chores, lighting her master's pipe, rearranging the pillows on the floor so that he could recline more comfortably, and removing his slippers. She turned around and looked at the Aga.

"What do you think, Fatmé?" the Aga could not refrain from asking. "Is it true that I look pale? Has my face changed?"

"What? Master think he turning pale? Why, he turning black . . . more black than my hide!" Fatmé snapped, perhaps pleased at the opportunity to pay him back for the many beatings she had received.

The *hanum* grabbed her slipper and threw it at the slave's head, but Fatmé had turned on her heel and made a hurried escape.

From that day on, the Aga lost his appetite and grew increasingly thin and pale.

He became dejected, malicious, and vile. Wherever he went he carried his extinguished pipe under his arm, ready to raise it and strike across the back anyone who might contradict him or annoy him with trivial questions.

Siraina Pantousa had left the village. She was afraid of what she had done. She had become afraid of her own tongue, her own eye.

It seems that others also had put the fear into her. The old woman who had declared a few days ago that "Turkey will not be done in" said to her: "They will hang you, my child. Who will protect you? Do you think they'll show mercy just because you're a woman? All he has to do is whistle and a thousand Turks will come pouring in, from over there and from up there too!" (She pointed to the western and the northern mainland.) "And our poor island will be awash with blood!"

[6]Wife (Turkish).

Aunt Siraina fled the village in the middle of the night. It was said that she was hiding in an extremely safe place, a cave with a second secret exit up in the mountains, a cave that nobody knew about except for one of her nephews who was a shepherd and brought her bread every three days.

She did remain safe, and lived until 1865. At the age of ninety she was still alive to tell the tale.

For two more weeks the Aga came out of his quarters every morning and went down to the mosque, chanted, *"La, Allah,"* and then went over to the kiosk.

"It is true that I've gone pale, that I've lost weight?" he asked each of the notables he spoke with.

"There's nothing wrong with you, Aga," they told him. "You are a little thin, but you shouldn't let that worry you. Forget about it. You'll see how quickly you'll get your old strength back. The air here will put roses back in your cheeks, it's good and hardy air!"

Such were the answers they gave him. Not that they were able to say anything else, for he was always ready to raise his pipe against them.

The third week, the Aga no longer left his quarters. He no longer had the strength. He was paralyzed with fear. He did not have the strength to touch the plates set before him on the table.

In vain did the *hanum* double her attentions, and Fatmé the Negress no longer dared say that her master was as black as her skin. The truth was that he was pale as wax and white as a shroud.

For two more weeks the ailing Aga did not go to the mosque. One morning during the fifth week after Aunt Siraina's prophesy, he made a valiant effort and left his quarters. He dragged himself into the mosque. Fatmé came with him and helped him climb onto the table.

He stuck his head out of the window and began chanting, *"La, Allah il'Allah, Allah Akbar Mohammed resul l'Allah."* He chanted it with all his might, and the call to prayer echoed down to the waves of the open sea. And far away the steep, deserted, hollow rock of the cape echoed it in a tone of mourning.

When he climbed down from the table he felt a great tiredness descend upon him. He sat shivering beside the table and mechanically opened the Koran that lay there. By a strange coincidence, he opened it to a page in the third chapter of the third Surah, his eye falling upon the words "Man dies at Allah's decree, in accordance with the Book in which the number of years he will live is written."

He grew dizzy, raised his hand to his forehead, and closed his eyes. He opened them again and read: "Allah has set us in flight from our foes . . . even if you hide in your abode, if your time to die is written in the book, then you will die. The arrow that you dodged in war will now seek you out."

He gritted his teeth and clenched his fist, furious that he could not go to battle for Islam and slaughter infidels.

He leafed through the Koran and found the following passage in the second Surah: "O Men of the Faith! Go to battle against the infidels who live along your borders, strike the infidels wherever you can. Go to battle until all evil is destroyed, until nothing remains but the religion of the one and only God."

After this the Aga, supported by Fatmé, returned to his quarters, entered his room, lay down on the soft divan, and never rose again.

Siraina, the prophetess, had foretold that he would not live forty days.

And the Aga died on the thirty-ninth day after the prophesy. He died of the prophesy, of its suggestion, of the enchantment of that woman. He died because he was ill.

As for the Sick Man,[7] chronically ill, now 444 years old, who will enchant him?

THE SEAL'S DIRGE

Beneath the cliff where the waves spray and the path from Mamoyiannis's windmill descends lies the cemetery, and the area to the west, where the shore juts out and the village urchins swim from morning to night all summer long is called Kohili, "shell," as it has the shape of a shell. Toward evening old Loukena, a poor, death-singed woman, came down the path carrying a bundle of clothes under her arm, to wash the woolen blankets in the salty waves and then rinse them in the small fountain of the brackish waters that trickle from the slate rock face and empties calmly into the waves.

[7]The declining Ottoman Empire, which had occupied Constantinople in 1453. Papadiamantis wrote "The Enchanting of the Aga" in 1897, 444 years after the fall of Constantinople, traditionally seen in Greece as the beginning of the Ottoman Empire.

She walked slowly, down the path, down the slope, singing a mournful dirge in a whispering voice, raising her hand to shade her eyes from the glare of the sun setting behind the mountain across the water, its rays caressing opposite her the small enclosure and the tombs, bleached, whitewashed, shining in the sun's last blaze. She thought of the five children she had buried one after the other in that threshing floor of death, that garden of decay, many years ago when she was still young. Two girls and three boys, all in their infancy. Ravenous death had scythed them down. Death finally seized her husband too, and she was left only two sons, who had moved to foreign lands. One, she had been told, had gone to Australia. He had not sent a letter in three years. She had no idea what had become of him. The other, the younger, traveled the Mediterranean on ships, and still remembered her from time to time. She was also left a daughter, married now with half a dozen children. Old Loukena was working alongside her in her old age, and it was for her that she was walking down the path, down the slope, to wash the woolen blankets and the clothes in the salty waves and then rinse them in the fountain of the brackish waters. The old woman bent over the side of the low, sea-eaten rock and began the wash. To her right lay the smoother and less abrupt slope of the earthen hill on which the cemetery stood, and from whose sides rotting wood rolled toward the all-embracing sea from the unearthings, in other words from the digging up of human remains, and the removal of young women's golden slippers and gold-embroidered clothes that had been buried with them, of tresses of blonde hair and other spoils of death.

Above her head a little to her right, in a hidden hollow next to the cemetery, sat a young shepherd who had just returned from the meadows with his small flock, and who, without considering the mournfulness of the area, had taken his flute from his bag and begun playing a merry shepherd's tune.

The old woman's dirge fell silent at the sound of the flute, and the villagers returning from the meadows—the sun had set in the meantime—heard the flute but could not see the flute player who was hidden among the bushes in the deep hollow on the hill. A schooner was preparing to put out to sea and was tacking across the harbor. But its sails were not filling and so it did not reach the open water past the western cape. A seal meandering through the deep waters close to the shore, perhaps hearing the old woman's whispered dirge and enticed by the young shepherd's loud flute, swam into the shallows, taking pleasure in the sound and frolicking in the waves.

A small girl, one of the old woman's grandchildren, her name was Akrivoula, nine years old, her mother had perhaps sent her, or more likely she had slipped away from under her mother's watchful eye, and hearing that her grandma was down at Kohili, washing clothes by the shore, went to look for her so she could play a little by the waves. But she did not know where the path began by Mamoyiannis's windmill across from the cemetery, and, hearing the flute, she went toward it and found the hidden flute player. Listening to the music and admiring the young shepherd, she saw in the twilight of the approaching darkness a small path that descended steeply, quite sharply, and she thought that that was the path her grandma had taken, and so she began going down the steep slope to find her by the shore. By now night had fallen. The little girl descended another few steps and then saw that the path was becoming even steeper. She called out in fear, and tried to scamper back up the slope. She had come to the rock that hung above the waves twice the height of a man. The sky darkened, clouds hid the stars, the moon was on the wane. She tried to find the path by which she had come down but could not. She turned back toward the edge of the rock and tried to continue her descent. She slipped and—splash—fell into the waves. The sea was as deep as the rock was tall, a good two fathoms. The sound of the flute covered her cry. The shepherd heard the splash, but he could not see the base of the rock and the edge of the shore. Furthermore he had not seen the little girl, he had barely felt her presence. As night had already fallen, old Loukena had finished her wash and was climbing up the path back toward the house. Halfway up the slope she heard the splash, turned, and looked into the darkness in the direction of the flute player. "It must have been him," she said to herself, for she knew the boy. "Not only does he wake the dead with that flute of his, now he's also throwing stones into the sea to pass the time. What a loner and misfit that boy is!" And she went on her way. And the schooner continued tacking back and forth in the harbor, and the young shepherd continued blowing on his flute into the silence of the night. And the seal that had swum into the shallows found the little drowned body of poor Akrivoula and began swimming around it in a dirge before its nighttime feed. An old fisherman, versed in the voiceless language of seals, translated it into the words of man:

Akrivoula lies among the seaweed wild,
Death-singed Loukena's daughter's child,

Garland of sea flowers in her hair,
Her dowry of sparkling shells so rare,
And the old woman still sheds bitter tears
For the infants lost in distant years.
Man's troubles and sorrows never end.

LOVE IN THE SNOW

The heart of winter. Christmas, New Year's, Epiphany.

He got up in the morning, slipped into his old jacket, the only piece of clothing left from his years of prosperity, and made his way from his old half-tumbled-down house to the marketplace by the sea.

"Pangs of passion, not trickling gruel, through my veins gush hot and cruel. Love is young with lust, not old with rust," he mumbled loudly enough for the neighbor's wife to hear.

He sang these words so often that the neighborhood girls nicknamed him "Uncle Yannos, young with lust."

But he was no longer young, nor handsome, nor did he have a brass coin to his name. All that had disappeared years ago, along with the ship, the sea, Marseilles.

He had begun his career when he first set out to sea in his cousin's boat, in the same jacket he was now wearing. He had attained part ownership of the vessel from his share of the profits, and later he had managed to purchase a ship of his own and had had good runs. He had worn English felt, velvet vests, top hats, watches with gold chains. He had made money. But over the years he had squandered it all on the beguiling *phrynes* of Marseilles, and nothing remained but the old jacket that he wore over his shoulders when he went down to the shore in the morning to set out as a crewman on a three-master or a small freighter, or to go out into the harbor on another man's boat to catch an octopus or two.

He had nobody in the world. He was completely alone. He had been a married man, a widower, had had a child, and was left childless.

And late in the evening, at night, at midnight, he would return to the old half-tumbled-down house after drinking a few glasses to forget or to warm his bones, pouring out his pain in song:

"Little path, little path
Long and narrow down the slope,

One day you will lead me
To the neighbor's wife, I hope."

Other times he sang in happy lament:

"Neighbor's wife, neighbor's wife,
Gossiping night and day,
Never have you whispered
'Why don't you come my way?'"

Heavy winter, for days the sky hung low. Snow in the mountains, sleet on the plains. The morning was like the ditty:

"It's raining, it's snowing,
The morning's dark and dour,
The priest has found his hand mill
And has begun to grind the flour."

It was not the priest who was grinding flour with his hand mill but the neighbor's wife, gossiping night and day of Uncle Yannos's song. She was the miller's wife, and was busy grinding flour with a hand mill. It must be added that the local gentry thought it was beneath them to eat bread kneaded with flour ground by the watermill or the windmill, preferring flour that had been ground by hand. So the gossiping miller's wife had clients near and far. She sparkled, had large eyes and varnished cheeks. She had a husband, four children, and a small donkey that carried the sacks of ground flour. She loved them all—her husband, her children, her donkey. Only Uncle Yannos she did not love.

Who was there to love him? He was alone in the world.

He tumbled into love with the gossiping neighbor's wife so that he would forget his boat, the beguiling *phrynes* of Marseilles, the sea and its waves, his misery, his lust, his wife, his child. And he tumbled into wine to forget the neighbor's wife.

Often when he returned in the evening, at night, at midnight, the jacket slipping off his shoulders, his shadow, long, tall, and thin, penetrating the long and narrow path, and the snowflakes, white flies and tufts of cotton, whirling in the air and tumbling onto the earth, often he saw the mountain whiten in the darkness. He saw the window of the neighbor's wife closed, mute, and the hatch gleaming dimly, dully, and heard the hand mill still rattling, heard the hand mill fall silent, and heard her voice grinding. And he thought of her husband, her children, and her little donkey, all of whom she loved, though she never gave him a second glance, and he felt like a bee smoked out with its swarm, like an octopus flushed out of its hole, and gave himself up to philosophical thoughts and poetic images.

If love had darts . . . had snares . . . had fire . . . its darts piercing the windows . . . warming hearts . . . laying its snares upon the snow . . . old Feretzelis would catch a thousand blackbirds with his noose.

He imagined love to be very much like old Feretzelis on the high, pine-shaded slopes laying traps in the snow to ensnare innocent hearts like half-frozen blackbirds searching the olive groves in vain for one last olive. The tiny, pelletlike fruit had disappeared from Mount Varantra's wild olive trees, as had the myrtle from the fragrant bushes of the Mamous Gorge, and now the cheerful thrushes and the twittering little blackbirds with their black plumage and sweet wax-colored beaks fell victim to the snares of old Feretzelis.

That evening as he returned, not too heavy with drink, he glanced at the windows of the gossiping neighbor's wife and shrugged his shoulders.

"Only the Almighty will pass judgment upon us. . . . Only Death will part us," he murmured, adding with a sigh: "And the grave alone will unite us."

But before he returned home to sleep he always sang his ditty:

"Little path, little path
Long and narrow down the slope,
One day you will lead me
To the neighbor's wife, I hope."

That evening the snow had spread a sheet over the long and narrow path.

"White sheet . . . whiten us in the eyes of the Almighty . . . whiten our innards . . . so that we will not have a black heart within us."

He vaguely saw an image, a vision, a waking dream. It was as if the snow smoothed and whitened all things, all sins, all that was past—the ship, the sea, the top hats, the watches, the chains of gold and the chains of iron, the whores of Marseilles, the dissolution, the misery, the shipwrecks—covering them all, purifying them, enshrouding them; covering them so that they might not stand naked as if fresh from an orgy or a foreign feast before the eye of the Judge, the Ancient of Days, the Thrice Holy One. Whitening and enshrouding the path, long and narrow down the slope, with its stench, the old, crumbling house, the dirty, ragged jacket; enshrouding the neighbor's wife gossiping night and day, and her hand mill, and her politeness, her scheming, her garrulousness, her sparkle, her varnish, her paint, her smile, and her husband, her children, and her little donkey—covering all, whitening and purifying all!

That evening, the final evening, night, midnight, he returned home more drunk than ever.

He could barely stand on his feet, barely move or breathe.

Heavy winter, crumbling house, shattered heart. Loneliness, dullness, a world that is harsh, bad, ruthless. Ruined health. A body tormented and worn, vitals spent. He could no longer live, feel, find joy in anything. He could not find solace or warm himself. He drank so that he could stand up, he drank so that he could walk, he drank so that he could fall. His feet were no longer steady on the ground.

He found the path, he recognized it. He steadied himself on a cornerstone. He swayed. He leaned with his shoulders against a wall, bracing his legs.

"If only fire had love! . . . If only traps had snow!" he murmered.

He was no longer able to form a logical sentence. He strung words together.

He swayed again. He steadied himself on a doorpost and bumped against the door knocker. The door knocker rapped loudly.

"Who is it?"

It was the door of the gossiping neighbor's wife.

Obviously, he was, for better or worse, trying to enter her house. How could anyone think otherwise?

Upstairs, lights and people were flitting about. It seemed preparations were under way. Christmas, New Year's, Epiphany were approaching. The heart of winter.

"Who is it?" the voice repeated.

The window creaked. Uncle Yannos was standing beneath the balcony, hidden from view. No one's there. The window slammed shut. Had they only waited another moment!

Uncle Yannos stood propped up by the doorpost. He tried singing his song, but from his drowning mind only shipwrecked words came.

"Gossiping neighbor's wife, little path, long and narrow . . ."

He barely managed to voice his words. Almost inaudible, they disappeared in the droning wind and whirling snow.

"I too am a path," he murmured, "a living path."

He lost his grip on the doorpost. He swayed, staggered, slumped down, and fell. He lay in the snow, his long body sprawled across the whole width of the long and narrow path.

He tried to get up, but was gripped by numbness. He found a horrifying warmth in the snow.

"Fires did have love! . . . The traps did have snow!"

And the window had closed only a moment earlier. Had the gossiping woman's husband waited a moment more, he would have seen the man lying in the snow.

But he did not see him, nor did anybody else. And snow fell upon the snow. And the snow whirled. And the snow piled up, grew two hand spans deep, rose in a mound. And the snow became a sheet, a shroud.

And Uncle Yannos turned white and fell asleep beneath the snow, so that he and his life and his deeds might not stand naked and completely bare before the Judge, the Ancient of Days, the Thrice Holy.

From Master of the Sea

José Sarney

Translated from Portuguese by Gregory Rabassa

TRANSLATOR'S NOTE

JOSÉ SARNEY IS A FORMER president of Brazil and governor of the state of Maranhão, where this novel takes place. He is currently a senator from the state of Amapá, which lies between the mouth of the Amazon and French Guiana and is the scene of his second novel, *Saraminda,* which deals with a mysterious woman who is involved in the fight over gold between French and Brazilian prospectors. *Master of the Sea,* whose first chapter is presented here, describes the life of Cristório the fisherman and his companions. There is a good picture of life on the coast of Maranhão, seen both in the clarity of naturalism and through the gauze of what has come to be called magic realism.

* * *

IT WASN'T DAY AND it wasn't night on the waterfront of Mojó. Instead, the dim light of early dawn.

When Antão Cristório arrived to go out, the water still hadn't left its trace on the sand. A lifeless high tide, just before the ebb. He walked along on those broad, triangular duck feet of his, with their big spread-out toes digging into the ground and kneading it into footprints. His body was solid, stocky, strong, and stiff, and his long arms swung unrhythmically. The lines of his muscles were clear as they divided arm from forearm, thigh from leg, chest from belly. He had on his old straw hat and was wearing his fishing shorts, frayed and grimy with sea salt. His face was broad, with a flat nose and slack jaw. His leathery mud-colored skin had been tanned by sun and sea.

"Good morning, Captain Cristório," Bertolino greeted him.

"Did you say captain? Captain is your whore of a mother. Everybody knows I don't like people to call me captain on Fridays," he retorted dryly and sternly, with the steady flapping of the sail he was carrying on his shoulder, on his way to his small boat, a *biana.*

"But, Captain! . . ." Bertolino tried to explain.

"Didn't I just tell you I don't like people to call me captain on Fridays? Go back to your whore of a mother. And if you say it again I'll cut your tongue out."

That's the way it was. Clear and clean. Bertolino swallowed the insult. He knew that words weren't casual matters there. In fact, they were things. Many a time blood had been spilled on the sands of Mojó. Everything always started the way it does at sea. A touch of breeze, a touch of talk, a storm.

Cristório had good reason for hating Fridays. It was on a Friday that his son Jerumenho had been murdered. Cristório had come back from fishing, weary and sad, and scarcely had time to lie down when he heard his cousin Garatoso's voice calling him:

"Captain Cristório, Captain Cristório . . ."

Only God knows what happened that night. The times are long gone, but there's reason to remember. Fights during festivals, fights over love. Jerumenho, twenty years old, strong and healthy. Saint John's night festivities. He was singing the song for the *bumba-meu-boi* bull dance and everybody was dancing. Maria Dina was leading the revelers. Night comes on, three nights, and the partying goes right along. A liveliness in the air makes everybody feel good. There's the smell of women, cane liquor, darkness. The dancing heats up, desire heats up, and Dina arrives, all in heat. She rubs herself here, looks for a man there, feeling the urge all over to give into desire and fun. Jerumenho comes along, swaying, strutting; they head off toward the hiding place.

"Come on, Dina."

She follows. It's all she's been thinking about and wanting. Jerumenho, with his drive, drives. This way, that way. That way, this way. She moans. The party and her husband are not far away. It's all happiness and she wants to know the unknown.

Jerumenho was always whispering words of love to her:

"Sweet-smelling night flower. August moon. God made you and God preserves you."

She listened. Her woman's instinct was awakening and it kept seeing his body wanting hers. She could feel it in the thrusting words and in the hints coming from sturdy hands.

That night everything happened as it happens. Fate. A schottische starts to play, gives a touch here, rolls over there, then comes the deviltry of body needing body. The oil lamp was burning. Yellow light, the kind that rises out of the big wick and reaches up high, lighting up the night with anything goes.

"How about doing a little shuffling? How about it?"

She heard nothing and she heard everything, and she was leaving, leaving sideways—all at once they were in the underbrush. A carpet of leaves. Stars and desire. Mouth to mouth, mouth next to mouth, member to member. Smell to smell. And love was being born out of flesh, one and the same.

Jerumenho takes out his mainmast. Maria Dina lifts her skirt and the stars shine in the night sky. The fields open up. Woman, female, and African rites of *terecô*. Come and go, up and down, rise and fall. Rub together and start all over again. Possession, the full miracle of those sweet nights. The pleasures of the body.

Hard to know what devil's tricks brought Carideno, her husband, along on that outing, but in the middle of everything Jerumenho feels the broad blade of the fish knife in his back and the frigid warmth of a strange sun, and life pours out of him along with the flowing blood. Dina hugs him, hugging night and death, and he loses his mainmast, then silence.

It didn't take long for the shouting to start:

"Somebody's been killed, there's blood here, there's blood!"

Shouting, a desire to know what's not known follows after the happening that happened.

Love and death. The *bumba-meu-boi* group is roaring:

Get yourself up, ox, and come.
You stamp your hooves too.
If the lady of the house can be mounted,
the daughters can be mounted too.
He gave a bellow, he just gave a bellow,
I've already gobbled all three . . .

This was the night of the *bumba-meu-boi* dances and their flowery decorations. Jerôncio, the Cazumbá, leader of the merrymaking, had said even before the young ones arrived:

"Things are going to get pretty hot today!"

On Friday nights you've got to look at the stars. They're blue, sometimes yellow. They ride goats and horses in the empty spots where there are holes in the sky. That's where the demons live. They look down at the earth and have a consultation to see what place they can lay their hand of misfortune upon as it quivers like the dew, in order to cast night's net when day is done.

There's a deep silence. Ants move slowly along. The branches of the *imbaúba* trees are motionless. People run to find out what's behind that mysterious shouting:

"He got laid but he got no pleasure" was what a woman looking at the scene said.

Jerumenho was lying in a pool of blood. Arms open, night closed. That was when Garatoso took off and went to tell Cristório. He'd scarcely started when he stopped and stood stock-still in the middle of the road because he'd heard a voice:

"Don't tell my father that I didn't put up a fight. I was held back. It was a spell of Dina's. And I only saw the night glow of that hair."

"Who's that talking?"

"It's me, Jerumenho."

"You're dead!"

"I'm dead but I can see life. And I'm leaving it."

In the house next door by the side of the road, Zeferina, a local property owner, heard voices and woke up. She made out a shadow speaking to her through the blinking lights:

"Who's there?"

"It's me."

"Who?"

"Jerumenho."

"Aren't you out at sea with Tandito, son?"

"No, I'm in death. I want you to give me a piece of lacework, with lots of flowered squares, so I can make a love charm for Dina, Carideno's wife."

"Where are you?"

"In the world of the horseflies. Flying."

"Stop your sinning. Are you a soul?"

"No. I'm people."

"I can't see you."

"Never will. I'm not anything anymore."

Night comes on and everything is sorcery—and in the distance people are singing and dancing to the songs of the *bumba-meu-boi* that lend enchantment to the nights of mystery.

"Captain Cristório, come quick. . . ."

"What the devil are you calling me like that for? I'm coming." And he came out of the house into the front yard.

"Jerumenho's been killed!"

"What kind of terrible news is this?"

"He's been killed."

"Where?"

"At Faustino's dance."

Cristório fell silent. Brow wrinkled, teeth clenched, he went into the house. Jerumenho was his companion at sea. He was the one who would hang onto the halyard, share his silences, roll up the net. He'd grown up in the canoe, there were so many days and nights they'd spent together in it since he was a boy. Cristório lowered his head, put on his rough cloth shirt, tightened his rope belt, put on his hat, and came out crushed:

"Let's go, Cousin Garatoso. It's God's will and I have to obey."

They got there. A handful of people were around the body. They'd already lit some candles by the foot of the *tamborila* tree where they'd gathered together. Blood was flowing from the wound onto the ground. Jerumenho's face couldn't be seen. He was lying prone. Cristório asked for a sheet. They went to get one. He wrapped his son's body, lifted it onto his shoulder, and headed home. He arrived there. The silence was heavy. He'd left without telling anyone. He stopped in front of the house with the warm body on his back. Only then did he shout for his wife:

"Camborina, wake up! Camborina, Camborina!" His voice was firm and sharp, just like the command to cast a harpoon.

He stood waiting for a while. The door opened. Camborina, in the shadows and not knowing what it was all about, asked:

"What kind of fish is that you're carrying on your back?"

"It's the body of your son Jerumenho."

A wail of grief cut through the night. He went in, laid Jerumenho on the kitchen table, and repeated:

"It's God's will," and he added with rage, "Shit!"

The lamentations, the prayers, and the sadness started up. The news was spreading and friends were arriving. The business of the dead began: coffin, shroud, and grave. Cristório on top of everything. He did it all as though he were getting things ready to sail out. Cristório shed no tears. From time to time he would go over to the body, lift the sheet that covered the face, look, turn his eyes away, and leave.

He put a pot of water on the fire, mixed some warm water in with the cold, picked up some old pieces of cloth, and began to clean his son's corpse. He took off the faded blue pants.

"I'd like for you all to leave!" he ordered his children and neighbors.

He ran his hands over the naked flesh, covering the skin with love. He washed the feet. He turned the body over carefully. It was still bleeding so he placed a cloth over the wound. He went to the bedroom and took the boy's duffel bag down from the hammock hook. The clothes were all washed and carefully rolled up. He pickd out a pair of khaki drill pants and a white shirt. He thought that he really ought to be wearing his old shorts from all those fishing trips. Camborina was weeping, kissing her dead son, and praying to God. Her lamentations flowed through the house like rain in the gutters. There was a brisk wind shaking the old cashew tree in bloom, its branches spreading out over sky and ground in the backyard by the green trees where the guinea hens slept.

Cristório came back. The body was covered by a sheet and he pulled it off. He stood staring at his son as if for the first time. The teeth were barely showing through a half-open mouth. He took hold of the lips and tugged on them three times. He cleansed the face once more. He kissed the forehead. The eyes were closed and the hands hung limply off the table.

He looked at the muscles, began to inspect the body all over. He lifted the arms, pulled on the hair in the armpits. He squeezed the wet cloth so the dirty water would run out and he wet it again in the pot. He slowly washed the mainmast, groin, thighs, legs. He smoothed down the hair, closed the hands, and crossed them over the chest. He began to get him ready. Camborina wanted to help.

"No!" he shouted. "I want to do it by myself!"

He unrolled the pants and began to dress the corpse. First one side, then the other. He remembered the shorts and took everything off. He got the old fishing shorts that his son used to wear in the boat and put them on him. He pulled the cord belt tight and tied it. Then he began working with the pants again. Next, the shirt. He raised the body, hugged it, and only then did he ask Camborina:

"You put on the shirt. No. First clean up the rest of the blood on the table."

He put the arms into the sleeves and slowly went along buttoning the shirt up to the neck.

He brought the feet together, tied them with a strip of cloth and did the same with the hands over the chest. He went to the bedroom, got a comb, fixed the hair, and left a forelock. The hair was brown, neither straight nor curly. Sunburned, smelling of sweat and heat. He got a lump in his throat, combed Jerumenho's hair once more, kissed his face. There were no tears in his eyes. He went to the kitchen and got a knife and a ball of twine. He measured the body three times. He calculated one hand span beyond the feet, another beyond the head. He took the knife, cut the twine, and said in a loud voice:

"Garatoso, take this measurement. For the size of the coffin."

He covered him with the sheet, pulled up a stool, and sat down. He stayed there for the rest of the night and the day that followed, without eating or drinking, without moving a muscle until it was time for the burial on the afternoon of that day, which was still that early dawn for him.

The way to the cemetery was long and difficult. The coffin was being carried by hand. At the cemetery some old women were chanting funeral laments.

Oh, mother of souls,
Friend of the Mother of God,
Rosemary of the field,
Saint Luke and Saint Jerome,
Help me, mother of souls,
Friend of the Mother of God.

Clumps of wild lilies stood around those poor graves. Cristório was silent, then he turned to Garatoso and asked:

"Where's the house of the woman Jerumenho was on top of?"

"A league up the road, near Mojó harbor."

"Well, I want to go there. . . ."

"Don't do anything foolish, cousin! Let time pass."

"I want to talk to her. Then it will be her husband's turn. It'll be a short talk."

"Get that idea of revenge out of your head."

"Let's be on our way."

The coffin arrived at the cemetery. They laid it on the ground where some straggly grass was growing. Camborina went along supported by her children and friends. A great sob arose from all their throats.

"Open the lid," Cristório said.

Jerumenho appeared. His face with its bitter lips. Camborina knelt down, laid her head on her son's chest, crushing the red flowers from the plant in the backyard that had been shaped like a chalice.

"Camborina," her sister Germana said, "accept the will of God."

"Oh, God, why wasn't it me?" she answered with despair.

Cristório kept his eyes fixed on the grave. He wasn't speaking to anyone. No one was speaking to him. They began to say the prayers for the dead. That was the task of Gertrudes, a black granny from the village, well versed in the art of burials:

Lazarus saw his resurrection, Jerumenho will see his.
Lazarus believed.
We believe in the resurrection of the dead.
Oh, Mother of God . . .

Evening was coming on. The sobs grew deeper. There was a breeze that smelled of lavender. The leaves of the cashew trees were curling.

Before he closed the coffin, Cristório ran his hand over his son's face. He kissed him for the last time and said:

"God wished it. God wishes it. God be praised."

A woman tried to console him:

"Jerumenho was so good . . ."

"Shut up, for God's sake, he's dead now," he answered harshly.

The grave was open, and beside it a mound of earth. The grave diggers were ready. An old spade, worn out from the task of covering the dead, was perched, exhausted, on the gravel.

The shouting started. Throats were too small for the deep wails of sorrow. Jerumenho was being lowered. The ropes at the head and foot of the coffin were slowly being released. It reached the bottom. Ropes were pulled, groaning against the wood. Everybody went over and tossed in flowers and green sprigs. That smell of lavender was filling the air. The breeze was the same. Camborina fainted. Germana was raising her hands. Cristório was like a wooden stake.

The spadefuls of earth were shoveled in. The first, when it hit the boards of the coffin, made a hollow sound and Cristório felt a shiver and a hot flash that ran together all through his body, from his feet to his head.

The wake had been a long one. People came from all the surrounding area. Everybody talked about the crime and how good Jerumenho was. After the grave had been filled, a mound of earth was formed and more green sprigs were thrown onto it, jasmine, faded roses, yellowed carnations. Camborina lit a candle that the wind immediately blew out. They all stuck their candles into the ground and tossed more flowers on.

Night was falling. The sun was disappearing. The horizon was red, like a dying fire.

Camborina, hunched over, held up, looked at the ground:

"My darling son!" And she fainted again.

Cristório took Garatoso's arm and said:

"Let's go, cousin. I want to get to the woman's house before the dark of night."

And without speaking to anyone, all sadness and grief, he went off, walking toward the unknown. He took the road to Mojó. Farther on he glanced to the side and saw a shadow. It was going in his direction. He heard sounds, as if they were voices. He went off onto the path. His steps led him into the bushes.

"Papa Cristório, I didn't put up a fight because I wasn't able."

It was Jerumenho. Beside him was Terêncio, the uncle who'd died of fever the winter before. Behind him Varizinha and Batesta, the sisters who'd died of childhood illnesses, little children. Batesta had a long face, gentle eyes, the same ones Cristório had seen in the white coffin when, over twenty years ago, they'd taken her to the cemetery. She'd died with her eyes open, and her father's hands had pulled the eyelids down to cover the sightless look.

"Papa Cristório, you have to caulk the boat and repair the net. I was going to do it today but I couldn't. Watch out for Seasick Sandbar. It's tricky so you've got to stay awake."

There was a cashew tree loaded down and a strong smell of fruit. Cristório tried to catch hold of his son, but there was only wind. He couldn't understand what was going on. He stopped and asked:

"Did that woman call you and not tell you she had a husband?"

"She said she had a husband but that her husband was out fishing."

"God save your soul. You're a real blessing for those girls."

Terêncio was fat. It seemed he was eating too much.

"Terêncio," he said, "your wife's getting married again. The husband's a working man."

"I can't make it. My feet are stuck in the mud of the swamp."

"So how come you're here?"

"I came here carried in Jerumenho's arms."

"Where did you all go?"

They'd disappeared.

Cristório heard a snapping of branches and a crowd of people in the bushes. He went back to the road and found Garatoso.

"Did you hear? Did you see?"

"I didn't hear anything. You went into the woods because of your belly, naturally. At this time of day a person's guts can't take so much pain."

Cristório was silent.

"Is the woman's house far?"

"Just around a couple more bends in the road."

In fact, a few hundred yards ahead a shack could be seen, closed tight with no sign of life. Cristório went up and knocked:

"Anybody home? Anybody home?"

A great silence. Cristório went ahead and opened the door with a kick, revealing a room with a dirt floor off the bedroom. It was all one single motion. A terrified woman was there. It was Maria Dina, her eyes puffy from so much weeping, wearing a blouse and petticoat. Cristório glared at her with eyes of hate:

"Are you the woman who was under Jerumenho yesterday when he was killed by Carideno?"

"Don't kill me, for the love of God! It wasn't my fault! It was love. We did it without thinking about any trouble."

Cristório looked at her from the side. Twilight was settling now, and objects and people were turning hazy. He looked at her again, his eyes wide open and his hands trembling. Everything he'd suffered that day had left marks on his injured body.

"Take off your clothes, get naked, and lay down."

"Don't kill me, please don't kill me . . . ," Maria Dina begged, feeling the weight of those eyes.

"Take everything off, right now!" Cristório commanded in a voice of hatred.

Maria Dina began to get undressed. She was shaking, overcome with terror. First she took off her blouse, and her breasts stood out. Then she removed her skirt and plain cotton panties. She didn't know what she was doing or why. She was following orders. Cristório didn't move. Emerging from those rags was a young body, broad hips; covering her parts was dark hair the color of a boat, dark and light like that, like the sails of his boat all stained with mangrove mud.

Cristório drew out his fishing knife. It was broad and a foot long, his ever-present companion for fishing. Honed on aerolite, it was what he used to open up the bellies of big fish with a sure cut, not swerving, but steady and precise. He used the reverse of the blade as a club, strong blows to kill catfish, break their spines, smash their heads. Dina's face was showing a terror that was coming out of her eyes just as if fear were an animal that had taken shape and motion as it tried to flee.

Cristório looked at that body. It was thin but firm. Its nakedness was not so clear in the half-light of evening, but there was enough for him to see the woman. Hate and desire were growing together in his guts. He grabbed the knife, clutched the handle, lifted it up, and struck it into the mud wall with all the strength of his rage.

"Open your legs, woman! You stray bitch, I've come to finish what Jerumenho started!"

And night fell with tears and terror.

Seven Poems

Pierre Martory

Translated from French by John Ashbery

Translator's Note

Pierre Martory was born in Bayonne, France, on December 1, 1920, of a Basque mother and French father who was an an army officer. He spent much of his childhood in Morocco, where his father was posted, and returned there often as an adult. After passing his *baccalauréat* he enrolled at the Ecole des Sciences Politiques in Paris in the fall of 1939, but was forced to flee the Nazi army in June 1940. He joined the French army and was shipped to North Africa, where he ended up fighting alongside the Allied forces in what had become the Free French Army. After the war he held a number of jobs, first at the unlikely-sounding Biarritz American University, then as an airlines clerk in Bordeaux and Paris, as assistant to the anthropologist Marcel Griaule, reporter at *Le Monde Diplomatique,* and finally as arts editor of *Paris Match,* where he remained for twenty-five years. He died in October 1998.

His novel *Phébus ou le beau Mariage* was published by Denoël in 1953 to respectable reviews (a second completed novel, *Un jeune Homme attachant,* remains unpublished). Meanwhile he wrote poetry almost constantly throughout his life, publishing only a few poems in little magazines when he was briefly part of a group of poets (including Hubert Juin and Pierre-Jean Oswald) who met regularly at a café on the Ile St. Louis to read their work aloud to each other. As his executor, I have been classifying his papers, beginning with a school copybook containing more than one thousand lines of poetry written in Tunisia during the war. Of the poems translated here, "Music" is dated 1948. The others are from a typed manuscript titled "La Lyre d'Aloès," which appears to date from the early 1950s. It is dedicated to a friend, Simone Bitterly, with the line "*en attendant une édition sérieuse*"—until there is a real edition. A handwritten note from the publisher Seghers is inserted in the manuscript. Dated simply "Tuesday," it announced the acceptance of six of the poems for publication, but adds, "Unfortunately we can't give you a date—perhaps in a month, two months, or six months." This seems to have been typical of his dealings with French publishers.

He has had better luck in America. Poems of his have appeared in *Poetry,* the *New Yorker, American Poetry Review,* and a number of smaller publications. A collection, *Every Question but One,* was published in 1989 by Ground Water Press. Sheep Meadow Press has published two collections: *The Landscape Is Behind the Door,* translated by me, and *Veilleur de Jours,* in French.

* * *

EARLY MORNING

Is it you? It's night. The stairway has folded. The doors are soldered to their frames. The clocks killed. The midnight sky had no moon worth bothering with. Is it you? It's for me. It's not you. Till tomorrow, then.

Then I met you on the sidewalk and ants in your brain. "They didn't want me but they stole all I had. If they had wanted me to I'd have given them everything."

Then you put on your last dress. "I don't know. I don't want to, not by the boulevards" and as I was sleeping between noon and dawn you climbed up to the roof passing my room. You climbed the wall like another lizard.

You slip into the sunlight without a sandal or a comb. Give what they took from you. Is it you that pile. A cotton cloth covers the day's hole.

THE BUYING BACK

I came down into the square of sunlight to choose from among the black products of the other earth the one that would shake my body black from sleep the one that would wash all my limbs the one that would nourish my hunger for all things the one that would sing exotic refrains the one that would teach me a language of which I would understand nothing.

I wanted him to be strong and with good teeth I wanted him to be named Foolhardiness and to know how to smile and dance sometimes in the moonlight and invoke a deity whose picture would decorate his room instead of a mirror.

So amid the chained horde the copper the marble the ebony the lapis and the perfumes of those bodies ripening at noon I found only a woman who would fill the canvas of my reasonable desires

I bought her I signed her deed of liberation I called her Quasi-Foolhardiness I wanted to put her to the test, she asked me to bathe her to put her to sleep to sing her a sentimental song in the language of my country that she didn't know.

UNNATURAL HISTORY

An anachronistic chimera camouflaged with rhinestones, as scrawny as one could wish, was hawking her chandelier (crystal pendants) before the lighted facade of a porcelain shop and the vendors of fresh newspapers jostled her without her seeming to mind the noise of the street the slow motion of the houses or the rotation of the sky.

The stream carried a boat made of straw veiled with silk. The paper to read love on flowed on the waves toward the open sewers like a weekday between the hour of the wolf and the hour of the shepherd. Pedestrians placed their feet on the studded crosswalks of evening. Each signal to go forward was pinned to their lapels.

Then the parade of witches passed, barely noticed. On the float of an angelic choir, marshmallow sweetness of catarrhal voices. Their painted eyebrows their labeled teeth their fingers weighed down with green fingernails. When they cried Evoē the echo from the walls came back, "One hundred francs." Never an echo from the horizon Achtung.

And the silence draped the statues with the red of sincere modesty. Far from the desiccated hay the matches the ardent bodies—these arsonists. Night slept, vying with the neon signs. The martyr's crown was bestowed on the patient since she had vomited all the contents of her poor-box onto the pavement

Emptied like a sack flipped over like a cuttlefish the bone one now saw was white flowed in a river napping with cream the cake of her viscera. She slowly decided to die and entering heaven's gate asked the porter as a favor to have her stone engraved with a series of Roman numerals and that it be used as a sundial.

COMMON CAUSE

The accomplices ran through the streets, and without it needing to be advertised, they were already waiting before the doors, already armed, already arrested, already condemned, already punished, all those who wanted to accompany me into the shadows.

One didn't have to choose the youngest the most open the plumpest the most bewitched each one was going to have his share of my sins They penetrated a body I was followed by that mob

When I wanted to point out my victim they had already put a hood over his head I could only make out the shape and the voice
When I wanted to choose the blade they handed me a revolver when I wanted to release the bullet my fingers squeezed the neck
in the sack and they burst out laughing when I was called murderer.

Then they continued on their way with hands thrust deep in my pockets Then they took turns kissing me in front of my door I have the traces of those mouths on my chest They sang all night all dawn all day under my window before my eyes in my sleep

I went down into the street I took my place in their queue No one will have chosen me I will penetrate a single body I knew they would repeat my gesture of the night before I laughed to see what it was that was dead whose face they had never seen

Pierre Martory

THE MAIN THING IN A FACE CAN BE READ ON A FREEZING DAY

The main thing in a face can be read on a freezing day
The apparatus of inspiration the hands the keys the trees
The bunch of behaviors stored up time after time
And embroidered with blazing initials
With butterflies without discretion
Now that within these limits of cold
Your head is sleeping young-old poet
Now that within the limits of their flesh at zero
Your lips and your cheeks remain starched
Now that you move your tongue
On the mirror of your palate
The main thing in your face can be read like a newspaper.

LITANIES

May it please the shower of gold to cover me for I am cold from soft metal
May it please the shower of gold to cover me for I am cold from soft metal

May it please the shower of water to cover me for I have faith of metamorphosis
May it please the shower of water to cover me for I have faith of metamorphosis

May it please the harsh idea to nourish me for I thirst after my false loves
May it please the harsh idea to nourish me for I thirst after my false loves

May it please the afternoon to suffice me for I've had too much of my dark days
May it please the afternoon to suffice me for I've had too much of my dark days

May it please the near here to open for me for I've knocked at its door in vain
May it please the near here to open for me for I've knocked at its door in vain

May it please the calm sea to swell for I've trapped too many sea lice
May it please the calm sea to swell for I've trapped too many sea lice

May it please the incarnate soul to show itself for I have believed in the incarnate soul
May it please the incarnate soul to show itself for I have believed in the incarnate soul

May it please the firm hand to show itself for I've drawn the rusty blade
May it please the firm hand to show itself for I've drawn the rusty blade

May it please the lover the loved to lie to itself for I've known the weight of the lie
May it please the lover the loved to lie to itself for I've known the weight of the lie

May it please the man in tears to bruise himself I've howled the cry of my dreams
May it please the man in tears to bruise himself I've howled the cry of my dreams

MUSIC

You are drumming I don't know what percussion of forests and grief into my skull

O hands beginning the ceremony of circumstances to be borne in mind

And it's not a people not the lone outpouring of a hermit on his tower

who harangues, above expectant ears, the sadness of my mornings and the overlong days that are my due

And it's not an appeal coming from some place I'll be able to reach some day

with a huge effort of attention like a reward for my function of being that makes the gold leaves vibrate that indicates at which crossroads in my memory a majestic sign is hiding or revealing itself

noise from the pile of other tall columns of silence   sparse ruins of silence

between the stones of the ceiling under the undecipherable allegories the ancient psalm is being played that doesn't need to be remembered in order to be loved nor loved in order to be remembered

I hear a woman walking on the leaves of summer that has passed

I hear amazement sighing before the deforested clearing, open like an avenue in a poor neighborhood

I hear the door of a temple turning on its hinges

And the portico filling with the vibrant turbulence of accumulated presences like a basin under the thread of water from a fountain

wind that enters my ear and flattens me against a tree like a wet cloth

wind that fits my body to the stones

then a torn song waiting for the throat that will give it life

faces surround the measuring tools, a pack of hounds longs to hold the calm prey in their teeth

face and wind form the sheaf of pointless allusions that allow the comings and goings of emptiness

> urgent silence   cork of silence bobbing on the sea   scales to weigh the peaks and hollows of deep waves
>
> revolve revolve   smashed waves   that torment thousands of hopes condemned to be never anything but hopes yet gathered together like a group of communicants
>
> be my lasting substitute for a machine for living   instruments overflowing with possible miracles

I'm listening to a single being placed before the teeth of a piano that can revive the oldest flames and calls to the conclave of our joy the dead who've already turned to the dust we breathe

I hate the order of the clandestine world I want to intuit the meaning of all signs

I want to leave outside in every snow the unwanted children of a solitary outburst of feeling

Night that creates a decoy tower where cannon shots reverberate night filtered through the hours with immobile strolls dives into yesterday flights above tomorrow

I'm listening to one person placed in front of the pictures stolen from an extinct family album that is constructing the scenery of so ancient a custom

The lover with the object of his love
The mother present at the dying of her youngest son

Pathetic unwinding of spirals whose end is lost in a tangle of misfortunes

And I grow lighter from what makes me a contemporary of myself
The sac of my flesh, the garment of feeling

And I lie down on the cloud about to burst into rain that will irrigate the illusory fields of eternity

And I make my bed of fallen leaves   an ambience scented with the lightest effluvia   a never-ending evening with this brother who comes to me each time a train of particular waves is set in motion

The Guest
Yoko Tawada

Translated from German by Susan Bernofsky

Translator's Note

I first encountered Yoko Tawada in 1991 in an Austrian literary magazine called *manuskripte* that had published a very short piece of hers (and one of the first she'd ever written in German) called "Das Fremde aus der Dose" ("Canned Foreign," *Fiction International* 24, 1993). In it, Tawada writes about the difficulties of reading the world in a foreign language. The narrator of her story becomes obsessed with a sort of desperate literalism, buying a can in a supermarket because of the Japanese woman printed on its label and being surprised to discover it contains only tuna fish. In "The Guest," too—the novella whose first four chapters are excerpted here—Tawada's main character struggles to read a world written in a language that seems just beyond her grasp. The items she sees at a flea market become bearers of meaning that she can move beyond only after she's found an interpretation to contain them. The ensuing chain of interpretations produces the narrative we are reading. The "flea" of the flea market becomes a literal creature that the narrator imagines has lodged in her ear (perhaps because of the German expression—not explicitly mentioned in the story—"to put a flea in someone's ear," which means to put a notion into a person's head). The penetration of the body via the ear canal naturally suggests impregnation (thanks to the Virgin Mary) as well as another case of irregular (and cross-cultural) engendering, the tale of Mme. Butterfly. The chain of associations has brought us back to Japan, though it is a Japan seen darkly through a European glass.

Yoko Tawada's work straddles two continents, two languages and cultures. Since the mid-1980s (she moved from Tokyo to Hamburg in 1982, at the age of twenty-two), she has been writing in both languages, and has published a good ten books in each: stories, short novels, poems, and works for the stage. The interlingual space her texts carve out for themselves draws attention not only to the different ways in which different languages signify, but also (perhaps as a corollary thereof) to how strange it is that there should be signification at all. If some things around us (a clock, the cover of a book, street signs) must be read to be understood, who's to say we needn't do the same with other sorts of objects: a jacket, a radio, a candlestick, a face? This faux-naive view of the universe turns an ordinary street scene into a place of wonder and makes the plight of the foreigner struggling to understand a new physical as well as linguistic world appear to be a plausible metaphor for the human condition.

* * *

1.

ONE WINTER AFTERNOON—I had an ear infection—I walked through an underground passage that led from a subway station to a street with many shops. I had a three o'clock appointment with my ear doctor, whose office was at the end of the street. How late was it? I wondered. Just before the entrance to the passage I'd seen a clock mounted on the side of a kiosk. The clock was missing the numbers three and seven. Beside the clock stood a man who was just taking the missing numbers from his tool kit so as to affix them to the clock's face. The woman inside the kiosk shouted to him how nice it would be to be able to see the correct time again. All at once it seemed strange to me that the numbers were arranged in a circle, since ordinarily numbers are always written from left to right.

As I entered the artificially lit passage, I realized I'd forgotten to check what time it was. It was flea-market day in the passage. The people standing on either side of the aisle inspecting the items offered up for sale looked to me as though they'd come from a dream. Their voices echoed as if from a great distance, and their bodies lacked contours. The night before I had dreamt of a flea, or of a market. When I woke up from the ear pain, I felt as though there were a flea leaping about in my ear. I remembered a story in which a young woman developed an earache during a coach ride. I can't remember if she was the main character in the story or whether it was only that her pain made me think of her as a heroine. Her mother and her lover pour water into the painful ear, shift her head back and forth several times, then pour the water back out. When they do so, a damp flea leaps out of her ear. The woman faints, and her mother screams for help, while her lover seizes the flea—his prey—between his fingertips and pops it into his mouth.

The flea market was like an illustrated encyclopedia. The ground was crowded with small objects of copper, colored glass, rubber, beechwood, paper, nylon, and other materials. On the wall of the passage, which bore several years' worth of posters advertising concerts and demonstrations, a number of jackets and coats were displayed for sale. They had been thoroughly cleaned, some of them even ironed and fitted out with new buttons, but I realized that their previous owners had left behind invisible traces on the clothing. These traces frightened me. It wasn't some contagious illness I was afraid of, but rather the stories of lives unknown to me. A dark gray jacket, for example, which I noticed straight off, reminded me of a neighbor whose life remained a mystery to me although I'd known him for ten years. He wore a similar jacket, the left pocket of which was pulled slightly out of shape. What did he always carry in it? Every morning he left his apartment, and returned every evening at six o'clock. I knew only the name of the bank he worked for, nothing more. Every so often I noticed, emanating from his apartment, the smell of singed hair.

A hoarse voice addressed me from the left, polite and threatening at once. I shouldn't just look at the jacket, I should try it on. It's true it was a man's jacket, but it would be just right for me. I said nothing and, making no move to touch the jacket, stayed where I was. A short while later a gaunt-looking man with a guitar case appeared. He stopped before the jacket, placed the case on the ground beside him, and without the slightest hesitation tried the jacket on. Apparently he was not at all afraid of its former owner. At the time I didn't yet know that even jackets fresh from the factory already have life stories unknown to me and are not like blank paper. The traces are well hidden, but sometimes one can discover them by accident. Once I purchased what seemed to me in the store a perfectly ordinary radio, but at home that night when I turned it on, it emitted a strange noise. The sound resembled the hoarse scream of a male voice. Then there was a brief scratching sound. I inspected the radio with my magnifying glass and discovered in one of the buttons a splinter of fingernail. It was embedded like a fossil in the black plastic. Probably someone working on the assembly line had been attacked by a machine and lost a fingernail, or even a whole finger. The attack was probably classified as an accident. During the quality-control check, the finger had been discovered and removed, but no one had noticed the fingernail. I dug it out with my pocketknife and buried it in the garden. Since then, there have been no more inappropriate sounds from my radio.

At the flea market, no one tries to hide the traces hidden in an object. The stuffed animals with their somewhat squashed faces observed me ironically, furiously, or disdainfully. Paperback novelettes with faded covers still bore coffee stains and greasy fingerprints from their first readers. The books can never forget their readers, though the readers have no doubt forgotten all about the books' contents. Even more than the traces on these objects, the order in which the items were arranged fascinated me. An iron and a candlestick stood side by side, as though there were some relation between them. I was even able to think how this proximity might be deciphered: The iron produces heat and the candlestick light. Each takes the place of the sun, which from the underground passage is never visible.

The interior of my ear is never illuminated by the sun either. It doesn't want to be illuminated, not even by the ear doctor's artificial light. For eardrums can receive sounds only in the dark. How late was it? Would I still be able to get to the doctor's on time? A pair of ice skates and a clock lay side by side, as though challenging me to guess their relation. I stood before them until I had found a solution: ice skates and clock—both turn in circles. When the skaters twirl on the ice, their skates have to turn with them. When ice skaters twirl, they look like the dolls in music boxes, which you wind like a clock.

At the end of the passage I discovered a book between a black umbrella and a sewing machine with a treadle. I don't know why this book in particular drew my attention. I picked it up, and noticed its slight warmth in the palm of my hand. On the book's cover I saw letters that were written not from left to right, but in a circle. I asked the man who was standing there hawking his wares in what language the book was written, since I don't know of any language whose letters are arranged in a circle. He shrugged his shoulders and said it wasn't a book, it was a mirror. I refused to look at the thing he was calling a mirror. Maybe it isn't a book, I conceded, but I would still like to know what's going on with this writing.

The man grinned and replied: To our eyes, you look exactly like this writing. That's why I said it was a mirror.

I rubbed my forehead from left to right, as though rewriting my face.

2.

The ear doctor, Dr. Mettinger, had his door half open and was waiting for me in his consulting room. Like all the other doctors who have treated me in this city, he wanted to speak with me alone behind closed doors, as though I had an illness of which no one else should hear. I stopped just before the threshold, unable to take another step, although I was already fairly accustomed to being alone in a room with a strange man, for in this city even the vegetable and fish shops have doors that separate them from the life of the street. I stared at the silver door handle sticking out of the white, smooth door. Surely it will be cold if I touch it, I thought, and then the warmth of my own hand will feel unpleasant. It will be slippery in my moist hand and refuse to let me grip it. The doctor's assistant, observing me from her post at the reception desk, called to me that I was standing in front of the correct room. But I wasn't at all interested in whether it was the right or wrong room.

Come in, Dr. Mettinger said in a peremptory tone. At this, my legs began to march like the legs of a robot. I didn't feel the sort of fear people in this city call claustrophobia. It wasn't the room's enclosedness that troubled me, but rather the strange quiet within it. Unlike the underground passage where I'd seen the flea market, it had neither sounds nor voices nor superfluous objects. There was no trace of any of the patients who had been treated in this room. Since I spent a moment occupied only with gazing around me, Dr. Mettinger withdrew his right hand, which he had been holding out to me.

Have a seat, Ms. . . .

He broke off his sentence and sat down himself at his desk to look for the insurance certificate where he could check my name. As he attempted to pronounce it, I tried to find the best place to put my chair. I didn't want to sit too close to Dr. Mettinger, and pushed the chair a little to the right so I could sit diagonally opposite him. Then I fixed my eyes on his white coat, exactly the way I fix my eyes on a white sheet of paper before I begin to write. I told him I had an earache. As though there were a flea in my ear, I wanted to add, but instead said: There's a flea living in my ear.

I beg your pardon? Dr. Mettinger asked, looking startled. For a moment, the muscles of his face forgot to hold the individual pieces of flesh together. Dr. Mettinger was not a fat man, but now his flesh appeared superfluous and useless. Why was he startled? Perhaps I had mispronounced the *l* in the word "flea," and Dr. Mettinger had heard an *r*. My tongue surreptitiously probed my hard palate to check whether I'd really said an *l*. I can distinguish between these two sounds only with my tongue, not with my ears, for my sense of touch is more highly developed with respect to the foreign language than my hearing. My doubt over whether I'd pronounced an *l* vanished again as the doctor asked me where I'd gotten the idea that a flea might be living in my ear. I answered that I knew from a story that such things could happen. He got up abruptly, strode to the window, and shifted a vase of flowers a little to the left so that the sun could shine directly on his desk.

Excuse me, it was a little too dark for me, even though the weather today is splendid, he said in a friendly voice and picked up his big fountain pen. The expression "the weather today is splendid" bothered me for some reason. The fountain pen began writing on a sheet of paper; it was thicker around than my thumb and had a middle section that looked like a golden ring.

How long have you had the earache?

I told him I'd woken up in the middle of the night because of a burning sensation in my left ear. On Dr. Mettinger's desk lay three stacks of paper that reflected the sun's glare. The letters vanished in the strong light. While Dr. Mettinger was taking notes, I remembered that the night before I had dreamt of a fire on a sheet of paper. One by one the letters went up in flames, and only the ones containing an enclosed space—like *O, P, D, Q,* and *R*—remained unharmed. So I hadn't dreamt of the flea or the market after all, I had been mistaken, and only now realized what my dream had really been about.

Dr. Mettinger informed me that he would have to examine my ear. As he spoke, he gazed attentively into my eyes, as though searching for something. I couldn't imagine what.

Yes, I said uncertainly and turned to the side so that he could see my painful ear better.

Uncover the ear, he said in a tone both severe and apprehensive. I pushed back my hair to expose the ear, realizing as I did so that my ears were protected by my hair. I hadn't been outside with exposed ears at all. How then was it possible for someone to have put something in my ear that caused me pain? Dr. Mettinger took an instrument that resembled a small telescope or spyglass from a drawer. Then he gazed into my ear with it and held his breath. After a while he began to groan, laid aside his spyglass, and said: You're pregnant.

The doctor's face reddened. I assumed he was furious. A foreigner like me simply showed up at his office, rather than going to a gynecologist, and forced him to make a diagnosis that lay outside his area of expertise. I remembered that this city was full of people who specialized in a particular field and wanted nothing to do with anything else. I couldn't explain to Dr. Mettinger why I'd gone to him and not a gynecologist. Both of us remained silent until I discovered a calendar hanging beside the window. On this calendar all the days of the year were marked, even this day in December, but there was not a single day on the calendar on which I could have become pregnant. It took me a moment to realize this. The calendar looked strange to me all at once: The dates were arranged in such a way that every month formed a square. It occurred to me that ever since I'd stopped working in an office, I no longer thought of a month as being square, but rather like a moon, a circular motion that gave my body its orientation. It was no longer important to me whether a day was a Sunday or a Monday.

The numbers on the calendar had to break free of the lines of the weekdays, form circles, and sketch out moons.

Please look again to be sure if I'm really pregnant; it really isn't possible. Could you have confused a flea with an embryo?

Dr. Mettinger took up his spyglass again and this time poked it deeper into my ear.

What do you see? I asked in a severe tone to subdue a feeling of uneasiness.

I see a stage in a theater, he said now in a childish voice.

Try to say more precisely what it is you see. I heard him inhale deeply and then say: I see a building near a harbor, an officer, and several women.

The doctor's assistant called to him from outside that there was an important phone call for him, but he didn't hear her voice.

What do the women standing there look like?

I asked a few more questions, although my curiosity was abating, for I suspected the doctor of being an inexperienced theater-goer; when the women entered, at the latest, he would see only old, familiar, boring pictures. His voice became somewhat higher as he reported: The women have on long dresses, silk, what do you call them, oh, that's right, kimonos, and one of them has a knife in her hand. Now she's just plunged it into her belly, a red stain spreads on the white silk, it gets bigger and bigger.

I groaned and simply pushed his hand away.

Dr. Mettinger, that is Madame Butterfly; what you describe is not original.

He turned red, and his lips twitched to seize on words that might still be said. I didn't wait any longer but rather left his office without so much as a goodbye.

3.

The book I'd bought at the flea market was not a book at all, but rather a box containing four cassette tapes. I ought to have realized this when I saw the circle of letters on the cover. The text turns in a circle, rather than being read from left to right. "A Novel," I read on the title page. Under these words stood the title and the author's name in tiny, unclear letters.

I inserted the first cassette into my tape recorder and pressed the button. A female voice began to read from the novel. After a while I realized I was now in the landscape of the novel. Although the plot did not interest me at all, I entered the novel the way one might mistakenly enter a house that has neither doors nor walls. I hadn't noticed a threshold where I might have paused to consider whether or not I wanted to go in. I began to be afraid of the voice and turned off the tape recorder.

Why couldn't I take pleasure in this voice? After all, I had been looking for a text whose letters would disappear as they were read, like the many novels I read as an adolescent. In those years I went to the neighborhood library almost every day, picked some novel or other, and found a seat in a corner of the reading room. My reading was always the same: For the first half hour, I had to struggle against a wall of words. It was strenuous work, but I didn't lose patience, knowing that sooner or later I would gain entrance to the novel. I read and read without knowing why I should be interested in what I was reading and where the novel was taking me. Soon the speed of my reading increased and the letters vanished before my eyes, as during a train ride. When the train accelerates soon after departure, the trees closest to the tracks disappear, and one sees only the distant landscape.

It has been years since I last read a novel whose letters I could make disappear. Probably this has nothing to do with me, but with the city: The only books here are written in a foreign script. As long as I've lived here I've been unable to enter novels. I read and read, but the alphabet never vanishes before my eyes, but rather remains like iron bars or like sand in salad or the reproduction of my face in the glass of a night train's window. How often my own reflection in the glass has kept me from enjoying a nocturnal landscape. Even when there was nothing much to see, I would have liked to gaze into the darkness, not at my own mirror image.

Why had it never occurred to me that a tape recording could be the magic means for erasing the letters in a novel? Finally I had succeeded in eliminating the alphabet. I should have been happy.

I turned the tape recorder back on, this time trying to listen to the voice without losing my distance from it. But I couldn't. Either I heard nothing at all, or I was plunged into the novel.

As I turned off the machine, furious, the doorbell rang. It was my new neighbor, who had moved into the building approximately a week ago. I recognized him by the sunglasses that hid his eyes. He asked whether I had a little salt. This was the second time a man had asked me for salt in this city. The first time, a man sitting at the next table in a restaurant where only a few tables had salt shakers had asked: Have you got salt?

He had a cello case and a portable music stand next to his table. With his eyes closed, he shook the salt shaker over his salad plate. I thought I could hear the grains of salt falling on the leaves. The man was not afraid to act with his eyes closed. I had often made the discovery that people carrying musical instruments around with them are not afraid of certain things. I saw on the leaves of his salad white grains of salt that for a moment glittered strangely but soon became transparent.

I filled a teacup with salt for my neighbor and gave it to him. He asked whether I had a visitor. His lips were smooth and slightly moist, though his skin was dry.

No, no one's visiting, I replied, noticing at the same time that there was a voice coming from my kitchen. It was the voice from the tape recorder, which I had already turned off.

I don't have a visitor, but sometimes it happens that there is suddenly a woman there and . . . I don't mean a woman, but actually just a woman's voice. Because the voice can get in anywhere and . . .

A woman? he asked suspiciously.

No, a voice, not a woman.

He didn't ask any more questions. When I had said goodbye to the neighbor, I returned to the kitchen. The tape recorder was running on its own. I sat down on the chair and pretended the voice wasn't bothering me. I tried to think about the man in sunglasses. "Sunglasses," "professionally," "how old," "thin," "salt," "lips," "tennis shoes." . . . The questions had to be formulated, and they would have to be asked when I saw him again. But I had no idea what I wanted to know about him, what I wanted to think about him, what it was even possible for me to think, for the voice from the tape recorder forced me to return to the novel. The plot was boring, but the voice wouldn't let me go. It determined the temperature of the room in which the novel was set. It determined the smell of the main character's skin. And the figure's gaze was also determined by it.

What an incredibly tedious novel, I said aloud, but it didn't help. As if chained down, I sat on the kitchen chair listening to the voice. After the first side of the tape was finished and the tape player turned itself off, the voice went on speaking in my head. I could no longer recognize the words, but the voice itself became clearer and clearer.

That night I made myself a cup of tea and by mistake put salt in it. I had to dump out the tea in the sink. I gazed for a long time into the hole of the drain, into which the brown spiral of tea was being sucked. I don't know how long I stood there looking at the hole without making a new cup of tea. I was no longer able to measure time, for time passed more quickly when the voice inside me sped up. When it spoke in staccato, time stuttered. Sometimes it stopped, and I took deep breaths so as not to suffocate. At twelve o'clock the voice suddenly vanished. The very same moment, my radio alarm turned on automatically. The news. I ran over and switched the radio off.

4.

Once the voice from the tape recorder had taken possession of my life, I became sensitive to every sound that came from a machine. I noticed, for example, that my typewriter clacked in an irregular rhythm, although the distance between the characters was constant. Only between words did it leave a particularly large space in which a whole character might have fit. But the typewriter fell silent not only between words but at other points as well, and when I listened to the sound while typing I could no longer understand the meaning of the words.

Ty pew r ite r!

The music of this clacking produced a text that was different from mine, words incorrectly divided in a stumbling rhythm.

At the time I regularly wrote short articles that were published as a series in a Japanese women's magazine. When the editor had first called me up to ask whether I could write something about holidays in Germany, I'd immediately said no. I'm not an ethnologist, and have never occupied myself with this sort of topic. The editor said she wasn't looking for scholarly essays but just everyday observations that would make sense to her readers. I wound up taking the job for financial reasons. But as soon as I started working on the first article I realized what a difficult job it was. The first topic was birthdays, which are perhaps the most important holidays of all, since even people who try to ignore Christmas like to celebrate their birthdays.

There was a lot for me to write about, since there are many phenomena that interest me, but I was unable to explain any of them. For example, I wrote that a neighbor of mine—although she was already twenty-two years old—was visited on her birthday by her mother, who hugged and kissed her as though she'd just been born.

So that the readers of the women's magazine wouldn't get the wrong idea, I added that it was often considered normal here in Germany to kiss one's mother. Even adults are permitted to kiss their mothers, celebrate their own birthdays, and receive birthday presents from their mothers. The difference between childhood and adulthood wasn't as clearly demarcated in Europe, I wrote, and then crossed out the sentence. Since I'm not an ethnologist, I wasn't sure I was qualified to make such a statement. If I were an ethnologist, I might have known why birthdays here are so important.

Why do people celebrate birthdays? Because they've lived another year without dying? Here, too, I didn't attempt an explanation, but instead wrote that you weren't allowed to congratulate a person before the actual day of the birthday, since that brought bad luck. Then suddenly an explanation for the celebration of birthdays occurred to me. Perhaps people celebrate their birthdays because this is a day when they can distinguish themselves from everyone else. Unlike the others, they have a special relationship to this day. I wrote that people here were in search of something that distinguishes them from other people.

Three minutes later I realized that many people share the same birthday and crossed out the sentence. It also occurred to me that people here like to talk about their zodiac signs. But a sign doesn't belong to a single person; everyone shares his sign with approximately a twelfth of mankind. Thus my supposition that birthdays distinguish people from others couldn't be right. So I wrote only that people here like to celebrate their birthdays and talk about signs of the zodiac, especially late at night after a long discussion about politics.

I was dissatisfied with my first article, since I hadn't been able to explain any of what I described. But the editor said I didn't have to explain anything at all, since there was usually no explanation for superstitions. I promised to write about Christmas the next time, and then about German Unification Day.

Since I didn't have my own typewriter, I often visited Martina, a student who lived across the hall. In a sort of ritual I asked her every time whether by any chance she could work without her typewriter for a few hours. I had never seen her writing anything. Nor had she ever mentioned anything about some paper she was working on. Whenever I came to her apartment, she said she wasn't working at the moment because she lacked the necessary calm. Except for a salt shaker on the table, all the objects in her apartment looked as though they'd never been touched. Martina once explained to me that she hardly ever used anything in her apartment since she often slept elsewhere. Nevertheless I could not understand why her apartment looked like a hotel room that had not been slept in for months, a hotel room no longer in use because the traces of some unfortunate incident could not be removed.

Today her alarm clock began to jangle at the very moment I was about to pose the usual question. Instead of turning it off, she closed her eyes. I could see her lips moving. It looked as though she were counting numbers soundlessly. After a while she walked over to the alarm clock with deliberate slowness and pressed its button. Finally the clock was silent.

Although I hadn't said a word, she gave me a horrified look, as though I'd reproached her. With both embarrassment and pride she then answered a question I hadn't asked. It was an exercise. She was practicing enduring sounds that seemed to announce catastrophe without being overcome with hysteria or panic.

Once a week Martina went to a therapist. Every sound that leapt into her ears—an alarm clock ringing, the squeal of car brakes, even the voices of strange children on the street—made her think she was no longer able to protect herself from anything.

What do you want to protect yourself against?

Martina did not answer my question. Instead she answered a question I hadn't asked:

No, I don't want to.

I said nothing, and Martina told me that a few days before she'd been on her way to the subway station and just before she reached the entrance she'd heard a little girl shout: Papa, c'mon!

Martina couldn't see her because the little girl was standing in one of the tunnels to which the stairs led. Martina only heard the voice, and was unable to go down the stairs. Then she went home again. She no longer had the strength to visit the girlfriend with whom she'd had a date. The girl's voice had plunged into her ear like an invisible hand grenade and then had exploded silently inside her body. After this incident Martina didn't leave her apartment for three days and didn't talk to anyone.

Carefully I hinted that I, too, had once been possessed by a voice. She had no way of knowing I was describing my current situation. She didn't seem at all interested in the situations of other people. But it wasn't all that bad to be possessed by a voice.

Quite the contrary, I eventually came to take great pleasure in it, I said in an intentionally cheerful tone, which did nothing to change Martina's dour expression. She looked at me, but it was clear she hadn't understood what I'd said. I suggested she always wear her Walkman when she went out so her ears would be protected. She took the Walkman from her desk drawer and tried it to see if it still worked. I asked her whether she'd spoken with our new neighbor yet.

What new neighbor do you mean?

Martina said she hadn't seen any new neighbor.

When I was about to return to my apartment, Martina's boyfriend arrived to pick her up. With his appearance, the oppressiveness in the air vanished. I took a long deep breath. At the same time I missed my tape so badly that I immediately said goodbye to them and went back to my apartment with the typewriter.

I couldn't type a thing that day, nor for many days after, because the voice from the tape recorder became louder and louder, until eventually it drowned out the clacking of the machine. Several times a day I turned off the tape recorder, but it kept turning back on by itself.

Don't you want me to write?

For the first time I asked the voice an audible question.

Or do you have something against written characters?

No answer came. I placed my hands on the pause button of the recorder to silence it. Then my radio clock automatically began to speak. I couldn't understand the technical connection between the two machines. News.

I couldn't bear the voice of the clock radio very long, either. But not because I didn't want to hear any other voice but that of the tape player. On the contrary, the radio briefly liberated me from the voice of the novel. From the radio, new voices entered my apartment: the voices of politicians, the voices of dock workers, the voices of men of letters. . . . But I didn't listen for long. I kept returning to the voice of the novel and wasn't sure whether or not I really wanted to escape from it.

From Flowers of Evil

Charles Baudelaire

Translated from French by Keith Waldrop

Translator's Note

Why am I spending my time on a version of *Les Fleurs du mal?* Easy: I have not been satisfied with any translation[1] I have read. There are a great many—no doubt many more than I have dug up—going back to the Victorians. (How unfortunate neither Rossetti nor Swinburne took on Baudelaire.)

The harder question: Why in versets?

What are the alternatives?

The old phrase "in the original meters" is not helpful. A French meter, alexandrine or other (Baudelaire uses various meters), cannot be followed in English. An English alexandrine, for instance, has the same number of syllables as its French namesake, but no other relation.

Another tack is to claim, for instance, that the alexandrine is to French poetry what heroic verse is to English. This makes sense to me. At any rate, it seems reasonable to translate metrical poems in meter.

Reasonable. But not for me.

And I do not find anyone who has really done it well. Arthur Symons tried sometimes—not consistently—to work, not just with a meter, but with the classical French device of alternating masculine and feminine rhymes.

> Stinginess, Sin, Stupidity, shall determine
> Our spirits' fashion and travail our body's forces,
> And we shall feed on the corpses of our remorses
> Like the beggars who nourish their own vermin.

It is hard to believe, with this first stanza of *Flowers of Evil,* that Symons—on his own—was a competent poet. I think he was trapped

[1] I don't mean there is no single poem well translated. I am thinking of the whole collection or a substantial part of it.

by an idea of duty, that he must somehow match (match *exactly*) the formal qualities of the original—which, however, he was quite incapable of doing. It is the analog of another (and opposite) mistaken idea: that one must be as literal as possible, even if that means word for word.

There is another possibility: free verse. This would mean not meter into meter, but at least verse into verse. . . .

But at this point (having tried, by the way, several kinds of verse) I was struck by other considerations. In translating any particular text, there are particular values to be considered, particular, that is, not to a theory, but to this piece at hand. Something is bound to get lost in transit and some things are more precious than others, and one must decide, in a text to be translated, what is more, and what is less, precious.

Some poems can be translated into prose, not without loss, but still retaining a great deal of their value. Long narrative poems are often cases in point. I like enormously the prose version of *Orlando Furioso* by Guido Waldman.

Even with lyric poetry . . . I must admit that, after looking through many versions of the Greek Anthology, I have generally gotten more from the Loeb "literal" translations.

J. M. Synge translated a dozen poems of Petrarch into prose, the most beautiful Petrarch in English.[2]

> All things that I am bearing in mind, and all things I am in dread of, are keeping me in troubles, in this way one time, in that way another time, so that if I wasn't taking pity on my own self it's long ago I'd have given up my life.

There are poets whose work, handled this way, can survive hardly or not at all: Verlaine, Heine. . . . Or try to imagine prosing Auden's

> As I walked out one evening
> Walking down Bristol Street . . .

Is *Les Fleurs du mal* in this category?

But meanwhile, I had been working in another direction. The Bible was so early and so pervasive an influence that my first impulses to write came often in the shape of versets. This strange hybrid, hovering between verse and prose, has always haunted me. Many of my

[2]Putting aside, of course, the great Wyatt imitations.

first effusions were versets, biblical to the point of blasphemy.

French poetry is full of versets, from Judith Gautier's versions of Chinese poetry, through Claudel, Segalen, Perse, to Jean Grosjean and Paol Keineg, both of whom I have translated.[3]

Not everyone admires the Carlyle-Wicksteed Dante, but I have always liked and still continually go back to it. Each tercet of Dante's terza rima is made into a separate but continuous prose, a sort of prose stanza. Some of these stanzas contain more than one sentence; some sentences take more than one stanza. They are, in other words, not quite prose, not quite verse—precisely, versets. I have seen Carlyle's *Inferno* (he was, by the way, John Carlyle, Thomas's younger brother) referred to as a "scholarly" translation, but—not allergic, as some are, to Victorian English—I find it beautiful.

My interest in translating Baudelaire goes far back and I have, over the years—decades—tried meter and rhyme, free verse, prose. . . . In an attempt to make a prose version of one of these poems, I somehow tricked myself into making versets. It seemed, when I realized what I was doing, a ridiculous thing, but what is a little flirt with the ridiculous, compared with the immense impossibility of translating any literary text? For some time now, I have continued. I have, in various states, the first eighty or so poems. Off and on, I flip open my Pléiade and work on another. . . .

* * *

TO THE READER

Stupidity, error, sin, stinginess—they fill our minds and torment our bodies, and we nourish our comfortable remorse the way beggars feed their lice.

Our sins are headstrong, our repentance faint-hearted. We make our confession firm and full and saunter back into the mire, confident in cheap tears to wash us clean.

On the pillow of perdition Satan Trismegistus lulls the mind, spellbinds it, and the fine metal of our will is quite vaporized by this clever chemist.

[3]Jean Grosjean, *Elegies;* Paol Keineg, *Boudica.*

It's the Devil holds the strings that move us! We find allure in loathsome objects, each day another step toward hell, unhorrified, downward through stinking shadows.

Like some rake, sunk to slobbering, gumming the brutalized tit of a superannuated whore, we grasp in passing a clandestine pleasure to squeeze hard, as on an overripe orange.

Huddled, teeming, like gut-worms by the million, a clutch of Demons make whoopee in our brain and, when we breathe, Death floods our lungs, an invisible torrent, muffled in groans.

Rape, poison, the knife, fire—if these have not yet embroidered with absurd design the banal story of our sorry destiny, it's merely that our soul is, alas! not bold enough.

But among jackals, panthers, bitch hounds, apes, scorpions, vultures, serpents—monsters yapping, howling, grumbling, crawling—in the foul menagerie of our vices

there is one still uglier, meaner, filthier! Without grand gesture, without a yawp, he would gladly shiver the earth, swallow the world, in a yawn.

Who? Ennui! Eye brimming with involuntary tears, he dreams of gallows while puffing on his hookah. You know him, reader, this dainty monster—hypocrite reader—my fellow—my brother!

CORRESPONDENCES

Nature is a temple whose columns are alive and sometimes issue disjointed messages. We thread our way through a forest of symbols that peer out, as if recognizing us.

Like long echoes from far away, merging into a deep dark unity, vast as night, vast as the light, smells and colors and sounds concur.

There are perfumes cool as children's flesh, sweet as oboes, green like the prairie. And others corrupt, rich, overbearing, with the expansiveness of infinite things—like ambergris, musk, spikenard, frankincense, singing ecstasy to the mind and to the senses.

GIANTESS

Back when Nature in her zestful sway daily brought forth child monsters, I would like to have lived with a young giantess, like a voluptuous cat at a queen's feet.

I would have liked to watch her body blossom, along with her soul; free to grow into her terrible games; to divine a dark flame brooding in her heart through the damp mists aswim in her eyes;

to survey at leisure her magnificent parts; climb the slope of her enormous knees, and sometimes, in summer, when the unhealthy sun

tires her till she stretches out across the landscape, to sleep nonchalantly in the shade of her breasts, as in a quiet hamlet at the foot of a mountain.

CARRION

Recall, my soul, the thing we saw that fine mild summer morning: there at a bend in the path, loathsome carrion on a bed sown with cobbles,

legs in the air, like a lewd woman, scorching and sweating poisons, reeking belly split open nonchalantly, cynically.

The sun beat down on that rotten meat, as if to be sure it was well done, and to render unto Mother Nature a hundredfold all she had joined together.

And the sky watched that superb carcass blossom like a flower, the stench so strong you thought you might fall in a faint on the grass.

Flies buzzed around the putrid belly, from whence black armies of larvae came gushing like a viscous liquid along those tatters of life.

All of it came down and reared again, like a wave, or bubbled up; it seemed the body, inflated with vague breath, lived and multiplied.

And the world gave out a strange music, as from wind and running water, or like the rhythm of grain as the winnower turns and shakes it in his fan.

Those shapes faded and were no more than a dream, a rough sketch slow to appear on forgotten canvas, which the artist can only complete by memory.

Behind some rocks, an anxious bitch dog eyed us angrily, waiting for the moment she could get back to those bones for the mouthful left.

—And to think, you will be like that filth, like that horrible stench: you, my eyes' guiding star, sun of my life, you my angel, my passion!

Yes! such you will become, O queen of graces, after the last sacraments when, under the grass and the gross flowering, you mould with the other bones.

Then, O my beauty! tell the worms that feed on you with kisses, that I have kept both the form and the divine essence of my loves-in-decay!

EVENING'S HARMONY

Now comes the time each flower, trembling on its stem, evanesces like incense from a censer; sound and scent revolve in the air of evening; melancholy waltz, vertiginous languor!

Each flower evanesces like incense from a censer; the violin quivers like a heart aggrieved; melancholy waltz, vertiginous languor! The sky is sad and beautiful as an extreme shelter.

The violin quivers like a heart aggrieved, a tender heart which hates the vast black void! The sky is sad and beautiful as an extreme shelter; the sun is drowned in its own blood run cold.

A tender heart which hates the vast black void garners any vestige from the luminous past! The sun is drowned in its own blood run cold. . . . Your image in me gleams as from a monstrance!

AFTERNOON SONG

Although your evil eyebrows lend you an air odd and unangelic, come-hither-eyed witch,

I adore you, my frivolous, my terrible passion! with the devotion of a priest for his idol.

Desert and forest are rank in your uncouth hair; your head leans as to enigmas and secrets.

Scent prowls over your flesh as above a censer; you are enchanting as evening, somber and warm nymph.

How your sloth outdoes the strongest potion, how you know just the caress to bring the dead to life!

Your hips are in love with your back and your breasts; pillows delight in your languid postures.

Sometimes, to appease your mysterious rage, you lavish earnest bites and kisses;

you lacerate me, Dark-Hair, with derisive laughter, and then on my heart you train your eye, tender as moonlight.

Beneath your satin slippers, under your charming silken feet, I place my highest joy, my genius, my destiny,

my soul that you heal, you: light and color! burst of warmth in my dark Siberia!

Charles Baudelaire

REVENANT

Like an eagle-eyed angel, I will come back to your bedchamber, slipping soundlessly to you through night shadows;

And I will give you, dark beauty, kisses cold as the moon and the caresses of a snake from a seething snake-pit.

In livid daybreak, my side of the bed, which you'll find empty, will retain its cold till evening.

Others may have taken by tenderness your life, your youth, but as for me, I shall win you by terror.

Two Poems

Giacomo Leopardi

Translated from Italian by Jonathan Galassi

Translator's Note

After coming to the end (I think) of more than twenty-five years' involvement in translating Eugenio Montale, I found myself looking for another writer to work with/against/for. Translating for me has always been avocational, an exercise aimed at enhancing my own expressive skills, as well as a way of deepening my understanding of another literature (and of writing itself). Translating poetry has always, for me, been fundamentally a way of trying to write poetry, and I've generally found it productive to be working on translation and my own poems more or less simultaneously.

After Montale, I didn't see a route forward, really (lots of Italians have had the same problem!), so I found myself gravitating backward, to the dominant nineteenth-century Italian lyric voice, who himself greatly influenced Montale and almost everyone else. Leopardi is a daunting and enthralling mixture of the archaic (his diction), the classical (his linguistic and philosophical roots), and the modern (his anxiety). To my mind, most of the many English translations miss the directness and nobility of his austere rhetoric—and I'm firmly of the belief that in translation, more is always better. The challenge is to try to make something that sounds plausible to me, and see if it can be useful to others. A caveat: The versions presented here are provisional only, and I take no final responsibility for them.

* * *

Giacomo Leopardi

THE SETTING OF THE MOON

As in the solitary night,
Over silvered countryside and waters,
Where zephyr sweetly breathes.
And far-flung shadows
Project a thousand vague shapes
And chimeras
On quiet waves
And branches, hedges, hills, and farms;
Reaching the horizon,
Behind Apennine or Alp, or on the endless
Breast of the Tyrrhenian,
The moon descends; the world goes colorless;
Shadows vanish, and a single darkness
Swallows hill and valley;
Night goes blind,
And singing, with a mournful melody,
The carter on his way salutes
The last glimmer of fleeting light,
That led him on;

So youth fades out,
So it abandons
Mortal life. The shadows
And the shapes of glad illusions
Flee; and distant hopes,
That prop our mortal
Nature up, give out.
Life lies deserted,
Lightless. Setting his sights on it,
The confused wayfarer seeks in vain
For goal or reason on the long road
Ahead of him; and sees
Man's home itself is truly
Alien to him, and he to it.

Our miserable fate was judged
Too happy and delightful up above,
If youth, whose every good's
The outcome of a thousand pains,

Should last for life;
The sentence that condemns
All animals to death seemed far too mild
If first they were not given
A half-life far crueler
than fearful death itself.
The eternal gods imagined
(Worthy work
For deathless minds)
The worst of all afflictions:
Old age, in which desire
Is unfulfilled and hope extinguished,
The fonts of pleasure dry,
Pain ever greater, and with no relief.

You, hills and shores,
The splendor having fallen that transformed
The veil of night to silver in the west,
Will not stay orphaned long;
For on the other side
Soon you'll see
The sky turn newly white, and dawn arise:
After which the sun,
Flashing with potent
Fire everywhere,
Will bathe you and the ethereal fields
In floods of light.
But mortal life, once lovely youth
Has died, is never colored
By other light or other dawns again.
She remains a widow to the end; and as for night
which hides our other times,
The gods made burial its terminus.

Giacomo Leopardi

TO THE MOON

O graceful moon, I can remember, now
the year has come around, how on this hill
I came to gaze at you in misery:
And you hung then above those woods
as you do now, illuminating all.
But your face was clouded,
and wavering to my eyes, thanks to the tears
that filled them, for my life
was torment: and it is, it doesn't change,
beloved moon of mine. And yet remembering
helps me, and the fresh return
of the time of my unhappiness.
Oh in youth, when hope
has a long row to hoe
and memory is short,
how gladdening recalling past things is,
though they were sad, and though the pain endures!

From Anna Karenina

Leo Tolstoy

Translated from Russian by Marian Schwartz

Translator's Note

Reading *Anna Karenina* in Russian, one is struck by the vigor and beauty of its language, quite distinct from the masterfully told tale. This power can be attributed in part to Tolstoy's purposely unconventional style, an important aspect of the Tolstoyan technique that Formalist critic Viktor Shklovsky referred to as *ostranenie* ("making strange"). Tolstoy breaks literary "rules" with impunity—repeating key words to hammer home a crucial observation, mimicking French syntax, using length to slow down the text at a critical moment to force the reader to dwell on an argument, for example. We see a striking instance of this last device in the first long paragraph of the novel, with the list "spouses, family members, and servants," which appears in almost identical form three times in the space of two sentences: at the end of one and at the beginning and end of the next. The temptation is to replace one or more of the repetitions with a pronoun, but it is a temptation to be resisted. Indeed, we must treat this repetition as intentional. Tolstoy uses what might be viewed as excessive repetition to emphasize that the significance of Stiva's misdeed was not that Stiva was bad, but that his betrayal profoundly touched those closest to him. Without this repetition, the implications of Stiva's adultery for the family and household amount to little more than Stiva's own personal predicament.

The famous opening sentence—so famous, indeed, that English speakers who have never read the novel can quote it—also holds out dangerous snares, principally the urge to tidy up Tolstoy's sentence and make the two halves balance perfectly, which they don't in Russian. Here as throughout the novel, Tolstoy is concerned with making the words convey his precise meaning and is not afraid to use an almost clumsy phrase (*pokhozhi drug na druga*) to achieve that end. In the first half of the sentence he assiduously avoids a snappy aphorism that would imply that happy families are "all alike," so alike as to be indistinguishable; rather, he says, they merely resemble one another to the point of being much less interesting than their unhappy counterparts. The best translation of this sentence into English is the most straightforward one.

More difficult from the standpoint of English translation is the crucial second sentence, which launches a thousand pages of narrative and derives much of its force from being short, syntactically natural, and trochaic; that is to say, it scans. I have turned this sentence around grammatically in order to achieve a short, syntactically natural English sentence that also scans. One additional point about this sentence: The word for "confusion" (*smeshalos'*) is the same used in the Bible for the Tower of Babel story. This subtle association ties us back to the idea of biblical references first raised with the epigraph and reinforces our consciousness of Tolstoy's prominent religious and moral concerns.

In *Anna Karenina,* Tolstoy fought to be language's master and ultimately, I think, he won; he made the Russian language serve him and his overriding moral imperative. I try in this new translation to demonstrate to English readers this linguistic dimension of *Anna Karenina* through close attention to Tolstoy's vocabulary and syntax and through straining against convention, much as the author did, in order, I hope, to recreate the aesthetic experience of reading Tolstoy's masterpiece.

* * *

Vengeance is mine, I will repay.

PART ONE

I.

ALL HAPPY FAMILIES RESEMBLE one another; each unhappy family is unhappy in its own way.

The Oblonsky house was all confusion. The wife had found out about her husband's affair with the French governess formerly in their employ and had informed her husband that she could not go on living in the same house with him. This had been the state of affairs for three days now, and it was keenly felt not only by the spouses themselves but by all the members of the family and the servants as well. All the members of the family and the servants felt that there was no sense in their living together and that travelers chancing to meet in any inn had more in common than did they, the members of the Oblonsky family and the Oblonsky servants. The wife would not leave her rooms, and the husband had not stayed home for three days. The children raced through the house like lost souls; the English governess quarreled with the housekeeper and wrote a note to a friend asking to find her a new position; the cook had walked off the premises yesterday, during the midday meal; the scullery maid and the coachman had given notice.

Three days after the quarrel, Prince Stepan Arkadievich Oblonsky—or Stiva, as he was called in society—at his usual hour, that is, at eight o'clock in the morning, awoke not in his wife's bedroom but in his study, on his leather sofa. He rolled his plump, pampered body over on the sofa springs, as if hoping to fall back into a long sleep, while he hugged the pillow tight and pressed it to his cheek; but then he jumped up, sat on the sofa, and opened his eyes.

"Ah yes, now how did that go?" he mused, trying to remember his dream. "Ah yes, how did that go? Yes! Alabin was giving a dinner in Darmstadt; no, not Darmstadt, something American. Yes, but then Darmstadt was in America. Yes, Alabin was giving a dinner on glass tables, yes—and the tables were singing '*Il mio tesoro*'[1]—no, not '*Il mio tesoro,*' something even better, and there were tiny decanters, and they were women, too," he recalled.

Stepan Arkadievich's eyes twinkled, and he lapsed into reverie, a smile on his face. "Yes, that was fine, very fine. And there were so many excellent things in it, even awake you could never put it all into words and ideas." And noticing the strip of light coming in at the side of one of the curtains, he swung his legs off the sofa and felt with his feet for the slippers his wife had embroidered on gold morocco leather (a gift for his birthday last year), and out of a habit of nine years, still seated, he reached for where his dressing gown hung in the bedroom. Only then did he remember how and why he came to be sleeping not in his wife's bedroom but in his study. The smile vanished from his face, and his brow furrowed.

"Oh, oh! Oh!" he groaned, remembering all that had transpired. And his imagination called up once again each and every detail of the quarrel with his wife, the full desperation of his position, and most agonizing of all, his own culpability.

"No! She would never—could never—forgive me. And what is even more horrible is that it is all my fault—all my fault, yet I am not to blame. Therein lies the full drama," he thought. "Oh, oh!" he

[1]My treasure (Italian), from Mozart's *Don Giovanni.*

moaned as he recalled the impressions this quarrel had left with him that were the hardest to bear.

Most distasteful of all was that initial moment when he, returned from the theater, cheerful and content, carrying an enormous pear for his wife, failed to find his wife in the drawing room; to his surprise, he did not find her in the study, either, but at last did see her in the bedroom holding the unlucky note, which revealed all.

She, Dolly, in his eyes a fretful, restless, and far from bright woman, sat perfectly still, clutching the note, and gave him a look of horror, dismay, and outrage.

"What is this? This?" she asked, pointing to the note.

And at that memory, as often happens, what pained Stepan Arkadievich most was not so much the event itself as how he responded to these words of his wife.

In that instant something happened to him that tends to happen to people caught out in something that is altogether too shameful. He had no time to prepare his face for the position in which he now stood before his wife upon the discovery of his guilt. Instead of taking offense, making a disavowal, trying to justify himself, begging forgiveness, even feigning indifference—anything would have been better than what he did do!—his face, quite involuntarily ("the reflexes of the brain," thought Stepan Arkadievich, who was fond of physiology), suddenly, and quite involuntarily, broke into his usual good-natured, and thus foolish, smile.

He could not forgive himself that foolish smile. When she saw this smile, Dolly reeled, as if she had been struck, and with her characteristic temper unleashed a torrent of harsh words and ran out of the room. She had refused to see her husband ever since.

"That stupid smile of mine is to blame for everything," thought Stepan Arkadievich.

"What am I to do, though? What am I to do?" he mumbled to himself in despair, but found no answer.

II.

Stepan Arkadievich was always honest with himself. He was incapable of lying, of telling himself that he repented of his deed. He could not now repent that he, a handsome, amorous, thirty-four-year-old man, was not in love with his wife, the mother of his five living and two dead children, who was only one year younger than he. He repented only that he had not done a better job of concealing this fact from his wife. Nonetheless, he was sensible of the full gravity of his situation and felt sorry for his wife, his children, and himself. Perhaps he could have done a better job of concealing his sins from his wife had he anticipated the terrible effect this news would have on her. Clearly he had never thought the matter through, but he had had the vague notion that his wife had guessed long ago that he was not faithful to her and that she was simply turning a blind eye. It had even seemed to him that she, a worn-out, aging, no longer beautiful woman who was in no way remarkable, the simple, merely good-natured mother of his family, ought to have indulged him out of a sense of fairness. The exact opposite proved to be the case.

"Oh, it's horrible! Oh, my! Simply horrible!" Stepan Arkadievich repeated over and over to himself, but he could conceive of no remedy. "And how fine everything was before this, how well we lived! She was content and happy with the children, I never interfered in the slightest way, I left her to manage the children and the household as she pleased. True, it was not good that *she* had been a governess in our own house. Not good at all! There is something common, vulgar even, about making love to one's own governess. But what a governess!" He enthusiastically recalled the mischievous black eyes of Mademoiselle Roland, and her smile. "It is true, though, that as long as she was in our house, I never took any liberties. Worst of all, she is already . . . You'd think it was all on purpose! Oh my, oh my! But what, what am I to do?"

There was no answer other than the general answer that life offers to all the most complicated and insoluble problems. And this answer was to live for the demands of the day, that is, lose oneself. He could not lose himself in dreams now, or at least not until night came, and he could not return to the music sung by the decanter-women; consequently, he would have to lose himself in the dream of life.

"Then we shall see," Stepan Arkadievich told himself. He stood up, put on his gray dressing gown with the blue silk lining, and tied the tassels in a knot, filling his broad chest with air. His turned-out feet bore his plump body as effortlessly and confidently as ever to the window; he raised the blind, and rang loudly. At his ring, Matvei, his old friend and valet, entered carrying his clothes, his boots, and a telegram. The barber followed Matvei in with his shaving kit.

"Are there any papers from the office?" asked Stepan Arkadievich, picking up the telegram and seating himself at the mirror.

"On the table," replied Matvei, looking inquiringly, solicitously, at his master, and after a moment's hesitation, added with a cunning smile: "They've come from the stable owner."

Stepan Arkadievich said nothing in reply, only glanced at Matvei in the mirror, but from the glance in which their eyes met in the mirror it was obvious how well they understood one another. Stepan Arkadievich's glance seemed to ask: "Why are you saying this? Don't you know?"

Matvei put his hands in the pockets of his jacket, drew one foot to the side, and regarded his master silently and good-naturedly, smiling just barely.

"I told them to come this Sunday and not to disturb you or themselves pointlessly before then." It was a statement he had evidently prepared in advance.

Stepan Arkadievich realized that Matvei was trying to make a joke and thus attract attention. Ripping open the telegram, he read it, trying to piece together the typically disjointed words, and his face brightened.

"Matvei, my sister Anna Arkadievna will be here tomorrow," he said, momentarily halting the sleek, plump hand of the barber, who had cleared a pink pathway between his long, curly sidewhiskers.

"Praise God," said Matvei, showing by his response, that like his master, he appreciated the significance of this arrival, that is, that Anna Arkadievna, Stepan Arkadievich's beloved sister, might be able to effect a reconciliation between husband and wife.

"Alone or with her husband?" inquired Matvei.

Stepan Arkadievich could not say because the barber was working on his upper lip, so he raised one finger. Matvei nodded into the mirror.

"Alone. Ready a room upstairs?"

"Inform Daria Alexandrovna, wherever she instructs."

"Daria Alexandrovna?" Matvei echoed, as if dubious.

"Yes, inform her. And here, take the telegram, give it to her, and do as she says."

"You want to give it a try," Matvei thought, but he said only: "As you wish, sir."

Stepan Arkadievich was already washed and combed and was preparing to dress when Matvei, stepping slowly in his creaky boots, returned to the room with telegram in hand. The barber had left.

"Daria Alexandrovna instructed me to inform you that she is going away. 'Let him'—that is, you—'do whatever he pleases,'" he said, laughing only with his eyes, and putting his hands in his pockets and cocking his head to one side, he fixed his eyes on his master.

Stepan Arkadievich did not respond immediately. Then a good-natured and somewhat pathetic smile appeared on his handsome face.

"Eh? Matvei?" he said, shaking his head.

"It's all right, master, things will sort out," said Matvei.

"They will?"

"I'm certain of it, sir."

"You think so? Who is that there?" asked Stepan Arkadievich, hearing the rustle of a woman's dress outside his door.

"It's me, sir," said a woman's firm and pleasant voice, and from behind the door poked the stern, pock-marked face of Matryona Filimonovna, the nurse.

"Well, what is it, Matryosha?" asked Stepan Arkadievich, walking toward her.

Despite the fact that Stepan Arkadievich was wholly to blame before his wife and was himself sensible of that fact, nearly everyone in the household, even the nurse, Daria Alexandrovna's principal ally, was on his side.

"Well, what is it?" he said dolefully.

"You must go to her, sir, and apologize again. Maybe God will grant it. She's in agony, it's a real shame to look at her, and you know very well the whole household is a shambles. Have pity on the children, sir. Apologize, sir. What can you do! It's time to pay the piper. . . ."

"But she's not going to accept. . . ."

"You have to do your part. God is merciful, pray to God, sir, pray to God."

"All right, run along then," said Stepan Arkadievich, suddenly blushing. "Well, let's get dressed, shall we?" he said to Matvei, and he flung off his dressing gown.

Matvei, puffing at an invisible speck, was already holding the readied shirt by the collar, and with obvious satisfaction he slipped it over his master's well-groomed body.

III.

Once dressed, Stepan Arkadievich sprayed himself with eau de cologne, tugged at the sleeves of his shirt, and in an accustomed gesture deposited his cigarettes, his wallet, his matches, and his watch with the double chain and seals into his various pockets, gave his handkerchief a quick snap, and feeling clean, fragrant, healthy, and physically cheerful, despite his misfortune, and with a slight spring in his step, went into the dining room, where waiting for him was his coffee and, next to the coffee, the letters and papers from his office.

He read the letters. One was quite nasty—from the merchant who was buying a forest on his wife's estate. He had had no choice, the forest had to be sold, but now, until he and his wife were reconciled, the entire matter was out of the question. Even more distasteful was the fact that this interjected his financial interest in the pending transaction into the reconciliation with his wife. And the idea that he might be guided by this interest, that for the sake of selling this forest he might seek a reconciliation with his wife—the very idea was an insult.

When he had finished with the letters, Stepan Arkadievich drew the papers from his office closer, read rapidly through two files, made several comments with a large pencil, and pushing the files aside, began drinking his coffee; over his coffee he unfolded the still damp morning newspaper and began to read.

Stepan Arkadievich took and read a liberal newspaper, not a radical one, but one that advocated the orientation maintained by the majority. And despite the fact that science and art and politics held no particular interest for him, he firmly maintained the same views on these subjects that were maintained by the majority and by his newspaper, and he changed them only when the majority changed them, or, rather, he did not change them at all; they changed in him on their own, without his noticing.

Stepan Arkadievich chose neither his own orientation nor his own views; rather his orientation and views came to him on their own, just as he did not choose the style of his hat or his frock coat but chose those which were being worn. And for him, living as he did in a certain society, and given his need for some mental activity, such as develops quite naturally in one's mature years, possessing opinions was just as essential as possessing a hat. If he had any reason for preferring the liberal orientation to the conservative, to which many others of his circle held, then it was not that he found the liberal orientation more sensible but that it was a better fit with life as he led it. The liberal party said that in Russia everything was bad, and indeed, Stepan Arkadievich did have many debts and money was definitely in short supply. The liberal party said that marriage was an outmoded institution in need of restructuring, and indeed, family life afforded Stepan Arkadievich little pleasure and forced him into lies and hypocrisy, which were so repellent to his nature. The liberal party said, or, rather, assumed, that religion was merely a check on the barbarous portion of the populace, and indeed, Stepan Arkadievich could not stand through even a short service without his feet aching, and he failed to comprehend what purpose all those terrifying high-flown words about the other world served when it could be so very gay to live in this one. At the same time, Stepan Arkadievich, who loved a good joke, occasionally enjoyed confounding a humble soul by pointing out that if one was going to take pride in one's stock, one should not stop at Riurik[2] and deny our very first forebears—the apes. This liberal orientation had become habit for Stepan Arkadievich, and he liked his newspaper, as he did his cigar after dinner, for the light haze it produced in his head. He read the lead article, in which it was explained that in our day it was utterly pointless to raise a hue and cry about radicalism supposedly threatening to swallow up all conservative elements and the government supposedly being obliged to take measures to crush the revolutionary hydra, that quite to the contrary: "In our opinion, the danger lies not in any imaginary revolutionary hydra but in hidebound tradition, which impedes progress," etc. He read another article, too, a financial article that alluded to Bentham and Mill and made some insinuations about the ministry. With his characteristic quick mind, he caught the implications of each and every insinuation: by whom, at whom, and on what occasion it had been aimed, and this, as always, afforded him a certain satisfaction. Today, however, this satisfaction was poisoned by the memory of Matryona Filimonovna's advice and by the fact that his household was in such a bad way. He also read about Count Beist, who was rumored to have traveled to Wiesbaden, and about the fact that gray hair is a thing of the past, and about the sale of a light carriage, and about a certain young person seeking a position; however this information did not afford him his usual understated, ironical satisfaction.

Having finished his newspaper, his second cup of coffee, and his buttered roll, he stood up, brushed the crumbs off his vest, and patting his broad chest, smiled radiantly, though not because he had anything particularly pleasant in his heart—his radiant smile was evoked by his excellent digestion.

This radiant smile immediately reminded him of everything, though, and he lapsed into thought.

Two children's voices (Stepan Arkadievich recognized the voices of Grisha, his younger son, and Tania, his eldest daughter) could be

---

[2]According to the Primary Chronicle, the first prince of the Slav tribes.

heard outside his doors. They had been pulling something and had dropped it.

"I told you not to put passengers on the roof!" the girl scolded him in English. "Now pick it up!"

"Nothing is right," thought Stepan Arkadievich. "There the children go racing about unsupervised." And he went to the door and called to them. They abandoned the box that had been serving as a train and went to their father.

The girl, her father's pet, ran in boldly, threw her arms around him, and dangled from his neck, laughing, as always, and reveling in the familiar scent of cologne that came from his sidewhiskers. Kissing him, finally, on his face, which was flushed from his bent posture and which beamed with tenderness, the girl let go and tried to run off, but her father held her back.

"How is Mama?" he asked, running his hand over his daughter's soft, smooth neck. "Hello there," he said, smiling at the thriving little boy.

He was conscious of the fact that he loved the boy less and so always endeavored to be even-handed, but the boy sensed this and did not respond to his father's cold smile with a smile of his own.

"Mama? She's awake," replied the girl.

Stepan Arkadievich sighed. "Which means she didn't sleep again all night," he thought. "Well, is she cheerful?"

The little girl knew that there had been a quarrel between her father and mother, and that her mother could not possibly be cheerful, and that her father ought to know this and that he was pretending, inquiring about this so lightly. And she blushed for her father. He realized this straightaway and blushed as well.

"I don't know," she said. "She didn't tell us to study our lessons, but she did tell us to take a walk with Miss Hull to Grandmama's."

"Well then, run along, my little Tania. Oh yes, just a moment," he said, detaining her nonetheless and stroking her soft little hand.

He took a box of candies from the mantelpiece where he had put it yesterday, and gave her two, selecting her favorites, a chocolate and a fondant.

"For Grisha?" said the girl, pointing to the chocolate.

"Yes, yes." And stroking her little shoulder one more time, he kissed the roots of her hair and her nape and let her go.

"Your carriage is ready," said Matvei. "And there is a lady petitioner," he added.

"Has she been here long?" asked Stepan Arkadievich.

"About half an hour."

"How many times have I instructed you to inform me at once!"

"I had to let you finish your coffee," said Matvei in that amiably gruff tone with which it was impossible to be angry.

"Well then, show her in quickly," said Oblonsky, frowning in irritation.

The petitioner, the widow of Staff Captain Kalinin, was asking for something not only impossible but incoherent; nonetheless, Stepan Arkadievich, as was his custom, had her sit down and paid close attention to all she had to say, without interrupting, and then gave her detailed advice as to whom she should appeal to and how she should go about doing so. He even dashed off a note for her in his handsome, sprawling, and precise hand to a personage who might be of assistance to her. Dismissing the captain's widow, Stepan Arkadievich picked up his hat and stopped to think whether he had forgotten anything. It turned out that he had not forgotten anything except the one thing he would have liked to forget—his wife.

"Ah, yes!" He bowed his head, and a miserable expression came over his handsome face. "Should I go or shouldn't I?" he said to himself. And an inner voice told him that there was no point in going, that this could only mean hypocrisy, that fixing, mending their relations was impossible because it was impossible to make her attractive and desirable once more or to make him an old man incapable of love. Other than hypocrisy and lies, nothing could come of it now; and hypocrisy and lies were repellent to his nature.

"Though I will have to eventually; after all, things cannot remain as they are," he said, trying to give himself courage. He squared his chest, took out a cigarette, lit it, took two puffs, dropped it into a mother-of-pearl ashtray, and with quick steps passed through the gloomy drawing room and opened the other door, to his wife's bedroom.

NOTES ON CONTRIBUTORS

ESTHER ALLEN edited and translated the *Selected Writings* of José Martí, forthcoming from Penguin Classics.

JULIA ALVAREZ's novels include *In the Time of the Butterflies* (Penguin) and *How the García Girls Lost their Accents* (Plume). "Anita's Diary" is an excerpt from her forthcoming novel for young adults, *Before We Were Free* (Knopf). She has also written two other books for young readers, *The Secret Footprints* and *How Tía Lola Came to Stay* (both by Knopf).

LOUIS ARAGON (1897–1982) was an active participant in the French Dada movement and later a principal member of the Surrealists. His poetry collections include *Feu de joie, Le Mouvement perpétuel, La Diane française,* and *Le Voyage en Hollande.* In addition to his poetry, he wrote novels, essays, and a long study of Matisse.

HANS ARP (1887–1966), a k a Jean Arp, is best known as a visual artist associated with both the Dada and Surrealist movements. He was also the author of hundreds of poems, written in both German and English.

ANTONIN ARTAUD (1896–1948) was active in the Surrealist movement until 1930. All of his writings have been collected in the multivolumed set *Oeuvres Complètes,* published by Gallimard, and English-language collections include *Artaud Anthology, Black Poet and Other Texts,* and *Selected Writings.*

JOHN ASHBERY's most recent book is *The Vermont Notebook* (Granary Books). He is the Charles P. Stevenson, Jr., Professor of Languages and Literature at Bard College.

PAUL AUSTER's most recent works are *The Red Notebook* (New Directions) and *The Story of My Typewriter,* with paintings and drawings by Sam Messer (Distributed Art Publishers). His tenth novel, *The Book of Illusions,* will be published by Henry Holt in September.

CHARLES BAUDELAIRE (1821–1867) wrote some of the best art criticism of his time, translated Poe, and published, in 1857, *Les Fleurs du mal,* which created—according to Victor Hugo—"un frisson nouveau." His poems in prose were published as a volume two years after his death.

MICHAEL BERGSTEIN is managing editor of *Conjunctions.* These three requia are from a larger work in progress.

SUSAN BERNOFSKY has translated two books by Robert Walser and a volume of memories by Gregor von Rezzori. Forthcoming translations (with Yumi Selden) include *Where Europe Begins* by Yoko Tawada (New Directions), *The Trip to*

Bordeaux by Ludwig Harig (Burning Deck), and *Celan Studies* by Peter Szondi (Stanford University Press). She teaches at Bard College.

In 1924, ANDRÉ BRETON (1896–1966) published the first manifesto of Surrealism, and from then until his death was the chief organizer and theoretician of the movement. He broke with the Communist Party in 1935 and soon after met Diego Rivera and Leon Trotsky in Mexico prior to moving to New York and founding the magazine *VVV* with Marcel Duchamp, Max Ernst, and David Hare. He published numerous collections of poetry and prose.

ROBERT QUILLEN CAMP is a playwright and performance artist. His plays will appear in forthcoming issues of *Conundrum* and *Chain.*

MIGUEL DE CERVANTES (1547–1616), one of the supreme figures in literary history, perfected and defined the modern novel; although he wrote in a variety of genres, his great achievement remains *Don Quixote.*

MAXINE CHERNOFF is the author of six books of poems and six books of fiction, most recently *World: Poems 1991–2001* (Salt Publications) and *Some of Her Friends That Year* (Coffee House Press).

PETER COLE's most recent book is *Selected Poems of Solomon Ibn Gabirol,* which received the 2001 TLS-Porjes Prize for Translation from Hebrew. *The Poetry of Kabbalah,* edited by Aminadav Dykman and Moshe Idel, is forthcoming from Penn State University Press.

PETER CONSTANTINE's most recent translations are *The Complete Works of Isaac Babel* (W. W. Norton), *Within Four Walls: The Correspondence Between Hannah Arendt and Heinrich Blucher, 1936–1968* (Harcourt Brace), and *Elegy for Kosovo* (Arcade Books), by Ismail Kadare. His translations of *Six Early Stories* (Sun & Moon Press), by Thomas Mann, was awarded the PEN Translation Prize, and *The Undiscovered Chekhov: Thirty-Eight New Stories* (Seven Stories Press) received the National Translation Award.

LYDIA DAVIS is the author of *Break It Down, The End of the Stay, Almost No Memory* (all Farrar, Straus & Giroux), and, most recently, a collection of stories titled *Samuel Johnson Is Indignant* (McSweeney's). Her translation of *The Way by Swann's* will appear from Penguin UK this fall.

ROBERT DESNOS (1900–1945) was one of the most important members of the Surrealists. His principal collections of poetry include *Corps et biens: poèmes 1919–1929, Fortunes,* and *Contrée.* Active during World War II as a member of the Resistance, he was arrested by the Gestapo in 1944 and died shortly after the liberation in a German concentration camp in Czechoslovakia.

FYODOR DOSTOEVSKY's (1821–1881) first novel, *Poor Folk,* was published in 1846 to great acclaim. In the early 1860s he edited two magazines, *Time* and *Epoch,* in collaboration with his brother Mikhail. But both magazines were closed by the censors, and in 1864 his wife and brother both died, leaving him in charge of their families and deeply in debt. In that same year he wrote *Notes from Underground,* which was the prelude to the five great novels that crowned his work:

Crime and Punishment (1866), *The Idiot* (1868), *Demons* (1872), *The Adolescent* (1875), and *The Brothers Karamazov* (1880).

In longer and more mutable form, RIKKI DUCORNET's "The Deep Zoo" was first presented at the University of Houston in 2001, and then at the Institut Charles V, in Paris, on the occasion of "Un Symposium sur la Litterature Americaine Contemporaine: Imagination Alive Imagine."

PAUL ÉLUARD (1895–1952) participated in the activities of French Dada and later was a major presence in the Surrealist movement. His principal collections of poetry include *Capitale de la douleur, La Rose publique, Les Yeux fertiles,* and *Corps mémorable.* His *Selected Poems* is available in English.

KAREN EMMERICH is a graduate student of comparative literature at the Aristotelian University of Thessaloniki, Greece. Her translation of Vassilis Vassilikos's novel *Glafkos Thrassakis* is forthcoming from Seven Stories Press.

MICHAEL EMMERICH has translated works of various genres from both contemporary and pre-modern Japanese, including Yasunari Kawabata's collection of short stories *First Snow on Fuji* and Banana Yoshimoto's *Asleep.* His translation of Yoshimoto's novel *Goodbye Tsugumi* is forthcoming from Grove Press.

REA GALANAKE, born on Crete in 1947, is one of Greece's foremost contemporary authors. Her third novel, *Eleni, or Nobody,* received the Greek equivalent of the National Book Award in 1999, and four of her nine books have been published in English translation.

JONATHAN GALASSI's translations of Eugenio Montale's poetry include *Collected Poems 1920–1954* (Farrar, Straus & Giroux) and *Diario Postumo* (Turtle Point Press).

PETER GIZZI's books include *Artificial Heart* (Burning Deck), *Periplum* (Small Press Distribution), and *Music for Films* (Paradigm Press). He has two chapbooks out this spring: *Fin Amor,* with artwork by George Herms (Tougher Disguises Press), and *Revival,* with photography by David Byrne (Phylum Press).

EDITH GROSSMAN has translated works by major Spanish-language authors, including Gabriel García Márquez, Mario Vargas Llosa, Julían Ríos, and Mayra Montero.

RICHARD HOWARD is a poet and translator from the French. He teaches literature in the School of the Arts at Columbia University.

GIACOMO LEOPARDI (1798–1837) is generally considered the greatest Italian poet of the nineteenth century.

TAN LIN is the author of two books of poems, *Lotion Bullwhip Giraffe* (Sun & Moon Press) and *Box* (Atelos). He has taught English, creative writing, and art history at the University of Virginia, Cal Arts, and currently, New Jersey City University.

MAURICE MAETERLINCK (1862–1949) was a Belgian writer of poetry (*Hothouses*), plays (*Pelleas and Melisande, The Intruder, The Blue Bird*), philosophical works (*The Treasure of the Humble, The Double Garden*), and nature studies (*The Life of the Bee*). He was awarded the Nobel Prize for literature in 1911.

The founding father of Cuban independence, JOSÉ MARTÍ was killed in battle in 1895, at the age of forty-two. His *Complete Works* fill twenty-seven volumes.

PIERRE MARTORY (1920–1998) was raised in Morocco and later, as a student in Paris, fled the German occupiers in June 1940. He fought in the Free French Army in North Africa, and after various jobs became arts editor of *Paris Match,* a position he held for twenty-five years.

T. M. McNALLY is the author of a collection of stories, *Low Flying Aircraft* (University of Georgia Press), and the novels *Until Your Heart Stops* (Villard) and *Almost Home* (Scribner). He teaches at Arizona State University in Tempe.

BREON MITCHELL is director of the Lilly Library and professor of Germanic studies and comparative literature at Indiana University. His most recent translation was a new version of Franz Kafka's *The Trial,* published by Schocken Books.

RICK MOODY is the author, most recently, of *The Black Veil: A Memoir with Digressions* (Little, Brown) and *Fair Use: Poems* (Base Canard).

ALBERTO MORAVIA (1907–1990) was the outstanding Italian novelist of his time, author of *The Time of Indifference* (1929), *The Woman of Rome* (1947), *Boredom* (1961), and many other works of fiction. He was also a prolific critic and travel writer.

BRADFORD MORROW's new novel, *Ariel's Crossing,* has just been published by Viking. He is a professor of literature at Bard College.

ROBERT MUSIL (1880–1942) was the author of two novels, *Young Torless* and the important epic *The Man without Qualities,* as well as a number of short stories and miscellaneous pieces, two plays, *The Visionaries* and *Vinzenz,* and a considerable number of essays on European culture. Born in Austria-Hungary, he lived in Vienna and Berlin, and died in exile in Switzerland.

DMITRI NABOKOV was born in 1934 in Berlin and came to the United States as a young child with his parents. Following his graduation from Harvard and service in the U.S. Army, he became a worldwide opera and concert performer (as a basso), and translated most of his father's Russian stories, plays, and novels into English.

VLADIMIR NABOKOV (1899–1977) was born in St. Petersburg and educated in French and Russian literature at Trinity College, Cambridge. In 1940 he moved to the United States, where he pursued a brilliant literary career as a poet, novelist, critic, and translator while teaching at several colleges and universities. His landmark novel *Lolita* was published in 1955 and was followed by dozens of other remarkable stories and novels, including *Pale Fire* and *Ada.*

RON PADGETT's books include *New & Selected Poems* (Godine), *Great Balls of Fire* (Coffee House Press), *The Straight Line* (University of Michigan Press), and *You Never Know* (Coffee House Press). His memoir/biography of his father, *Oklahoma Tough* (University of Oklahoma Press), will appear next year.

Recently Padgett was made a Chevalier dans l'Ordre des Arts et des Lettres by the French government.

ALEXANDROS PAPADIAMANTIS (1851–1911) is considered Greece's foremost prose writer. Among his best-known works are the novel *The Murderess,* and the collection of short stories *Tales from a Greek Island.*

OCTAVIO PAZ (1914–1998) was awarded the Nobel Prize in 1990. Among his many books available in English are *Collected Poems 1957–1987, Sunstone* (both from New Directions), *In Light of India, The Other Voice,* and *The Double Flame* (all from Harvest Books).

BENJAMIN PÉRET (1899–1959) was an active Surrealist from the beginning of the movement, publishing, in 1923, what many consider the first Surrealist fiction, *Au 125 du boulevard Saint-Germain.* All of his poems have been collected in a two-volume *Oeuvres Complètes,* published by Éditions Losfeld.

RICHARD PEVEAR and LARISSA VOLOKHONSKY have translated works by Nikolai Gogol, Leo Tolstoy, Anton Chekhov, and Mikhail Bulgakov, as well as six books by Fyodor Dostoevsky. Their translation of *The Brothers Karamazov* won the PEN/Book-of-the-Month Club Translation Prize in 1991; their translation of Dostoevsky's *Demons* was a finalist for the same prize in 1996. They live in Paris.

BURTON PIKE is professor emeritus of comparative literature and German at the Graduate School of the City University of New York. He edited and co-translated, with Sophie Wilkins, Robert Musil's *The Man without Qualities* (Knopf), and edited and co-translated with David S. Luft *Robert Musil: Precision and Soul, Essays and Addresses* (Chicago). He also edited *Robert Musil: Selected Writings* (Continuum).

MARCEL PROUST (1871–1922) was the author of *Les plaisirs and les jours;* an unfinished novel, *Jean Santeuil,* first published in 1954; translator of John Ruskin's *The Bible of Amiens* and *Sesame and Lilies;* and, most famously, author of the masterpiece *À la recherche du temps perdu.*

GREGORY RABASSA is the translator of some forty novels from Spanish and Portuguese. His latest is *The Return of the Caravels,* by António Lobo Antunes (Grove Press). He teaches at Queens College and the Graduate School of CUNY.

JOAN RETALLACK's books include *Mongrelisme* (Paradigm Press), *How to Do Things with Words* (Sun & Moon Press), and *Afterrimages,* from Wesleyan Press, which also published her book on and with John Cage: *MUSICAGE.* Paradigm Press will bring out the complete *Memnoir* this summer, and *The Poethical Wager,* a book of essays, is forthcoming from the University of California Press. She teaches at Bard College.

DONALD REVELL is the author of seven collections of poetry, most recently of *Arcady* and *There Are Three* (both Wesleyan Press).

PIERRE REVERDY (1889–1960) was the quintessential poet of cubism. Most of his poetry is contained in two cumulative collections, *Plupart du temps* and *Main d'oeuvre.*

ELIZABETH ROBINSON's recent books include *House Made of Silver* (Kelsey Street Press) and *Harrow* (Omnidawn). *Pure Descent* was a 2001 winner of the National Poetry Series and is forthcoming from Sun & Moon Press.

JOSÉ SARNEY is a former president of Brazil and former governor of the state of Maranhão. He is presently senator from the state of Amapá. *Master of the Sea* is his first novel.

MARIAN SCHWARTZ's most recent translation is *The Billancourt Tales*, by Nina Berberova (New Directions). Her new translation of *Anna Karenina* will be published by Seven Stories Press. Schwartz is the current president of the American Literary Translators Association.

ELENI SIKELIANOS's most recent book is *Earliest Worlds* (Coffee House Press).

PHILIPPE SOUPAULT (1897–1990) was a prolific novelist and essayist. Founder of the review *Littérature* in 1919 (with André Breton and Louis Aragon), he was active in French Dada and a central figure of Surrealism in its early years, though eventually drifted away from the movement. His principal collections of poetry were published in a single volume by Grasset in 1973.

JAMES TATE's most recent books are *Memoir of the Hawk* (Ecco Press) and *Dreams of a Robot Dancing Bee* (Verse Press).

YOKO TAWADA was born in Tokyo and later moved to Hamburg. She has made a name for herself in the literary worlds of both Germany and Japan, publishing at least ten books in each language (she writes now in the one, now in the other). Her many awards include the Akutagawa Prize in Japan and the Adalbert von Chamisso Prize in Germany, the highest honor bestowed upon a foreign-born author.

UWE TIMM was born in 1940 in Hamburg. He has published several novels, including *Midsummer Night, The Invention of Curried Sausage, Headhunter,* and *The Snake Tree* (all New Directions). *Morenga* is also forthcoming from New Directions.

LEO TOLSTOY (1828–1910) wrote *War and Peace* and *Anna Karenina* within a decade of each other. In subsequent years, Tolstoy spurned first fiction in general and then fiction that did not serve his Christian message, though this later period did yield yet another masterwork, *The Death of Ivan Ilyich.*

KEITH WALDROP has translated the work of Anne-Marie Albiach, Claude Royet-Journoud, Dominique Fourcade, Paol Keineg, and Jean Grosjean, among others. His most recent books are *Haunt* (Instance) and *Semiramis If I Remember* (Avec Books). He is the publisher of Burning Deck Books (with Rosmarie Waldrop) and teaches at Brown University.

ROSMARIE WALDROP's most recent books of poems are *Reluctant Gravities* (New Directions), *Split Infinities* (Singing Horse Press), and *Another Language: Selected Poems* (Talisman House). Northwestern University Press has reprinted her two novels, *The Hanky of Pippin's Daughter* and *A Form/of Taking/It All,* in one paperback. Her memoir, *Lavish Absence: Recalling and Rereading Edmond Jabès,* is forthcoming from Wesleyan University Press.

WILLIAM WEAVER is a Bard Center Fellow at Bard College. Translator, biographer, and critic, he has published English versions of many Italian writers, including Umberto Eco, Italo Calvino, and Alberto Moravia. He has written extensively about nineteenth-century Italian opera and theater.

ELIOT WEINBERGER's most recent books are a collection of essays, *Karmic Traces,* and a translation of Bei Dao's *Unlock* (both from New Directions) and his edition of Jorge Luis Borges's *Selected Non-Fictions* (Viking Press).

A paperback reissue of PAUL WEST's *The Place in Flowers Where Pollen Rests* is forthcoming from Voyant. His most recent books are a memoir, *Oxford Days* (British American), and a novel, *Cheops: A Cupboard for the Sun* (New Directions). The University of Tours will devote a symposium to his work in October 2003.